THE HOME-WRECKER

USA TODAY BESTSELLING AUTHOR

SARA CATE

Cover design: Emily Wittig

For history's most epic home-wreckers—
Francesca and Paolo

Dear Reader

Above all, this is a story about a family finding their way to love and acceptance. There is a happy ending but some things along the way that you should be aware of.

There are elements of their story that could be triggering to some readers, such as: infertility, religious trauma, homophobia, biphobia/bi erasure, cancer, and the death of a parent. There is also some graphic teen violence, bullying, and domestic violence. There is on-the-page cheating in this story. Please read with caution if any of these listed topics are potentially triggering to you.

As always in my books, the kink and elements of BDSM are entirely fictional and meant to be read as fantasy, not reality. Should anything in my novels serve as inspiration to you, you and your partner(s) are responsible for your own research and safety.

I hope you enjoy Caleb, Briar, and Dean's journey of family, acceptance, and religious recovery.

If the idea of breaking vows and giving into temptation excites you, this might be the book for you.

Enjoy!

Love always,

Sara

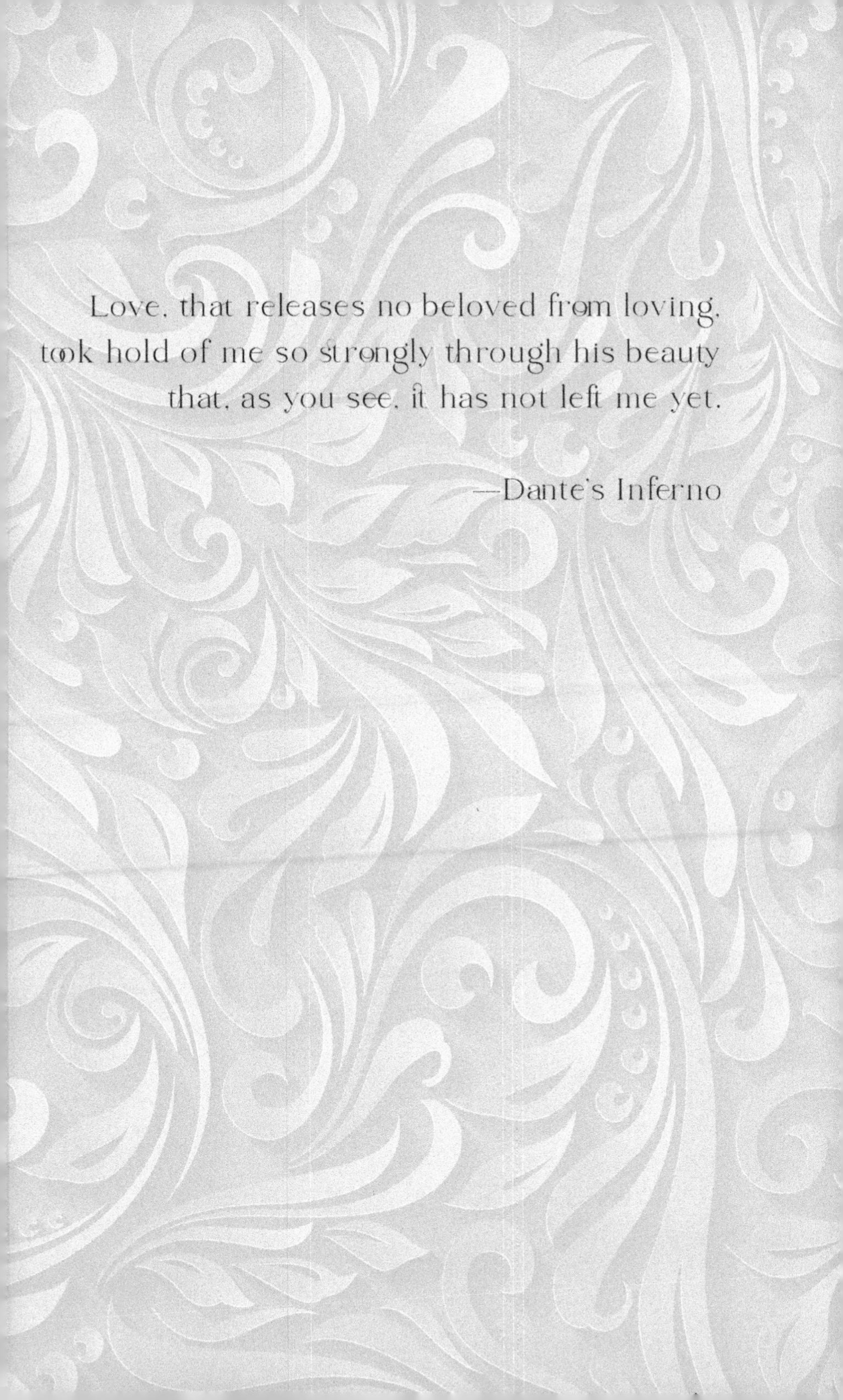

Love, that releases no beloved from loving,
took hold of me so strongly through his beauty
that, as you see, it has not left me yet.

—Dante's Inferno

PROLOGUE

Caleb
21 years old

"Good game, son." My father's hand lands heavily on my shoulder as we make our way to the parking lot from the football field. The campus is still buzzing with energy from our big win against Amarillo College.

I glance up, my hair still wet from the shower, as I search my father's expression for something that resembles pride, but his eyes never truly make their way to me. He's still staring straight ahead as we walk toward our cars. My mother is beside him, beaming with a smile as she glances my way.

My fourteen-year-old brother Isaac and his best friend are straggling behind us.

Meanwhile, I still fight the urge to look for Luke. For the first eighteen years of our lives, my twin brother was always by my side. We had our own secret language, and no matter what our father did, I could convey everything I was feeling to my twin with one glance.

If Luke were here now, I'd give him an eye roll that would say,

I'm calling Dad's bullshit. He has no clue if it was a good game. He probably wasn't even watching it.

But I can't because Lucas is currently seventeen hundred miles away in Ithaca, New York. Our family is well-off now that Dad is a big-deal preacher, but I didn't want to leave home or Isaac.

Besides, football managed to get me a partial scholarship at Austin State, a small state college with a Division II team and a decent prelaw program. So I don't mind living at home for now.

Luke is smarter than me, anyway.

"Caleb, sweetheart. Your father needs to run by the church. Can you take the boys through a drive-through on your way home?" my mom asks softly as she finds her way toward me, wrapping her thin arm around mine.

I let out a scoff as I glance back at my little brother. My head is pounding, and I just want to collapse into my bed, not chauffeur a couple of teenage boys around town.

Not to mention, I'm a little bit tired of feeling like the oldest kid in the family. I may still live at home to save money, but I'm twenty-one years old.

As soon as I graduate and my tuition's paid, I'm out of here.

I want to argue, but my dad is right here. And I don't need to start with him tonight. It would just kill my good mood after our big win.

Reluctantly, I nod. "Yeah, Mom. I can take 'em."

She stands on her tiptoes and kisses me on the cheek. "Thank you, my sweet boy."

"You're welcome, Mom."

"Drive safe. See you boys at home," she says.

Before we part ways so they can head to Dad's Lexus and we can head to my hand-me-down Civic, my mother calls toward us. "Dean, are you sure it's okay with your dad if you spend the night again?"

My brother's best friend shrugs. "Yes, Mrs. Goode. He doesn't mind."

"Good," she replies sweetly.

As the three of us walk left through the dark lot, I hear my father grumble to my mom about how he'll be feeding "Isaac's little friend" once again, which makes me wince because he's still within earshot.

"Come on. You guys want Mickey D's?" I ask, trying to talk over my father's voice in the distance.

"Yeah!" Isaac answers enthusiastically.

His friend just shrugs. "Sure."

As we get into the car, I peer through the rearview at the kids in the back seat. My dad wasn't lying. Dean has been staying over a lot more than usual lately, but I can't say I'm surprised. His dad is, like, sixty years old and is raising him alone. And everyone knows he's got a drinking problem.

The car ride is quiet, at least for me. The passenger seat is empty as my brother and his friend laugh about something on their phones in the back. I don't pay much attention, and to be honest, I don't want to.

Sometimes, I worry about Isaac. He's nothing like me or Lucas or Adam. It's like he wants to be different, and I know how much my dad hates that. He acts out on purpose. Makes comments just to ruffle Dad's feathers. I wish he'd just stay in line sometimes. Be normal. Be like the rest of us.

As we pull up to the fast-food restaurant, I groan when I see how massively long the drive-through line is.

"It'll be quicker just to go in," I say as I whip into one of the front parking spaces.

"Cool with me," Isaac replies.

After I put the car into park, I pull my phone out of my pocket just to check for any messages. Isaac and Dean both have their doors open when a loud crash echoes through the car, and I'm knocked forward in my seat, nearly smacking my face into the steering wheel.

"What the hell?" Dean shouts.

I quickly flip around and check on my little brother and his friend, but they're both fine with their seat belts still on. They're wearing wide-eyed expressions and clutching tight to the headrests of the front seats. Through the back window, I see a Jeep Wrangler with its reverse lights on, close enough to my car to be in the trunk.

"Fuckers," I mutter to myself as I jump out of my seat.

I'm rounding the side of my car when I see the passenger wearing an Austin State jersey with the number forty-four on the back. It belongs to our star wide receiver and resident asshole—Sean Butler.

Then I hear yelling.

"What the fuck is wrong with you?" he bellows inside the Jeep.

"I'm sorry! I didn't see them!" a female voice shrieks in return.

I walk up to the window in time to see my teammate rearing back a hand in anger. I quickly knock on the glass.

Sean turns toward me with clenched teeth and narrowed eyes. He shoves open the car door.

"Goode," he says with a sigh. "Thank God."

"Are you guys okay?" I ask. Peering around Sean, I spot a head of blonde hair draped forward in the driver's seat.

"My idiot girlfriend doesn't know how to use a rearview mirror, apparently."

My brow furrows at Sean, and I don't respond as I watch the girl behind the wheel slowly look up toward me. When our eyes meet, I lose all sense of space and time.

I don't normally attend my team's parties or hang out with any of the players. I never fit in with that crowd. Maybe if I did, I would know Sean's long-term girlfriend by now. Which would be much better than being struck silent in the parking lot with my brake lights shattered at my feet.

She is by far the most beautiful girl I've ever seen. Round blue eyes, a delicate button nose, and full pink lips.

"I'll have my dad just take care of this, if you don't mind, Goode. That way, we don't have to get insurance involved."

"Yeah, sure," I mutter, still staring at the beauty in the other seat.

"I'm sorry," she mumbles sadly.

"It's okay," I reply. "You're not an idiot."

Her mouth lifts in a crooked smirk. Then she rolls her eyes, glancing at the back of her boyfriend's head, making me smile.

Tearing myself away from her gaze, I look at the back of my car to see that most of the damage is to the bumper and one taillight. The car was falling apart anyway.

"Hey, no worries. Accidents happen," I say, noting that his Jeep barely has a scratch.

"Yes, well, accidents wouldn't happen if someone would just watch where she's going," Sean says with a grimace in his girlfriend's direction.

I peek over him again. "I'm Caleb," I say directly to her.

Behind me, I hear someone snicker. Looking over my shoulder, I notice my brother laughing to himself.

"I'm Briar," the girl replies awkwardly.

"Nice to meet you, Briar. And seriously, no worries. I need a new car anyway."

She gives me a tight-lipped smile while Sean's expression grows even more disgruntled.

"Let's go, Briar," he mutters coldly as he bats her arm with the back of his hand.

She waves softly at me before they pull away. I'm staring at the damage left, but my eyes aren't exactly focused on my car. I'm still staring at her face in my mind.

"Real slick."

I glance up from my car to see my younger brother laughing at me.

"What?" I ask with a tilt of my head.

"I'm Caleb," he says, mimicking my voice in a teasing tone.

"Shut up," I say with a chuckle as I walk toward the door of the restaurant.

"You were totally hitting on that guy's girlfriend," he urges.

"Was not," I argue.

"You kinda were," Dean adds.

I laugh to myself, shaking my head as I relive the whole encounter in my head.

Was I?

"That guy was a dick anyway," Dean adds, and I stop in my tracks. Staring down at my brother's best friend, his foul language

takes me by surprise. I'm not used to hearing fourteen-year-olds cuss in my family.

But he's right. That guy was a dick.

"Fuck yeah, he was," I reply.

Dean smirks as I pull open the front door. The three of us decide to just eat here instead of taking it home. I've never really been able to bond with my younger brother that much due to our seven-year age difference. But tonight, we're actually getting along.

And it makes me miss Luke a little bit less.

During the entire meal, I can't get that blonde out of my head. While Isaac and Dean continue to joke and laugh while staring at Isaac's phone, I just keep thinking about what I need to do in order to see her again.

Part One
The Husband

One

Briar

The woman sitting across from me has the same sandals as I do. And so does the woman on my right, but she needs a pedicure. I should invite her to go with me to the nail salon tomorrow, but I think she has a baby. No one wants to take a baby to the nail salon.

To be honest, I don't even remember the woman's name.

"Briar."

I blink, lifting my eyes from the floor to stare at the woman leading Bible study across from me.

Shoot. I think she asked me a question.

"We were just discussing the end of Proverbs 31. Did you have anything to add?"

I swallow. "No. I'm sorry."

"No need to apologize," she replies with a forced smile.

Sitting back in my seat, I scan the women in our circle, noticing the way they glance at me nervously before looking back down at their Bibles. Ever since my father-in-law was caught in a sex club scandal and arrested for assaulting my brother-in-law's girlfriend, everyone at my church looks at me as if family scandal is a disease you can catch. As if I was in that sex club with him or I was the one holding down that poor woman as he punched her.

It might not be the same church, but word gets around. If it weren't for my perfect mother and straitlaced sister dragging me to these meetings, I probably would have stopped coming months ago —or maybe more.

My sister, Juliet, side-eyes me for not paying attention as she shifts in her seat.

"Before we end tonight's meeting, are there any prayer requests?" the leader of the group says, folding her hands in her lap.

I wince as my mother raises her hand.

"Yes, Mrs. Rockford."

My mother reaches over my sister's lap and squeezes my hand as she says, "My daughter, Briar, and her husband, Caleb, are still trying to conceive. It's been a tough road. If we could bring together the power of prayer for them, we'd be eternally grateful."

My stomach turns.

The women all nod in unison as the group leader leans toward us with an expression of nerve-grating sympathy. "Absolutely."

Everyone bows their heads and closes their eyes. I do the same.

But halfway through the prayer, I open them and peer upward at the people around me. While studying each of their somber faces, furrowed brows, and pressed lips, I try to feel *something*. Gratitude, hope, faith, love...anything.

"Amen," the woman says.

"Amen," the rest of us reply in unison.

"Thank you," I add quietly.

After everyone rises from their seats and says their goodbyes, my sister and I make our way to the parking lot first. Our mother has a way of lingering. She loves to strike up conversations with all of the other women, even though most of them are closer in age to Juliet and me.

I feel my phone buzz in the pocket of my sweater, and I pull it out to see the notification.

It's a fertile day! Get busy!

My fertility tracker likes to make jokes, but I'm not laughing.

"There's a woman in our PTA who said she cut all sugar and processed foods for six months, and she got pregnant after trying for years," Juliet says like the haughty know-it-all she is.

I let out a sigh. More unsolicited advice from my older sister.

"Thanks. I'll think about that," I mutter flatly.

She shrugs in a way that tells me she's disappointed with my response. As if I'm not appreciative enough of her gracious benevolence. "Just saying. That stuff is basically poison anyway. No wonder our bodies don't work the way they're supposed to."

My sister drones on, but I tune her out. She and my mother have a tendency to speak around me in a way that I'm not sure they realize hurts. The little comments about *my* body. The constant complaints about *my* fertility. The pining and wishing for another baby—*a boy this time.*

I don't argue. I don't speak up. I take it all in stride and sweep it under the rug—as the women in our family so often do.

I track my cycle. I have sex with my husband. I do everything to hold up my side of the bargain *for them.*

Caleb and I were really excited for another baby around the time Abigail turned three. We were riding that parenthood high when our lives were filled with toddler milestones and joy with every *new* thing having a baby brought. Now, Abby is six and a half and she's the love of our lives, but, to be honest, the idea of starting over scares me. The high has worn off.

Juliet and I wait by the car as Mom finally emerges, carrying a tray of cookies. She's wearing a bright smile as she says goodbye to the other women. I wait for the moment when she wipes the grin off her face and says what's *really* on her mind once she's out of earshot of the others.

"That woman actually brought up your brother-in-law," she mutters as she unlocks her car. "How embarrassing. Your husband's family has become the laughingstock of the whole town. The nerve of *her* bringing up your family drama as if her husband hasn't cheated on her five times in the past decade."

There it is.

"Mother," Juliet says in warning.

"What did she say?" I ask.

"She said she'll be praying for Adam Goode's soul and that he ought not to be associating himself with that woman and her...club. Like she has room to talk."

I climb into the back seat of my mother's car and slam the door. I'm not exactly looking forward to a car ride back to my house when I'm sure the two of them will do nothing but chastise Adam's girlfriend, Sage, for owning a sex club.

Again, I stay quiet.

Instead, I stare out the window for the rest of the drive.

When we reach my house, my mother stops at the curb.

"Thanks for the ride," I say as I open the door and move to climb out.

"Briar," she says, stopping me as I glance up at the front seat. "Just stay away from Adam and that girlfriend of his. They are nothing but trouble; we don't need that in our family. Just as bad as his father, if you ask me."

"I know," I lie.

As I step out onto the sidewalk and slam the door behind me, I want to tell my mother that Adam and Sage are my family, too. I see them every Sunday at Caleb's mother's house. I *like* Sage.

But I can't tell my mother that.

When I let myself in the front door of the house, it's quiet. Looking down at my watch, I see that it's eight thirty, and silently, I pray that Abby is asleep. After dropping my keys and purse on the entryway table, I go into the kitchen and immediately pour myself a glass of wine. Until there's a possibility that I'm pregnant, I can still have a glass for now.

Standing in the dim room, leaning against the island, I soak up the silence and enjoy the warmth from the wine as it travels down my throat.

I hate that I'm dreading tonight. I don't *dread* having sex with my husband. I love Caleb. I love his body and the way he touches me. I love sex with him.

But somewhere in the past three years of shots and schedules and doctors, the light has gone out. Any day now, I expect him to say he's done. And part of me fears that he has been done for a while but won't say it.

Done with me or with the trying or all of it.

At this point, those two things feel like one and the same. I have become *this*. I am the *trying*.

Taking my unfinished drink up the stairs, I hear the soft lullaby playing in Abby's room. Peeking my head in, I feel a smile grow across my lips as I stare at my husband sprawled out on our daughter's tiny twin bed, a unicorn book splayed open on his chest, and six-year-old Abigail cuddled up on his arm.

Leaning against the doorframe, I sip my wine as I stare at them. Seeing him like this definitely helps to turn my mood around.

Caleb has always had a way of getting Abby to sleep. Even as a baby, he would lay her on his chest or let her use his bicep as a pillow, and moments later, she was asleep. Memories like that make me miss having Abby as a baby. The sweet memories.

Not the colic or the sleepless nights, or the blowout diapers, or the exhaustion that burrowed itself into my bones like a tumor.

"Hey," he mumbles in a raspy whisper.

"Hey," I reply with a smile.

"She's out," he says.

"Like a light."

Slowly, he works himself out from under her. She rolls over sleepily, and he tucks the plush purple blanket around her tiny body. Carefully, he creeps out of her room, avoiding the small toys and creaky spots on the floor like land mines as he makes his way to me.

Meeting me in the doorway, he gives me a soft grin and presses his lips to my cheek.

"How was Bible study?" he asks in that fake-interest way he always does.

Although Caleb grew up in the church with his father literally running his own and becoming a worldwide famous preacher, Caleb doesn't care about God or religion at all anymore. Deep down, I think he thinks that bothers me, but it doesn't. I love how independent he is from his family. I think that's what I've always loved about him.

He takes the glass of wine from my hand and drinks a sip before handing it back to me. The silence between us starts to grow awkward, like a wilting rose.

Sometimes I wonder if it's just me. In his mind, is everything between us as perfect as it was seven years ago when we could barely keep our hands off each other? When I could see the way he would light up whenever I entered the room.

Doesn't he feel us dying, too?

I avoid looking him in the eye so I don't have to face it. Instead, I turn away and head to our bedroom. He follows, and we move through our nightly routine in thick, tense silence.

I floss my teeth. He takes his supplements. I put on moisturizer. He tosses his shirt on the floor next to the hamper.

Same as every night.

At some point, I know I need to remind him of what we have to do. But I can't bring myself to speak those words.

When we climb into bed, I let the opportunity slip away. He pulls out his laptop and I pick up my book. But even as my eyes settle on the words on the page, I don't read. Instead, I fantasize about a different life for us. I conjure up a fairy tale in my head of what Caleb and I were supposed to be. Happy. Connected.

I reminisce on the way it felt when we first met. When I thought Caleb was going to save me. When it felt as if he was my liberation, my safe space, my truth.

And in my fantasy, we don't have sex to conceive. Our lives look more similar to that of his brother and his girlfriend. Caleb wants me. He *needs* me. I belong to him in a way that's not based on scripture. Silently lying next to my husband, my body starts to heat up just thinking about it.

I know deep down that I should be able to express my desires with him, but I'm afraid we might be too far gone. And that's a harsh truth I don't want to face.

Two

Caleb

Theo Virgil shared a new post.

The small notification on my phone catches my eye in the dark bedroom. Without clicking away from the open case file on my laptop, I swipe open the Instagram app on my phone and wait for it to load.

Glancing to my left, I watch Briar as she reads her paperback with the small book light attached to the top.

She doesn't even notice me.

I look back at my phone, hiding the screen from her, and there he is.

Now dark-brown hair, piercing blue eyes, standing against a brick wall. It's clearly a posed photo. On his face is an expression of nonchalance. Uncaring, not quite bored, but not entirely indifferent either. Head tilted back, staring at the camera through his hooded eyes. I swallow as my eyes scan the image, absorbing the features of this new photo.

He's letting his facial hair grow to a scruff, unkept mess, but it looks good on him. Even his hair is wild and untamed.

Our father would hate it.

But our father will never see it because Theo Virgil is a stranger to Truett Goode. A nobody. Some random indie songwriter in Nashville, Tennessee, and certainly not the child he banished nine years ago.

All it took was a little digging, and I found him. Now, I just watch him as a protective but silent older brother.

Every photo *Theo* posts is like a piece of driftwood cast into the ocean, and I am the collector standing on the shore, picking up every little bit that I can.

He doesn't know I follow him, and he doesn't know I'm watching his every move. Every show. Every Instagram story. Every like, every follow, every comment. If he's tagged in something, I see it. If his songs are played, I hear them.

And hovering somewhere nearby is that message button, lurking like a bad omen that I'm too afraid to touch.

Beside me, Briar clears her throat. As she closes her book, I swipe to close the app on my phone.

"So..." she starts, cautiously setting her book on the nightstand. "It's the tenth."

She doesn't look into my eyes as she says that, stating the day of the month as if we're late on our mortgage payment or she's hinting that I missed our anniversary. But I know exactly what she means by stating the date. She's signaling to me that we have to try and make a baby.

I hate how uncomfortable she looks, chewing on her bottom lip, waiting eagerly for my reaction.

I hate that I set the tone for this entire thing.

I hate that I don't have a clue whether or not she *wants* to have sex, just that we have to. It's up to me not to appear disappointed or uninterested.

Slowly closing my laptop, I mentally encourage myself to give her the enthusiasm she needs.

"A fertile day," I say, forcing a smirk on my face.

I love my wife, and there's not a single day I regret that it's her warm body filling the space on the other side of my bed. But when I roll over and tug her under me, I know deep down that I'm doing it because a stupid fucking app on her phone has told her that we have to have sex and not because either of us truly wants to.

Just once, I'd like to have sex with my wife for the sake of fucking.

Her legs fall open, and I cage her in with my elbows on the pillow on either side of her head. In the dim light of our room, I stare down at her and try to remember what it felt like in the beginning. When we were new, the weight of this situation didn't loom over us, showering us with tension and guilt every time the pressure built too high.

I wish I could say *I love you* to her, but that would be too intimate and personal. And what we're about to do is anything but.

Lifting her oversized tee, I try to move farther down her body, but she grabs my arms and stops me.

"You don't need to do that," she says despondently.

I lift my head and stare at her, perplexed. "Let me at least make you feel good. I want to make sure you get off."

She tugs me upward again. "I don't need to get off to make a baby."

"How romantic," I mutter with a sigh.

"Caleb..." Her tone is pleading, and when I look up at her, I decide to swallow down the argument building inside me.

I hate this. I hate that my wife has to bear this and won't even let me make it better for her.

But I can't tell her I hate it.

"Not even if I want to?" I murmur against the tender, warm flesh below her breasts.

"It's late, Caleb."

Fuck, this is humiliating. Having to beg my wife to let me lick her pussy, both of us knowing full well that ten years ago, she loved how ravenous I was for her. But now it feels like we're just performing roles in a well-rehearsed play. And doing a shitty fucking job of it.

Instead of burying my face between her thighs, I kiss her lips as if I'm trying to revive something long past dead. She tries to play along, humming against my mouth, but the performance is weak. And when she reaches between us to stroke my cock to life, I swallow down another dose of mortification.

Once she decides it's hard enough to get the job done, she shimmies down her panties and puts me where she wants me. I spit into my palm to lube her up, but it feels like I'm touching a stranger. Staring at the headboard, I thrust inside her. There's not a single moan from either of us, and it's fucking depressing.

Deep down, I know she wants this to be over as fast as it can, so I lift up and thrust faster. She has her eyes closed, and it makes me miss the days when a fire would burn between us, caught in the throes of passion together. When the connection we shared felt like the biggest, most powerful thing in my life. Bigger than God. Bigger than my father and the church. Bigger than life and bigger than death.

Briar gave me something to believe in.

She *was* something to believe in.

But somewhere in the past seven years, she's plummeted away from me as if the weight of something pulled her under the surface beyond my reach. I don't know if it was me or her or the birth of our daughter or this baby we're so desperately trying to have. Or maybe all of them combined.

Time is the shackle dragging her down to the ocean floor.

In order to come, I have to imagine she's staring up at me. In my mind, she's the twenty-one-year-old who was off-limits, and fucking her was nothing more than a pipe dream. I have to imagine that what we're doing is a sin.

My orgasm is silent and pathetic and fills me with shame instead of pleasure. I don't miss the look of relief on her face afterward. Once I pull out and roll off her, she lifts her knees to her chest and stays that way for a while to keep my precious semen inside.

"Good night," I say awkwardly before rolling over. I wish I could say more.

I miss you.

I still love you.

I need you.

You mean everything to me.

These sentiments die before they reach my lips. They wouldn't make it over the wall between us anyway. She's already miles away.

Three

Dean

"Such a good fucking girl, aren't you?" I mutter through my teeth as I slam into the woman on her knees in front of me. She whines and moans with her face pressed into the mattress.

"Yes," she cries. "Harder."

I pick up my pace, practically bruising her backside with my hips. Her wrists are pinned together behind her back, held in place by my hand.

With every thrust, I gauge her reactions. She doesn't pull away or make any noises of pain. She's not shaking or trembling; from what I can tell, she feels good.

Mentally, I'm aware that there are only about twenty minutes left in our session, which means I need to start wrapping this up so we have time for aftercare.

Digging my free hand into her hair, I hoist her upright and bring my mouth to her ear. "Let me hear you come for me."

"I'm almost there," she says through panting breaths.

I quickly lean down and snatch the vibrator off the bed, clicking it on while I keep up my thrusts. When I press the low power of the wand against her clit, she starts bucking in my arms.

"That's my girl," I say in her ear. "Come on my cock. Don't you dare let me down."

She lets out a screaming wail of a moan as her body tenses. It sounds feral and wild. Once I know she's just about finished, I realize it's time to focus on myself.

I hate having to come at work. And I realize how ridiculous of a complaint that is. Most guys would think my job is a dream.

But my focus isn't getting myself off. That's what makes me good at my craft. It's the reason I'm scheduled months out. I'm not here to shoot my load. I'm here to be the best at what I do.

And judging by the way my client is howling and quaking with her ass in the air for me, I'd say I am the fucking best.

But as much as I hate it, I have to come in order for her to be satisfied. If I don't get my orgasm, then she will take it personally or assume it's not over until I do, neither of which is true.

Shutting my eyes, I take myself somewhere else. I drown out the noise and sensations of the moment. It has nothing to do with this beautiful creature in my bed. She's stunning and fun, and I genuinely like her a lot.

But for some reason, there's a block.

And it's been getting worse. Although I'm trying not to think about that. My sessions over the last few weeks have been difficult. Men, women, couples, groups...doesn't matter.

Sadie suggested I see a therapist about it. Or take some time off.

There I go again...getting lost in my thoughts and no closer to my climax.

My client's orgasm has ended, and she's melting into the mattress while I'm trying to finish.

Come on, Dean. Figure it out.

"Come inside me," she purrs, thinking it's what I need to finish.

"You want me to fucking come inside you?" I ask with a grunt. "Want me to fill you up?"

"Yes, yes, yes," she mumbles into the mattress.

Of course, this is all just talk. The only thing I'm coming in is a condom. And that's if I come at all.

Shutting my eyes again, I take myself to a few of my favorite memories, hoping one will get me there.

I'm so close, but it's downright cruel how much my orgasm will tease me. It hovers just out of reach—like it always does.

After a few more minutes, I do what I've resorted to doing over the past few weeks.

I fake it.

I'm not proud of it. But as I shudder and moan through a jizz-less orgasm, I silently pray my client won't pick up on it and start canceling her sessions.

When I'm done, I pull out and roll over to remove the clean condom and take it to the trash. My client has maneuvered to her back, staring at the ceiling, looking entirely satisfied and well-fucked. Her cheeks are red, and her hair's a mangled mess.

"How are you feeling?" I ask after I've picked up my black briefs from where they lie folded on the chair. As I slip them on, she gives me a soft smile and a nod.

"I'm wonderful."

On my way to the mini-fridge to retrieve her water bottle, I notice the time. Ten minutes left. Perfect.

I unscrew the cap as I reach the bed. "Be a good girl and sit up for me."

She gives me a flirtatious smile as she sits up on the bed, resting against the headboard. "Thank you," she murmurs as she takes the water. After the first sip, she looks at me with her lips pressed together. "My friend was right about you."

One side of my mouth lifts into a smirk. "Oh yeah? I hope that means you enjoyed yourself."

She chuckles to herself as she glances down. "I never imagined I'd do something like this."

Sitting on the bed, I reach out to her and touch her hand. "What do you mean by that?"

When she looks back up, she gives me a shrug. "I didn't just want sex," she says before chewing on her bottom lip. "But most guys I date just don't get it. Even if I told them what I wanted, they didn't take me seriously or take the time to make sure I even finished. It's pretty sad if you think about it. Having to pay someone to put your needs first."

That is fucking sad, but I don't say it. "I'm here for you anytime," I reply because what else am I going to say? That normal men being shit in the sack keeps me in business. That I'm glad she can't get a good fuck because then I know she'll come back and shell out another six hundred bucks.

It is fucking sad, but that's life. Life is fucking sad.

I'm just here to give orgasms when I can to make it a little less fucking sad.

"Thank you," she says, her mouth screwed up in a soft smirk.

After our session, I walk my client to the door. A security guard will ensure she gets to her car safely.

On my way back, I notice my pink-haired boss practically jogging across the club toward me.

"Dean," she calls before I can disappear back into my room.

Begrudgingly, I turn around to face her. "Sage."

"We just scheduled your last appointment for August. You are booked for the next three months." She says this with pride and excitement as she grabs my arm and gives it a squeeze. Then she leans in as if to tell me a secret. "You're by far our most popular escort out of them all."

That is not a secret. She knows that.

We all know that.

But Sage is kind and doesn't want to hurt anyone's feelings.

"Thanks," I reply politely. "I'm happy to add another opening in my week."

Emphatically, she shakes her head. "Absolutely not. You're already putting in eight sessions a week. Your dick is going to fall off if we add any more."

I smirk at her as I lean against the wall. "I appreciate your concern for my dick."

She playfully punches my arm.

"And you know...your mental health," she adds. "How's that block going?"

My face screws up at the mention of it. My inability to climax has become a public topic of concern at the club. Not that I mind. I'm not ashamed. "It'll pass."

"Things like that don't just pass, Dean. You're working too hard." She puts her hands on her hips as if that makes her look more authoritative. She's far too adorable to come across as assertive, but that's what I like about her. Sage doesn't give a shit about most things people concern themselves over. Images, norms, expectations, reputation.

Which is why she's less worried about my performance as one of her employees and more about my health as her friend.

"I'll figure it out, Sage. I promise."

She delicately rests her fingers on my forearm as she leans toward me. "Please take care of yourself. If you need time off, say the word, and we'll move things around."

"Thanks," I reply with a tight-lipped smile. I'm brushing off her offer before she can even get the words out.

Behind Sage, I notice the club manager, Sadie, rushing toward us with an expression on her face I don't like. Her eyes are wide and pointed directly at me.

"Dean," she says, sounding exasperated. "There was a call for you."

My blood runs cold as my spine straightens. Immediately, I think of my father. Ever since his lung cancer progressed to stage four, he's been staying with me.

"Who was it?" I ask, bracing myself for the news. But what comes out of her mouth takes me by surprise.

"It was the fire department. There was a fire at your house."

"Oh my god!" Sage replies, lifting her hand to her mouth. "Was anyone hurt?"

My teeth clench as I wait for the answer, but Sadie is quick to shake her head.

"No. Your dad got out okay. Everyone is fine, but they need you to go there *now*."

Maybe I waited to hear that my dad was okay before the anger started to set in. Maybe I didn't.

And as I dash toward my room to grab my phone and keys, I start to fume. Because I already know exactly how that fire got started, and I know exactly who to blame.

Four

Dean

"I'm just glad everyone's okay." Adam Goode stands in front of what's left of my house. And while I normally like my boss's boyfriend, right now, I'd like to deliver a hard right to his handsome fucking face. The last thing I need at this moment is his positivity bullshit.

Sure, I'm also glad my father wasn't hurt in the fire, but I'm still fucking pissed it happened in the first place.

The gray smoke continues to billow from the hole left above my garage, even though the fire has long been put out. Firefighters are still dousing it with water, and I can't tear my eyes away from everything I own being ruined even more. If it wasn't burned, it's being soaked.

My father groans from the ambulance, and it's the only thing that steals my attention away.

"Is he okay?" I ask as I approach where they have him resting on a stretcher in the back of the truck. His oxygen tank is still sitting at his side, the tubes in his nose and a blood pressure cuff on his arm.

"Vitals seem fine," the paramedic replies.

"I'm so sorry, son," my father mutters.

I don't reply. What would I say?

It's not your fault. *It was.*

It's okay, Dad. *It's not.*

We'll be fine. *We won't.*

He's still dying. Now he's just dying and homeless.

I've caught him smoking in his room a few times before, and it wasn't just the fact that he's still fucking smoking and drinking that pissed me off. It was the fact that when I caught him smoking, he was passed out with the cigarette still between his fingers and ashes all over his chest.

I warned him that he'd burn the house down. He's lucky he didn't get the flame close enough to his oxygen tank.

But he doesn't listen to me. He *never* listens to me.

And he's *always* so sorry, which only makes me feel like an asshole for being so angry at him.

"We got you two a room at the hotel for a couple of nights," Sage says with her phone in her hand as she approaches us. I didn't ask her and Adam to come, but they insisted. And I hate to say it, but their kindness grates on my nerves.

"You didn't have to do that," I mutter indignantly. I fucking hate charity.

"We know, but we want to help," she replies.

My shoulders tense as I bite my tongue. Because what the fuck are we supposed to do after those two nights? Where will we go?

As if the cards weren't stacked against us enough, now I have to tend to my terminally ill father in a hotel room.

Adam takes a step closer. "Do you happen to know anyone else in the area who could give you a place to stay while they do repairs?"

"No," I mumble.

I despise the expression on Adam's face. I can tell just by the way he's concentrating that he's trying to come up with a solution for me, and I want to tell him to stop. Not being able to stand being helped is a stubborn, useless trait of mine, but I'd rather sit here and struggle alone than let anyone else help me, especially out of the goodness of their heart.

But that's just how the Goode family is. They're a church family through and through. I was around them for a couple of years as a kid. From the age of twelve to fourteen, I practically lived at the Goode residence because I was best friends with Adam's youngest brother, Isaac.

That is until I was shoved out of his life for being a bad influence and told to never return. A few years later, he vanished into thin air during our senior year of high school. Turns out the God-fearing patriarch of the family wasn't so altruistic when it came to his gay son.

I hated his father even before that day, and I've hated him ten times more since then.

I have nothing against Adam. He was so much older than us growing up that he was moved out before I even started coming around. But if I ever see that other Goode brother again, I swear...

"Caleb's got a room for rent, doesn't he?" Sage says enthusiastically to Adam, who immediately nods.

Meanwhile, I'm frozen in place at the sound of that name.

"That's right. He does," Adam replies. "I'm sure he'd be willing to offer it to a family friend in need."

A family friend.

"It's upstairs, though," Sage adds. "Won't that be a problem for Dean's dad?"

"Oh yeah..." Adam puts that contemplative expression back on his face.

My teeth are clenched so tight my jaw hurts. I scratch the back of my neck without responding to their offer. I need this conversation to end right now before I explode.

"You guys mind if we talk about this tomorrow? I need to get my dad to the hotel so he can rest."

"Of course," they respond in unison.

"Can we offer you a ride?" Adam asks.

I shake my head. "No, thank you. I, uh, appreciate all of your help, though."

After helping my dad to the car, I make sure everything is squared away with the fire department before pulling away from the rubble of my home.

†

I stand by the bathroom door, listening intently in case my dad falls and gets hurt. He is still insistent on showering himself, although I've offered to help. When he finally comes out, he's gasping for breath, like he's just finished climbing ten flights of stairs.

"You okay?" I ask with a hand on his back as I guide him to the first bed.

"I'm fine," he rasps breathlessly as he leans against the headboard in the thick sweats I bought at the store on the way to the hotel.

He looks so elderly now. I'm used to having a dad so much older than the dads of other people my age. When I was growing up and had friends with dads in their thirties and forties, my dad was already in his late sixties. He and my mom had me when he was almost fifty. She wasn't interested in raising a child at her age, so she ran off with some guy she met when I was only seven.

From that point, it was just me and a man who should have been enjoying his retirement. A man who most people assumed was my grandfather. A man who sacrificed everything for me.

I know that everyone in our town assumed my dad was a shitty father. That he drank too much and didn't provide me with the life I deserved, but they were wrong. He's not perfect, but no one is. The truth is that he was the best dad he could have been.

And now he needs me, and I can't do shit about it.

After my dad is settled, I take a quick shower and order some food. Then I sit at the desk and open my laptop.

"Son," my father mutters in his gravelly, breathless voice across the room.

"What, Dad?" I ask, not looking up from the claims page on my insurance company's website.

"You should take that place."

"Huh?" I ask, not entirely paying attention.

"Take the place that man offered you."

"You heard him," I reply without glancing up. "It's on the second floor. Those stairs would kill you."

Not to mention, the room is owned by the one person in this town I hate. But I don't tell my dad that part.

"I don't mean for me, Dean. I'm mean for you."

Finally, I do look up. "What are you talking about? Where the hell are you going to go?"

"The retirement community can take care of me, so you don't have to. And they have hospice there when the time comes."

"Fuck that," I mumble, shutting down the argument. "I'm not leaving you to some fucking nurses. I will take care of you."

"Goddammit, son. Will you just listen to me? I'm tired of being..." He pauses to catch his breath, his eyes fluttering closed as he fights the urge to pass out.

"Jesus, Dad. Calm down." I shut my laptop and cross the room toward him, checking the settings on his oxygen tank.

When he finally settles down, he's wearing an expression of frustration. And I get it. I'd hate to be in his shoes. I'd hate feeling so helpless that others have to take care of me. I hate the thought of needing anyone.

I will never let myself get to this point, though.

But I also won't have a stubborn-as-fuck grown kid to relentlessly keep me alive, either.

"I'm serious, Dean," he rasps. "I'm done. You're twenty-six. You shouldn't be taking care of an old man who smoked too much and lived like a goddamn fool. My insurance and retirement fund will cover it. Just call them."

"I said no, you stubborn old fucker."

"I'm not backing down from this fight," he says with a grunt. "You can either take me to that home, or I'll call a taxi myself. You hear me? Now go. Call them."

I stand upright and cross my arms over my chest. Inside, I'm fuming, but this anger burns like pain. And fear.

What if I drop him off at some retirement home, and he passes away without me there?

What if they're too busy with someone else and they don't get him his medicine on time?

Why doesn't he think about these things like I do?

"You won't be able to smoke there, you know," I say indignantly.

He waves me off. "Like they could stop me."

"Come on," I argue. "This is ridiculous. We don't need to put you in a home. We'll figure it out. Can't you just give me a chance to figure it out?"

"I'm the one who fucked up, son. Why should you have to pay for it?" he says. When he talks a lot like this, he starts to get out of breath. I hate the way his skin turns gray, the way it is now.

"Dad, stop—"

He puts up a hand, cutting off my words. As I kneel down in front of him, I feel a lump building in my throat. He looks so miserable.

I watch him struggle through nasty coughs for a while, and when he finally gets through it, he turns his glassy stare toward me. The look in his eyes is pleading, and I realize that I have to give in.

The nurses at the home could give him real care. They could have doctors on hand. They'd keep him comfortable, and it's a lot more than I can offer at the moment.

"Son," he rasps. "Please."

With a heavy sigh, I nod. "Fine. I'll call them first thing in the morning."

"Thank you," he mouths before resting his tired eyes and letting his head flop onto the pillow.

I return to my laptop when he's asleep but can't focus on the insurance page. I'm dreading that call tomorrow. I'm dreading the moment when I have to leave him at the home. I'm dreading the moment when I have to take Adam Goode's stupid charity.

I just keep thinking that doing the right thing feels a lot like failure.

FIVE

Caleb

I love Mondays. The only people who can't stand Mondays are people who toil away at jobs they hate. Lucky for me, I love my job. So I love Mondays. What I can't stand is a tired Thursday or a lazy Friday, but on Mondays, the work is fulfilling. The email inbox is full, and there's always something that requires my attention. And I love to feel needed.

There's an open case file on my computer and a to-do list three miles long.

"Jules, any word from the medical examiner on that Hawkins case?" I call through the open door toward my secretary.

"Not yet," she replies.

Just then, my cell phone rings and I glance down expectantly. I nearly pick it up in a rush of anticipation, but I pause when I notice my brother Adam's name on the caller ID.

I stifle a groan as it rings again.

"Is that them?" Jules calls.

"No," I mutter lowly. "Shut the door, would you, Jules?"

"Yep," she says with a forced smirk as she pulls my office door closed between us.

Lately, it feels like one fire after another with my family—especially Adam. Ever since he discovered our father owned a sex club and was harboring some pretty dark secrets, it feels like our family's drama has turned into a never-ending charade. It's like the most dramatic season of television, and I'm *this close* to unsubscribing altogether.

The world-famous preacher wasn't just exposed as a swindling cheater and a liar. No. On top of that, he was arrested for attacking Adam's girlfriend, Sage, at a party last year. He put her in the hospital and practically shattered her trachea into pieces.

Naturally, my father posted bail and is on house arrest until the DA's office decides on his charges and brings him to trial.

I love working in law, but God, I hate how slow the process is. Put him behind bars, or don't. At this point, I don't care. I just want this limbo we're in to be over. Just when it feels like things are starting to calm down, the next shoe drops.

"You're on speaker," I say after hitting the button on my phone. My older brother's voice echoes through my office as he replies in a somber greeting.

"Hey."

"Please tell me you're calling to invite me to a birthday party or tell me that you've won a million dollars," I respond with a chuckle.

"Is it ever good news anymore?" he replies.

I let out a despondent sigh while rubbing my brow. "I wish. What's up?"

"Do you remember Dean Sheridan?" he asks.

The bounce in my knee stops immediately, and my head pops up as I stare in confusion at my phone. That's nowhere near what I expected to hear.

Dean Sheridan.

That's a name I haven't thought of in a long time.

Dean was my brother's best friend growing up. Or maybe they

were more? But while I was going through college, the kid practically lived at our house.

Clearing my throat, I respond, "Uh, yeah. Why?"

There's a twinge of concern in the back of my mind, wondering if something might have happened to him. Or that maybe he has some news about Isaac.

"Well, he's been working at Sage's club for the past few months."

My brows pinch inward as I stare at my phone on the desk. "Working how?"

Technically, it's none of my business, and probably not why my brother is calling, but I can't help my curiosity. Adam's girlfriend owns a sex club. So unless Dean is a bartender or bouncer, there's really only one type of *work* he could be doing there.

"What do you think, Caleb?" my brother snaps defensively. "Does it really matter?"

"I'm not judging," I argue.

"Yes, you are— Listen, this isn't why I'm calling."

"Then why are you calling?" I ask with annoyance. Ever since my brother had his little mental breakdown, sexual awakening, or whatever it was last year, his high horse has gotten even fucking higher.

"Dean had a fire at his house last night. He's okay, but the place looks like it'll be demolished. Which means he needs a place to stay for a while."

I let the line go silent as I wait for him to elaborate. I'm not exactly sure what any of this has to do with me. Or why he thinks I should be the one to help Dean.

I hardly know the guy. The last time I saw him, he was only fourteen. He's gotta be, like...twenty-six now. And we didn't exactly part ways on good terms.

"Okay..." I say, letting my voice trail.

Adam continues, "I know you and Briar have that extra room above the garage you guys have considered renting out."

Everything inside me tenses.

While it's true that Briar and I do have an extra room above the garage—equipped with its own bathroom and kitchenette—and it is true that we have considered putting it up for rent for extra income, letting a sex worker from my brother's girlfriend's sex club live there doesn't sound exactly like a great idea.

Okay, so maybe I am being judgmental.

Growing up in a religious family, there were two constant themes in our upbringing. One was compassion and charity toward others. Loving thy neighbor and all that shit.

The other was righteousness. Be good. Follow the rules. Don't stray from the path. Essentially, don't be like *them*.

The former was really my mother's work. And the latter was my father's.

My mother is a fucking saint. My father is a judgmental prick.

Guess which way I lean?

"I don't know, Adam," I grumble. I don't say it out loud, but I immediately think of Abby, my six-year-old. I've got a little girl to protect. I can't just be inviting strangers onto our property, even if it's not in our home. I barely know this guy.

Immediately picking up on my hesitation, Adam says, "I get it, Caleb. I understand you have a family to protect, but Sage and I can vouch for this guy. He's a hard worker. He's honest. And it's not like he'd be living in your house."

I don't respond, letting the line go quiet again as I consider what he's requesting.

He probably should have known that had he gone to Briar with this request, she would have accepted without an ounce of distrust. Like my mother, my wife is a fucking saint.

But I'm not.

And that's when Adam hits me with the real gut wrencher.

The unspoken thing.

The grief-shaped elephant in the room.

"Besides," he starts quietly. "This is Isaac's friend."

"Low blow," I reply.

"I know, I know," he mumbles.

The line grows quiet once again and thick with tension. There's a moment in our silence when I wonder if Adam is thinking the exact same thing I'm thinking—a tie to Isaac's past is a tie to Isaac.

My brother has no idea that I see Isaac's face on a phone screen every single day. But I have my suspicions that Adam is looking for him, too, although we've never really spoken about it.

And yet, here we are, eating up crumbs our brother left behind.

Renting that room to Dean Sheridan is not going to bring Isaac back into my life. But I'd be lying if I said it didn't feel like, in some small way, I'd have a piece of him.

Then I remember the last night I saw Dean Sheridan. It's possible he's grown out of his teenage resentment toward me, but not likely. If it's anything like it was twelve years ago, he hates my fucking guts. I doubt he would even accept a room for rent on my property. Even if I let him stay there for free.

But I decide not to tell Adam that part. He doesn't need to know all the dirty details of what went down before Isaac left.

The phone line has been quiet for a few minutes when Adam tries one more tactic.

"Listen, if you don't want to help the guy, then don't help him," he says condescendingly.

I quickly cut him off. "Oh, don't play that holier-than-thou shit with me, Adam. I picked you up from the county jail last year, remember?"

He doesn't respond, and I let him hear my throaty chuckle. He should know better than to try and manipulate a lawyer.

But without another response from him, I know the ball is now in my court.

"Let me talk to Briar about it, okay?" I say to at least appease him for now.

"Of course," Adam replies.

"And you're sure this guy doesn't have any other place to go?" I ask.

"I'm sure."

If I remember correctly, Dean didn't have a lot of family. Just a very old dad who, I assumed by this point, has probably passed away. So, I don't find it hard to believe that he doesn't have a lot of family to fall back on.

And I know that if my brother could take him in, he definitely would. But he and his girlfriend live in an apartment with an annoying three-legged dog.

"I'll get back to you later, okay?" I add to end the conversation.

"Sounds good," he replies with a sigh.

It's like ever since he brought up Isaac, the tone of our conversation has gotten a little more melancholy.

"Thanks, Caleb," he says.

"Don't thank me yet."

The line goes dead, but I don't move for a moment. I just sit in my chair and stare straight ahead, caught somewhere between the past and the present.

The day Isaac left nine years ago feels so far away, but the pain of that year hangs over us like a dark cloud. One of these days, I wish it would just rain down on us and disappear, but it doesn't. It just hovers there, blocking the sun, threatening us with a downpour that we might not recover from.

We can't let go. There is no letting go of someone who just runs away. There is no grief process, no funeral, no goodbye, no see you later.

There's just me sitting on the porch of my parents' house one night after Sunday dinner, listening to my seventeen-year-old brother spill his heart out to our parents, only for my father to wave a Bible in his face, threaten him with an eternity in hell, and throw him out the door.

Most days, it feels like I'm still sitting on those porch steps, and part of me worries that I always will be.

I don't know how long I sit here in silence, staring at nothing at all. But it's my secretary, Jules, who knocks on the door and finally steals my attention.

I glance up at her expectantly as she opens it.

"What's up?" I ask, trying to shake off the mood.

"I just heard an update on your father's case," she says carefully.

That piques my interest.

I sit up tall in my chair and stare at her as I wait for more. "And?"

"The DA is charging him with attempted murder."

My mouth goes dry as I gape at her.

We've been waiting weeks for this call. And it could have gone either way. Attempted murder obviously being the more severe of the charges.

But I gotta admit, I'm a little surprised.

I'm astounded that my father didn't have one single good connection in the DA's office to get him a lesser charge. If I know anything about the man, it's that he knows exactly how and who to manipulate in his favor. He's been churching up blackmail since I was a kid.

So, for him to get the highest sentence possible nearly knocks me out of my seat.

I must stare at Jules for far too long because she finally asks, "Are you okay?"

Stammering, I reply, "Yeah, I guess."

"Not what you expected, huh?"

"Not at all," I reply.

"You think he's gonna fight it?" she asks, her arms crossed, leaning against the doorframe.

"Oh, abso-fucking-lutely, he's gonna fight it. My father taking responsibility for his actions? Not likely." I lean back in my office chair, steepling my fingers in front of me as I try to imagine what the man must be thinking right now. I bet he's fuming.

"Do you think that lawyer of his can pull it off?" she asks, pressing the question.

Immediately, I tense.

My father has had the same lawyer for as long as I can remember. He's a grease stain of a human named Wilford Carmichael. I've despised the man since I was a teenager.

Why a good Christian pastor needed a slimy defense attorney was beyond me. What did my father have to defend?

Obviously, now it makes a lot more sense.

But with the news of these charges, it's obvious Carmichael has about as much skill in a courtroom as he does merit as a human being.

Which is to say none at all.

"You know what I'm thinking, right?" Jules asks.

I let out a groan of frustration. "That he's going to ask me to help him get a lesser charge."

"I'm amazed he hasn't already," she replies.

At this point, I'm sure my father wishes that it was his good son, Adam—you know, before their big falling out last year—who was the skilled defense attorney and not me.

The last person in our family, aside from Isaac, who would be expected to defend my father's good nature, would be me.

We don't exactly get along, and we honestly never have.

I have never looked up to Truett Goode the way my older brother did. I just didn't see the appeal. He never came across as impressive or powerful to me. He's always just seemed like a selfish old man who loved power, attention, and fandom. The man who taught us not to worship false idols and yet proceeded to parade around as if he were one.

"So what are you going to say if he does?" she continues.

"Fuck, I don't know, Jules. Am I really the best man for the job?"

This makes her laugh as she leaves my office with her eyebrows raised and her head shaking.

"Not even close."

Six

Briar

21 years old

Sean's arm is slung over my shoulder as he walks me to my next class. He doesn't have a ten a.m. course, but he insists on walking me around campus as if I'm not safe here by myself.

"What are we doing tonight?" I ask, glancing up at him. Secretly I hope he has something planned for just us. A movie, a date, or even just being alone at his apartment. But lately, getting my boyfriend to even express interest in me feels like pulling teeth.

I throw out the line, and he never takes the bait.

"I'm going out with the guys. There's a fight on tonight. I told you that, babe."

I nod. "Sorry, I forgot."

He chuckles and playfully tugs on my hair. "My little dumb blonde. Always forgetting."

Forcing a laugh in return, I shake it off.

I can be such a ditz sometimes.

When we reach my building, I stop at the door, but he insists on walking me all the way in. After I open it, I feel him following me. My art history class is in the big lecture hall, and there are plenty of open seats, so I don't have to rush in. Technically, I'm not even in *this class. I'm the TA, so I don't need to find a good seat.*

"You have two more minutes," Sean reminds me when I try to kiss him goodbye.

I settle against the cool white paint-covered brick wall as he crowds me like he's protecting me from something.

Then, I spot a familiar face entering the building.

My eyes follow Caleb Goode, and my heart picks up speed when I notice him walking straight toward us.

"Goode," Sean says, addressing him as he turns away from me. The two guys greet each other with a casual handshake and chest bump thing. And when Caleb glances at me, I have to look away. "What are you doing here?" Sean asks him.

Caleb points toward the door. "I had to switch to art history," he says. "I didn't have enough humanities credits to graduate."

Sean scoffs. "That's so fucking lame. Like you need this shit in the real world, right?"

Caleb only chuckles uncomfortably, and I bite the inside of my cheek.

"I don't know a single thing about art history," Caleb says, and I can feel his eyes on me again.

"I can help you," I reply in a soft stammer.

"You're in this class?" he asks.

My lips tug into a crooked smirk. "This is my major. I'm the TA."

Caleb's expression doesn't change as he nods. "Lucky me."

Swallowing the strange feeling building in my throat, I glance down at my watch. "We should go in. Class is starting."

Sean slaps my ass and kisses my cheek before shoving me toward the door. Then he turns to Caleb. "She'll make sure you pass. It's the least she can do after fucking up your car the other day."

Leaving them behind, I enter the classroom and head toward the front. The professor is a woman well into her sixties, and she's nice. Most of the semester already, I've spent just watching and helping where she needs it. But it's laid back. This means I get to spend three hours a week just listening to someone talk about art, and as boring as that sounds to most, it's like heaven to me.

When I glance up at the door and watch Caleb walk in after talking to Sean, he gives me an awkward wave. Caleb has the kind of face you don't forget. He's not just handsome. Sean is handsome. Henry Cavill is handsome.

Caleb is...unforgettable.

And it's so much more than the features of his face—the sandy-brown hair he keeps combed back and the sharp cheekbones and the warm hazel orbs.

It's the light in his eyes. The gentleness of his smile.

I hope that whoever ends up with him appreciates that.

Sean talks about how strange Caleb is because he never hangs out with them or flirts with the cheerleaders at practice, but I don't think he's strange. When he looks at me, it's like he actually sees me.

Caleb takes a seat toward the back, and when the professor starts talking, I head up the stairs and slide into the seat next to him.

"Aren't you supposed to be teaching or something?" he whispers.

I smile as I rest my chin in my hand and keep my eyes on the screen portraying Degas. "Not really. I mostly help grade papers."

"Sounds boring," he replies.

"I love it." After a moment, I add, "I'm sorry about hitting your car."

"I don't care about my car," he replies under his breath. When I glance toward him with a soft smile, I see something like hesitation on his face, like he wants to say more, but he doesn't.

"I can still help you in this class," I say, looking into his soulful eyes.

He stares back, and the warmth from his gaze makes me feel as if I'm melting. "Thank you."

†

Present day

. . .

"Okay, pour the chocolate chips in now."

Abby's tiny hands grip the side of the mint-green porcelain bowl as she dumps two cups of miniature chocolate chips into the batter.

"Like that?" she asks.

"Perfect," I reply, patting her gently on the back.

Then I hand her the wooden spoon with a smile.

"You want to try to mix it too?" I ask.

"Yes, I'll do it," she replies proudly.

She struggles at first. And soon, chocolate chips are flying all over my kitchen. I wince when I hear one fall behind the stove.

So I step behind her and hold the spoon over her hand. "You're doing a great job, but let me help."

Together, we mix chips evenly through the batter, and she starts to fidget with anticipation for the next step.

In the distance, I hear the garage door opening, and I glance at the clock to see that it's just past three thirty, which means Caleb's home early.

"Now what?" Abby asks excitedly.

I hand her the ice cream scoop with the floral pink handle, and I show her how to form the batter into perfect cookie-sized balls.

She pops a dollop of batter into her mouth with a mischievous smirk.

Together, we giggle as she says, "Yum!"

Behind us, I hear the door open and look over my shoulder to see Caleb walking in. He drops his keys and wallet on the entryway table as Abby squeals with joy.

"Daddy's home!"

There's a serious expression on his face that he quickly hides with a bright smile for our daughter.

"Hey, peanut!" he greets her as he crosses the kitchen toward us. First, he kisses the top of Abby's head and then my cheek. "How are my girls?"

"We're making chocolate chip cookies!" she shrieks.

"Looks delicious," he says with a fake smile for her.

After standing up, he lets his grin fade away and makes brief eye contact with me before escaping to our bedroom. Not only can I tell he's had a hard day of his own, but I also have to break the news to him that the two-week wait has closed, and I took a test today. Negative, again.

"Okay, peanut," I say to Abby, "I want you to fill this whole tray with these little cookie balls and call me when you're done."

"Okay, Mama," she replies.

After brushing my hands on my apron and pulling it over my head, I follow Caleb up to our room.

"You're home early. Everything okay?" I ask with concern when I find him peeling off his work shirt and draping it over the chair in the corner.

When my husband turns toward me, I can practically see the tension dripping from his shoulders. I feel like he's aged twelve years in the past twelve months. The last year has been hard on us all.

Typical for Caleb, he often carries all of this tension alone. Just once, I wish he would unload all of that worry and anxiety and let me help him carry it.

"Nothing you really need to worry about," he replies, and my mouth sets in a thin line.

"Caleb, talk to me."

With a shake of his head, he mumbles, "It's just work stuff."

"Okay, do you at least want to talk about it?" I ask.

"Not really."

Standing near the door, I watch him as he peels off his belt and slacks, throwing them haphazardly onto the bed before sliding into a pair of his black joggers.

As he turns toward me, he looks as if he's just remembered something. "Actually, there is one thing I need to talk to you about."

I lean against our dresser. "Okay, hit me."

It takes him a moment to reply as if he's trying to gather his words or decide how he's going to phrase them—which has me a little concerned.

"Adam called me today," he says plainly.

Uh-oh.

"Apparently, there's a guy who works at Sage's club who had a fire at his house last night. He basically called to ask if we'd let this guy stay in our rental room above the garage, but I told him that's crazy, right? The guy's a—"

He pauses, staring at the door as if he's watching to make sure our daughter is out of earshot. Then he whispers the next two words.

"Sex worker."

Maybe if he had told me this a year ago, I'd respond with shock or horror. But after everything, I'm not sure anything could surprise me now.

"What did you say?" I ask without much reaction.

The way he phrased that question made it sound as if he's already told his brother no or that he wants me to side with him and tell him how crazy that is, although, to be honest, it's not all that crazy to me.

"Well, I mean, I told him we have a little girl to protect here," he says, waving his hand toward the kitchen where Abby is still working on the cookies. "I can't just let strangers come stay at our rental room."

I nod to show that I hear him and then carefully reply, "I thought that was the whole plan of the rental room."

"Yeah, but not...sex workers."

I put up my hands to stop him. I know my husband is not that ignorant. Whatever is really bothering him has to be more than that. Subtly, I work around the topic.

"Okay. Let's forget that part for now. Sage *owns* that club, and we trust her immensely. So just because somebody works there doesn't mean they're dangerous, Caleb."

This only makes him look more frustrated.

"I know, but fuck, it makes me uncomfortable."

"I understand, but it's not fair for you to judge somebody you haven't even met," I reply.

He scratches the back of his neck for a moment before glancing at me.

"Actually, I have met him."

"Oh?"

"He was a...a friend of Isaac's," he stammers.

"Oh."

Now we're getting somewhere.

The room grows silent as Caleb and I stare at each other. His younger brother Isaac has been a red-button topic for as long as I've known Caleb.

It was a couple years before Abby was born when Isaac ran away from home without a word. To say his family has harbored some pretty deep scars from the entire thing would be a grand understatement.

So I tread lightly on the topic.

"Is the reason you want to say no to this because the guy works at the sex club or because..." My voice trails off as he looks up from the floor to my face. The weight of what I'm implying lies heavily between us.

That my husband can't bear to be around somebody tied to Isaac.

That the guilt of even seeing him might be too much to handle.

That he feels any guilt at all.

"I don't know," he mumbles to himself.

Dropping into the chair in the corner, he props his elbows onto his legs and runs his fingers through his hair.

A piece of my chest aches to see him in so much distress. It's as if I can feel the anxiety that courses through him as it courses through me, too.

Quietly crossing the room, I brush my fingers through his soft brown hair and pull his head toward me, letting him rest it against my lower belly. For a moment, he allows himself to melt into me.

As I caress my fingers down his neck, I speak gently. "I can't make this decision for you. I know how hard it is, but just keep in mind that we can always protect Abby. No matter who rents that room above the garage. And whatever you decide, you don't have to decide it alone."

He wraps his large arms around my legs, tugging me closer. And even though I know he's struggling, I love this feeling.

I love knowing that he needs me.

I love feeling as if we're in this together.

I miss this.

I can only imagine the river of thoughts, feelings and fears running through Caleb's mind right now. I just wish he would voice them. I wish he'd let me hear every single one.

But I know better.

I know that my husband is strong but silent. He sees his purpose as protecting us, no matter the cost. And I know to him that means to bear the burden alone.

But just once, I wish he would let *me* protect *him*.

"Mama," a small voice calls from the kitchen. "I'm done."

"Okay, peanut. I'll be right out," I holler back.

Caleb tilts his head up toward me, and I stare down into those disarming eyes I fell in love with ten years ago.

With a shrug, I say, "I think it'd be fun to have someone new around. I'm sure your mom would love to help me fix up the room for him."

Caleb's expression turns contemplative. I don't know the reason he finally changes his mind. Maybe deep down, he sees helping this man as a way of helping his brother. Or relieving himself from some of the guilt he feels.

But with a soft nod, he finally says, "I'm going to tell Adam yes, then."

My smile softens. "Okay."

"Okay," he echoes.

Then I run my fingers through his hair again and lean down to press my lips to his.

As I pull away, I add, "By the way, I took a test today."

His expression changes before he winces. "Fuck, Briar. I completely forgot. I'm so sorry."

"It's okay," I reply, rubbing his shoulder and acting like it's not a big deal. "It was negative, of course."

"Why didn't you wait for me?" he asks with sympathy on his face.

I just shrug in response. Because I hate his disappointment, I think. Because we are incapable of relying on each other for some reason. Because if I take the test alone, then I don't have to act devastated by the results.

Instead of saying any of that, I just force a grin. "Everything's going to be okay."

I watch the muscles in his jaw tic as he clenches his teeth and swallows, fighting off emotion.

Solemnly, he replies, "I know."

Seven

Dean

14 years old

As the lights of the theater dim, I set my elbow on the armrest between Isaac and me.

He bumps mine off and replaces it with his own. "Don't even think about it," he mutters, and I stifle a smile.

There's an empty seat on his other side where his brother will be sitting once he gets back from getting popcorn.

"Did you talk to him?" I whisper as the first credit starts playing.

Isaac glances toward me and then down to his lap. "No. It's a stupid idea."

"No, it's not," I argue. "He'll totally have your back."

"It doesn't matter," Isaac says under his breath.

"Yes, it does." My voice grows louder, and I notice a couple in front of us glance our way, so I shrink down in my seat.

"You wouldn't understand, Dean," he murmurs. "So just drop it."

My teeth grind as my brows pinch together. I should tell him that I do understand. The only part I don't get is why he's bending over backward for a family that can't love him and accept him the way he is.

Just then, I spot his brother climbing the stairs toward our seats.

"Here," Caleb says as he places the bucket on his brother's lap. "You're in the middle, so you have to hold it."

"Thanks," he mutters with his eyes on the movie screen.

"What's wrong with you?" Caleb asks before glancing at me as if I'm to blame.

I shrug in response.

"I'm trying to watch the previews," Isaac whispers angrily.

When Caleb offers me a comforting smile, I try to let the whole thing roll off my shoulders. I want to press the topic some more, but Isaac is too scared to even try.

Out of his whole family, his brother, Caleb, seems like the most down to earth. He hangs out with us a lot now. He's even made subtle comments that make me think he'd be cool with it.

At some point, Isaac is going to have to come out. I just figure his brother seems like the best person to come out to.

†

Present day

I dread every single mile of road I cover between my ash pile of a home and Caleb Goode's house. It's only seventeen miles, but it might as well be another planet. Because, of course, Caleb has settled his family in a cozy suburban neighborhood outside of the city.

What am I doing?

That's been the phrase of the day. I muttered the same thing to myself this morning as I rummaged through the remnants of my home to salvage what I could—a small heap of smoke-stained belongings now piled in the trunk of my car.

And I said it again after driving away from my dad in the nursing home.

What the fuck am I doing?

As I make the final turn onto Caleb's street, I mutter a curse to myself. Naturally, Caleb's house has a picket fence out front. The front yard is a deep and vibrant green. The house itself is a two-story with a white-painted brick exterior and ivy growing up the side.

I pull my car into the curved driveway, staring up at the small apartment above the detached garage.

What on earth compelled me to agree to this? There must have been something, aside from the fact that they've offered to let me live in the rental for free. I can't help but wonder if, deep down, I'm agreeing to live in close proximity to this pompous asshole who ruined my life when I was only fourteen for a more obtuse reason.

Like, maybe finally facing him for the first time in twelve years to tell him what an ignorant, selfish, homophobic piece of shit he is.

As soon as I turn my car off, I spot movement through the window of the apartment over the garage. A few moments later, a woman emerges from behind the small building and rushes toward my car with a warm smile.

She's wearing a pair of high-waisted blue jeans, loose around her calves, and a soft white V-neck T-shirt.

What a little trophy she is.

She beams at me, soft and acquiescent, as I open my car and climb out.

"You must be Dean," she says with her delicate hand extended toward me.

For the first time all day, I find myself smiling.

Reaching out, I hold hers softly. "And you must be Briar."

"It's so nice to meet you," she replies politely. "And I'm so sorry to hear about your house. That's just awful."

I force myself to swallow. "Thank you."

In the distance, I hear a door closing. Just as I drop Briar's hand, I spot Caleb appearing from the backyard to greet us.

At first glance, I'd consider Caleb rather forgettable. A typical white man in his early thirties, wearing a pair of black slacks and a tight polo. But as he gets closer, I swallow my resentment at just how handsome he's grown over the years.

Symmetrical features. Enigmatic hazel eyes. Long lines and warm tones. It's infuriating.

When his eyes meet mine, I take pride in not betraying a single emotion. If anything, my expression screams indifference.

You mean nothing to me, Caleb Goode.

He bristles at my reaction. Then cordially puts out his hand.

"It's been a long time. Good to see you again."

I let his hand hang in the blank space between us for a moment, hoping it'll make him sweat before I finally reach out and shake it, being sure to squeeze it enough to inflict a little pain without seeming too rough. He winces.

I watch as his jaw clicks when he releases my hand. Then he shoves his own into his pocket. "I'm sorry to hear about what happened to your house. Briar and I are happy to help."

If he thinks I'm going to thank him, he's crazy.

"Yes, of course," she chimes in. "Please know that you are welcome here as long as you need. Caleb and I are just happy to help in any way we can."

"I appreciate that," I reply, keeping my gaze trained on her. "Please, let me offer you compensation."

"Absolutely not," Briar says, cutting me off with a wave of her hands.

"That's very kind of you. But I won't be staying longer than three months. By then, my insurance claim should be settled, and I'll find a new place." My tone is emotionless as I let my gaze rake over her face.

She really is beautiful in a remarkable sort of way that might go unnoticed by most. She seems like the type of woman who thrives on blending in. Her hair hangs just past her shoulders in delicate waves with streaks of warm gold with platinum blonde.

Her makeup is subtle. Some blush on her cheeks and a little liner around her glossy lips. She really is pretty.

Just then, a small child bounds out from the backyard. I practically jump when she comes flying toward us. Her tiny feet pitter-patter on the stone-paved driveway before she wraps her arms enthusiastically around Briar's legs.

"Oh yeah," Briar says as she strokes the child's brown hair. "This is our daughter, Abby. Abby, this is our friend, Dean. He's going to live in the apartment above the garage."

The little girl smirks up at me bashfully. "Hi," she mumbles.

I clear my throat. "Hello."

I don't know why it didn't occur to me that Caleb Goode would have a child. I mean, naturally, he's in his thirties. He's married. He lives in suburbia.

Why wouldn't he have a kid?

And maybe it's because I literally haven't been around children since I was one, but I'm not exactly great around kids. I don't know how to talk to them or how to treat them.

I don't even know how old this girl is. She could be three or eleven, for all I know.

She's missing her two bottom front teeth, her hair is pulled into two neat, braided pigtails, and she has a spatter of freckles across her cheeks.

There's an awkward tension now among us since the little girl has joined us. And I briefly wonder if it's because I'm not reacting to her the way that I should.

Am I supposed to ask her a question? Am I supposed to be talking to her? Should I shake her hand?

Finally, it's Briar who breaks the silence.

"Well, why don't we show you upstairs, and then you can unpack your things?" she says brightly.

I can feel Caleb's scrutinizing gaze on me as she turns to walk toward the apartment. He's probably wondering what I'll do next. Or maybe he's also questioning why I'm here and why on earth I agreed to this.

The entrance to the apartment upstairs is around the back of the detached garage. There's a set of black metal stairs with a railing that leads to a small porch and a door to the apartment.

"You'll have your own key," Briar says as she opens the door.

I follow her in and notice that the apartment looks larger from the inside than it does from the outside. It's a basic studio with a bed on the opposite wall and a good amount of shelves framing each side.

There's a small blue couch in the middle and a mounted TV on the wall to my right. The kitchenette on the left is simple but enough to get me by. I'm not a big cook as it is, but it's nice to at least have a fridge and a small cooktop.

"The bathroom is over here," she says as she moves deeper into the apartment, pressing open the bathroom door to reveal a basic sink, toilet, and single shower.

"It's perfect," I mutter flatly.

The apartment seems well stocked with blankets, pillows, towels, and things of that sort. And most of it looks new, which means they must have just bought everything in here...for me.

Should I appear more gracious? I never asked for any of this.

"I filled the fridge and the pantry with food to get you by for now. I hope it's enough, but if you need anything, please let me know," Briar says in a sweet, singsong tone.

"It's more than enough," I reply, without looking her in the eye. My chin is held high, but I can't seem to meet her gaze as she offers me so much more than I expected. This makes me incredibly uncomfortable.

"And, of course, you're welcome to join us for dinner. I cook nearly every night," she adds, fiddling with the diamond necklace hanging over her chest.

"That's incredibly kind of you," I reply.

Then I hear Caleb in the doorway. "I'm sure he has a life, honey," he says, almost mockingly. "He doesn't want to hang out with us—a boring suburban family, right?" I can feel him looking at me, but I don't meet his eyes. "I mean, surely he works nights, don't you?" he adds.

This time, I finally do look at him, and not because he's speaking to me, but because I can't help but feel as if he's trying to taunt me. His tone is patronizing, and I didn't think it was possible, but I think I hate this guy even more now.

I don't reply to his question. I'm not going to entertain some close-minded, ignorant humor just because I'm a sex worker, and he thinks that's beneath him.

Instead, I turn back toward his wife.

"I'd love to join you for dinner," I say with a smile, "and I would be happy to hang out with a boring suburban family."

Then I add a wink for good measure.

This makes her cheeks turn a light shade of blush pink, and I almost feel bad for a moment for toying with her in order to annoy her husband, but I can't help it. I don't feel bad at all.

Briar holds her hands tightly in front of her before stammering uncomfortably.

"Why don't we go ahead and get your things out of your car?" she says.

"That won't be necessary," I reply. "There's really nothing in my car I need." Not to mention, it all smells like smoke, and I don't want to contaminate this clean space.

"Oh no," she says sadly. "Well, is there anything that you need? New clothes or...or...well, anything, really?"

"You're being far too kind," I shoot back with a slight chuckle.

"Come on, Briar," Caleb says in a deep tone. "Let's let him get himself settled here and get out of his way."

"Of course."

After she passes by me toward the door, she stops and turns back to say, "Oh, I forgot. You have free access to the pool anytime you'd like it."

"I appreciate that," I reply.

"All right, we'll leave you then," she says before disappearing through the door. The little girl gives me one more small wave before following her mother.

And then, just like that, I'm alone.

Standing in the middle of the apartment, I take a look around. I appreciate how tidy it is here. And she's right, I will need some new clothes eventually. But for now, I just need some rest after the day I've had.

Slipping off each shoe, I place them together near the door. Then I drop onto the bed, resting my head on the pillow.

As I let my eyes close, I feel a sense of renewed purpose settling into my tired bones.

I don't know if that fire was a blessing or a curse, but here I lie on Caleb Goode's property, feeling as if I'm meant to be here. Maybe this is my chance to finally close a door that's been haunting me for twelve years.

All of the hatred and resentment I've been harboring for that man has been like poison swirling under my skin, but now it feels as if atonement is just within my reach. The opportunity to cure myself of what's plagued me for so long.

I'm not the revenge type, but if I were, the idea of making him suffer the way I did would be too tempting to ignore. It wouldn't even be hard. I have everything he cares about at the tips of my fingers now.

I'd just have to flirt with his wife a little. It would drive him crazy. I bet she would melt like wax in my hands. But that's not me. I'm not some vindictive guy who needs to toy with innocent women in spite of some rich prick.

Never in my life have I ever wanted to hurt someone, but God, I do want to hurt him. I want to get him back for everything he did to me when he chose to do nothing at all.

And for what he did to Isaac.

But lucky for him, I'm not that type of guy.

Eight

Briar

"He seems nice," I say as I pull the throw pillows off our bed.

Caleb lifts his gaze to my face and tilts his head to the side skeptically. "Nice? I don't know if I'd call him that."

My brows furrow inward. Sure, I was just making simple conversation, and Dean does seem, at best, mysterious, but I sense some real contempt in Caleb's reaction, too.

"What would you call him?" I ask.

He tosses one of the pillows on the floor. "Suspicious."

"His house just burned down, Caleb. I didn't really expect him to show up with a smile on his face."

"He could have at least been gracious. There's something about him that I don't trust. I want you and Abby to stay away from him while I'm gone. Keep the doors locked."

I let out a scoff. "You're being ridiculous."

"I'm being protective," he replies defensively.

I level a glare at him, and after a moment, he relents with a sigh. "I'll give him a chance, but for now, let's just be on the safe side."

"Fine," I mutter as I climb under the covers.

We go through our normal routine. He pulls out his laptop. I pretend to read my book. He makes a comment about the weather or dinner or the house. He rolls over with an expression of disappointment. At least tonight, we can skip the lifeless sex since I won't be ovulating for a few more weeks.

I toss and turn for what feels like an hour. Caleb is fast asleep next to me, and the space between us might only be inches, but it feels like miles. It's so prominent that I can't stand to even be in the bed anymore.

Careful not to wake my husband, I crawl out from under the covers. It's practically a nightly ritual at this point—like I have a secret second life that takes place when everyone else is asleep.

Normally I'll watch TV and eat all the snacks in the kitchen. Sometimes, I'll scour anything interesting on the internet that I can find, or I'll start up a conversation in one of my online art forums. But tonight, none of that interests me.

Instead, I stand near the window of our bedroom on the second floor, and I stare at the illuminated window over the garage. Our new tenant is awake, the young, handsome stranger who's renting the apartment.

As I'm staring out the window, it suddenly dawns on me that I forgot to give Dean the key to the apartment.

I mean, sure, he could lock it from the inside, but if he needed to go anywhere, he wouldn't be able to lock it from the outside. And while I'm sure he doesn't really need it in the middle of the night, I figure he's up. I'm up. I might as well take it out to him now.

I guess I could also check to see if he needs anything while over there. I just want to be a good host.

Quietly tiptoeing through the house, I sneak out the back door by the kitchen, grabbing the apartment keys on my way. About halfway across the yard, I realize how crazy this is, but I've always been a night owl, and I assume he is, too, so maybe he won't think it's too odd.

I walk lightly up the stairs until I reach his apartment. Through the door, I can hear the TV playing. It's a laugh track to something that must be a sitcom.

Gently, I knock, and it only takes him a few moments before he opens the door.

Dean is standing in the narrow opening in the same loose jeans and weathered gray tee he had on earlier. Colorful tattoos peek out from the sleeves of his shirt, and I notice what seems to be nipple piercings poking through the fabric.

Something I did not notice earlier. Suddenly, I'm wondering if he has anything else pierced.

My eyes catch on his chest before I lift them to his face.

"Sorry to bother you," I mumble. "I just realized I hadn't given you the keys, and I saw you were up."

I jingle them between us, and he glances down with a small nod.

"Thanks," he replies, reaching out and taking them from me.

Dean is handsome in a different way than Caleb is. He's young and has a grit to his appearance that I find incredibly attractive. His dark hair is buzzed short, and he has sharp cheekbones and a sculpted jawline.

Where Caleb has life behind his eyes, it's almost as if Dean has none, and it makes me want to bring him back to life. I want to uncover what he's hiding behind those hooded, dark-blue irises.

"Are you getting settled in okay?" I ask.

He noticeably relaxes against the doorframe as he responds. "Yeah, took a nice long nap today, so I'm feeling a lot better."

"That's good," I reply. "I'm sure you've had a really rough few days. How is your dad?" I add cordially.

His eyes glisten as if he appreciates me asking that.

"He's doing well, thanks. He's all settled in at the home."

"Good," I say. "I imagine that must have been hard on you."

Something compels me to reach out and rest my hand over his in a comforting sort of way, but he instantly bristles at the touch, so I quickly pull away.

Why am I acting so strange?

His eyes glance toward the window of our house that leads to our bedroom.

"Well, I should—"

"Can't sleep?" he asks, cutting me off.

"No," I reply, crossing my arms over my chest. "I'm always such a night owl. I think it comes with being a mom. These late hours are all I really get to myself, and I'll pay for it in the morning."

His expression lights up with interest.

"What do you like to do?" he asks in a slow, almost sultry tone.

"Um," I stammer, "mostly watch TV. Maybe scroll on my phone. You know, brainless stuff."

"Me too," he replies cheekily.

Then he steps away from the doorframe, letting it open and reveal the small apartment where the television is playing.

"Would you like to come in? Maybe watch a show with me?"

I know I shouldn't.

My mouth even opens to utter those words. *No, thank you. I should get back to bed.*

But I don't.

I mean, what's the harm? I could use the company. It's just watching a show. And I'd like to get to know our new tenant, this mysterious old friend of Caleb's brother. Maybe if I know more about him, I can help defend his character to my husband, who seems so set on his ways of distrusting him.

"If you're sure you don't mind," I reply nonchalantly.

"Of course not," he chuckles.

As he steps back from the doorframe, allowing me access to the apartment, I squeeze in carefully to avoid brushing against his chest.

"Make yourself at home," he says with a half smile.

"What are you watching?" I ask as I make my way toward the couch.

"Ah, just some old *Friends* reruns."

"Classic," I murmur.

He moves toward the kitchenette area and awkwardly points to the fridge. "You already know this, but there's a bottle of wine chilling in the refrigerator. Would you like a glass?"

"Oh, that's yours," I reply, putting my hands up. "I didn't know if you liked wine or beer, so I went ahead and put both in there."

"I'm more of a wine guy," he says, shooting me another wink like he did earlier today. Once again, it has me blushing.

"Noted," I reply, clearing my throat.

As he pulls out the bottle, I go to the cabinet where I know I placed two wineglasses earlier today. Deciding it would be unfair to make him drink alone, I set them both on the counter as he uncorks the bottle and pours us each a glass in comfortable silence.

Normally, in situations like these, I feel pressured to make conversation. But honestly, I kind of hate small talk, so I'm relieved that the air between us isn't thick with tension.

It's actually kind of nice.

After handing me my glass, he gives me a crooked smirk as he holds up his and says, "Cheers."

I tap mine against his before taking a sip.

His eyes are on my face as I take my drink, but not in a predatory sort of way. It's more of a kind and curious way.

Dean seems so harmless. And I have experience with dangerous, cruel, selfish men.

Or should I say *man*?

My high school boyfriend, who turned into my college boyfriend, Sean, was possessive and manipulative. And at the time, to my young, naive, lovestruck mind, that was the sincerest form of affection.

I thought he was possessive of me because he loved me so much. Wanted to control me because I meant so much to him.

His love was a cloak over my eyes, and it was eventually Caleb who helped me lift it.

Dean moves to the couch, and I follow. He takes one side, and I take the other.

For a while, we sip our wine in silence and watch an episode of the show, laughing at all of the appropriate moments. But then a commercial break comes, and I feel obligated to make conversation.

"So you work at Sage's club?" I ask, instantly regretting the question after it comes out of my mouth.

He nearly chokes on his wine.

Coughing, he replies, "Um, yeah, I do."

"You don't have to elaborate," I say, stuttering apologetically. "I was just making small talk."

"No worries," he says with a lazy smile. "It's okay. I'm not ashamed or embarrassed to talk about it if you're not ashamed or embarrassed to hear about it."

"Of course not," I reply quickly. "I like Sage. I think she's great. I've never been to the club, but I'm sure it's wonderful."

God, I sound like a bumbling idiot.

"It is nice," he replies plainly. "I didn't see it before she got ownership and changed a few things, but I'm really impressed with how she runs it now."

"That's good," I say. "She's a smart girl."

"Yeah, she is."

"Have you..." My words trail. "...been in this business for long?"

"About two years." Now it's his turn to blush, and the color looks so nice on his tan cheeks.

"But I like my job, and I'm good at what I do."

My eyes widen as I turn my gaze toward the TV.

He's good at what he does?

I've let too much time pass without responding, but honestly, I have no clue how to even reply to that. He just admitted that he's good at sex. What am I supposed to say?

"I mean...as long as you're happy, that's all that matters, right?" I say, which is such a generic response, but it's all I can come up with at the moment.

"Exactly," he replies. "And what about you?"

I turn my gaze back toward him, my eyes a little wider. "What about me?"

His lips pull into a sly smile as he turns his gaze downward bashfully. "I just meant, are you happy?"

"Oh." I laugh nervously to myself. "Yeah, uh, I am...happy."

Why did I just stutter so much? It definitely did not sound convincing.

And judging by the tight-lipped smile he's giving me as he nods, I can tell he's thinking the same thing.

So, I feel the need to elaborate.

With a sigh, I continue, "I am happy. I love getting to stay at home and raise our daughter. It's just..." I let my words trail to take a breath. "Caleb and I have been trying to conceive for nearly three years now, and it's been rough."

"I'm sorry to hear that." The expression on his face appears sincere and compassionate, which is nice. It's better than pity.

The commercials are still playing, and we both turn our attention back to the TV. I know that neither of us is really watching them, though. The air grows thick with tension, but suddenly, I find myself chuckling quietly.

He snaps his gaze toward me. "What's so funny?"

"Nothing," I reply with another chuckle. "It's just that..." Awkwardly, I pause. "It's just that we're both sort of talking about sex, but in two very different ways."

The word *sex* comes out of my mouth, feeling like the most uncomfortable word I've ever uttered.

One side of his face lifts into a mischievous smile, and he keeps those hooded eyes trained on my face as he replies, "Yeah, I guess you're right. We're both having a lot of sex. You're doing it for a baby, and I'm doing it for money. Either way...it's still fun."

I have to force myself to swallow, my blood running hotter through my veins as he stares at me. And there's a voice in my head that is screaming, *You should go.*

And this time, I listen.

Quickly, I gulp back the rest of the wine in my glass and stand from the couch.

"It's late. I should really go. Thank you so much," I stammer as

I move toward the kitchen, "for letting me crash...your uh...TV watching...time."

Oh my god, what am I saying?

He chuckles from the couch. "Of course, anytime. No worries. I love company."

I drop the empty glass in the sink before rushing to the door. "Okay, well, I'll be home all day tomorrow. You know, in case you want me—I mean, need me." With a wince, I open the door. Behind me, I hear him chuckle again, and I feel like a colossal idiot. Before leaving, I add, "Just let me know if you need anything."

He stands from the couch and waves at me as I leave. "No worries, Briar. Again, thank you."

With that, I close the door, pressing my back to the surface of it as I struggle to catch my breath. That was humiliating and dangerous, and I had absolutely no business even being in there.

What is wrong with me?

But as my blood pressure starts to settle and the cool night air seeps into my pores, I realize that while it was sort of reckless, it was also really nice.

And honestly, when was the last time I did anything reckless?

Nine

Caleb
21 years old

If anyone had told me two weeks ago that I'd look forward to my art history class each week, I'd call them crazy. But here I am, waltzing to the humanities building with a smirk on my face because I know in just a few minutes, I'll get to see her.

Briar has been helping me with the coursework. Do I really need the help? Not entirely. But the first time I leaned toward her during class and whispered, "What was this period called?" she gave me that sweet smile and leaned so close I could smell the flowery scent of her perfume. "Baroque," she whispered softly before nudging my shoulder. From that moment, I was hooked.

Now, I ask every period. Every artist's name. Every style.

If Briar's boyfriend wasn't such a prick, I might actually feel bad for flirting with her so much. But there's no way she's actually happy with him. He's controlling and selfish and so fucking full of himself.

I would treat her so much better than him. She just has to know that.

Turning the corner in the quad to head toward class, I hear a familiar voice up ahead. I scan the crowd of students coming and going and spot her familiar blonde locks.

Then my stomach sours.

She has her arms wrapped around Sean's midsection, and she's staring lovingly into his eyes. There's a smile on her face as he dips his head toward hers and kisses her on the mouth.

I feel myself slowing as I watch them, a swirl of nauseating emotions landing in my gut like lead.

What is she doing? Why is she with him?

As I pass them by, the smile on my face has morphed into a clenched-jaw scowl. Neither of them even notices me. It's like the wind has been knocked out of my chest.

I hurry to the classroom and take a seat in the back, slamming my book on the table in frustration. Briar doesn't make it into the room until after class has already started. And when she takes the seat next to me, her cheeks are tinged pink, and she's biting her bottom lip to hide her smirk.

My gaze is focused on the front of the room where the professor is talking. Even when Briar looks at me and nudges my shoulder playfully as a greeting, I don't turn in her direction.

None of this is her fault; I have no good reason to be mad.

But I am.

I'm mad at her for letting that asshole have her heart when she deserves so much better. I hate that, because of him, I can't tell her how amazing she is.

This morning, I actually let myself believe that I was one step closer to having her as my girl. Now I know the truth. It's all a delusion, and Briar will never be mine.

†

Present day

. . .

The house is quiet as I pour my morning coffee. Abigail is out of school for the summer, which means she and Briar get to sleep in a little bit later.

It's only seven thirty in the morning as I stand in the kitchen, staring out the window that looks over the backyard. I'm replaying the events of yesterday when a ghost from my past showed up at my house.

Dean Sheridan has changed a lot.

Sure, he was only fourteen the last time I saw him, but it's more than the transformation in his size and appearance. He carries himself with a sense of bitterness and regret now.

I had a feeling he still harbored resentment toward me, but I was surprised to see just how much he showed it. He couldn't even be cordial or polite to me.

I have no idea why he took the apartment in the first place. Is this how it's going to be? Is he really going to hate me the entire three months that he stays here?

I wish I could just tell him that for everything he hates me for, I hate myself ten times more.

He thinks he's angry at me? He has no idea. I've been beating myself up for the past nine years. Nothing I do now is going to right that wrong.

I'm just about to turn away from the window when movement in the yard catches my eye.

Staring through the glass, my jaw drops with surprise as I watch Dean emerge from the apartment in nothing but a pair of tight swim shorts.

Incredibly revealing tight swim shorts.

My mouth goes dry as I watch him cross the yard and bend into a squatting position near the edge of the pool to dip his hand in and test the temperature.

This feels like an intrusion. He has no idea I'm standing here, gawking like a pervert. But he's barely been here a day, and already, it feels like the walking embodiment of sex has just infiltrated my otherwise innocent family home.

When Dean stands up again, I get a good look at the tattoos covering his sculpted arm like a sleeve. It's a collage—a colorful tiger with some black-and-white flowers and a bright sun at the top.

Dean has a narrow build. His face still carries a boyish look, hardened by time and life. Nothing like the youthful kid I once knew.

I don't know why I'm still standing here watching him as my coffee cup grows cold in my hand. It doesn't make any sense. I don't know if it's curiosity or interest, but I can't tear my eyes away.

That is, until his head turns, and his gaze meets the window I'm staring through.

Our eyes meet for just a moment, and I quickly fumble, spinning away from the window, full of embarrassment.

Could he see me watching him?

Should I go out there and say something?

Just then, my phone on the counter starts to vibrate. Quickly, I pick it up and let out a groan when I see the name.

Truett Goode

"Fuck," I mutter to myself.

I bet I know exactly what my father's calling for, and to be honest, I expected this, but that doesn't mean I'm prepared.

So, after a few rings, I swipe the decline button.

A moment later, I hear steps coming down the stairs, and my wife appears in her pajamas. She has that precious, sleepy look about her. Her hair is a mess. Her eyes still squint as if she's not ready to fully open them, and she gives me a gentle smile.

"Morning," she squeaks with a yawn.

When I see Briar like this in her purest and most natural form, without a hint of worry or anxiety on her face, it makes something in my chest swell.

God, I love her so much.

The day is still new, which means we haven't erected that wall between us yet. Setting my coffee cup down, I reach for her, pulling her against my chest and planting a kiss against the side of her head.

"Good morning," I mumble against her hair.

The voice in the back of my mind chants a familiar cadence—*she's mine, she's mine, she's mine.*

"I was hoping I would catch you before you left," she says softly. I love the way it feels when she wraps her arms around my waist, pressing her face into my neck.

"I'm glad you did," I reply.

"How are you feeling today?" she asks. "With our new tenant."

"Fine," I reply, which feels like a lie. "I don't really see how it'll affect us."

"Exactly," she agrees. "It feels good to help someone out."

"I love you," I mumble softly.

Turning her face up toward me, she gives me a gentle smile, and I lean in to press my lips to hers.

My phone begins to buzz again. Before Briar can turn to see the name on the screen, I quickly flip it over, hitting decline again.

Worrying about my father is the last thing she needs right now. She has enough on her plate, but I see the way she glances skeptically at the phone, wondering who it could have been that I so quickly declined.

"Just work," I mutter to cover it up.

"Don't work too hard," she says, crossing her arms in front of her chest.

"I might be taking on another case," I stammer.

Her arms fall to her sides. "Are you sure about that? It seems like you've been working a lot lately."

"I'm sure," I reply with a hint of defensiveness.

Even though I'm trying to protect her from stressing or worrying, it's almost like she just stresses and worries twice as much.

As I take the last sip of coffee in my cup, I watch the window behind Briar to see Dean jumping headfirst into our pool. He emerges a moment later, swimming laps to the other side.

The thought of leaving Briar and Abigail here with him has me feeling a little unsettled.

"What are your plans today?" I ask.

She shrugs. "I don't know. Probably take Abigail to the library for story time. Maybe go out to lunch. Nothing exciting."

"Good," I reply nonchalantly. Secretly, I'm pleased to hear that they'll be out of the house for most of the day, but I don't tell her that part.

"Just be careful," I say.

She gives me a knowing smirk as she tilts her head to the side. "Yes, of course, dear. We'll be fine."

I press my lips to her forehead again. "I love you."

"I love you too," she replies as I grab my keys from the entryway table.

I'm not even in my car by the time my father calls again. My phone is buzzing on the center console. I know the longer I avoid him, the worse it's going to get.

"Hello, Dad," I say in a disgruntled tone after hitting the answer button.

My father's deep voice echoes from the car's Bluetooth speaker. "What kind of son declines his father's call?" he says with his thick Texas drawl.

The question is rhetorical, but part of me still wants to reply—the son of a lying, cheating, criminal father, of course. As much as I would love to say that, I don't.

"It was early. I was in the shower. What do you need?" I reply.

"I'm sure by now you've heard of these absolutely ridiculous charges they're bringing against me."

"I heard," I reply shortly.

"Wilford and I think we've got a case against the DA for religious discrimination because someone in their office must be some Christian-hating, liberal, biased idiot."

"Then I'm sure Wilfred can defend you in court and get you off on those charges."

"I ain't letting these goddamn charges even come to court, son. You must be out of your mind."

He sounds so tired, his tone ragged and exhausted.

"So you're gonna fight the charges?" I ask as I get on the freeway.

"Absolutely," he says, sounding more confident than I would in his situation.

"It won't be easy," I reply.

"I know. That's why I need you."

"Me?" I ask, even though I saw this coming from a mile away.

"We can appeal those charges before they make it to court. Who better to plead my case than my own son? One of the best defense attorneys in Austin, Texas."

I want to tell him to fuck off. I want to tell him I hate him and that I hope he lands behind bars for the rest of his life. Not just for what he's done to Sage but what he's done to our entire family.

I want to wring his neck for what he did to Isaac alone.

But I am not Adam. I don't do rebellious. I don't like to cause a scene.

I've made it my entire life by staying off my dad's radar. Always careful, never pleasing him too much and never angering him too much. I coasted somewhere in the middle. My mission was to be so inconsequential that he barely noticed I was even there.

If I weren't a lawyer, he would not be on the phone with me right now. His calling to ask for my help has nothing to do with our relationship and everything to do with my position. So I have every reason to turn him down, to tell him to fuck off, to wish him well, and to never speak to him again.

So why can't I? Why can't I just utter those words?

Why can't I just hang up the phone and move on with my life and pretend he doesn't even exist? Why does it feel like, deep down, there's a part of me that's still searching and hoping for his approval?

I don't need it. I don't want it. I don't care about it, and yet here I am, struck silent when all I know I really need to do is hang up the phone.

But I am a good lawyer, and I know I could easily get those charges lessened. It's like I'm already building the case in my head, but I can't seriously do that. I can't possibly defend him when it was my own brother's girlfriend who he attacked.

I couldn't possibly betray my family like that.

"I'll send you my location," he says when I don't respond. My thoughts are deafening, but my mouth stays quiet.

"Okay," I mutter without knowing why.

"Be here in an hour," he demands as if I'm still a child and he has any power over me.

The line goes dead without a goodbye. And I find myself driving into the city with a sense of confusion and irritation.

I won't help that man. It's not my job as a lawyer or as his son. But a part of me is curious to hear what he has to say. Maybe I just want to see how pathetic he is in person again. It's been nearly nine months since I've laid eyes on him. And he is still my father, after all.

Ten

Briar

After Caleb leaves for work, I try to savor the last few minutes of silence that I can before Abby wakes up. In a perfect world, I'd use this time to do something meaningful, like praying, journaling, reading my Bible, or cleaning. Instead, I scroll on my phone and turn my brain into short-attention-span mush.

But not without guilt.

As I get up to take my empty coffee cup to the sink, I notice movement in the water of the pool. Seeing Dean pop his head out from under the surface, I feel my lips twitch with a slight smile.

Planting his hands on the surface of the pool deck, he hoists his wet body out of the water, droplets cascading down his chiseled pecs and abs.

Suddenly, the grip on my mug has grown so tight that my hand aches.

He climbs out in nothing but a pair of tight swim trunks. They hug his thick thighs and barely graze his hip bones. Just a couple inches lower, and they'd reveal—

Stop it.

I turn my gaze downward and rush to the sink. Scrubbing the inside of my coffee mug, I try not to look back up again. There's nothing wrong with just looking. I'm sure Caleb looks at women all the time.

With a man like Dean walking around, it's nearly impossible not to sneak a glance. It's not like I'm going to do anything scandalous. I'm just admiring him.

When I lift my gaze again, I let my eyes rake over his body. Sculpted abs, rounded shoulders, and a thin tuft of hair below his navel that I can barely see from here. He's taking long, heavy breaths, sucking them in and out in a steady rhythm. His arms are winding around him as if he's warming himself up.

I assumed he was swimming to relax or cool off, but he seems like he's gearing up for a workout. I watch as he dives headfirst into the pool, disappearing below the surface.

Glancing back down at the cup in my hand, I notice it's clear of soapy bubbles, so I set it on the drying rack before looking back out at the water and waiting for Dean's head to pop back up.

Maybe I'll go out there and offer him some coffee when he's done with his swim. Or what if he's hungry? I could make him breakfast. I have to make some for me and Abby anyway.

The water in the pool starts to settle from the waves of his jump, so I squint my eyes to find where he might have resurfaced. I glance around the yard, wondering if maybe I missed him getting out entirely. He's nowhere to be seen.

The water is flat and quiet now.

Another five seconds go by.

Another ten.

Another fifteen.

"Oh my god," I mutter as I shut off the running water and bolt for the door leading to the backyard. My hands are still soaked as I sprint across the grass. I half expect to find blood or a floating body.

When I reach the pool, I see his form at the bottom of the deep end, huddled against the floor.

Terror and adrenaline boil inside me like water in a kettle about to explode.

"Dean!" I scream, hoping he'll suddenly respond, but he doesn't move.

I don't think. I just act.

Without another thought, I dive headfirst into the water. Immediately, I swim to the bottom and reach for him. As I wind my hands around his bare waist to drag him to the top, he gapes at me with a shocked expression on his face.

He's just sitting at the bottom of the pool, legs crossed and arms moving slowly to hold him there. I don't take any time to question it. I just bounce my feet off the floor, hauling us both to the surface.

As soon as our heads pop out together, I shriek. "Are you okay?"

"What are you doing?" he stammers breathlessly. I'm still holding him as if he's drowning. My breasts are pressed to his back, and my hands are holding his firm pecs as I kick us both toward the edge. My fingertips graze the stud piercing through one of his nipples.

"What am I doing?" I ask in a panic. "I'm saving your life."

"I wasn't drowning," he mutters indignantly. As we reach the edge, I finally let him go, and we both hold on to the pool deck and stare at each other, each working to catch our breath.

"Dean, I watched you dive into that pool five minutes ago!"

He lets out a huff as he hoists himself out of the pool. Then he leans over and reaches a hand toward me. When I slide my palm against his, I'm taken aback by how quickly and easily he drags me out of the water and onto the deck.

I'm also instantly aware that I'm still in my pajamas, which are thin and soaking wet. And I don't have a bra on. His gaze flashes downward at the sight of my cold, perky nipples through the translucent fabric. Quickly, I cross my arms across my chest.

"I'm sorry for scaring you, but I wasn't drowning," he says. Water drips from his stern brow, down the straight slope of his nose, and over his full, pink lips.

"What were you doing then?" I ask, trying to make sense of it all.

He lets out an exasperated sigh, staring upward as he confesses, "I just like to practice holding my breath."

My head tilts. "Holding your breath?"

"I have strong lungs."

That is the strangest thing I've ever heard.

"You do know that diving into someone's pool and disappearing under the surface for minutes at a time is cause for alarm, right?" I sound like his mother, and I don't like it.

That makes him chuckle. "Yes, I suppose so."

When he smiles, it's disarming. It makes me forget the words hanging on my lips. It quiets my mind and disables my entire system.

"I apologize," he adds as the smile fades and his face relaxes into a less stern and softer expression. "It was nice of you to jump in and save me."

"Anyone would have done it," I reply, which makes him chuckle again.

"What's so funny?" I ask.

He shakes his head as he stares at the ground. More water drips over the soft tan skin of his face, and I'm mesmerized by it. I wonder what it would feel like to run my tongue along his brow line or lick the moisture from his cheek.

Stop it, Briar.

When he looks into my eyes again, I lose my train of thought.

Then, he says, "Not just anyone."

I'm staring dumbly at him as he rushes to the pool chair, where he left a folded towel. Immediately, he wraps it around my shoulders and rubs my arms to warm me up.

We're so close that I can make out the array of cool gray tones in his eyes. And the faded freckles on his face. And the stubble he needs to shave off on his jaw.

I've been staring at him too long.

Say something, Briar.

"I'm glad you're okay," I mutter.

His lips stretch into a smile again. In turn, I find myself smiling too.

"Mom, I'm hungry!" a small voice shouts from the house's back door.

I tear myself away from Dean and turn to find Abby watching us in her pajamas.

"Coming, peanut!" I call before glancing back at Dean. "I should go make her breakfast. If you...get hungry or want coffee, just knock." I gesture toward the house with my thumb as I back away, leaving him dripping next to the pool.

"Thanks," he mutters awkwardly.

"Oh, your towel," I reply, pulling it from around my shoulders and handing it back to him. I'm fully exposed in my soaked pajamas again, which makes him smirk as he lets his gaze scan the length of my body.

It feels both evasive and arousing.

I have to force myself to swallow as I move toward the house.

"I'm making lasagna tonight if you're hungry," I stammer, nearly tripping over one of Abby's toys in the yard.

He shoots another one of those disarming smiles as he scratches his head. "Thanks, but I have to work tonight."

I can feel the flames in my cheeks as I reply, "Oh. Okay. Well, another time then."

Instantly, I turn away from him, rushing to where Abby is standing on the back deck, waiting for me.

"Mommy, why were you swimming in your pajamas?" she asks with her face screwed up in confusion.

"I wasn't, honey. I was just...helping our new friend."

She waves to Dean with a cheesy grin on her face, and I glance back at him to see his awkward wave to her. I quickly usher her into the house, and she immediately goes to the couch with her tablet and starts watching a video. Meanwhile, I run up the stairs to get out of these wet clothes.

"Can I have cereal?" she calls after me.

"Yeah," I reply. "Just let me change first, okay?"

After closing the bathroom door, I get a look at myself in the mirror. I look ridiculous. My wet hair is plastered against my head, and my nipples are on full display through this thin top.

Letting out a groan, I clap my hands over my face.

That was humiliating.

What am I even doing? Did he think I was flirting with him? *Was* I flirting with him?

First, it was last night in his apartment. And now today in the pool. He hasn't been here a full twenty-four hours, and I feel like he's flipped my life on its head.

Why do I act so strange around him? I love my husband and would never cheat on him. And it's not like a good-looking guy in his twenties would want anything to do with a thirty-three-year-old suburban mom.

Jeez, Briar. Get a hold of yourself.

But even as I'm drying my hair and changing into some dry clothes, I can't stop thinking about the entire encounter. Replaying everything he said. Remembering how his body felt against my fingers, as if the memory is imprinted into my skin.

There's nothing wrong with that. Thinking about another man isn't cheating.

Even if I let my imagination get away from me, thinking about him going to work tonight and picturing in great detail everything that entails.

Eleven

Dean

"Give me a color."

I yank the man's mouth off my cock with a punishing grip on his hair. He sucks in a lungful of air before gasping his response. "Green, Sir."

"Good boy," I mutter in response. "You're being such a good boy."

He smiles up at me proudly.

"I think my good boy deserves a reward," I add. "Are you ready for your reward?"

"Yes, Sir," he says with a grin. Then, his expression changes into somber concern. "But can I make you come first?"

Fuck.

I had a feeling he was going to ask me that. He has no idea how much I wish I could let him make me come first. But that's just not in the cards for me lately.

What sucks is this poor guy is going to think he's done something wrong. And there's really nothing I can say to him to explain that I can't come. And it has nothing to do with how *good* he is.

And everything to do with how fucked in the head I am at the moment.

"Seeing you come is what I really want," I say, softly stroking his head.

I don't miss the hint of disappointment on his face.

"You're not going to let me down, are you?" I ask.

"No, Sir." He shakes his head emphatically.

"Good. Now, be a good boy for me and lie on your back."

"Yes, Sir," he replies. Obediently, he moves into a lying position with his arms stretched over his head. His dick is hard, jutting upward as it leaks precum into the tip of the condom.

The entire time I'm stroking and sucking his cock, fondling his balls, and licking the tight rim of his asshole, I do it knowing that I'm making up for the fact that I can't give my client one hundred percent of what he really wants.

And that is to please me.

This might be his first night with me, but I know clients like him. He's a people pleaser with a raging praise kink. Which means my pleasure is just as important as his.

He's paying me to come at the same time he's paying me to make him come.

Judging by the way he's moaning, writhing, and sweating on the bed as I draw him excruciatingly slowly to the brink of ecstasy, I've done enough to make this session worth it for him. When he finally fills the condom and shudders out his release, he's a mess.

"You're amazing," he mumbles twenty minutes later as he slips on his shoes and smiles at me from the chair.

"I'm glad you're satisfied," I reply frankly.

He smirks to himself with a shake of his head. "You should give yourself more credit," he adds. "I'm not just satisfied."

Leaning against the wall, I ask, "What are you, then?"

Lifting those handsome blue eyes up to my face, he says, "Blown away."

My eyebrows jump upward. “Blown away is good.”

“Blown away is *very* good.”

We both laugh for a moment and then he stands up and takes a step closer. My smile fades as I feel him reach for me, placing a hand on my waist.

“Is there a rule against grabbing a drink after your session?” he mumbles softly.

“I’m afraid there is,” I reply without looking him in the eye.

He nods as if he understands, but it still makes me feel like shit. Every once in a while, this happens, and it’s my least favorite part of my job. When my client and I share a moment, a laugh, a smile, something that makes them feel as if I could ever be more for them, I wish I could explain...

I’ll never be more for anybody.

“Damn,” he says. “Well...thanks for blowing me away. Next time, maybe I can do the same for you.”

“See you next time then,” I reply, forcing a smile on my face as I watch him leave the room. For a while, I’m stuck to the wall, too lost in my thoughts to move. Wondering if I should chase after him. What would happen? We’d have a few laughs. We’d fuck for fun a few times. Maybe, by some miracle, I’d actually get off.

Then what? Would he introduce me to his family? Take me to his home? Make a real boyfriend out of me?

No thanks.

Sooner or later, he’d end up disappointed. And the only way to avoid disappointment is to expect nothing at all.

I only have the one client tonight. So, after our session, I spend a few hours helping out around the club, ordering more supplies for my room, and planning some of the BDSM sessions that Sage has asked me to demonstrate for our patrons.

For some reason, I keep looking at the clock. I don’t really keep strict hours at my job. I work for my clients and then pick up small tasks here and there, but I don’t really clock in or clock out.

So it’s strange to feel restless, like I’m eager to get back home.

Although right now, my home is a one-bedroom apartment above a garage in a suburban neighborhood.

My first few days at Caleb's have been interesting, to say the least. I've hardly seen him at all, but his wife, on the other hand, has definitely taken a keen interest in me.

They don't call them desperate housewives for nothing.

My first night, she was knocking on my door past midnight, and it's almost midnight now. Will she be back again?

I smile at myself as I think how angry Caleb would be to know that his wife was hanging out with me while he slept.

Or that I've seen how perky her little tits are under her wet clothes.

Scheming to get revenge against Caleb by seducing his wife was almost a joke at first. It wasn't a serious plan, but suddenly, it's as if she's fallen into my lap, and I can't ignore that.

She's making this too easy.

"Hey there." I feel a soft hand drift across my back.

I'm sitting alone at one of the tables in the back of the club when Sage takes the seat across from mine. With her bubblegum-pink hair, tattoos, and face full of piercings, Sage doesn't look like the kind of girl you'd expect to be with the pastor's son—but alas, she is.

"How's your dad?" she asks with concern.

"He's good. Thanks," I reply. "I actually just spoke with him earlier today. He's all settled and already complaining about one of the nurses who bosses him around too much."

She lets out a soft giggle. "I'm glad he's doing well."

"Yeah, me too."

"And what about you?" she asks pointedly.

"I'm fine," I say with a shrug.

"That apartment at Caleb's is working out?"

"It's perfect," I reply. "Caleb and his wife are very..." My voice trails for a moment. "...accommodating."

"I hope they're treating you with respect," she adds with a stern expression.

Which makes my brow furrow.

"Of course they are. Why would you ask that?"

She lets her head tilt to the side. "The Goodes are not like us, Dean."

"You don't think I know that?" I reply with a snicker. "You realize I basically grew up around these people, right?"

"I keep forgetting that," she replies with a shake of her head. "They're still new to me. They mean well, but you should have seen them when I started coming around."

"Yeah, well, I don't know if Caleb Goode is a big fan of mine," I add with a coy smirk.

"No, that's not you," she replies, waving her hand. "Caleb doesn't like anyone. How's Briar been?"

The corner of my mouth lifts into a crooked smile. "She's been great."

"What's that supposed to mean?"

I can't help but laugh. "It just means she's been very hospitable, the perfect Southern host."

I don't miss the way Sage rolls her eyes. "I'm sure she has. I like Briar. I really do. But the woman strives for perfection. Perfect house, perfect husband, perfect children, perfect life."

I blink down at the table, remembering how Briar came to my room last week, opening up about some of the struggles she and Caleb have had over the years. It's not my business and definitely not for me to share. But I wish I could tell Sage that Briar's life probably isn't as perfect as she thinks it is.

"Maybe having you around will help her loosen up a little bit," she says. "I'd really love to see her let go. I'm sure she'd be a lot happier if she did."

"You don't think she's happy?" I ask. I have this nagging curiosity now when it comes to Caleb's wife. As if she's like an onion, and I'm desperate to peel back all the layers.

Because Sage is right. Briar does present herself and her life as being perfect, but it's not real. There has to be a real person in there somewhere.

"I think she wants everybody to believe she's happy," Sage replies. "But that woman gives so much. It just makes me wonder if she's asking for what she deserves in return."

Interesting, I think to myself.

Sage lets out a big sigh as she stands from the table. "Well, anyway, I'm glad it's working out over there, and I'm glad your dad is doing well. Let me know if you need anything here at the club, but if not, I'm gonna head out for the night. Sadie's got it from here."

"Yeah, I think I'm clocking out too," I say as I stretch my arms over my head. "It's been a long couple of days."

"Of course," she replies. "Take care of yourself, Dean. And again, let me know if you need anything at all."

"Thanks, Sage," I reply.

During the entire drive back to the house, I can't stop thinking about Briar. After such a short period of time, it's like she's chiseled her way into my brain. For somebody that I thought was so predictable, the idea that there's more to her than meets the eye is incredibly intriguing.

After parking my car in the driveway, I climb out and walk toward the back of the garage when I spot movement on the back porch of the house.

I freeze when I spot Briar sitting on the patio chair, holding a glass of wine in her hand and staring at her phone in the other. It's half past one in the morning, and I did not expect her to still be up.

When she hears me approaching, she lifts her gaze and finds me in the dim light from the moon.

"Hey," I say. "Can't sleep again?"

"You caught me," she replies groggily.

I make my way over to the back porch. She's curled up on one of the patio chairs around the table with a throw blanket draped over her legs. She's already taken off all of her makeup. And she has her hair piled on her head in a messy bun.

"How was work?" she asks.

"Work was work," I say.

She presses her lips together and gives a slight nod. Judging by the look in her eyes, talking about my job makes her slightly uncomfortable but curious enough to want to know more. I know she's afraid to ask.

"You want a glass?" she asks, holding up her wine.

I should say no, but I don't.

"Sure, what the hell."

As I take the seat across from her, she goes inside to get another glass. After filling it from the bottle on the table, she hands it to me.

"I hope you like merlot."

"More of a malbec guy myself," I reply, swirling the glass and taking a sip.

"How sophisticated," she says, looking impressed. "I'm more of a...whatever catches my eye at the grocery store type of woman."

"Fair enough." Giving her a subtle smirk over my glass, I notice how easy it is to be around her. She's far more comfortable now than she was after that pool rescue fiasco. Maybe it's the wine.

I assume the wine also gives her the courage to ask what's on her mind because she leans forward and looks deep into my eyes. "Can I ask you a personal question?"

"Of course," I reply bluntly.

"What made you become a..." She stumbles on the word, her fingers touching her lips as she starts to blush. "I don't know the right word to use."

"Escort," I say to finish her sentence. "Or sex worker, I guess. But hooker is just offensive."

She lets out a short laugh, clearly from embarrassment. "Sorry, I didn't mean to offend you."

"You didn't," I say to ease her nerves.

"But I'm just curious. What do you do? I mean...is it just sex? Or is there...more that you provide?"

Leaning back in the chair, I bring the wine to my lips as I contemplate my answer. "Well, technically, I'm providing an experience my clients don't know how to find anywhere else. Sex is intimate, but they don't know how to ask for what they want from the people they're with. But for some reason, it's easier to ask a professional."

I watch the movement in Briar's throat as she swallows, a knowing look in her eyes as if she understands. "That makes sense," she replies. And then, in a low whisper, she adds, "And what exactly...do people ask for?"

There is a glossiness to her eyes as she stares at me across the table. The tension between us grows thick. So thick that even I have to force myself to swallow.

"Some people want me to praise them, control them, punish them, or just...fuck them. Most women who come to see me just want to be with a partner who makes them come. Who puts their needs first. Who gives them the attention they deserve."

Briar hasn't moved an inch. She's practically frozen in place, and her breath has grown shaky. When she finally blinks, picking up her wine to take a large gulp, I notice the quiver in her hand.

The space between us is silent. "I don't judge you, you know?" she says as she sets down her glass.

"Excuse me?"

Finally, her eyes meet mine again. "You probably think that I do, but I don't. Especially when you explain it like that, I just think...if you're happy doing it, then that's all that matters."

"I am," I say, but it feels like a lie on my tongue.

"Good," she whispers.

We sit together in comfortable silence, letting our gazes meet without it feeling charged or uncomfortable. For the next few minutes, we each finish our drinks. She doesn't ask me any more questions, although I wish she would. I wish this conversation could go further.

I want to know what she would ask of me if she could hire me. I want to know what Briar wants. What she needs. I imagine myself praising her. Having her at my feet. Looking down at those beautiful blue eyes. Feeling her lips wrapped around my cock and calling her mine.

"I should get to bed," she says after her glass is emptied.

I swallow my disappointment.

"Sleep well," I say as she stands from the table.

"Feel free to finish the bottle. Stay out here as long as you'd like."

"Thanks," I reply.

Before walking away, she rests her hand on my arm and pauses there for a moment as she gazes down into my eyes. "Night, Dean."

"Good night, Briar."

When she pulls her hand away and disappears into her house, I feel the absence of her touch on my skin. This woman has found a way to make me miss her in such a short amount of time.

I do finish the bottle of wine after she's gone. And while I drink it, something becomes increasingly clear to me. I want her.

I want to seduce her. I want to make her mine. I want to have Briar Goode at my mercy and in my bed.

Then I want to see the look on Caleb's face when he finds out.

It's funny, really. I've only wanted two people in my entire life. The first time, it was his brother.

And now, it's his wife.

Part Two
The Protector

Twelve

Caleb
21 years old

I hoist my duffel bag onto my shoulder as I exit through the locker room door to the parking lot. I nearly miss the blonde sitting on the block wall outside the stadium until I hear a delicate voice calling my name.

"Hey, Caleb."

I spin around to find Briar grinning at me. She waves a hand, and I freeze in my tracks to wave back.

"Hey," I reply dumbly.

Briefly, I consider leaving it at that, continuing to my car, and driving home. But she said hi to me first. So, I feel compelled to stop and talk to her for a moment. Even if I know it's only friendly conversation and nothing else.

"If you're waiting for Sean, he wasn't even in the shower yet when I left," I say, nodding toward the locker room.

She shrugs. "He always takes forever, but we had plans to grab dinner, so I'll wait."

"You shouldn't have to wait alone," I reply as I drop my bag on the concrete.

"You don't have to do that," she says, but her argument feels weak and there's a subtle warmth on her face as if she actually wants me to stick around.

"I want to," I add. When our eyes meet, I wonder if this is normal. Do other guys look at her and feel this intense pull? Are we truly just friends or is there an inkling of hope that she likes me half as much as I like her?

When she bites her bottom lip and gazes at her feet, I feel a thread of hope.

"You're doing great in art history," she says to make conversation.

"Only because you're helping me." I give her a nudge on the shoulder.

"I'm not doing that much," she says with an eye roll.

"Yes, you are. You have a gift for this stuff. You seem to really like it."

"I do." She smiles to herself.

"Is that what you want to do with your life after you graduate? Work at a museum or something?" I ask, taking a seat on the low wall next to her.

She stares listlessly at the dimly lit parking lot in front of us. "I don't know..."

My brow furrows as I turn toward her. "So, what do you want to do?"

With a shrug, she says, "I'm sure Sean and I will get married and have some kids, and I think I'd be happy. I really want a family."

The words Sean and married in one sentence make my skin crawl. She can't seriously be considering spending forever with that condescending asshole? I wish I could just grab her by the shoulders and shake some sense into her.

And I hate that she thinks she has to give up her passion for a family. "So what?"

"So what?" she replies with a laugh.

"Yeah, so what? Get married. Have some kids. You can still do all

of that and work in a museum or paint or teach idiots like me why they should appreciate Van Gogh."

Her head falls back as she lets out a laugh. "I know that."

"Do you? Because it sounds like you're getting an art history degree to throw it away."

She knocks my shoulder with her own. "I'm not throwing it away. You're being such a jerk tonight."

She slings the insult with a smile on her face.

"I am not," I say, bumping my shoulder against hers.

When our eyes meet, hers are still crinkled with her grin, and I get lost in them for a moment. Then we're staring at each other for too long. And if she weren't someone's girlfriend, I'd lean in, take her lips, and make her mine.

"Don't marry him," I whisper.

Her smile fades. "What?"

Swallowing down my discomfort and looking away, I add, "I just mean...don't marry anyone and sacrifice your dreams, Briar. You should do whatever you want with your life."

Just then, the door opens, and I see Sean emerging from behind Briar, but she doesn't look toward him. Her eyes are glued to my face as she sternly replies, "I plan to." Then she stands from the wall and walks toward him.

"Hey, babe," Sean says as he slings an arm over her shoulder and tugs her against his body. I have to look away when he presses his lips to her cheek.

Sean's eyes meet mine over the top of her head, and his expression isn't warm or cordial. "Thanks for watching my girl, Goode."

I clench my molars as I glare back at him.

He takes her mouth in a kiss, and I feel hatred like nothing I've ever felt burn inside me. It's like he's kissing her to spite me, but there's nothing I can do about it.

As they make their way to the parking lot, I stay on the brick wall. Alone.

†

Present Day

I can't sleep. I'm sitting up in my bed, texting Luke. My twin is practically nocturnal, so when I can't sleep, he's the first one I text. The conversation starts innocently enough until he starts asking about last week's meeting with our father.

How was it?

I hated every second of it.

He's living in some piece-of-shit apartment in the city.

I heard that he can't access the church funds anymore.

He's broke.

He's lost a lot of weight too.

And I think he has a drinking problem.

Careful. You almost sound sympathetic.

Fuck you.

I don't give a shit about him.

He can rot to death in that apartment for all I care.

Did he ask you to help him?

Of course.

And?

I stare at my brother's text and replay everything my father said. Of course, I didn't agree to help him, but I also didn't tell him to fuck off like I wanted to either. He got into my head, and I'm not proud of it.

I stood by silently while he droned on and on about how I should be a good son and help him. He quoted a Bible verse about family and told me how a man's duty is to his parents before his brothers. I even sat in silence as he talked shit about Adam and Sage, and I let him.

He tried to open his mouth about Lucas once, and I shut him down fast.

Other than that, I barely said a word the whole time. I left him with an *I'll think about it*, and I've been trying to shake the whole encounter all week. But I can't say that to Luke. I'm too ashamed to admit that I didn't say no on the spot.

. . .

I told him no. Obviously.

Good.

He doesn't deserve your help.

I know.

If I were you, I wouldn't let Adam find out you took that meeting.

He's already pissed enough as it is.

He needs to calm the fuck down.

He's not the only one who has to deal with our father.

What if it had been Briar and Adam took a meeting with him?

My brow furrows as resentment builds inside me. Luke is always so smart, so analytical, and acts like everything is tit for tat. And I know he's right. If Truett laid a finger on my wife, and my brothers even dared to take his side, I'd cut them all off without hesitation—or worse.

But I don't need Luke serving up that much logical reasoning to make me feel like an even bigger asshole than I already feel.

I know.

But I'm not helping him.

I would never do that.

Trust me, I know you wouldn't.

Get some rest.

You get pissy when you're tired.

Fuck you.

Fuck you too.

You're still awake.

So why don't you get rest?

If you can't sleep, then I can't sleep.

Twin sense.

That's not a real thing, liar.

Yeah, I know.

But if you still want to talk, I'll stay up.

No, you have an early class.

Go to sleep.

Night, Caleb.

Night, Luke.

Trying to stay mad at him, I set my phone on the nightstand. He's right, of course. I do get pissy when I'm tired, but sleep hasn't been easy this week. There's just too much going on.

On top of that, Briar has been in a strange mood.

The one guy in Texas who hates me is living a couple hundred feet away. And if that wasn't strange enough, I can't get the image of him in those tight swim trunks out of my head. I'm certainly not against finding a man attractive. I've found plenty of men attractive in the past—that doesn't mean anything.

But this one in particular has really haunted my mind for the last week. Because Dean is very, *very* attractive, and it's bad enough worrying about my wife around him. I don't need to fantasize about him myself. Talk about a mess.

Flipping onto my back in bed, I turn to see the empty space next to me. My wife has always been a night owl, and it's not unheard of to feel her absence at night, especially if it's not a fertile day.

But when I can't get back to sleep, I climb out from under the covers. Walking to the window, I peer out over the yard toward the room above the garage. The lights are off, so I assume Dean is either asleep or at work.

Just then, the bedroom door opens and Briar walks in. She pauses when she spots me as if she's surprised to see me up.

"Hey," she mumbles before walking to the bathroom. "I didn't expect you to be awake. It's late."

I take in a deep breath as I turn toward her. "Couldn't sleep. What were you doing?"

Her brow furrows as she stops to glare at me. "Having a glass of wine and enjoying the peace and quiet. Is that okay with you?"

"It was just a question."

"Well, it sounded like an accusation," she argues.

I take a step toward her. "What exactly would I be accusing you of?"

She looks taken aback. "I don't know, Caleb. You're the one with the tone."

"And you're the one being defensive."

She lets out a huff of frustration as she spins away from me, putting the bathroom door between us.

She's slipping away.

I don't know what to say anymore. Which is a recurring theme, it seems.

Instead of standing there like an idiot, I walk out of our bedroom. I end up in the kitchen, filling a glass with water and rubbing my brow as I drink it. If I thought it would help, I'd reach for something stronger.

That's when movement on the porch catches my eye. I'm frozen in place as I watch Dean lift a glass to his lips. A glass from *my* kitchen. A glass full of *my* wine.

Glancing down to the sink, my eyes catch on an empty wine-glass, and it's not hard to put everything together from there. She was up in the middle of the night, drinking with him. Part of me wants to march out there and throw him off my property, but for what? Talking to her? Being near her? Being here in general?

I did this.

I'm not intimidated by a man who's been here a week. She's my wife. We have a life together. We have a child together. She wouldn't jeopardize that.

I just walk upstairs instead. Briar is in bed when I get to our room. She's lying on her side, facing me as I climb in next to her. She stares into my eyes for a moment, and I wish I could place the expression on her face.

What are we doing? Who are we anymore?

Does she even still love me?

I want to scream at her. I wish she would tell me how to make this better, and I would do it.

After a few minutes, she rolls over and falls asleep, but I lie awake. I don't ask her if she was with him or bother accusing her of anything. And maybe I should be mad, but I'm not.

Perhaps I'd be angry if I wasn't so terrified.

Thirteen

Briar

"Abby, no splashing," I say from the pool deck.

"Sorry," she replies breathlessly as she pops her head out of the water. Then she and my niece, Felicity, dive back in together. Their little feet kick water all over me and my sister.

Juliet is sitting in the pool chair next to me. She's wearing a wide-brimmed hat and large round sunglasses and sipping sweet tea out of a Mason jar.

My sister is the only friend I have left. And I enjoy spending time with her, especially without our mother around. Juliet naturally sides with her on most things. And the two of them make me feel like the odd one of the bunch.

We used to have more friends over for playdates or game nights. Our neighborhood was a much friendlier place before everything happened last year with Caleb's family.

Now, Juliet is the only one who still comes around.

Abby and Felicity are swimming in the pool, diving to the

bottom to retrieve the little sticks that we have to toss in every five minutes.

"Are you signing Abby up for ballet again this year?" Juliet asks.

"She doesn't want to do ballet," I reply with a sigh.

"Oh, that's a bummer."

Overhearing our conversation, Abby pops out of the water and pulls the goggles off her eyes.

"Mommy, I want to do karate," she says enthusiastically.

"I know, peanut. Daddy and I are going to sign you up for karate," I answer proudly.

Already, I can sense my sister gearing up her argument with the way she purses her lips and plasters a fake smile on her face. "Are you sure you don't want to be in ballet with Felicity, Abby? There are a lot of little girls in there."

"I'm sure," my daughter replies, and I smile proudly at her.

Juliet gives me a shrug as if to say she tried, and I appreciate her for not pushing the topic more. My parents constantly pressed us to do things we didn't want when we were kids. I remember wanting to go to theater camp in middle school, but my mother insisted I was more suited for cheerleading, so that's what I did.

I even had myself convinced that I loved it.

"So," Juliet starts in a hushed tone. "Kyle told me about you-know-who."

My sister and I have made a deal not to talk about the scandal or anything revolving Truett Goode in front of our kids. It usually means we have to speak in code, but we've gotten pretty good at it by this point.

"And his *attempted schmurder* charges," she adds.

I'm wringing my hands in my seat. I had to hear about the charges through social media instead of from my husband, but I didn't have the heart to press him about it. I know that Caleb is carrying a lot of stress over his father's case and what happened to Sage.

But I wish he'd open up to me about it. I wish we had that kind of marriage where we could lean on each other in moments like this. Instead, he's closing himself off entirely.

I glance sideways at our kids in the pool as I reply, "Yeah, I know."

"Have you and Caleb talked about it?" she asks.

Letting out a disgruntled sigh, I shake my head. "Not really. I don't think he wants to talk about it."

Instead, it's been hovering around us for over a week, like an ominous elephant in the room.

"I'm not gonna lie," Juliet says. "I was sort of hoping they would have gone with a lesser charge. It'd be so much less complicated. I'm ready for the day when we can forget this whole thing ever happened."

"I know," I mumble to myself, although I know our family will never forget about it. But I don't argue with her. I think what she wants is for me to agree with her, but deep down, I'm glad he was charged with attempted murder. I hope he's found guilty, and I hope he spends the rest of his miserable life in jail. I don't care that he's my husband's father or my daughter's grandfather.

"Oh my god," my sister whispers under her breath, disrupting my train of thought.

I follow her gaze and spin toward the garage to see Dean walking down the stairs with his keys and phone in his hands.

He's dressed casually today in a pair of tight jeans and a loose black shirt. His tattoos peek out from the sleeves, but it's the aviators on his face that add to the look and have my sister and I speechless as we watch him approach us.

He lifts a hand awkwardly in greeting, and we return the gesture.

Standing from the pool chair, I take a clumsy step toward him.

"Dean, this is my sister, Juliet," I say, gesturing to her. "Juliet, this is Dean Sheridan. He is the new tenant in our garage apartment."

"Nice to meet you," he says politely, with a curt nod.

"Yeah..." she stutters. "Nice to meet you, too."

The air grows awkward quickly as it's obvious just how much she's checking him out. Suddenly, I find myself standing between them as if I can block her view.

"Dean," Abby calls from the pool. "Look how long I can hold my breath!"

With that, she plunges her face under the water, and I glance up at him sheepishly.

"I told her what you were doing in the pool that day, and she's been practicing ever since."

Abby only lasts about twenty seconds before she pops her head up for air.

"Very impressive," he says flatly.

"Good job, honey," I add, to boost her confidence. Then I turn back toward him. "Is everything okay?"

He nods. "Yeah, it's fine."

I swallow my disappointment. Just once, I wish he would need something that I could provide.

"Okay, sorry, we won't keep you," I say to him. "But let me know if you need anything."

After he shuffles in place for a moment, he waves goodbye and gets into his car.

It's awkwardly quiet for a few minutes after he pulls away before my sister starts.

"Well, he's interesting," she says.

"Yeah."

"And not very good with kids."

"I mean, he's young," I say, defending him.

"He's also *very* good-looking," she replies quietly.

"Is he?" I reply, staring forward. "I hadn't really noticed."

She starts laughing, and I chuckle to myself.

"It would drive Kyle crazy to know a good-looking young man like that was living on our property while he was gone all day."

My laughter dies as I start to pick at my nails nervously.

Is it driving Caleb crazy? I mean, the other night, he did act a little strange when I was up late, and I suspect he might have seen Dean was also up late, but why wouldn't he just say something?

Is it weird that I sort of wish it was driving Caleb crazy? Maybe a little jealousy would do him some good. I want him to start acting like my husband.

Pick a fight about Dean. Be territorial. Lose his mind.

Tell me how much I belong to him.

He doesn't do any of that.

And the more I think about it, the more depressed I feel.

"Yeah," I lie. "It drives Caleb crazy too."

Fourteen

Caleb

It's well after eight thirty at night when I finally pull my car into the garage. Briar is at Bible study tonight, and Abby is over at my mom's. I sit behind the wheel for a while instead of getting out.

My life feels like one fucking mess after another.

I haven't responded to my father since our meeting last week.

I haven't even talked to Briar about it.

My wife is miserable, and I don't know if she's unhappy with me or she's unhappy in general, and I have no idea how to fix it.

The only thing I do know for sure is that inviting Dean Sheridan to live on my property was a fucking mistake. I spend all day at work, unable to focus because I know that back at my house, he's alone with my wife and daughter.

Yeah, he might be in the apartment, but he's still there.

And to make matters worse, I know that Briar likes him. I trust my wife. I know that what we have is stronger than anything he might tempt her with, but the idea that he's here grates on my nerves every minute of the day.

I finally climb out of my car with a sigh. But as I walk toward the house, I find myself pausing and looking up at his apartment instead. Since moving in, he and I haven't been alone or spoken a word to each other. I have no clue what I would even say to him, but this feels like an opportunity to at least say *something*.

So I quietly climb the steps up to his place. There's a window next to the door, and while the curtains are closed, there is a sliver of light shining through. Just as I pass the window, I pause when I see Dean inside.

It's not the sight of Dean on the couch that stops me in my tracks.

It's the sound.

Through the thin walls and glass pane, I can just make out his low moaning grunts.

There's only an inch of space between the curtains, but it's enough to make out exactly what Dean is doing. With his head hanging back on the blue sofa, the quick stroking motion of his arm is unmistakable.

Seconds pass by as I stand there, watching without reason. I could easily walk away or knock and make my presence known, but I don't. I find myself watching for far too long.

With every pained-sounding cry of his, I am more and more enthralled. And I certainly can't ignore the thickening of my own cock behind my zipper.

My lips part as I stare in awe.

As I watch the way he struggles, I feel the urge to bite my bottom lip. By the look of his violent stroking, it almost appears as if he's abusing his own cock. And the sounds that are coming from his mouth are not sounds of pleasure. It's almost as if he's trying his hardest to come, but he can't.

When I force myself to swallow, my mouth is as dry as a desert. But I can't tear myself away. I just stand there and wait, gawking at him like some sort of pervert.

What is wrong with me?

What is wrong with *him*?

Just come already. Why is he struggling so hard?

After what feels like forever, he lets out a disgruntled "Fuck!" before dropping his arm and collapsing against the couch in frustration. He lets his head fall back as he stares at the ceiling.

Holy shit.

I move away from the window and hide behind the door, giving him a few moments before I decide to knock. Besides, I have a raging issue of my own that I need to give time to go down before I'm ready to face him. It would be awfully suspicious if he opened his door to find me standing here with a stiff dick for no reason.

It's not surprising that watching him jack off made me hard. That would happen to anybody.

When enough time has passed, I finally tap against the wood. He lets out a grunt, and a moment later, he opens the door.

When our eyes meet, he's wearing a rueful scowl.

And I don't know if it's because *I'm* the one at the door, and he hates my guts, or if it's because he just yanked the fuck out of his own dick without getting his release.

"Can I help you?" he asks with a crass tone.

Fuck, why did I come here?

After the scene I just witnessed through the window, my brain has become foggy. I forgot what the whole point of me knocking in the first place was. And seeing what he just went through, I might be feeling a hint of sympathy for him and not really in the mood anymore to give him shit.

Then I remember him on my porch the other night, no doubt conversing with my wife. And something territorial takes over.

"I'm here to set a boundary," I say sternly.

His brows shoot upward as he stares at me in astonishment.

"Excuse me?" he asks.

This is just like any case at work, Caleb. Be stern and concise.

"The deal is that you can live here at this apartment because you need a place to stay, and I'm not taking that away. But I want you to know your place when it comes to my wife."

When his expression of astonishment morphs into a smug grin, my blood starts to boil. His full, pink lips stretch into a wicked smile, giving him two deep dimples on either side of his cheeks. And when his tongue peeks out to lick his bottom lip, my fists start to clench at my sides.

"I'm serious, Dean," I mutter.

He only laughs. "Oh, I'm sure that you are serious, but it sounds like a joke to me."

"This isn't a joke," I reply angrily.

"Yes, it is, because you're feeling insecure, right? And that's somehow my problem."

"I'm going to be your problem in a minute," I growl.

As he steps forward and meets my gaze, I fight the urge to grab him by the throat and shove him against the wall.

"Listen, Caleb," he says bitterly. "I haven't touched your wife. In fact, I haven't even tried because we both know that if I wanted to, I would have already."

"Lay a hand on Briar, and I'll fucking bury you in the backyard, you understand me?"

At my brutal threat, his eyebrows pop upward again, and he looks almost impressed.

"Tell me, Caleb, what exactly am I supposed to do if it's your wife who wants me?" he says.

I take a step forward, cornering him against the doorframe, and he stares at me with intensity. We're so close I can feel his breath on my face.

"My wife would never want you," I say in a growly, deep tone.

"Are you sure about that?" he replies with a grin that I want to smack off his face.

"Yeah, I'm fucking sure. You can try all you want, but Briar is loyal to me." My chest puffs up as I try to make myself taller, but he meets me eye to eye.

"If you're so sure, why are you here at all, then?"

I jab a finger in his chest. "Because I see the way you talk to her, and she's a good person, so she'll be nice to you. But I don't want you getting in her head or making her feel things she doesn't want to. She is my wife, and it's my job to protect her."

"From people like me?" he asks with a lopsided grin.

"Yeah, from people like you."

"Well, what if I told you it was your wife who knocked on *my* door?" he says.

"Like I said, she's just being *nice*," I grumble in return.

"Oh yeah, she's very nice," he replies in a sultry tone, and suddenly, his back is against the wall, and my forearm is pressed against his throat.

"Do you want to fucking play with me?" I shout in his face. "Because I'll kick you the fuck out of this apartment right now. Do you understand me?"

"Why don't you, Caleb? Why am I here?" he replies.

"Because she's a much better fucking person than I am," I say.

And although my arm is cutting off his windpipe, he still holds that smile.

When he presses on my chest, I let up just a little, so at least I don't kill him. I don't need to deal with that right now.

"So you think you really know her, huh?" he asks, and my brows furrow in confusion.

"Of course I fucking know her. She's my wife."

"Okay," he replies in a smooth tone. "Then why don't we make a little wager?"

At that word, I pause, my curiosity piqued. "The fuck are you talking about?" I grumble.

"Well, you're so sure that your wife doesn't want me, right?"

"I *know* my wife would not cheat on me," I say assuredly.

Again, he laughs, and I find myself holding back my fists. "You think you know her so well. I've only been here nine days, and I can tell you don't know shit about your wife, Caleb. But if you're so sure, then let's put it to the test."

"Put it to the test?" I stammer. "Are you seriously suggesting that we toy with my wife like she's a trophy to be won?

"Isn't she?"

"You're fucking insane," I mutter, stepping away from him.

"You're the one who started threatening me, shoving me against the wall, yelling in my face, and why? Because I talk to your wife? It sounds to me like you're a man who's a little insecure and is afraid his marriage is falling apart. So maybe, instead of coming over here and talking shit, why don't you fucking prove it, Caleb?"

"Prove it how?"

"Let's see how faithful your wife is. I won't even initiate it, and I bet she'll still want me."

Even as my blood boils, I do my best to keep calm. He's trying to provoke me, and it's not going to work. He's been here nine days. He thinks he knows Briar better than me? He's crazy.

"Fine. What do I get if I prove to you that my wife will not cheat on me with you?"

"Bragging rights," he shrugs. "And a faithful marriage."

"And that's all you want? Bragging rights?"

"That would be enough for me to know that I beat you. To know that I finally got back at you for what you did to Isaac."

My jaw clenches as my molars grind together. *What I did to Isaac*?

"Is there a better prize than that?" he asks.

"And how the hell am I supposed to know if she wants you or not? You think she'll admit that to me?" I ask with fiery resentment.

"Oh, trust me, Caleb. I will let you know. And I'll savor the look on your face when you find out."

"Fine, you arrogant son of a bitch," I reply sternly. "Do your best, but I promise you, Briar will never fall for you."

"We'll see about that."

He grins as he backs away from the door and then slams it in my face.

Fifteen

Dean

I'm burning with rage. That asshole seriously knocked on my door to accuse me of being a home-wrecker, completely unwarranted.

Yes, I've fantasized about seducing his wife, but I haven't actually done anything. Yet.

God, he infuriates me. Caleb Goode is the most self-righteous, arrogant, inconsiderate asshole I've ever met. I can't wait to see the look on his face when I tell him how easy it was to tempt his wife. He thinks he can just bully and control anyone he wants, but he can't control me.

I spend the rest of my night stewing in my apartment. Feeling this fired up nearly has me wanting to try to get off again. But I decide not to even bother. It's hopeless, and my efforts would be better spent proving that egotistical asshole wrong.

I hear a car door closing outside, and I peer out my window to see Briar walking up the paved walkway toward the house.

For a moment, as I watch her, I feel a hint of regret for playing her like a pawn in our game. She doesn't deserve to be used like that. But she also doesn't deserve to suffer through a lousy marriage.

If I could just make her see that, she'd be so much better off with someone who could please her...

As she reaches the house, I notice the way her gaze flits up toward my window. For a moment, our eyes meet, and she waves softly up at me. I wave back.

She scurries into the house, where her husband waits for her, and I bide my time. She'll come knocking. I know she will.

Until then, I busy myself with tidying up my tiny place. I check in on my dad with a quick phone call. He's still up and spends at least twenty minutes complaining about the same nurse as last time. I don't bother telling him that it sounds like he's in love, but I keep a smirk on my face the entire time.

His mood sounds better, but his voice is raspier, and he seems to be losing his breath more. It's almost as if his body is giving out faster than his spirit, a thought that makes me nauseous with grief.

After our call, I sit on the couch and scroll through my phone for a while. Somehow, I end up looking through flashback photos on Insta of my high school days. Most of the photos are of me and Isaac.

Seeing how happy we were only fueling my hatred for his brother. Isaac was more than my best friend. Everyone knew that. We might have started as friends, but it didn't take long until everything changed. For me. For him. For us.

Isaac was the catalyst. It was as if my life had completely ended and then began again with one kiss.

And if there's one truth that has kept me anchored to him after all this time, it's this—if Isaac's family had been different, we would have stayed together for a long time. We would have been happy. I know that in my heart.

We might have just been kids, but I meant as much to him as he did to me. He just didn't have a choice. His father threw him out. His brothers didn't save him. And because of them, he and I didn't stand a chance. I couldn't leave my father.

Even if Isaac had given me a chance, I still wouldn't have been able to go with him.

I don't know how long I sit on my couch and stew in my resentment when I hear the light tapping on the door. I glance down at the time on my phone, eleven forty-five.

Perfect.

I climb from the couch and rush to the front door, opening it to find Briar standing there with a bottle of wine in her hand.

"It feels weird to drink alone now," she says with a sheepish smile.

"No one should ever drink alone," I reply as I open the door to usher her inside. She makes herself at home, going to the kitchen to retrieve the glasses as I sit on the couch, angled toward the space she eventually takes.

The TV is on, but the volume is low, and I don't turn it up. I want her to know she's my focus tonight. I think that's what she wants, too.

"You didn't work tonight?" she asks as she takes a sip.

With a shake of my head, I reply, "Nope. I had two clients yesterday, though."

"Oh." Her cheeks start to turn pink at the mention of my work.

I let the moment grow more charged by the second as we stare across the sofa at each other.

"Tell me," I say, just above a whisper. "If you could hire an escort to do anything you want, what would you hire me for?"

Her eyes widen as she puts her lips against the rim of her wineglass. After a quick drink, she averts her gaze as she responds. "I don't know."

"Sure you do," I say. "There must be something."

"You mean like...sex?" Her eyes finally meet mine, and I find myself grinning with how adorable she is. So innocent and yet so... curious.

"Not necessarily."

"I don't know, then. I feel like there's a whole world of possibilities that I'm not even aware of. But...I'm married now, so...I never will."

"Don't say that."

"It's true," she snaps back with a chuckle. "Caleb and I don't have that kind of marriage, and the sex we do have used to be fun, but now it's all about trying to get pregnant. It's like all of the intimacy and pleasure has been sucked out of the act altogether."

Fuck, that's sad.

"Have you thought about telling him what you want?" The words slip out, and I realize once I've uttered them that giving her relationship advice is the opposite of my goal right now, but I can't help myself. Everything about Briar screams unhappy and afraid, even though she won't admit it.

Standing from the couch with a huff, she moves toward the kitchen for another glass. "God, no," she replies haughtily.

"Why not?"

She tries to laugh it off again. "Because I don't even know what I want."

I stand from the couch and move toward her. Something beyond the wager I made with Caleb is compelling me to help her. Maybe it's my own desire or attraction to her. Maybe it's because even in my line of work, I've never wanted to see someone discover what turns them on more than I want Briar to.

I want to watch her find a part of herself she didn't know existed.

So, without thinking, I just speak, changing my tone to a deeper, steadier cadence.

"Briar, I want you to kneel."

The hand lifting the glass to her lips freezes as her expression twists in confusion. "What?"

"You heard me. Get on your knees."

I watch the color drain from her face. "Why?" she whispers.

"Because I want to see if you'll do it. And I want to see if you like it."

"I shouldn't," she murmurs to herself. "Dean, I won't cheat on my husband."

"I'm not telling you to suck my dick, Briar. This has nothing to do with cheating. I'm just telling you to kneel."

At the mention of sucking my dick, her eyes go wide again before she quickly turns her gaze down to the floor.

"And what if I do kneel for you?" she asks.

"You'll be rewarded," I reply softly, wearing a casual grin.

I can see the contemplation on her face. The way she worries her lip and wrings her hands. She's at war within herself, a raging battle between what she wants and what she thinks she's allowed to want.

But ever so slowly, one side of that conflict clearly takes the victory as Briar moves to her knees. Her eyes stay averted from mine, almost as if I am the living embodiment of her own shame, and she cannot face me.

"Lovely," I whisper quietly to myself as I take in the exquisite way she settles into a submissive pose, hands folded in her lap, head bowed, shoulders relaxed.

She slips on submission like a well-fitting dress, immediately flaunting how fucking good it looks on her.

"Do you like it?" I ask, hearing the weakness in my own voice. Even I'm caught off guard by how sexy she looks in a kneeling position.

"Being on my knees?" she asks as if I'm speaking a different language, and I might as well be. This is as foreign to her as Portuguese.

"Being submissive."

She attempts a glance in my direction but immediately casts her eyes back to the floor. "I don't know."

"What if I was your husband, Briar? What if you trusted me enough to let me do whatever I want to you, and what if you knew that all of that would please me very much? Would you like that?"

The gentle curve of her throat moves as she swallows nervously. She deliberates her answer, almost as if she doesn't trust it herself. But it slips through her lips regardless. "Yes."

It rings with truth like an anthem.

"Have you ever told Caleb that?" I ask carefully as I take a step toward her, pacing around her slowly like a predator.

She shakes her head.

Reaching down, I touch her chin and guide it upward until she's staring right at me.

Fuck, she really is so beautiful with those big blue eyes, warm and honest. Something about Briar brings me comfort, makes me feel safe, and makes me want to test her limits and play with her.

"I like your voice. I want to hear it."

"No," she says assertively. "I've never told Caleb."

"Why not?"

"Because...it's not that easy."

"It's not easy to express to your husband what you want?" I genuinely don't understand. What is the point of marrying someone if she can't even tell him her desires?

Briar grows flustered. "What if he doesn't want what I want? What if he thinks it's silly or it changes things between us?"

I crouch down to look her in the eye. Brushing her blonde waves behind her ear, I give her a soft expression. It seems such a waste to me to have a beautiful wife like Briar and never truly know what she wants because she's too afraid to tell me. And the last thing I would ever want to do is help Caleb Goode, but I do want to help Briar.

"You know..." I say softly. "I could show you more. I could give you what you need without the sex. Without cheating on your husband."

I'm playing with fire, and I love it. I'm offering her something that will undoubtedly infuriate Caleb. But I have a soft spot for this woman. Someone else's wife. The wife of someone I hate.

Briar seems to lose her breath for a moment. She sways in her kneeled position, gazing into my eyes as if searching them for meaning. Then, suddenly, without warning, she scurries to her feet.

"That's very kind of you, Dean. Really. But I can't."

"Briar..." I call as she moves toward the door. "Don't go."

"I really should. I'm sorry," she stammers.

"Don't apologize. If you have to go, I understand. Just think about it, okay?"

Her gaze meets mine, and I see the anxious remorse on her face. She wants what she can't have, and I wish I could just set her free.

"I will," she mumbles.

And with that, she's out the door and scurrying down the steps toward her house. Even after she's gone, I find myself smiling. I meant for that to tempt her, but I can't help but feel like it may have had the same effect on me.

Sixteen

Caleb
21 years old

Briar is sitting on a chair at my desk in my bedroom, holding an index card with the word chiaroscuro *scribbled on the front. I let my eyes narrow as I stare at the word, biting my bottom lip.*

"Come on, Caleb," she says with an eye roll. "We've gone over this one."

"It's something about paint, right?"

She drops the card in her lap with an exasperated sigh. "You're doing this on purpose."

"Why would I act like an idiot on purpose?"

She's grinning to herself as she looks down at her lap, and I love the way it creates little dimples in her cheeks. She curls her wavy hair behind her ear like she always does when she has something to say, and I wait patiently for her to say it.

"I don't know," she replies. "To get me to stay and help you study."

I feign offense as I place my hand on my chest. "You think I'm that clever?"

With a giggle, she shakes her head. "You are smarter than you let people believe."

I give a shrug, trying to appear innocent. "I don't know what you're talking about."

We have our semester midterms next week, and it's true that I've been using them as an excuse to spend more time with Briar. We've been meeting outside of class alone, *and I'm running out of reasons to need her help. I'm dreading the end of the semester when I know I'll see her so much less.*

But I'm not trying to be manipulative. Briar and I have fun together, and I swear she looks forward to these study sessions as much as I do. She just seems to relax more when that dickhead boyfriend of hers isn't around.

"You know what?" I ask without answering the question on her flash card. "I'm getting hungry. You hungry?"

"Caleb!" she shouts at me while hiding a grin. "Answer the question!"

"I'm gonna order a pizza. You like pizza?"

Laughing, she picks up the calculator on my desk and flings it at me. I catch it in my hand as I climb off my bed, ruffling her hair before I set the calculator back on my desk.

"You get mean when you're hungry," I tease her.

Biting her bottom lip like she is right now drives me absolutely crazy. She's trying not to flirt with me, but she can't help it.

When I pick up my phone from the desk, she moves to snatch it from my hand, but I hold it out of her reach. She's pressed against my chest as we start to wrestle over control of the phone.

My free hand rests on her lower back, and she doesn't move away. Not even when I use it to press her body against mine. She's giggling and standing on her tiptoes, although she's nowhere near being able to reach my phone as I hold it over my head.

"You're such a jerk," she teases, shining those pearly whites at me.

"Come on," I mumble softly. "Let's get some food, and then we'll get back to studying."

Her struggle starts to die down, but my hand remains on her lower back, and her body is still flush against me. When her gaze lands briefly on my lips, my heart rate starts to pick up. The air in the room grows thick, and I find myself gazing down at her perfect pink lips with that little Cupid's bow between her nose and top lip.

I want to make those lips mine.

It's wrong of me to want Briar to cheat on her boyfriend with me. I know that, but I can't find it in myself to feel bad about it. They're not married, so it's hardly adultery. She doesn't belong to him. And besides that, he's not good enough for her.

Her reaching arm starts to lower, and the space between us grows more charged and electric. Her lips are only inches from mine, and I'm desperate to close the distance, but I don't want to make the first move. I want it to be her choice.

In a soft whisper, she says, "Tell me what chiaroscuro is, and I'll let you order a pizza."

I can't help but smile. Leaning in until our mouths are only a breath apart, I reply, "The use of contrast to create light in drawings and paintings."

The corner of her mouth tugs into a grin. "See, I knew you weren't an idiot."

Then she presses her hands to my chest and shoves me away. "Now, go order that pizza."

As I stumble away from her with a feeling of victory, I move toward the door. There's no denying this chemistry between us now. And though I didn't get that kiss, I still got something. And that something is hope.

"I'm gonna see if Isaac and his friend want some, too," I say as I pull open the door and walk down the hall toward my brother's room. Our parents are at the church tonight, so it's just us here.

My mind is still reeling from that almost kiss with Briar, so I'm not even thinking as I barge right into my little brother's bedroom.

I'm frozen in shock as I take in the sight of Dean quickly scrambling from the bed. Isaac jumps up from a lying position. They're both fully clothed, but judging by the way they were both horizontal a moment ago, they were definitely up to something.

"Holy shit," I stammer as I quickly turn away.

"Ever heard of knocking?" my brother shouts.

"What the fuck?" I reply with my back to them.

"Get out, Caleb!" Isaac bellows.

I don't know what to do, so I quickly slam the door closed again. And maybe shutting two horny teenagers back in a closed room isn't the greatest idea, but until this very moment, I thought Isaac and Dean were just friends.

I had my suspicions about Isaac, but I guess I just assumed this was a bridge we'd cross later when he's an adult, has moved out, and can do what he wants. Not now, under my father's roof.

My mind is reeling as I stand in the hallway, unsure of what to do now. I should send Dean home, right? I can't let this go on. My parents will be home at any minute. I can't let my father find out about Isaac.

Under absolutely no *circumstance can I let my father find out about Isaac. There's no telling what he'll do.*

Which means his friend has to go—for good.

†

Present Day

I can't sleep again. Briar is slumbering peacefully next to me in the bed, but I'm sitting here at three in the morning, staring at Isaac's picture on my phone.

He's on a mini tour right now, promoting an LP he put out, and I can't stop staring at the event listed in town, which is only half an hour away.

I won't go. It would be wrong of me to show up at his show and disrupt what he has going on, but at the same time...that's my brother.

Theo Virgil is chasing his dreams right now. He's free. What kind of monster would pull him back down to the depths of hell for his own selfish gain?

I'm sure he's seen the news. He knows by now that our father is about to go on trial for attempted murder, and I hope it makes him happy. But it feels strange that we aren't talking about this. He's not here to experience this with us.

Isaac deserves to live in peace, free from this family that hurt him so badly, but I also hate to feel as if he's missing the best part. The part he deserves to witness firsthand. The reckoning.

"Hey," Briar whispers from the pillow next to me.

I swipe to close the app on my phone and turn to face her. She looks so beautiful and peaceful, with her face on the pillow and her soft hair strewn around her head like a halo.

"What's wrong?" she asks.

"I can't sleep," I reply.

"Come here." The soft cadence of her voice is like a siren song, and I find myself melting into the mattress, falling helplessly into her embrace. Instead of holding her in my arms like I normally do, I cover her body with my own and press my cheek against her chest. She wraps her thin arms around me.

"Thinking about your father's case?" she asks.

"Among other things," I reply, not mentioning my argument with Dean tonight. Or my estranged brother's new tour schedule.

She rubs my back. "You don't have to do anything, Caleb."

I lift onto my elbows and stare down at her. "I know," I reply softly, trying to breathe in her comfort. When our eyes meet, it feels as if it's the first time we've stared at each other in months. "I don't think I have it in me to defend that man."

"Then don't," she whispers, touching my face.

"Deep down," I continue, "I know that I could help him, though. I could get his charges lessened."

She nods knowingly. "And you worry that you won't be doing your job if you don't help him?"

"He doesn't deserve my help," I add.

"I agree," she says with a furrow in her brow.

"But when you have the power to help someone, and you don't do it..." My voice trails as I let that thought drift off my lips.

"You are still a good man, Caleb."

Am I? I want to ask. Am I a good man? It feels as if, down every road of my life, I've fucked over others for my own selfish goals. I stole Briar from another man. I drove away my brother's friend.

For fuck's sake, I made a wager with a man tonight over my wife, treating her like the spoils of war.

Am I truly a good man? Do I even deserve her?

Do I care?

I have what I want, and maybe I've gotten complacent. Somewhere along the way, I stopped appreciating what I had worked so hard to get. She is my wife. I *won* her because I *fought* for her.

And now I'm being challenged again. I didn't lose her before, and I sure as fuck don't plan to lose her now.

"Say that again," I murmur, lowering my lips to hers.

"You're a good man, Caleb," she replies.

"You really believe that?" I ask as I press my mouth to hers.

She mumbles against the kiss. "Yes."

Tugging her bottom lip between my teeth, I bite down, making her yelp in pain. After releasing it, I take her mouth in a brutal, possessive kiss. Her fingers scratch at my back as I tangle my tongue with hers, owning her mouth as my hips grind between her legs.

As I skate my teeth along her jawline, she gasps quietly. Reaching the side of her throat, I mutter, "What if I'm not, Briar? What if I'm not a good man? Would you still love me?"

"Of course," she answers without hesitation.

"I don't deserve you." My lips trail lower, claiming every inch of her skin as I sink down between her breasts and over the softness of her belly.

"Yes, you do," she replies with a hum.

When I reach her hips, I kiss a line above the hem of her panties, causing her skin to break out in goose bumps as she writhes on the bed.

Slipping my fingers under the elastic band, I pull her underwear down in a quick swipe.

"Caleb," she whispers.

"Don't you dare stop me, Briar." Pausing with my mouth hovering over her sex, I stare up into her eyes. She's biting her bottom lip as her fingers comb through my hair.

"I'm not stopping you," she mumbles delicately.

"Good. Because this is *mine*, right?"

"Of course," she breathes.

"Then say it," I command in a way I've never done before.

Her eyes widen slightly in surprise, but she answers without hesitation. "It's yours."

With my arms hooked around her thighs, I spread her legs farther, and I bury my nose against her wet, pink cunt, inhaling her scent like the animal I am. She gasps again, and I feel her thighs try to press back together as if she's self-conscious about herself. But I only press them wider, running my tongue through her folds. I growl deeply as my lips latch around her clit.

Her back arches as she lets out a quiet, breathless moan. "Don't stop," she whispers.

I wouldn't dream of stopping. I need to feel her pleasure on my tongue. I need to taste this victory. It might have been over twelve years since I made Briar mine for the first time, but it's become clear to me tonight that I can never stop fighting for her.

I know her body because I've spent the last decade memorizing it. I know how to make her come because I am the only man on earth with the right to do so.

Ravenously, I suck her clit. Sliding my middle finger into the heat of her pussy, I feel the way her body trembles with pleasure.

Pride flows through me as she convulses through her climax. Dean thinks he can challenge me. I wish he were here right now to see how she comes for me.

My hips grind into the mattress at the thought. I imagine him in the chair by the window, watching as I prove him wrong. Briar is mine and no one else's.

"Caleb, come here."

Her gentle call pulls me from my thoughts. Moving with urgency, I climb up her body, tugging my boxers down only enough to release my cock. And as I plunge inside her, she hums with gratitude against my ear.

"Yes," she whispers.

My hands find hers, and I interlace our fingers, pressing them both into the mattress above her head as I thrust inside her. Her expression softens when I have her at my mercy, unable to move as I fuck her.

Our hips grind together in sync, and the faster I pound into her, the shallower her breathing becomes. My gaze lifts to the empty chair in the corner. In my mind, he's sitting there, watching me claim what's mine.

There is no competition. There's not a single doubt in my mind that Briar is mine and will always be mine.

My orgasm comes crashing through me like a tidal wave. Resting my forehead against hers, I shudder through the sensation. Her legs wrap around my hips as if she wants to keep me inside her.

When I finally pull out, she doesn't bother keeping her legs up to keep my seed inside. She climbs from the bed, and I see in the glint of moonlight the way it drips down her thighs.

This wasn't about making a baby. We needed this. For a moment, I feel a hint of relief that we've mended a crack between us. Is it enough to save our marriage? I don't know, but I have to believe every little moment is enough.

Before going to the bathroom to clean up, she leans over and presses her lips to my cheek.

"I don't care what you say, Caleb Goode. You're a good man to me."

My lips pull into a smile as I watch her walk away. It helps to know that because, if I'm honest, her opinion is the only one that matters anyway.

Seventeen

Briar

Curling my hair in the bathroom, I get a quick flashback of last night every time I look at my reflection in the mirror. A smirk tugs at my lips.

First, that moment with Dean when he told me to kneel—*and I did*.

Then, later that night, in bed with Caleb.

I needed that. No, *we* needed that. Sex without purpose other than intimacy and pleasure. When was the last time we did that? Months? Years? I nearly forgot how good it can be. Our sex life used to be fun, back when I felt like someone he couldn't resist. Back when my body felt like my own.

I still don't understand what happened with Dean, though. It wasn't about attraction or sex, but something acute and powerful happened to me when I looked up at him from the floor. I felt so cherished. Like all of his attention was hyperfocused on me.

I haven't felt that way since college. Since Caleb and I first met, I knew that he wanted me. It was his attention I fell in love with first.

The way his eyes would always find me. The way he made it seem like even when my boyfriend was there, Caleb and I were the only two people in the room.

From there, I fell in love with Caleb. His kindness, his humor, and his confidence. I felt so safe with him, and I knew from our very first kiss that I could spend the rest of my life comfortable and happy in his arms. Like he carved out a space just for me.

Being with Dean reminds me of those days. Like Dean sees me, too.

After my hair is curled and my makeup is applied, I slip on a pair of comfortable sneakers and throw my purse over my shoulder. Abby is with Caleb's mother, so I have the whole day to myself. It's been a long time since I've been able to just go where I want when I want, and I have the perfect day planned.

"Where are you off to?" a deep voice calls when I walk out of the house with my keys in hand. I spin around to find Dean coming down the stairs. He's dressed like he's going somewhere too. In tight black pants and a dark-green polo that hugs his muscled arms, it's incredibly distracting.

"Headed to the art museum in the city," I reply cheerfully. "There's a traveling exhibit from Lyon there this month, and I don't want to miss it."

"Art museum?" he replies with interest.

"Yeah, I know that seems weird..."

"Doesn't seem weird at all," he says, cutting me off. "Sounds lovely."

Holding my hand on my forehead to block the sun, I squint up at him as the words just slip through my lips. "Do you wanna come?"

For a moment, he appears surprised by the invite. "I don't want to crash your relaxing day."

"You wouldn't be crashing it," I reply. "If you let me show you everything I love there and talk about art for a couple of hours, I think I'd enjoy it even more."

This makes him smile, and the way his eyes light up makes my stomach flutter. Then he takes a step toward me, and when he turns his gaze back up to my face, I feel my skin flush with heat.

"I would love to hear you talk about something you love. Anyone who turns that down is insane," he says coolly. "I'll drive."

I have to force myself to swallow. "Okay then."

Dean climbs into his car, which is a sleek black BMW sedan. It smells like fresh leather and cologne on the inside, making my mouth water immediately as I sit down. The drive into the city is about forty-five minutes, and we spend the entire time avoiding anything awkward, like whatever the hell happened last night.

Instead, he tells me about his father and growing up in the city. I tell him about my family and college.

"I remember you a little bit," he says with one hand gripping the steering wheel. "But you and Caleb were just friends back then, right?"

"Um..." My voice trails. Most of the time, when people ask how Caleb and I met, I just tell them we met in college. It's a classic story of cheerleader meets star quarterback. I usually include how whenever he was on the field, I was constantly watching him, and whenever he ran to the bench, his eyes would find me on the sidelines.

Those things are all true. The part about me dating the captain of the team at the same time is purposefully omitted.

Usually.

"I was dating his teammate in college," I say as I stare out the window.

"His teammate?" Dean asks, sounding surprised.

"Yeah," I confess. There's no excuse or sweet way to frame the story in our favor.

"You broke up with that guy for Caleb?" Dean asks.

"Eventually," I say.

"Wow..."

When I turn to look at him in the driver's seat, he's wearing a smug expression as if he's intrigued by the story. And maybe that's why I told him a little more than I normally do. I knew he wouldn't judge me.

"Very sexy," he remarks before turning toward the road. I bite my lip between my teeth as I stifle a grin.

"It *was* sexy," I reply.

When we reach the museum downtown, Dean parks on the top floor of the garage down the street, and we take a shifty elevator down to the ground level. Walking to the museum and passing by other people on the street, I feel an odd sense of mischief being out and alone with Dean.

These strangers probably think he and I are together. And something is alluring and exciting about that. Technically, I'm not doing anything wrong, but the prospect of being *bad* excites me.

He pays for our tickets when we reach the building and even opens the door for me when we enter. The moment we're inside, I feel at ease. I've been to this museum more times than I can count. When I was pregnant with Abby, I would come all the time just to walk around and try to induce labor. People probably thought I was crazy, but if I had to get my steps in, I was going to do it around something that I loved.

I take Dean through the various permanent exhibits, showing him some of my favorite pieces. He shows interest and listens intently to every word I say. But when we make our way to the special exhibit, the one full of pieces I've only seen on computer screens and in textbooks, I can hardly contain my excitement.

"Oh my gosh." I gasp. "This is a real Vestier. I haven't seen this since college."

Standing in front of the painting, the woman's face staring back at me, I'm speechless. I can feel Dean's eyes on me, so I turn his way, giving him a quizzical look.

"What?" I whisper.

"You really light up here," he answers plainly as he leans in so close I get a whiff of his cologne.

Goose bumps erupt down the back of my neck. "I love it."

"I can see that," he replies, gazing into my eyes.

With a blush, I turn back toward the painting. That's when I notice the one on the far wall. With a gasp, I move toward the piece. A man and a woman lie together, their bodies draped in fabric that is so intricate it looks as if it's caught in time, swept up by the wind. Red blood drips from the wounds in each of their chests, and their lips are so close they nearly touch.

"Wow," Dean mumbles from behind me.

"I love this one," I reply as I swallow the emotion building in my throat.

"They're dead," he says in a low mutter, and I find myself smiling as I tear up.

"They're lovers. This was a real couple," I reply gently. "She was married to his brother, and when they were caught together, her husband killed them."

"That's depressing," he says. I can feel his chest softly touching my back.

Turning my head to gaze up at him, I reply, "I think it's beautiful."

Looking back at the painting, I stare at it, feeling as if I could stand here forever. The way they look caught in a storm together. The longing on their faces, as if they loved each other until their dying breaths.

I love how art captures those feelings we often can't describe. The pull on my heartstrings it evokes when, at its core, it's nothing more than colorful paint someone applied to a canvas three hundred years ago.

Growing up, my family always made me feel as if expressing deep emotions was somehow beneath us. The only feelings to be shown were love, faith, and gratitude, and even those were best displayed modestly.

Art was my outlet, even if I wasn't the one creating it. I could *feel* it. It's like magic to me how something so simple could evoke something so visceral.

And when I look at the two lovers in this painting, it makes me feel...desire. Deep, yearning, obsessive desire.

"What are you thinking?" Dean whispers into my ear, and it

jolts me from my thoughts. Turning toward him, I blink, and a tear slips over my cheek.

The corner of his mouth lifts into a coy smirk as he reaches forward and wipes it away with the pad of his thumb. Our faces are so close I can feel the warmth of his breath. Although there are people meandering around us, it feels as if he and I are alone in this room with this work of art in front of us.

"I was just thinking..." I whisper.

Then something happens. I can't explain it, and I don't understand it, but suddenly, time stretches on without us, and I feel caught in the same storm the couple in the painting is caught in.

Dean's eyes bore into mine as something electric and all-consuming passes through us. I wonder if he can feel it, too.

When his breath quivers and his lips part, I get my answer.

When his fingers touch the bare skin between my shirt and my pants, I suck in a delicate gasp.

"Go on," he breathes.

He tugs me ever so gently toward him, so we're practically embracing. To anyone around us, we appear to be like the couple in the painting, two lovers gazing longingly into each other's eyes.

My body is on fire, and the turmoil inside me is agonizing. It's as if my mind and my body want two different things, and there is no way to reconcile them.

I want him. In a physical, torturous, heart-wrenching way, I want him. Dean is everything I crave out of my life. Independent and headstrong. With one quick motion, he could cut the ties keeping me chained to this life.

But I love my husband, and I love my family.

I don't understand why I so desperately feel this need to be free from it.

Standing in this gallery, in *my* safe space, I don't belong to anyone here. I serve no one. I worship *no one.*

"Please, Briar," he whispers, his breath grazing my lips. "Let's get out of here."

Those words feel like a bomb that detonates and takes out

everything. It razes my entire life, and at this moment, I find it so alluring that I let it.

"Okay," I mumble in return.

He slips his hand in mine and tugs me toward the door. I barely see the art we pass as we rush through the museum. Thoughts swirl through my mind as we go, but I brush them away as if we're trying to outrun them.

Outrun the consequences. Outrun the guilt. Outrun the multitude of reasons I should not want this.

I'm not thinking. Only acting, and it feels good. After years and years of making the smart choice, the Christian choice, the moral choice, I forgot how good it feels just to make the carnal, selfish choice.

Dean and I are out on the street, hands linked and practically running to the car. He's wearing an expression on his face of victory and elation. His eyes sparkle as he slips his tongue out and wets his bottom lip. When his eyes rake over my body from top to bottom, I feel alive for the first time since college.

As we step into the elevator of the parking garage and the doors close us in, I feel my temperature rise. He turns toward me with hunger in his eyes as he corners me against the wall.

"Look at me," he commands, and I lift my gaze to his face. "Hands behind your back," he says, and the way he tells me exactly what to do sends chills down my spine.

Like the condensation on a glass of sweet iced tea left out in the sun, I melt under his scorching gaze. When his lips move toward me, my heart races and my head turns slightly. His kiss lands against the rapid pulse of my neck, and I forget how to breathe.

The arousal that courses through me is fervent and intoxicating. His lips are harsh against my skin, and my eyes fly wide open as his hands grip my waist with brutal need.

I'm lost in a torrent of desire.

His deep, sexy voice whispers in my ear, "You might be married to him, but you belong to me."

Blood rushes to my core, pulsing with need. With my hands still pressed obediently between my body and the wall of this elevator, I'm powerless. I'm his.

As his lips finally find mine, I hold my breath and jump head-first into this feeling. His mouth captures mine, and suddenly, we're alone on a planet of our own. We are the only two people who exist. He licks into my mouth, caressing my tongue and making it so I couldn't breathe if I wanted to.

Everything about this kiss is exquisite, like the stroke of paint on a canvas blending together to form a masterpiece.

But when I feel him grind the stiff length in his pants against me, the panic sets in. I feel his cock, and suddenly I'm flooded with dirty, terrible thoughts of what I'd like to do with it. I want to touch it, taste it, worship it, take it.

It's so, *so* wrong.

Like being doused in cold water, I gasp. Just then, the elevator chimes, and the doors open.

I lift my hands from behind my back and shove Dean to the side so I can rush out of the elevator. When I reach the open air at the top of the parking garage, I suck in a breath as if I've been underwater this entire time.

"What am I doing?" I shout to myself as I pace the open space.

"Briar," he calls toward me, but my mind is not open to listening at the moment. It's too caught up in passion and conflict.

"I love my husband," I argue. "I'm not stuck in some loveless marriage."

"I didn't say you were," he says.

"Then...what are we doing? Why did we do that?" I'm practically screaming, clearly hysterical from that heated moment.

Meanwhile, Dean is as cool as a cucumber, strolling toward his car with his hands in his pockets.

"This isn't a game, Dean!" I shout toward him.

When he spins toward me, he's wearing a twisted expression of frustration. "What do you want me to say, Briar? That I'm sorry? Because I'm not."

"You can't just...kiss married women, Dean."

"I just did," he replies smugly. "And don't tell me you didn't want it."

"I—" This isn't fair. My body wanted something my heart didn't.

Or did it? My heart wants Dean, too. Sweet, dominant, compassionate Dean. But wanting and having are two different things, and if loving Caleb is my crime, then not having Dean is my punishment.

His car beeps as he unlocks it. Then he opens the passenger door and looks at me expectantly, waiting for me to get in. The painful surrender on his face guts me.

"I won't touch you anymore, Briar. If you don't want me to, I'll respect that."

My throat starts to sting as I strangle the urge to cry. Without another word, I walk to the car and climb into the passenger seat. The drive back to the house is silent and uncomfortable, but there are no words to say that would erase the harm we've just done.

Eighteen

Caleb
21 years old

I'm passed out on my bed, the TV still playing across the room, when my phone starts buzzing on my chest. In a rush, I sit up and notice the name on the screen—Briar.

My fingers have never moved so fast to answer a call.

"Hello?" I stammer groggily as I glance at the clock on my nightstand. Twelve o'clock in the morning.

She sniffles into the phone line. "I'm outside," she whimpers.

"What?" I nearly bolt out of bed. "You're outside where?"

"Your house," she replies. "I know it's late. I just...didn't know where else to go."

"I'm coming," I say in a rush as I throw on a pair of sweatpants and quietly open my bedroom door. The house is silent. Luckily, my parents' room is on the other side, so I don't risk waking them.

When I tear open the front door, my heart lurches at the sight of Briar standing there, huddled against the cool breeze. Her nose is red, and there are blotches of pink splattered all over her cheeks. It's obvious from the swells under her eyes that she's been crying.

"Jesus, what happened?" I whisper as I go to her, wrapping her up in my arms.

She melts against my chest, sobs racking through her tiny frame as I hold her.

After a while, she finally murmurs, "Sean and I got into a fight."

It's wrong of me to perk up at that, but I do. I hate to see her hurting, but maybe this is what she needs to finally take the steps she has to take.

"Do you want to come in?" I ask, rubbing her back.

"Can I? Are your parents home?"

"They're asleep," I reply. "We just have to be quiet."

When she gazes up at me, her expression softens. I love the way she looks at me as if she needs me. And there's never been an easier choice in my life. Whatever Briar needs, I will give her.

"Okay," she murmurs.

Quietly, I guide her up to my room, closing us in and immediately feeling how charged the space between us feels. We're alone in the middle of the night.

Have I made it evident enough how much I want her? She has to know that, right? But now's not the time for wanting. She's upset, and I'm not going to be some perv who tries to make moves on her when she's in a vulnerable state. I'd never want her to be with a creep like that.

"Talk to me," I say as I take the chair at the desk. She slips off her shoes and climbs onto my bed, sitting cross-legged and staring down at her fingers.

"He accused me of cheating on him," she murmurs. "He's been loyal to me for three years, and I don't appreciate him, and if I really want to hang out with someone else, then I must not love him."

"He's playing mind games with you, Briar," I say. "And I'm not saying that to convince you to leave him, but he's making you feel bad for something you haven't even done."

Her gaze lifts to my face, a furrow in her brow, and it suddenly has me questioning everything.

"Have you?" I ask. There couldn't possibly be someone else.

Quickly, she shakes her head. "You know I haven't."

Silence grows between us as she chews on her bottom lip.

"Briar," I carefully whisper. "He's talking about me, right? He thinks you and I..."

Slowly, she nods.

My heart hammers in my chest, and the air in the room grows thick. I want to kiss her so bad it hurts. And I have no clue if she loves Sean or if she would see me as a fling, but all of the things I feel like I should care about at this moment, I don't.

But I can't bring myself to close the distance.

"Will you come sit next to me?" she asks with a softness in her tone.

My breath feels heavy and slow, and I can't ignore the way my cock twitches when she says that.

"I don't think that's a good idea," I reply quietly.

"Why not?"

"Because if I sit next to you on my bed, I don't know if I'll be able to keep my hands to myself."

I watch the delicate movement in her throat as she swallows. Her lips part as her gaze connects with mine.

"What if I don't want you to keep your hands to yourself?"

"If I start, Briar, I won't want to stop."

"I don't want you to stop."

There are no more questions in my mind. No more moral dilemmas or consequences to consider. There is just her and the consent to do what I've wanted to do for months now.

I move toward her, running a hand along her jaw and sealing her mouth in a kiss. She grabs my neck to pull me closer, but I don't want to rush this. I want to savor this kiss and the way her lips feel against mine.

As I climb onto the bed, she falls backward, so she's lying down, and I'm draping my body over hers.

Our kiss is ravenous. It feels like our first but also like I've been kissing her for years. Her mouth is mine and no one else's.

When her legs part and I feel them wrapping around me, I grind myself against her, and the soft moan she hums in my ear is the most beautiful sound I've ever heard.

Lifting up, I stare down at her and soak up the sight of her splayed out beneath me.

She's here. She's in my bed, and she's mine.

With her soft hands latched around my neck, she plays with the hair on the nape as she says, "I feel so safe with you, Caleb."

"You are safe with me, Briar."

Leaning down, I kiss her again. The next few minutes are full of touches, kisses, and need. And like I told her, I don't want to stop. And like she said, she doesn't stop me.

She doesn't stop me when I tug her shirt over her head.

She doesn't stop me when I peel down her pants.

She doesn't stop me when I touch her, sliding my fingers into her soaked cunt.

We are naked and alone, and there is nothing stopping me as I bring our bodies together.

Somewhere in the back of my mind, I realize that I'm being reckless with my own heart. As I thrust inside her, it feels as if I'm getting everything I want, but am I? At any moment, I could lose her. It could be in an hour, a day, or a year, but that's a pain I will eventually face.

Being inside Briar feels like heaven. Like we were made for each other.

Her body is clenched around mine. She's muffling her moans in the crook of my neck as I rock into her. The sensation of her shivering around me sends me over the edge, and I bite my own lip hard enough to stop me from crying out as I fill the condom between us.

When our bodies are spent, we lie in that position for a long time. She's busy catching her breath, and meanwhile, I'm too scared to see the look on her face. Did she regret that? Does she feel terrible?

It was wrong of me to take advantage of her during a time when I should have been consoling her, but I'm falling head over heels for this woman. There is no reason for my actions.

She is my reason.

After slowly lifting up, I stare into her eyes, checking for signs of regret or sadness. Softly, she smiles.

"Are you okay?" I whisper.

"I've been wanting to do that for a long time," she replies, fighting a wide grin.

I wish I could smile in return, but I don't understand what that means. Was I just a fling to her? Just something to check off her list?

Feeling like a fool, I decide to blurt out the truth. "I like you, Briar. A lot."

Her hand caresses my cheek. "I like you too."

I want to know more. I want to know if she'll leave him for me. I want to be sure that this meant as much to her as it did to me. Instead, I slide my dick from inside her and pull off the condom.

Then I lie back in bed with her and hold her tightly in my arms. After a few minutes, she falls asleep there, but I don't.

I can't help but feel like this was either the greatest or worst moment of my life. Because if she doesn't end up with me, then I will forever look back at this night as the night I had everything I wanted, only to have it ripped away. The catalyst of my earth-shattering pain.

But even knowing that it could end in heartbreak, I'd still do it again.

†

Present Day

I'm leaving the office early today. I'm struggling to concentrate on work. There's too much on my mind, and to make matters worse, Briar is home alone with Dean.

I'm playing with fire here. I *dared* him to try and seduce my wife. What the fuck is wrong with me? I hope Briar turned him down. I hope she humiliated him.

But with every ounce of confidence that courses through me is a hint of doubt. He is good-looking and young and so fucking suave.

I trust Briar, but anyone would have a hard time turning him down.

Halfway through my drive, my phone rings. A feeling of dread washes over me until I see it's my mother's name on the caller ID instead of my father's.

"Hello," I say with a chipper tone after answering it.

"Hello, baby," my mother croons through the phone in her sweet Southern drawl.

"Hey, Mom. How's Abigail? I hope she's not being too difficult."

"Oh, not at all," my mother replies. "She and I were just having a fashion show. Abby designs my outfits—"

"And Nana has to wear them!" Abby calls from a distance, overhearing our conversation.

My face stretches into a wide smile at the happiness in her voice.

"Sounds like you girls are having fun," I say.

"We are having so much fun," my mom replies.

It's nice to hear her so happy, too. It's been a tough year for my mother. My father's scandal, learning he was a regular at a sex club in the city, and then being arrested for attacking her son's girlfriend, my mother needs all the smiles and laughs she can get.

"Abby would like to know if she can stay another night," she says.

"Of course," I reply.

My mother responds with a soft hum of approval. Then it sounds as if she closes herself in a room so I can no longer hear the cartoons playing in the background.

"And how are you doing, baby?" she asks.

My throat grows tight, hearing the concern in my mother's voice. "I'm fine, Mom," I lie, hoping it keeps her from worrying.

"Have you heard from your father?" she asks gently.

I can't lie to her about that. Clearing my throat, I reply, "Yeah. I saw him last week."

"How are you feeling after that?" she asks.

With a heavy sigh, I say, "He asked me to help him."

"Of course he did. You're a damn good lawyer, Caleb."

"Aren't you going to ask me what I said?" I reply.

"No. That's your business," she says sternly.

"Isn't it sort of everyone's business at this point?" A sarcastic laugh slips through my lips.

"No, it's not." With that motherly tone in her voice, I swallow my laughter. "I won't pit my boys against each other. You're both grown and can make up your own minds. That is between you and Adam, and I won't get in the middle of it."

The line gets quiet for a moment as I contemplate her words. My gut is telling me not to even consider it. He is evil and vile, and he deserves the worst possible charge he can get.

But my head is saying that with everything I know about this case and that attack, an aggravated assault charge would be much easier to convict. He'd go to jail either way, but a heavier charge might cost our family more time and stress.

What does he honestly deserve?

My mother's voice cuts me off from my contemplation.

"Whatever you're thinking, Caleb, just remember this. You don't owe that man a thing. Make your decision based on what *you* want."

"Thanks, Mom," I mutter.

With that, she says her goodbyes and hangs up the phone while I'm left to overthink the entire thing through the drive.

When I get home, Briar's car is still parked in the garage next to my empty spot. Dean's car is nowhere to be seen, which gives me some sense of peace. At least she's here without him.

Climbing out of the car, I loosen my tie as I step into the house.

"Briar," I call from the kitchen. There's no response. Maybe she's sleeping upstairs.

Before jogging up the stairs to check on her, I stop at the

laundry room. I tug off my jacket and hang it on the rack for dry cleaning. Then I unbutton my shirt and toss it in the hamper.

As I riffle through the pile of clothes on the counter, I pause when I realize there is nothing in here that I recognize. But it's definitely men's clothes, obvious in the black silk briefs I'm holding in my hand.

For a moment, I'm confused. Then I realize these must be Dean's clothes.

He's doing his laundry in *our* house? Has Briar been doing his laundry for him?

For far too long, I stare at the briefs in my hand, my fingers delicately rubbing the soft fabric, imagining how tight they must look on Dean's ass and thick thighs.

Fuck, he's getting in my head again. It's been years since I even allowed myself to think of a man in his underwear. That was college behavior when locker rooms and communal showers started making me discover some things about myself.

So I get aroused by men sometimes. It doesn't matter. I'm married to Briar, and I have never acted on those desires, so what difference does it make?

A car door closes in the distance and spooks me. For some reason, my reflexes make me shove the underwear into my pocket rather than put them back in the pile of clothes where they belong.

I leave the laundry room in a rush to see who's outside. Going out through the back door, I watch as Dean and Briar stomp away from each other, him going to his apartment and her walking toward me.

She pauses at the sight of me standing in the backyard, home early from work.

"What are you doing here?" she asks.

"Where have you been?" I ask at the same time.

"We went to the museum in the city," she replies, trying to move past me.

"Together?"

"It was just a museum, Caleb," she snaps in return. Something is bothering her. I can tell. I know my wife enough to know her moods. And something has definitely set her off today.

Grabbing her arm, I turn her toward me. "What happened?"

"Nothing," she replies with fervor.

"Why were you alone with him?" I ask. I find myself searching her features—her lips, her cheeks, her neck, her hair—as if signs that he's touched her would be written on her skin.

She glares at me, and for a moment, it feels like she's a stranger.

"What's wrong, Caleb? You don't trust me?"

The pain etched in her expression makes me release her arm.

"Of course I do, Briar. It's *him* I don't trust."

"Right," she replies with a slight eye roll. "Because I'm so trust-worthy, right?"

Jerking her arm from my grip, she stomps out of the room and up the stairs. Meanwhile, I'm staring at her, dumbstruck, without a damn thing to say.

Nineteen

Dean

14 years old

Isaac's knee knocks mine on the couch. When he turns toward me with a grin, I do my best not to look his way. His brother is in his room, but after the incident last week with Caleb walking in on us, I don't feel comfortable doing anything here.

I already feel like Caleb might kick my ass if he sees me again. The look he gave me that night did not instill a lot of comfort. Before that night, I was sure Isaac could open up to his brother about being gay. Even if he couldn't come out to his parents, at least he had his brother.

Isaac's hand reaches for mine on my lap, but I jerk it away. "Your brother is home," I mutter under my breath.

"So," Isaac replies with a playful smirk.

"So, I don't need him walking in on us again. This time, he will surely kick my ass."

"He will not." Isaac laughs.

"Did you see his face? He looked like he wanted to murder me."

Isaac hangs his head back on the sofa. "He was just surprised."

"Yeah, surprised to find his little brother making out with a guy," I snap in return.

"You were the one who said he'd be cool with it," he argues.

"Well, I was wrong."

Isaac reaches for my hand again, intertwining our fingers as he rests his head on the couch and gazes at me through his thick lashes. My resolve starts to fade the more he looks at me like that.

"I don't like pretending you're just my friend," he mumbles.

I roll my eyes, trying to keep my gaze focused on the Spider-Man *movie playing on the TV. "You're so dramatic."*

This makes him laugh as he launches himself at me, pressing his lips against my cheek. Turning my face toward him, I try my best to look stern, but it doesn't work, and he launches again, this time pressing his lips to mine.

In the distance, a door closes. I shove Isaac off me and look toward the stairs. A moment later, Caleb appears, pauses near the bottom, and glares at me.

"What are you two doing?" he mutters angrily.

"Watching a movie," Isaac replies casually.

Caleb stares at me for a moment, heat and anger in his eyes. "Isaac, your friend needs to go home."

"What?" Isaac barks. "Why?"

"Because Mom and Dad said. You're failing math, and they said no friends over."

Bullshit. I know that's utter bullshit, but Caleb can't stand the thought of his brother with a guy, and he just wants to be rid of me.

"Isaac," Caleb calls in frustration when he doesn't respond.

"What is your problem?" Isaac groans.

"Mom and Dad are on their way home, and if they find you with a friend over, it's going to be my *ass."*

"Dude, you're twenty-one. They can't yell at you anymore."

"Wanna bet?" Caleb shouts in return. "Tell your friend goodbye, now*."*

"I'm out of here," I say as I climb up from the couch.

"No, don't go," Isaac complains as he follows me toward the foyer.

"I should really go," I say when I reach the door.

Isaac turns back to his brother with an expression of resentment on his face. "Caleb, you're such a dick!"

My gaze connects with Caleb's across the room, and it feels like we are the only two people in on the secret. I know exactly why he's kicking me out. It's not because he doesn't like me or Isaac is grounded.

It's because Caleb is no better than his father.

†

Present Day

Which one of them will knock on my door first? That's the real question tonight as I lie on the couch, wishing I had picked up an extra client this week to at least have an excuse to get out of here.

It's nearly eleven, and I know one of them will come knocking at any moment. It'll either be Briar, reeling from her desire and guilt, wanting to hash out her identity crisis with me as if it's my fault.

Or it'll be Caleb coming here to threaten some answer out of me. Or maybe just get in my face again because he seems to love that.

Either way, I can't quite figure out how I ended up here. Stuck in some married couple's quarrel—and not just any couple. This is the marriage of the man I hate. The only thing more confusing than that is the question of why I don't just leave.

Because I *want* them to knock. I want to see their faces. I want to feel a part of whatever it is they have going on.

And that's fucking stupid. I shouldn't want to be a part of their marriage. I really shouldn't give a shit what they have to fight about. That's between them. It has nothing to do with me.

Today with Briar was just about revenge—at least it was supposed to be. But I'd be lying if I said the exhilaration of running out of that museum together and getting her alone in that elevator didn't feel like the most exciting thing I've done in months. Pressing her against the wall had my dick more interested than it's been in a long time.

Briar is so refreshing. She's nothing like I first expected, but I suspect that beneath that good-girl, sweet, suburban facade is a woman dying to feel desired. Does Caleb not make her feel that way? The taste of her skin is still on my tongue, and every time I lick my lips, I pick up a hint of that delicate perfume she wore.

I must drift off to the memory of that kiss when a knock at the door wakes me—a *heavy* knock.

With a wicked smirk, I climb off the couch and walk over to answer it. My smile grows as I pull the door open, revealing a very disgruntled-looking Caleb.

"Can I help you?" I ask, leaning on the doorframe.

He shoves me into the apartment and slams the door behind him. "What did you do to her?" he snaps.

Crossing my arms in front of my chest, I keep my cool as I reply, "Nothing she didn't want."

"You motherfucker," he replies with a growl. The next thing I know, I'm shoved against the wall, and Caleb's sneering face is in mine.

So predictable.

"That was the deal, right? You told me I couldn't get your wife to want me, but guess what? It only took me one day. I touched your wife today. What are you going to do about it?"

Caleb's large hand is wrapped around my throat, although he's not squeezing enough to cut off the airflow. He pulls my body from the wall and slams it back like some angry gorilla. My head smacks the drywall, but not enough to knock me out. It knocks the wind out of me, but I'm aware that if he really wanted to hurt me, he would.

"I never told you to touch her," he mutters angrily.

"Then you should have laid out the rules of our wager because they were a little unclear."

"She's upset," he replies. "Did you hurt her?"

My brow furrows. "Fuck no, I didn't hurt her," I reply, shoving him away, but he doesn't budge.

There are only inches between his body and mine, and his presence is so overwhelming I can smell his cologne and make out the gold flecks in his eyes.

I don't bother fighting back, and maybe he expects me to. But this fucker isn't going to really hurt me. He's just trying to intimidate me; if we're honest, I love it. Makes me feel alive.

"Tell me exactly what happened," he says in a deep grumble.

"Can you let go of my throat?" I ask.

"No."

"Fine," I reply with a smirk. "But you should be careful. I normally get turned on by this sort of thing."

I expect him to react, but he doesn't. Instead, his eyes narrow and he glares at me expectantly.

"I kissed her, and she let me. That's all. The second things got too heated, she freaked out and pushed me away."

Caleb's expression turns contemplative, lips pressed together tightly. "You made the move, and she turned you down."

I let out a chuckle. "She wanted it."

"Clearly not," Caleb replies. The hold around my neck loosens, but his body still has me pinned against the wall.

"Believe what you want," I say with a chuckle.

My hand is on his chest, and my attempt to shove him is futile. He doesn't budge an inch. Instead, his body only crowds mine more. That's when I feel a bulge in his pants that makes my eyes widen.

He freezes.

At first, I think it is his dick, but I shift enough to tell that it's not the right shape or place to be his cock. But he's clearly uncomfortable anyway, which piques my interest.

"What is this?" I ask in a teasing tone.

We're staring into each other's eyes as I reach down to inspect what is currently pressed against my upper thigh. As my hand pats his pocket, he tries to pull away, but not before I can yank out whatever he's hiding there.

The teasing grin on my face fades when I take in the familiar sight and feel of my *own* underwear.

What the...*fuck*?

Almost immediately, my gaze snaps back up to his face. He's still staring at me, his jaw tight and his eyes narrowed.

Isn't he going to explain himself? Make up some stupid fucking story that explains why he would be stashing away my underwear? They got caught in the laundry together. He thought they were his own. *Something*.

But he doesn't. He just stares at me. Almost as if...he wants me to know he has them for a reason.

Well, isn't this an interesting new development?

Pressing my lips together, I ball the underwear in my fist as I take a silent step toward him. He starts to back up, but I wordlessly grab the belt of his pants, tugging him toward me.

Immediately, his hands go to my chest to push me away, but I don't move to touch him again. I just shove the underwear back in his pocket.

Our eyes meet in a loaded gaze.

Then I release his belt and step away. He takes that as his sign to leave and does so quickly, making it to the door before he pauses and turns back toward me.

"If you hurt my wife, I'll kill you," he mutters quietly.

"Noted," I reply, although he really didn't need to tell me that. I have no intention of hurting anyone.

The door closes loudly as he leaves, and I'm left alone in my apartment. A smile pulls across my face as I let everything hit me at once. What the fuck just happened?

Twenty

Briar

Today is one of those days when I don't want to get out of bed. I don't have to get up for Abby since she's still with Caleb's mother, Melanie, and I have nothing on my schedule.

It's just past nine when I hear movement downstairs. Perking up, I glance at Caleb's things on the nightstand. His watch and wallet are still sitting in the exact spot he left them.

Maybe he's going in to work late today.

After climbing out of bed, I get cleaned up quickly, hoping he might leave before I go down and I'll miss him. After throwing on some plain yoga pants and a loose tank top, my phone buzzes with an alert on the bathroom counter.

*It's your lucky day! Your first fertile day of the week. You know what to do. *Winky face**

"Ugh," I groan around my toothbrush, fighting the urge to toss my phone in the toilet.

There won't be any of that today.

After he saw Dean and I getting out of the car yesterday, Caleb and I awkwardly avoided each other for the rest of the night. I had nothing to confess to, and he didn't bother accusing me.

Why didn't he?

Does he care so little that he wouldn't at least fight me for more information? I obviously want my husband to trust me, but it would be nice to see him get a little fired up, too. Especially when it pained me so much to turn down what *could have* happened with Dean.

It wasn't even about the physical stuff with him. We have an emotional connection that I'm denying myself for a husband who barely acknowledges me. I'm so lonely in my own marriage it hurts.

Quickly, I jog down the stairs to find Caleb sitting at the dining room table with his laptop open. His eyes are framed with dark circles underneath, as if he didn't get much sleep last night.

"You're not going in today?" I ask as I pull the coffeepot from the machine.

"No," he mutters lowly.

I pour myself a cup of coffee and try to ignore the suffocating tension between us right now. I know he's staying home because he doesn't trust me alone with Dean.

But I'm not just going to tiptoe around this and pretend like everything is fine. I'm tired of sweeping things under the rug and letting the fuse go out. Dean has awakened something inside me that won't let me be passive anymore.

I'm tired of pretending our life is perfect while it falls apart.

"So, are you just going to work from home until he moves out?" I ask, gripping my coffee cup so tightly I'm afraid it could shatter.

"If I have to," he argues as he glances my way with a stern expression.

"What is that supposed to mean?"

"It means I don't feel comfortable leaving my wife alone with another man," he replies, narrowing his eyes at me.

"Maybe instead of always trying to protect us and bear every burden alone, you could just *talk* to me," I snap.

"Talk about what?" he replies. "You won't tell me what happened."

"Are you saying you don't trust me?"

"Should I?" he snaps back. The silence stretches out before he adds in a cold tone, "You've cheated before."

My eyes pop open in surprise. "Caleb," I bark at him. The pain of those words is etched on my face. I slam my coffee cup down on the counter. "I can't believe you would say that to me."

He stands from the table but keeps the island between us as he places his hands down on the granite surface. "It's true, though, isn't it?"

"How dare you use that against me now," I spit back, my voice growing louder. "I cheated on a terrible boyfriend to be with *you*."

"So look me in the eye and tell me that nothing happened with Dean yesterday."

Gripping the counter, I lean forward. "Nothing happened."

"Don't lie to me, Briar."

"I can't help but feel like you *wish* something happened with him yesterday," I argue back.

"Why would I want that? Why the fuck would I want another man to touch my wife?"

"I don't know," I shout, throwing my hands in the air. "But you brought this young guy to live at our house, and then you left me with him here like you were testing me. I think you *wanted* him to touch me."

"I think *you* wanted him to touch you," he bellows.

"At least someone wants to!"

"What the fuck is that supposed to mean?" As much as I hate the anger on his face, I love to see him riled up. Alive and fighting instead of breezing out the door and ignoring the massive fire blazing our lives to the ground.

"It means the only time we have sex anymore, Caleb, is when we have to. And even then, I see how much you hate it. Like it pains you to fuck me."

"We just had sex last week!" he argues.

"One time!" I scream.

"I always want you, Briar. But yes, this fertility stuff has taken all the spontaneity out of it. I don't like being told by an app when I can fuck my wife!"

"And that's my fault?" I cry.

"I never said it was your fault."

We're both worked up, tightly wound, and ready to explode. Caleb slams his fist on the counter as he glares at me. "This has nothing to do with our sex life."

"Caleb, right now, everything is about our sex life."

Ignoring my argument, he continues, "Tell me right now, Briar. Do you want him?"

"Why? So you can do *nothing* about it? Do you really even care?"

"Oh, I'll fucking do something about it," he spits in return, his voice booming now.

"What will you do, Caleb? What would you honestly do if I told you I wanted him?"

"Do you?" he yells.

"Yes! Okay? I do want him. And I nearly let him fuck me yesterday, Caleb. Is that what you want to hear?"

His face contorts into anguish. "Why?"

"Why?" I screech. "Because he *listens* to me. He pays *attention* to me. He makes me feel wanted and desired and like I'm more than just a fucking *body* to make a fucking baby! Now I realize that I should have let him fuck me. Because then, at least, you'd be mad for a good fucking reason. Then maybe you'd finally fight for me."

My tirade is so heated that I feel like the room around me grows fuzzy and out of focus. I don't even notice when the door to the kitchen opens until I blink and notice a third person standing on the other side of the kitchen island.

He's tall and shirtless in my periphery. My chest heaves from the outburst, and I'm staring at Caleb before glancing over at Dean.

"Jesus, I could hear you guys all the way in my apartment."

I force my eyes closed so I no longer have to face my husband.

"I'm sorry," I mumble. "You should go."

"Fuck that," he replies. "I'm not going anywhere."

"Yeah, fuck that," Caleb barks. "He should stay and explain why the fuck he tried to fuck my wife."

Dean lets out a haughty chuckle. "You know exactly why."

My eyes dance back and forth between them. "What's that supposed to mean?"

Caleb answers first. "You say I don't fight for you, Briar, but only days after he arrived, I was at his apartment, threatening him to stay away from you."

"You were?" I ask.

"And he *admitted* he was trying to seduce you," he adds.

My gaze lands on Dean. I should be angry about this, but in my mind, all I can think is—he wanted me.

Then I look back at Caleb. "That night...you and I..."

He nods.

"So, this whole time, your jealousy made us...stronger," I say, my skin still buzzing with energy.

"I've never seen two people with such terrible communication," Dean mutters.

He's right. We're a mess. We can't even express ourselves to the one person on this earth we should be able to talk to. Caleb's expression is tight and disgruntled as he nods in agreement.

Rubbing my forehead with a sigh, I turn toward Dean. "You should really go. You'll just make things worse," I say, finally looking up at him.

There's a pause of silence before his response.

"Or...I can make things better." He says it so plainly that I think I misunderstand him.

"How can you make things better?" Caleb snaps.

"Because I see what you two need even when you don't. Briar, Caleb *wants* to fight for you but is too afraid to lose you."

I glare at him in confusion as he turns toward Caleb. "And Briar's so busy giving you everything you want that you don't think to ask what *she* wants."

"What, are you our marriage counselor now?" Caleb replies with cutting sarcasm.

"No," Dean replies with a shake of his head. "I don't do that shit, but I heard enough from outside that door to know that this is about sex. And sex is something I do know."

I let out a scoff as I look away.

"You're both pent up as fuck. I see it. So, let me help you."

"Why would you help us?" Caleb asks, and I glance up toward him to see the sullen way he glares at Dean. He's as surprised as I am that Dean would do anything to benefit him.

"I don't know. Because I can't stand to listen to this shit anymore. And because I'm fucking good at what I do."

My eyes track toward my husband on the other side of the island, and I wait with bated breath for him to say something. I expect him to spout out more *touch her and die* bullshit, but the words that do finally come out of his mouth take me by surprise.

"All right. You're so sure you know what my wife wants, then prove it."

My lips part, and my head tilts as I stare at him in shock. "Caleb," I whisper. But he doesn't look my way. He's too focused on the other man in the room.

"You sure about this? Back out now if you don't want to go down this road," Dean says softly, looking back and forth between us.

Caleb and I stare at each other for a moment. What I know we both see are remnants of a relationship that was once built on passion and love. We used to believe that this marriage was the greatest, most important thing in the world, and I miss that version of us.

He must be thinking it, too, because after a moment, we each nod at the same time.

It's Dean who speaks next. "Good." Then, in a deeper tone, he adds, "Briar, come here."

I turn toward him in surprise, and the expression he's giving me now is the same as the one in the elevator yesterday.

I feel like I'm floating for a moment, too dizzy and disoriented to think. All I hear is the smooth, deep command, and rather than deliberate, I just do as I'm told. Somewhere in the back of my mind, I tell myself that this is okay. Caleb told him to.

Ignoring the fact that my husband is standing right there, I move toward Dean. When I reach his side of the island, he runs his fingers across my neck. Brushing my hair out of the way, he brings his lips to my ear. "Good girl."

Shivers rack through my body at those words. I swear my legs tremble as I lean into him.

"She listens so well, and she *wants* to please, don't you?" Dean says.

It feels impossible to swallow, but I manage it as he gazes into my eyes, waiting for my response. This is really happening. *How* is this happening?

"Yes," I murmur.

"This is what your wife likes, Caleb. She likes to be good. But she likes to be corrupted too, don't you?" Dean gazes into my eyes as he says those words, uttering them like they're strings of silk gliding down my spine.

Silently, I nod.

These are the things I want Caleb to know that I've never had the courage to say. I want him to take control. Stop treating me like his perfect little wife and start treating me like the woman I am. A woman he wants.

Dean is holding my face, and I feel like I'm caught in the same storm I was caught in yesterday. Desire so potent I could drown in it. This need is so all-consuming I'm drunk on it.

When he leans in and presses his lips to mine, I nearly lose the strength to stand. Clutching onto his arms, I let him lick his way into my mouth, fully aware of my husband standing just on the other side of the island.

Caleb's jealousy is what we need and that's what this is all for—and yet, it feels so wrong.

Dean's kiss is heady and intoxicating, as his soft lips make me forget my own name.

As the kiss comes to an end, I can't bear to open my eyes. I'm still clinging to him as he says to Caleb, "If you want her, come and get her."

My eyes pop open as I turn my head to find Caleb standing right next to Dean. I have no idea when he came so close, but he's now within reach.

"Briar, come here," he says in the same low command that Dean used, but his voice is laced with possessiveness and desperation.

Fiercely, he grabs the back of my neck and hauls my mouth to his, kissing me with heated passion and need.

And when Dean's mouth finds the side of my neck, I realize I must still be sleeping. This is nothing more than a dream, and I'd be a lucky woman if I never woke up.

"She wants to please you," Dean mumbles, just under my ear. "Tell her how to please you."

Yes. Tell me, and I'll do it. Anything.

Arousal blooms between my legs as Caleb pulls away from our kiss and grunts against my mouth. "Get on your knees for me, Briar."

My panties are practically soaked as I drop to the floor. I still can't believe this is happening, but it feels like the three of us are getting carried away down a river none of us want to swim against. We all want this. Maybe we all have wanted this for longer than we're ready to admit.

It's not even ten in the morning in my kitchen when I pull down my husband's zipper and see his hard cock behind his boxer briefs while another man stands next to him and strokes my hair.

"There you go, Briar," Dean mumbles, urging me on with the softness in his praise and commands. "She needs to hear how good she's doing," he tells Caleb.

"Attagirl," Caleb replies. "You look so good on your knees for me."

The effect his words have on me is unnerving. As if I really would do anything at all.

As Caleb's cock springs free of his pants, I stroke it softly in my hand, gazing up at him as I wait for his next instruction. I've never seen him remotely like this before, but it fits him.

My husband has held in so much over the years, but I never had the guts to urge him to let out everything he's hiding. And I know there is so much. This feels like just the tip of the iceberg.

"Tell her what you want," Dean says, prodding him.

"Worship my cock like it's the only one for you."

I don't hesitate. My lips wrap around Caleb's hard length, and I coat his entire shaft with my saliva, humming with pleasure as I move my mouth from the base to the tip.

"Holy shit," he mutters softly.

"Tell her. Let her hear you," Dean says to Caleb, persuading him to say more.

Caleb strokes my face, making a pained expression as he says, "You look so fucking beautiful with my dick in your mouth, Briar. Do you like it?"

My eyes water as his cock hits the back of my throat. Gagging, I pop my mouth off, and a string of spit hangs between the head and my lips. "Yes," I reply as I catch my breath.

Caleb thrusts back into my mouth, moaning at the sensation when I suck on the crown, rubbing my tongue along the underside like I know he likes.

And as I'm stroking his dick with my lips, I gaze up at him in adoration. This moment is fucking wild, and a moment ago, we were fighting, but now he's giving me what I want. And he's finally getting what he wants.

None of this would have happened without Dean.

As if he realizes it at the same time, Caleb glances over at Dean. Their eyes meet, their gazes locked for a moment.

Something about the way they're looking at each other makes me pause. It's intense and not entirely charged with hatred or rivalry. Then Dean reaches out, and his fingers brush the backside of Caleb's arm. My eyes widen as I wait for Caleb to react...but he doesn't.

Then, as soon as the moment comes, it's gone again. Caleb

focuses his attention back on me, and I start to wonder if that was all in my head. Maybe I'm making a big deal out of nothing, but I swear the look they shared held...lust.

They were just caught in the moment. We're *all* caught in the moment.

"She wants you to come down her throat. Don't you, Briar?"

Eagerly, I nod. My mouth sucks harder, and my lips tighten around him as my head moves faster. Immediately, Caleb's groans get louder and more desperate sounding.

"That's it, Briar," he mumbles. "I'm gonna come down your throat. My dirty fucking wife. *My fucking wife.*" His rambling becomes incoherent as he thrusts quicker into my mouth, and when I feel the head of his dick tighten, I wait for his orgasm.

With a loud moan, I receive a warm, salty stream in the back of my mouth. I've never swallowed before, so I try not to panic and quickly force it down, gagging and spitting as the rest unloads on my face.

Staring down at the floor, the sight of Caleb's cum dripping against the tiles gives me a burst of exhilaration. I'm kneeling between both of them after my husband just painted my face white, and I realize that I should probably feel dirty or bad for what we've just done.

But I don't.

For the first time in nearly ten years, I finally feel alive.

Twenty-One

Caleb

W*hat just happened?*

My wife is staring up at me from the floor, my cum covering her face. As our eyes meet, it feels like waking up from a wild dream.

Dean moves first, quickly grabbing a towel to clean her up as I reach down to pull her to her feet.

"Uh, are you okay?" I ask.

She seems taken aback by the question. "Of course I'm okay," she replies. "Are you okay?"

Am I?

"Yes, of course."

Dean stands nearby, watching our awkward exchange. "Good start," he mutters. "Now..."

Now...what? I think.

"You guys really suck at conversations," he says, crossing his arms.

Tilting my head, I give him an exasperated glare. "Not helpful."

Briar goes to the sink to rinse her face, and I swallow down my humiliation. This isn't us. We don't do crazy shit like this. We're a respectable, married couple. Not some kinky couple still in their twenties and down to experiment.

"I think what Dean is trying to tell us, Caleb, is that we need to talk about what we just did," she says, patting her face with a paper towel.

"Why?" I ask.

She lets out a sigh.

"You should talk about it," Dean replies, "so your wife doesn't start to feel ashamed of blowing you in the kitchen with another man involved."

My eyes widen as I turn back toward her. "Do you...feel ashamed?"

She shrugs. "No."

"There you go," Dean replies. "And what about you?"

"What about me?" I quip back.

"Did you like it?" Briar asks.

My gaze scans over to Dean. I know the question is not whether I liked the blow job—that's a given. The question is whether I liked seeing another man touch my wife, feeling jealous and compelled to reclaim her. Telling her what to do just to watch her please me so I can shower her with praise.

Did I like that?

To be honest, I liked it a lot fucking more than I expected.

Just as I open my mouth to reply, the doorbell rings, and we all stare at each other in shock.

"Shit. Your mom is bringing Abby back."

"I should go," Dean says, moving toward the back door.

Briar and I rush to clean up and compose ourselves, and I make it to the foyer first.

Abby barrels through the front door excitedly, and my mother trails far behind. "I'm going swimming!" my daughter shouts.

"Not without me or Mom," I yell in her direction.

"I don't think she ever runs out of energy," my mother says with an exasperated smile as she reaches the front door.

"I think you're right," I reply. "Thanks for keeping her for a couple of nights."

"Oh, anytime," my mom says. "She keeps me young."

I laugh to myself as my mother hovers near the door. I feel her looking at me with that comforting, motherly expression on her face.

When she reaches out and squeezes my arm, I tense. "And how're you doing, darlin'?"

How am I doing? Well, aside from the fact that my father is going to prison, my marriage is falling apart, my estranged brother's ex-boyfriend found *his* underwear in *my* pocket, and my wife gave me a blow job while another man watched in our kitchen this morning, I'd say I'm doing fine. Nothing out of the ordinary, right?

Of course, I don't say that. I just nod and give her a reassuring smile. "I'm okay, Mom."

"Good," she replies, looking pleased. "Well, I should get going. Don't forget about family dinner on Sunday."

"Of course," I say with my hand on the door.

After my mother leaves, I find myself standing there, frozen in place. I'm still reeling from whatever that was.

What was that?

I can't decide if I should feel good or bad about what happened. Was it wrong to take advantage of Briar? Or let another man touch her like he did? I'll admit that watching him kiss her felt like slapping some sense into me.

It was like finding a part of myself I didn't know existed but only getting a taste. I want *more.*

Finally leaving the front door, I walk up the stairs to find Abby clumsily putting on her bathing suit. Briar is there helping her, and the moment she hoists the straps over her shoulders, Abby takes off in a sprint as if she can't get in the pool fast enough.

"You need sunblock!" Briar shouts after her.

With our daughter gone, it's just Briar and me, and the

moment our eyes meet, there is a sudden tension between us. Was Dean right when he said we suck at communication? Why can't I just talk to my wife about what happened? It's definitely a *me* problem.

"I should...go with her," Briar says, rising from the floor.

"Yeah, of course," I stammer. There won't be time for that conversation today, not with our six-year-old around.

I try to go back to work on my laptop, but it's futile. There is too much swirling through my mind. Instead, I walk out back, where Abby is splashing in the pool while Briar sits on the side with her feet in the water.

"Daddy, look how long I can hold my breath!" Abby shouts, mispronouncing breath with an *f* instead of a *th* because of the missing teeth in the front of her mouth. A smile stretches across my face as I watch her.

She sticks her face under the water for no more than fifteen seconds. "Good job, peanut."

When she wipes away the wet hair stuck to her face, she looks up at the apartment above the garage. "Will you ask your friend to come swim too?"

Briar and I glance nervously at each other.

"No, honey. He's probably busy," Briar says softly.

"Can you just ask him?" she begs. "He can hold his breath for a long time. Mommy had to save him."

Briar chuckles to herself as I glance between them.

"Please, Daddy!" Abby whines.

"We said no," I reply, sitting on one of the chairs by the pool. "Stop begging, Abby."

Just then, she waves up at the apartment. "There he is!"

Briar and I turn to look up to find Dean staring out the window. A moment later, he steps out onto the landing outside the apartment. Awkwardly, he waves down at us.

"Will you come swimming with me?" Abby asks.

"Um..." Dean stammers. "I don't...think so."

"Please..." she whines.

"Abby, what did I say about begging," I say, scolding her just as Dean cuts in.

"Fine, I guess."

As he disappears into his apartment, Briar and I share another nervous look. After our morning, it feels unnerving to play with our daughter like nothing happened.

After a few minutes, Dean emerges in the same tight swim shorts he normally wears, and I have to force my eyes not to look. But Briar doesn't bother looking away. I see the way she watches him. The way she pushes her tits forward when he's near her. The look of desire on her face.

Her words play back in my head. How she accused me of *wanting* Dean to touch her. Of bringing him here with the intention to test her. Why would I do that? Why would anyone do that?

But she has a point. Why don't I fight for her more? Deep down, I know he's not trying to take her from me. After this morning, it seems quite the opposite is true.

So, how would I feel if they were to really touch each other? Jealous? No. Maybe a little left out. Maybe a little aroused.

Maybe a *lot* aroused.

"You have to relax," Dean says to Abby. "You flail around too much. Just take a deep breath and go under, but try not to panic."

"Like this?" she asks. With a big gasp, she pushes her face underwater and almost immediately starts splashing around and coming up a second later.

"That was terrible," he says, staring down at her with a furrowed brow.

Briar giggles, looking away from them as I feel myself fighting a smile as well. Dean doesn't talk to Abby like everyone else does. It's clear he doesn't have experience with children, and judging by the way he is with her, I don't think he even likes children. So, seeing him talk to her just makes me want to laugh.

"Come here," he mutters with a sigh. Taking Abby's hand, he leads her deeper into the pool. "We'll go down together, but just look into my eyes and try not to think about breathing. Just count in your head or something."

"Okay," she says with an excited giggle. He rolls his eyes as he takes her hands.

Watching as they each take a long inhale, I bite my lip as they sink down to the bottom together. This time, Abby doesn't flail and splash. And nearly thirty seconds go by before she swims to the top.

"Mom, did you see that?" she squeals. "How long was that?"

"That was so good, peanut!" Briar says with excitement.

"Thirty seconds," I call as if I was keeping time. "That's a new record."

Dean swims up and gives Abby a proud smile. "Much better."

"Thanks, Dean," she says between gasps for air. When she reaches the edge of the pool, she looks at him with a toothless grin. "Wanna race to the other end?"

He stares at her, confused. "I'm not going to let you win."

This only makes her giggle. "Ready, set, go!" She pushes her feet off the edge and swims as fast as her little legs can propel her across the surface. Dean is there before she reaches the middle, but she doesn't seem to care. She's all giggles and excitement. Even when he beats her again and again.

Until the very last round, when he claims he's running out of energy, and she manages to touch the edge before him.

After another hour of swimming, Briar makes sandwiches for lunch, and the four of us eat them on the patio. Dean is still in those barely there shorts, and Abby is still beaming at him after he spent all morning playing with her in the pool.

When her lunch is gone, she hops up from the chair. "Can I go inside and watch TV?"

"Yes," Briar replies. "Hang your bathing suit up in the bathroom."

"Yes, ma'am," Abby says, nearly bouncing in place as Briar continues, "And clean up your plate."

"Yes, ma'am."

"Okay, you can go." Abby starts to sprint away before Briar yells for her. "Wait! Come back."

"What?" Abby whines as she returns to where Briar is still sitting. Pulling her close, Briar presses a big kiss right on Abby's cheek with a smile. "Okay, that's all. You can go now."

With a giggle, Abby takes off with her plate in her hand, closing the patio door so it's just the three of us left outside alone.

Shit.

"Thank you for playing with her," Briar says softly, picking at her sandwich. "She really liked that."

"Of course," Dean replies. "She's a cool kid."

Hearing him say that, I smile. But then, no one says anything for a while, and what we did this morning hangs over us, bathing the space between us in tension.

It's Dean who breaks the silence first.

"Fuck, this is awkward. Let's just talk about it."

Briar's head snaps up and she stares at him as if she's waiting for what he'll say next.

"You first," he says to her.

"Me?" She points to herself.

"Yeah, you. What did you like about it?"

Her lips part as she stares at him with shock. Fidgeting in her seat, she glances toward the back door to ensure we're really alone before she says, "I liked being told what to do, and I liked being fought over a little."

A grin slowly forms on his face. Then he looks at me, but I stop him immediately.

"Don't bother asking. You know I liked it."

This feels like a conversation my wife and I should have had already, but conversations seem to be a problem for us. What I'm wondering as I stare at her is if she liked it because of him or if she liked it because it helped us break down a barrier between us. One where we feel comfortable expressing our desires with each other.

And honestly, what does it matter? It's not like this is going to become a regular thing. Because where does it end? If we bring this man into our bedroom, and then one thing leads to another, what was meant to help us communicate better will end in threesomes and an open marriage, and it all just sounds so messy.

And fucking hot.

"So when are we doing it again?" he asks.

My gaze lands on Dean with intensity. I should stop this, right? This can't end well.

Briar fidgets again. "Maybe this is what we need, Caleb." She must notice the discomfort on my face. "If we want to continue trying for this baby, and we don't want to be miserable doing it, then why don't we just go for it? You can't tell me that after this morning, you don't want to explore this more."

Her pleading eyes are on my face, and I feel the desperation in her tone. She's right. We do need to have sex anyway, so why not invite someone who seems to know how to make our sex life not so miserable?

"What about tonight?" I ask, deciding to just go for it.

"I had a client tonight, but they canceled on me. So I'm free."

"Wait, should we...pay you?" Briar asks, and something in me sours. I don't want it to be like that. I don't want this to be a transaction. It sounds so impersonal.

Dean shakes his head. "Fuck no. This isn't work for me."

"Then what is it?" she murmurs.

With a huff, he smiles at her. "Fun."

Twenty-Two

Dean

Briar: We're ready.

If you had told me two weeks ago, when I moved into this apartment, that I'd get here, about to help this married couple's sex life by showing them how to please each other, I would have been shocked—but only because I know Caleb Goode can't stand me.

I'm doing this for her. Even when Caleb and Briar fight, I can see how much they care about each other. They belong to each other in a way I used to find repulsive to even think about. I don't want to belong to anyone. I don't want to feel obligated to give anyone my time or attention.

But Briar is so refreshing. After this morning, I can see the way Briar silently pleads for more. The way she's dying for me to teach her dirty, bad, terrible things. She doesn't think she's allowed to ask for these things, but I can see the way she wants them.

He wants them, too. He's just too afraid to ask her for them. He always was a stubborn jerk.

When I walk over to the house, Caleb is standing outside the back door, waiting for me.

"You're not going to turn me away now, are you?" I ask with a coy smirk.

He doesn't smile in return. "I want to explain the underwear," he says flatly.

I pause. "I don't think you have to explain."

"It was a reflex. I don't know why I did it, but it doesn't mean anything."

"Sure," I chuff.

"I'm serious," he replies. "I didn't keep them to jack off and think about you, so don't get any crazy ideas in your head."

"Just so I know we're talking about the same thing here. You're telling me that you're *not* attracted to me, right? And you kept my underwear in your pocket by *accident*."

He hesitates, and I watch the rolling movement of his Adam's apple as he swallows.

"That's what I'm saying," he replies weakly.

Stepping forward, I place a hand on his chest. "Relax. I believe you. Because how fucked up would it be for you to out your brother and get him kicked out when he was only seventeen if you yourself were queer?"

"I didn't—" he starts.

For the record, I don't actually believe him. I know plenty of guys become major hypocrites when they hide their own identity behind ignorant behavior.

"Save it. I don't want to get into this tonight. I just want to help Briar. That's why we're doing this, right?"

"Right."

We're standing chest to chest, and he's gazing into my eyes as if he has something else to say. I don't back down or move away.

"This is for Briar," he mutters.

My lips twitch with a smile. Again, I don't believe him.

A moment later, the back door opens and Briar appears with a nervous expression on her face. She lifts a white monitor in her hand. "I figure we should go to your place. I have this in case she wakes up."

My brow furrows as I stare at the thing in her hand. I can't say I've ever had to worry about a kid waking up before, but this is a very real circumstance for them. With a shrug, I turn back toward the apartment, and I feel them follow.

It's not until we are inside that I notice Briar has on a little makeup. Her hair is curled, and she's wearing a black cotton dress that makes her ass look fucking delicious. More than anything, I find it sort of endearing that she got herself dolled up for this.

"Need a drink?" I ask as I go to the kitchenette. "You can have one to calm your nerves, but no more than that." When I turn back to find them staring at me with confusion, I add, "It's important to keep your head straight."

"Yes, please," Briar responds, going for the glasses in the cabinet.

Caleb settles on a beer from the fridge instead.

"So...what exactly are we doing?" Briar asks. Her eager curiosity is my favorite thing. She really is so innocent, yet so ready to be corrupted. I can't fucking wait to be the one to do it.

"We have to set some limits, which are up to you two. Briar, you obviously love to be submissive, so I can show Caleb how to be more dominant."

She looks stiff as a board as she watches me talk, her hand gripping the glass so tightly her knuckles are white.

"You and I won't have sex," I say, thinking it's what she needs to calm her nerves. But when she just looks more confused, I go on, "That's a hard limit, right?"

"Yes," she stammers. "Of course."

"Don't look so disappointed," Caleb says to me, his tone dripping with sarcasm, and suddenly I find myself swallowing a laugh.

"Look," I say to dissolve the tension. "You clearly like being the center of attention and Caleb found it arousing to watch us kiss. So for now, we can touch each other, but no penetration."

Briar chokes on her wine.

"Are you sure you're ready for this?" I ask, seeing her jittery reaction.

"I'm sure," she replies assuredly.

Then I turn toward Caleb. "Are *you* sure about this?"

His brow is set in a tense scowl as he looks between us. "No penetration. We are doing this to conceive, after all, so letting another man come inside you probably isn't the wisest thing to do."

"Right," I say before taking a drink.

I don't bother telling them that even if sex were on the table, they don't need to worry about *that* from me. I haven't seen my dick unload in...three months? Or is it four now?

"You call the shots," I say, looking at Briar. "If you want to stop, we stop. Just say the word, okay?"

"Okay," she replies.

Even after everything at the club, I've never been with a woman like Briar. She embodies everything that is *good* and *pure*. And I desperately want to be the one to defile her.

Which gives me an idea.

This entire time, Caleb has seen his wife as someone he's not supposed to disgrace. Someone he's supposed to protect. Someone he's supposed to keep pure and good.

But I'm willing to bet he would love ruining her as much as I would, as would she.

Leaning over, I delicately take the wineglass from Briar's hand. Stroking her hair, I say, "You are such a good girl, aren't you?"

Instantly, her shoulders press back, and she holds her head higher.

"Yes," she says with slight hesitancy.

"And you're going to do exactly as we say, aren't you?"

Obediently, she nods.

"Even if it's a little dirty?"

She tugs her bottom lip between her teeth innocently.

"Yes," she hums in response.

"First, I want you to strip down to your panties and your bra and go kneel in the middle of the room for me and wait. Okay?"

"Okay," she replies.

Caleb and I stand next to each other as we watch Briar pull off her dress and shoes. I see the way his eyes drink in her body, watching her with desire.

"You heard her," I say, glancing over at him. "She'll do whatever we want. So tonight, imagine she's not your wife. She's just a pretty little angel who has ended up at our mercy. Just think of all the depraved things we can do with her."

The effect this is having on him is apparent. His next inhale shakes with anticipation; his fists are clenched at his sides.

He tugs open the top button of his shirt, methodically working each one all the way down. The sight of his fingers slipping them through has me feeling unexpectedly entranced.

Briar waits patiently on her knees, staring down at the floor. She does look like an angel in those white lace panties and bra. Not a drop of ink on her porcelain skin.

After Caleb gets his shirt undone, he slips it from his shoulders, revealing his bare chest, and once again, it feels difficult to tear my eyes away. Caleb has a broad frame and thick arms that I didn't realize he was hiding under those loose-fitting shirts. It's obvious he works out, but probably not as much as he wants to.

Reaching over my head, I tug my own shirt off quickly. Caleb is already walking toward Briar, so I meet him in the middle of the room, each of us standing on either side of her.

"Is that what you want, angel?" he whispers. "You want me to pretend you're not my wife? You want me to make a filthy woman out of you?"

She turns her gaze upward and meets his. With a wicked little smirk on her face, she nods.

"Yes, I do."

He holds her delicately by her chin. And I watch with keen interest as he slides his hand up her jaw, slowly easing two fingers into her mouth. She sucks on them while staring into his eyes. And even though she just said she doesn't want to be his wife tonight, there sure is a lot of adoration on her face.

After pulling his fingers from her mouth, he moves them to the back of her head. Grabbing her hair at the scalp, he tilts her head back.

"I want you to take his cock out," he growls at her.

My blood pressure starts to rise, which is unexpected. I was supposed to be the calm, cool, and collected one here, but these two like to surprise me at every turn.

Caleb keeps a hand in Briar's hair as she crawls toward me. Shivers rack down my spine as she unbuttons my pants and tugs down the zipper. My cock is growing steadily in my pants, so by the time she eases down my briefs, the rigid length juts out toward her.

When her eyes land on the head of my dick, I let out a chuckle. "What's wrong, sweet girl? Never seen an uncut cock before?"

She licks her lips and softly replies, "No."

"That's okay. It likes to be touched just the same."

"Stroke his cock," Caleb says in a deep command I didn't know he was capable of.

A grunting sound escapes my body as she wraps her soft hand around me, slowly stroking while staring up at me through her thick hooded lashes.

I'm fucked.

What did I get myself into? We've only just started, and I'm already overwhelmed by how hot they are. I never get like this with clients.

But *they* aren't clients. I know them better than I know my clients. Maybe that's the difference. In my head, I've already associated this with fun, casual sex. Not work sex.

But I'm not really a fun, casual-sex guy. Because when I try to have fun, casual sex, it usually ends with feelings. And who the fuck needs that?

I let out another grunt as she flicks her wrist on the upstroke.

"Easy, angel," I murmur. "You'll have a mess on your face if you keep doing that."

She bites her lip innocently. "Sorry."

God, she's so fucking sweet.

What I don't understand is why Caleb is all of a sudden into me touching his wife. Just a few days ago, he practically broke down my door, threatening me to stay away from her. Now he looks like he could get off from just watching her work my dick.

"Open up, angel," I say.

Caleb is still grasping her hair as her lips part innocently.

"Tongue out," I add.

When her wet, pink tongue slips out of her mouth, I slide the head of my dick over the surface. The warmth of her mouth is intoxicating, and my eyes nearly roll back as I reach her throat.

"Now suck," I groan. When she wraps her lips around me and adds some suction, I let out a heady, raspy sound. Then, my eyes track upward to where Caleb is staring at me. His eyes are on my face, and our gazes meet while his wife slurps loudly on my cock.

He doesn't say anything or make a move. It's unnerving how he can just stare at me for so long.

I wish I could crawl inside his brain for just a moment so I could see everything he's thinking. I want to know if any of those thoughts are about me.

When I feel my balls start to tighten, it takes me by surprise. With a roaring sound, I grab Briar's face and pull her off my cock.

She stares up at me in shock as I take a moment to catch my breath and get my bearings.

I almost came. It was *right* there.

So why did I stop it? I've been wanting to come for so long, and with just a few minutes in her mouth, I nearly blew without warning.

"Your fucking mouth, angel," I say with a grunt. "You might be a good girl, but you suck dick like a very bad girl."

I don't miss the hint of pride in her expression. She might have played it off as sweet and innocent before, but it's pretty clear now that this woman is anything but.

Twenty-Three

Caleb

My wife had her lips wrapped around another man's cock. I should be full of rage and jealousy. Instead, I've never been more aroused in my entire life.

Tonight, however, she's not my wife.

It's amazing how that one thought changes things. And it's not that I don't want Briar to be my wife. That's all I want.

But if I allow myself to suspend reality, the pressure of being her husband seems to dissipate. I have myself convinced that I'm not at risk of losing her. That one wrong move wouldn't cost me everything. That I don't have to constantly protect her.

It's perfectly clear that she's safe; neither of us is going to hurt her. I don't need to protect her from Dean or myself. She could stop this at any moment if she wanted to.

But judging by the look on her face, she's enjoying this very much. Which really, *really* turns me on.

I knew my wife had a dirty side. She's human, after all. But something has held me back all these years from wanting to explore those things with her. If there's anyone on earth that I should feel comfortable asking or exploring things with, it's her. But there's just been a disconnect. And I think the same goes for her as well.

"Get on the bed, you dirty little angel," Dean mutters to her after pulling his cock from her mouth. "On all fours," he commands. "But first, I want you to take those sweet little panties off. Show us that pretty cunt of yours."

My heart beats harder in my chest at his words. He's talking to my *wife*. There's not a hint of hesitation in his tone. Why the fuck does this turn me on so much?

Briar crawls obediently across the floor. She moves into a standing position when she reaches the bed, gently sliding down her white lace thong. Her movements are slow and exaggerated—she knows we're watching.

And like a couple of dogs, we are. We're practically salivating.

Even though Dean hasn't told her to, she slips off her bra as well, unhooking it from the back and letting it fall to the floor. When she crawls onto the bed, perching her ass in the air and exposing herself to us, I feel my mouth start to water.

Licking Briar's pussy has always been my favorite thing to do. I feel like a fucking pervert for how much I love to bury my nose between her legs and inhale her scent.

The prospect of watching Dean do it is somehow even more enticing.

Walking over to her, I feel Dean following me. Reaching her backside, I spread her wide, and Dean presses down on her shoulders so her ass perks up farther into the air. He takes in the sight of her like an animal about to go in for the kill.

I've never seen her like this before, so filthy and uninhibited. Leaning down with a growl that emits from my chest, I run the surface of my tongue from her clit to her asshole, humming as I devour her and breathe her in.

"Oh my god," she mutters into the blanket on the bed. Rising up with her taste on my tongue, I look at Dean. "Come here," I mutter.

I hold the wet pink lips of her pussy open, showing her off, and gesture for him to do the same as I just did.

With a salacious grin, he leans down and licks the length of her cunt. But once he gets a taste, he can't seem to stop. His groans are loud and hungry, and the more he sucks and teases her, the more she writhes and whimpers on the bed.

My cock twitches in my pants, and I feel the precum dripping from the head. I've never been this turned on in my entire life.

I nearly forgot why we're doing this. How did this start? Does it even fucking matter? Because we're not going back. We can't undo what we've already done. And we certainly can't fucking stop now.

Hearing Dean devour my wife's cunt, I can't wait another second. Leaning down, I press my face next to his, licking her hole as he sucks on her clit. She's crying out in earnest now. We have her completely at our mercy.

"Oh my god, don't stop." She moans. "I'm gonna come."

At the sound of her pleasure, Dean and I both become frenzied with our movements. Licking faster, sucking harder, groaning louder. Our cheeks are pressed together when I feel the warmth of his tongue brush mine.

Instantly, I tense at the sensation. Pulling back for a moment, I stare at him, gauging his reaction. With his lips still wrapped around my wife's pussy, he gazes up at me.

Then, a brutal hand lands on the back of my neck, and he hauls me back toward her. A moment later, Briar begins to tremble and shake. Her face is pressed into the mattress as she lets out a long, groaning scream.

I'm so overcome by the sight that I don't see his next move coming. With his hands still on the back of my neck, Dean jerks my mouth toward his. It's brief, but it happens. Our tongues intertwine and our mouths collide. He bites my bottom lip, and my cock jerks again. My hand reaches out, wrapping around his throat, but I don't push him away. I melt into the sensation of his tongue licking into my mouth, owning it for a brief moment.

Then, just like that, he releases me. The kiss only lasted a second, but for me, it was monumental.

"She's not such a sweet angel now, is she?" Dean says, pretending like nothing just happened. "I think this dirty little angel wants you to fuck her hard."

I'm still frozen, reliving that quick kiss. The sensation of his tongue against mine is burned into my memory, but at the mention of fucking my wife, I jolt out of my trance.

Standing from the floor, I quickly undo my pants, letting them drop to the floor. My boxer briefs follow behind, and I stroke my cock lazily as I watch Dean do the same.

There's no denying how sexy that man is, especially in his tight black underwear. There are tattoos on his legs, and although he's not a large man, his muscles are still defined. He is clearly in good shape.

Dean climbs onto the bed by Briar's face, and I settle in behind her.

"How are you feeling, angel?" he asks, stroking her hair and lifting her chin so she stares up into his eyes.

"Good," she says in a breathy, pleasure-laced tone.

"Tell me what you want," he replies. "I need to hear you say it."

"I want you in the front and him in the back," she says without missing a beat. "And I want you *both* to fill me up."

Jesus fucking Christ.

Just hearing my wife utter those words has me wanting to come. Where did this come from? How long has she been stifling these urges? And why wouldn't she tell me? Did she think I would judge her? Like it wasn't the wifely thing to want? Just because we're married doesn't mean our sex needs to be boring.

I can't take another second without being inside her. I line my cock up with her glistening sex. Glancing up at Dean, I wait for the signal. For some reason, I need to feel as if he and I are in sync.

Licking his lips, he gives a curt nod, and I slide easily inside her. She lets out a soft moan, and I can hardly breathe with how good this feels.

Grabbing her hips, I ease out slowly just to the tip and then back in again. I want to savor this moment, this feeling of her like this—all three of us like this.

Thrusting slowly, I wait, watching them for the moment when Briar reaches for Dean's dripping cock. Her hand wraps around his rigid length, and my eyes focus on the glistening wedding ring on her fourth finger.

Pride swells in my chest, watching her take both of us. Knowing that she loves it, that she asked for it, that she's not afraid to express what she wants. This woman I married isn't just brilliant and beautiful and kind, but she's also the sexiest woman I have ever met in my entire life.

As Dean thrusts into her mouth, I try to match his rhythm, fucking her from behind. Using her cries and moans as a cue, I'm careful that I'm not too rough.

We keep this going for a while, changing speed and rhythm. The sound of her ass slapping against my hips echoes through the room. I'm trying to savor everything when even I know it's too hot to savor. I'm burning up inside.

She groans around Dean's cock, and my gaze scans his face. His jaw is slack, and his eyes are wide. He looks as if he's struggling to breathe, and if I were to guess, I'd say he's about to come.

I watch with rapt attention, desperate to see the moment when he unloads. I want to see the look on his face. I want to memorize it. I want to experience the pinnacle of his pleasure.

"Oh fuck, oh fuck," he groans. "Your mouth is fucking magic, angel," he says to her. "I want to come on your face. I want to come all over that pretty face of yours."

Her response to that is a high-pitched whimper around his dick as she picks up speed, slurping on him with her lips rolled under her teeth.

Inadvertently, my thrusts quicken as well. I'm rapidly pounding into her from behind when Dean jerks his body away from her mouth. The booming sound that comes from him is indescribable.

Replacing her lips with his hand, he jerks himself, trembling violently as his cock shoots one white jet after another of cum all over her face. It lands on her forehead, her nose, her eyes, her lips. The expression on her face is downright rapturous as she accepts every drop.

"Holy fucking shit," he mutters.

I think all three of us are shocked by the amount that comes out of him. But more than anything, I'm surprised to see how much he's enjoying this. When we came in here, I sort of thought he would be levelheaded and cool about everything, but he seems as taken aback by this as we are, committing to the moment, relishing in the pleasure.

He loves this, and I love that he loves this. Although I don't know why.

My own orgasm slams into me unexpectedly, and I let out some grunting sounds as I come inside my wife.

None of us move for a while. My orgasm doesn't seem to end, but when I'm sure my cock is spent, I shiver and let myself finally breathe.

Dean is staring at Briar with his mouth hanging open as if he's taking in the sight of her, surprised as to why her face is covered with his cum.

"Holy shit," he whispers to himself.

After a moment, Briar mumbles sweetly, "Could you maybe get me a towel?"

"Oh, fuck, yeah...shit, sorry," he stutters, jumping from the bed and rushing to the bathroom.

A moment later, he returns with a washcloth that he's dampened in the sink. With delicate care, he wipes her face clean.

"God, that was a lot. I'm so sorry," he stammers.

She giggles in response. "It's okay."

Slowly, I ease out from behind her, and she immediately moves to her back, extending her legs in the air, as she often does. A little still slips out, but I don't wipe it away. I take pride in the way she looks, with my seed dripping from her as if it were more than her body could hold.

After taking the washcloth to the bathroom, Dean returns and pauses in the doorway, staring at her with a confused look on his face. "What are you doing?" he asks.

She smiles up at the ceiling. "It's just something I do to make sure everything gets where it needs to go."

"Does that help?" he asks.

"Probably not," she replies with a shrug. "But I do it anyway."

Dean picks up his underwear from the floor and quickly slides them up his legs. I do the same with my own. I'm grateful for the way Dean seems to fill the silence when I'm too stunned to speak.

I still can't believe we did that. And yet, these two are just carrying on as if it were another regular Friday night.

"How are you feeling?" he asks her as he sits on the bed next to her.

"Great," she replies nonchalantly. "That was fun."

Fun? Did she literally call that fun, as if we just finished playing a board game? I Eiffel Towered my wife with a twenty-six-year-old male prostitute, and she called it fun.

"And how about you, big boy?" Dean asks, looking at me.

"What kind of question is that?" I ask with offense.

"A pretty normal aftercare question," he replies.

"Yeah, but why would anything be wrong with me?"

"Just answer the question," Briar says to me in a scolding tone.

"I'm fine," I reply with far too much aggression, making the sentiment much less convincing.

"Uh-oh, you don't sound fine," Dean says, and it grates on my nerves.

But I am fine, I think to myself. *Aren't I?* That was the hottest thing I've ever done in my entire life. I loved it. I definitely want to do it again.

But I have to admit—there is a hint of something inside me that says I'm not entirely *fine*. I just wish I knew what it was so that maybe I could express it to them.

"If Briar's fine, then I'm fine," I say, hoping it will be enough.

Immediately, Dean shakes his head. "No. That's not how you answer that question."

"What do you want me to say?" I argue, feeling myself getting heated. "I'm not hurt. That was great. I loved it. I'm fine."

"You just seem tense, that's all," he replies.

"Are you dealing with a little guilt?" Briar asks softly.

"No," I reply immediately, without hesitation.

And I'm not. I can tell that it's not guilt.

But maybe a little...regret?

"It's okay," Dean says, putting up his hands. "It's normal to have a lot of conflicting feelings after an intense sexual scene that maybe you can't quite define."

"Well, don't you want to talk about them?" Briar asks.

"Not really," I reply immediately.

"It might help to define them," she pushes.

"What if I don't want to define them?" I fight back.

"Caleb, stop," she argues. "We're doing this to help each other, remember? Because shoving down feelings and pretending they don't exist and hoping that they go away is how we got into that fight in the first place."

She climbs onto her knees and crawls toward me. Taking my hand, she looks into my eyes. "I felt closer to you tonight than I have felt with you in a very long time. Did you feel that too?" she asks.

The softness in her voice shatters me inside.

"Yes," I reply emphatically. I saw my wife in a new light tonight, and I think I've fallen even more in love with her.

"Are you afraid that you've hurt me?" she asks.

"No," I reply. "I trust you. I know you would tell me if I did."

"I would," she says with certainty. "Are you afraid this hurts our marriage?" she tries again.

"No," I say. "But..." The word comes out of my mouth before I even know what I'm about to say. It's just there, this *but*.

Her eyebrows perk up in interest as she waits.

"But it changes it, doesn't it?" I say. And there it is. The *change*. The not good, but not bad change.

"You don't like change," she says as if she knows my mind better than I do, and maybe she does.

I don't like change. I hate change. At the slightest hint of change, I turn silent, guarded, and irritable.

I know this about myself. Briar knows this even more. With a tight smile on her face, she strokes her hand down my bearded cheek. As she stares at me, we have a conversation with our eyes that words can't convey. She settles me, eases my worries, confirms my fears.

From across the room, Dean's voice chimes in. "I don't understand what's changed."

And I don't know how to answer that because I don't know either.

I just know that something has changed or something is *about to* change. I feel it. She feels it. And tonight confirmed it.

It's not a change in her or me or Dean, but a change in *us*.

Twenty-Four

Briar
21 years old

You have to talk to him.

Caleb's words have been echoing in my ears since he uttered them. I know he's right, but I can't bring myself to have that conversation with Sean.

It's been almost a month since that first night at Caleb's house. Nearly every night since he's snuck me into his bedroom after his family has gone to sleep.

I know it's wrong. No matter how terrible Sean can be, he doesn't deserve this.

And neither does Caleb.

But I can't bring myself to do what needs to be done. Once I tell Sean it's over between us, he'll know. He already had his suspicions about Caleb even before anything happened.

Now, if I break up with him and start dating Caleb, he's going to wreak havoc on us both. Sean doesn't take things lightly. He won't handle this well.

To him, we've made a fool of him. Someone bested him. I chose someone else.

All of this will drive him mad. I keep telling myself that I can keep things going like this. If I stay with Sean, Caleb will be better off.

Of course, I can't put off sex with my boyfriend without it raising suspicion. But every time Sean touches me now, a small part of me dies. And I worry it kills Caleb a little bit every time, too.

Walking across campus with Sean's arm around my shoulder, I paste a smile on my face and try to pretend as if everything is normal. As we reach the humanities building, I search for Caleb among the crowd moving to and from the main doorway.

Sean is going on and on about the football game this weekend. Everyone has been talking lately about how good Caleb's game has been. Even Sean can't shut up about it. And as the guy on the field who catches most of his passes, you'd think he'd be ecstatic about that, but I can feel the bitterness in his tone.

"You listening to me, babe?" he mutters next to me.

I blink and glance up at him. "Of course. You said you should make the finals."

"Wouldn't that be amazing?" He presses his lips to the side of my head, and I resist the urge to pull away.

Somewhere in the back of my mind, I assure myself that it's better for Caleb if Sean never finds out. I can't tell him. I won't *tell him.*

But I don't know how much longer I can do this.

Something in my chest warms as I spot Caleb walking toward us. Just seeing him now makes me feel safe. Like everything is going to be okay.

And I know it's terrible, but I can hardly wait until tonight when I know I'll find myself on his front porch again, silently sneaking into his bed just to be back in his arms.

Sean is still going on and on as we reach Caleb, but rather than stop and speak with him, Sean bumps into Caleb, knocking him hard against his shoulder without looking back or apologizing.

My jaw drops and I try to look back at Caleb, but Sean jerks me forward, forcing me to stay on the path to the building.

I can't ignore the very bad feeling in my stomach when we reach the classroom.

Maybe he didn't see him. It could have been an accident. But deep down, I know the truth.

That wasn't an accident at all. Sean's suspicions have turned serious.

When he leans down and presses his lips to mine, he kisses me harder than he normally does, knowing that Caleb is now in the hallway. He makes him watch.

When he releases me and I see Caleb stomp angrily into the classroom, I realize that there will be no easy way out of this for us. Eventually, Caleb and I will have to pay for our sins.

†

Present day

It's after midnight by the time Caleb and I crawl into our own bed. We don't say much to each other. It's not awkward, though—just comfortably silent.

That is, until we each rest our heads on our pillows, facing each other. The moment our eyes meet, everything that happened tonight hits us both at the same time.

A slow, blushing smile stretches across Caleb's face, and as soon as I see it, I can't keep my giggle back. Once I start, he starts. And the next thing we know, we're both laughing profusely in our dark bedroom.

"I can't believe we just did that," I say with wide eyes when the laughter finally dies.

"I can't either," he replies.

"Who are we?"

There's warmth in his eyes. "You were incredible. I've never seen you like that."

"*You* were incredible," I reply. "I didn't even know you were into something like that until tonight."

"But you liked it?" he asks.

"Caleb, I loved it."

His expression grows contemplative, and I wonder if he's thinking about Dean. If I liked it because of him or because of both of them. I don't know. But I secretly hope he doesn't ask me that because I don't know how I'll answer.

I loved Caleb being so dominant, but I also loved having them both like that. So, I can't say with any certainty that it was just Caleb.

To my relief, he just softly whispers, "I loved it too."

Over the past couple of hours, his mood regarding the entire thing has definitely lightened. I could tell he was very *in his head* about it. He truly was afraid this one night would change our marriage forever, and I find that incredibly...endearing.

Our marriage means that much to him.

I don't remember what we were even fighting about this morning.

For the first time in ages, I find myself rolling closer to Caleb. When he extends his arm, I rest my head on his shoulder, using his body as a pillow. His arm wraps around me, and I breathe in the comfort he brings.

Caleb has always been my safe space. My *home*.

Tonight solidified that. I would have never been so open or vulnerable with anyone else. And in this very moment, it feels as if the sky is the limit. What else can we do together? What more can we explore?

What more can Dean show us?

Because it's truly Dean at the helm. I put my faith in both of them, but Dean was the one who was leading the way. I wonder if he realizes how special he is in all of this. It's not just about another warm body in our bed. It's the energy he brings. The security and warmth.

When I drift off to sleep, I do so with the cadence of my

husband's heartbeat in my ear. For a moment, everything feels right. And I have myself fooled into believing that one night would be enough to fix everything.

The next morning hits like a tidal wave. Abby wakes up with a fever and an upset stomach.

As if that wasn't enough, Caleb comes downstairs around nine, staring at his phone with wide, frantic eyes.

"What is it?" I ask from the couch with Abby's head in my lap.

Caleb doesn't answer. He just ambles into the kitchen, and I take it as my signal to follow.

When we're alone, he looks up at me with an anxiety-riddled expression.

"My father made a statement," he says.

"What did he say?" I ask, stepping toward him and touching his hand.

Reading his phone, he continues, "After serious contemplation, I've decided to separate from my current legal team and plan to fight these charges with the help of the most prominent and successful defense attorney in the city of Austin, my son, Caleb Goode."

I feel the blood rush from my face as Caleb's eyes drift up to mine. The shock and terror I feel in his expression shake me to my core.

"Oh my god," I mumble. "You didn't agree to this..."

He shakes his head emphatically. "No. Fuck no. Briar, I *can't* help him."

My arms move to pull him in, wrapping him in comfort. I hate to see him with such fear and worry. I wish I could take it all from him.

"I know you can't," I reply. "And you don't have to. It was just a statement. He lied, Caleb."

"That's all he does," he mutters into my shoulder.

I hold Caleb for a while, rubbing his back and feeling him breathe into my neck. As much as I hate this for him, I feel a sense of relief that he's finally leaning on me. He's letting me in.

"Mom!" Abby calls from the living room.

Caleb pulls away. Before going to Abby, I take his face in my hands and force him to look me in the eyes. "This doesn't mean anything, Caleb. You can make a statement of your own on Monday after you meet with your team. This can be fixed."

I watch the tension in his shoulders melt away as he nods. Then he leans forward and presses his lips to my forehead. "You really are an angel," he whispers.

A smile stretches across my face. As my eyes meet his, he gives me a quick wink.

Then, at the unmistakable sound of our daughter vomiting in the living room, we both jump into action. We rush toward her together, consoling her as she sobs. Caleb pulls her into his arms and cradles her against his chest, not caring about the mess.

"I'll get something to clean this up," I say as I touch his shoulder.

As he's carrying her to the bathroom and I'm gathering up the towels, we pass each other in the hallway.

"How quickly things go back to reality," he says with a despondent smirk.

"Always," I reply.

And it's true. The fantasy never lasts long—but the reality isn't half-bad, either.

Twenty-Five

Dean

Trying to focus on work feels impossible.

Ironically enough, my clients tonight are a hetero couple. But it's nothing like last night.

Work is work, and fun is fun. And while this couple is lovely and very enthusiastic, it's not the same—not even close.

I'm just a toy for these two. I'm just a thing they reach into the nightstand drawer to retrieve when their relationship needs an extra buzz. I don't feel wanted. I don't feel special.

And that's fine. This is my job. It's not like a barber wants to feel an emotional connection with his clients. So what the fuck is wrong with me?

I never, *ever* compare work to real life. But I can't seem to get Briar and Caleb out of my head tonight. It's making me bitter and resentful.

It's mostly that kiss with Caleb that I can't get out of my head. That brief but powerful moment when our tongues touched, and I know it was a huge deal for him. I found myself caught up in the heat of the moment when I pulled his mouth to mine, but I didn't stop to think how that felt for him. But he didn't panic or pull away —he kissed me back.

And I can't stop thinking about it, even with tonight's clients.

This couple is nothing like them. The wife likes to watch as I suck off her husband. And he likes to watch as I spank her ass and call her a *bad girl*. But then that's it. They both get off (I don't), and they leave happy. I get paid, and it's fine.

Everything is fine.

Except Briar and Caleb are everywhere I turn. When it's another woman with her lips around my cock, I see Briar. When I'm kissing another man, it's Caleb's warm tongue I feel.

I knew it was reckless to get into bed with those two. Everything was so personal and real.

And I want more, which is stupid. And dangerous.

I'm going to get all attached to them, and then it's going to end, and I'll have that shit to deal with. Right now, that's the last thing I need. It's bad enough I'm dealing with being homeless and my dad dying in some nursing home.

Now, I have to worry about getting my stupid, fucking heart broken.

Get your shit together, Dean.

This is why I don't do relationships.

But whenever I try to focus at work, my mind returns to them.

How Caleb is clearly covering up his own sexuality just because he's married to a woman.

My underwear in his pocket? He can't tell me that was an accident.

What I don't understand is, if Caleb is harboring some deep, hidden desires, then why was he such an asshole to me and Isaac all those years ago? Especially when I thought he'd be the most supportive, was that part of his own personal biphobia?

I know people who struggle with their own identity can be the ones throwing stones at others, but that's not the vibe I get from Caleb. I just don't understand.

My shift runs late Saturday night, and I don't end up getting home until three in the morning. Which means I sleep half the day away on Sunday. Around noon, I wake to a soft knock on my door.

Climbing off the couch in a pair of basketball shorts, I go to the door without a shirt on, expecting it to be Briar or Caleb. But when I open it and find Abby, I glare down at her in confusion.

"Hi," she says, swaying as if she can't hold still. "I threw up."

"Gross," I reply. "Just now?" With a look of disgust on my face, I glance around the stairs to see if there's a mess I have to call her parents to clean up.

"No," Abby says, hanging on the railing. "Yesterday."

"Did you come over here just to tell me that?"

She coughs. "Yeah."

"You're not going to throw up now, are you?"

Wiping her nose, she shakes her head up at me. "I feel better."

"Good," I reply. Glancing around the yard, I look for Briar and Caleb, but there's no sign of them. "Where are your parents?"

"They fell asleep while we were watching *Frozen*."

"They did?" I smirk down at her. "Did you keep them up all night?"

"Yeah." Then, without a pause, she adds, "I'm hungry. Do you have any snacks?" She's practically hanging upside down on the railing as she talks.

"Depends," I reply, crossing my arms in front of my chest. "Are you going to throw up in here?"

Hopping down, she stares up at me with bright eyes. "No, I promise. I feel all better now, and Mommy said my fever was gone."

With a sigh, I press the door open. "Fine. Come in."

She bounces into the apartment and goes straight for the cabinet. While she's digging through my assortment of chips, I grab a shirt from the couch and throw it on. Then I find my phone and text Briar to let her know Abby is here. Hopefully, she has her phone on silent so she can get some sleep.

"Will you make me some ramen?" Abby asks as she pulls out a package.

"That's spicy," I reply, taking it from her.

"Ooh, I love the spicy one. Please!"

"Didn't your dad tell you not to beg?" I say, pulling a saucepan from the lower cabinet.

She shrugs with a sheepish expression and watches as I fill the pot with water and put it on the stove.

"Do you have any kids?" she asks innocently.

"No."

"Why not?"

"Because I don't want kids," I reply.

"Why not?"

I let out a chuckle as I turn to face her, leaning against the kitchen counter. "Because they're annoying and ask too many questions. And gross. Wash your hands."

Her jaw drops as if I've offended her. Within a second, she shrugs it off and goes to the sink, stepping on her tiptoes to reach the soap. I watch as she scrubs her tiny fingers and then rinses them before drying them on the gray kitchen towel on the counter.

"How long are you going to live here?" she asks.

"I don't know."

"Did your house burn down?"

"Yeah," I reply plainly.

"Do you have a wife?" she says, hanging this time on the handle of my refrigerator.

"No. Don't hang on that."

She lets go and drapes herself over one of the chairs instead. "Do you have a girlfriend?"

"No," I say with my brow furrowed. "You know you shouldn't assume boys only have girlfriends. Some boys have boyfriends."

She pauses in her swinging and stares at me as if she's deep in thought. I don't know if that was inappropriate to say to a kid, but it's not on me if her family hasn't prepared her for the real world. She should know that kind of stuff.

Without skipping a beat, she asks, "Do you have a boyfriend?"

Chuckling, I shake my head. "No. Do you ever hold still?"

"Nope." Hooking her fingers on the countertop, she hangs from it like a monkey in a tree.

"You should join gymnastics or something," I reply as the water starts to boil. Unwrapping the ramen, I drop the noodles into the water and give them a quick stir.

"I want to do karate," she says.

"Karate is good."

"My gigi said karate is for boys. She said it's not ladylike."

I freeze. "Who the fuck is Gigi?" I ask, realizing a moment too late that I probably shouldn't cuss around her. But honestly, it sounds like Gigi is saying worse shit than fuck.

"Gigi is my grandma."

"Your mom's mom or your dad's mom?"

"Umm..." She thinks for a moment. "My mom's mom."

"Well, Gigi is wrong, and no offense, but she sounds sexist."

"What's sexist?" she asks, and I wince as I turn the stove off and start mixing the flavor packet into the noodles.

"It means she thinks boys can do things girls can't do, and she's wrong. Plenty of girls do karate, and the term *ladylike* is utter misogynistic bullshit, so don't listen to Gigi."

With that, I set her bowl of ramen on the counter. "Now, sit and eat."

"What does misogynistic mean—"

"No more questions," I snap, which makes her giggle.

Leaning against the counter, I watch her pull the noodles from the bowl with her fork, blowing on each one. Her tiny legs are constantly bouncing, and it's like she's dancing to music in her head that no one else can hear.

Most kids are annoying, but I have to admit...this one is pretty cute.

It makes my blood boil to think of someone telling her she can't do something because she's a girl. I hope Briar and Caleb don't stand for that shit.

Abby eats her ramen without asking more questions. When she requests to watch TV, I put on *Friends* because she said she's never seen it. She laughs when I laugh, even though I know most of the jokes go over her head.

After her ramen is gone, she climbs onto my couch next to me and props her feet on the ottoman next to mine. Her feet dance as we watch, and in the middle of the second episode, the front door opens.

Briar walks in, looking frazzled and apologetic.

"Oh my god, Dean. I'm so sorry," she mutters. "I don't know what happened. We just passed out."

"Relax. It's fine. She ate some spicy ramen, and now we're watching TV."

"She didn't get sick, did she?" she asks, looking concerned as she runs the back of her hand over Abby's forehead.

There are dark circles under Briar's eyes, and her hair looks like she could use a shower.

"Nope," I reply, ruffling Abby's brown, messy locks.

"Come on, Abby," Briar calls. "Let's go back home and leave Dean alone."

Furrowing my brow, I touch Briar's arm. "Leave her. She's fine. You need a shower and some rest. I'll let you know if she gets sick again."

"You don't have to do that," she replies, shaking her head.

"I know I don't."

Staring into my eyes, I see hers begin to moisten with tears. Then she licks her bottom lip before tugging it between her teeth, and I suddenly find myself wanting to reach out and kiss her.

Of course, I don't. Not with Abby around, but when I gaze down at Briar's lips, I think she gets the message.

Her cheeks blush, and she leans in very subtly.

"What would we do without you?" she whispers.

My mouth stretches into a smile because I felt that. I'm not sure if she's referring to watching Abby or what we did Friday night, but it's nice to feel needed. For a guy who's usually alone and likes to be alone, I could get used to being a part of a family like this.

"Go take a shower. Come back and get her in a few hours. We'll be fine."

Her hand squeezes my arm. "Thank you so much."

"Don't mention it."

After Briar leaves, Abby and I binge a couple more episodes of *Friends*. She asks a thousand more questions. Then she asks to draw and I pull out a single black pen and some junk mail for her to scribble on.

And when she draws a picture of everyone in her family together on the back of an old bank statement, I definitely should not be so touched by how she includes me—but I am.

Part Three

The Home-Wrecker

Twenty-Six

Caleb

"We have dinner at my parents'...er, I mean my mother's tonight," I say, stepping out of the shower. Briar just woke up from a long nap, and judging by the look on her face, she'd rather spend the rest of the night in bed than go to someone else's house.

"Mind if I skip it?" she asks, looking run-down.

"Of course not," I reply, kissing the side of her head. "I'll take Abby. You relax. Take a bubble bath."

"Are you sure?" Her expression is etched with concern. And I know deep down she's thinking about the news we got the other day and how she doesn't want me to have to face my family alone.

"I'll be fine. It's just dinner."

"Okay, I appreciate it," she mumbles to herself as she turns the faucet on the tub. "Just grab Abby from Dean's before you go."

I get ready in a rush, noticing the time. My hair is still wet as I jog up the stairs to Dean's place. Knocking on the door, I hear laughter inside.

"Come in," Dean calls, and when I open the door, I find him and Abby sitting on the couch, each of them with a video game controller in their hands and what looks like *Grand Theft Auto* playing on the screen.

Shaking my head, I walk into the apartment and stand behind the couch as my six-year-old daughter hijacks a fictional Impala on the screen.

"Briar would have your head if she knew you were letting her play this," I say with a cold, hard stare in his direction.

He lets out a laugh as he shrugs. "I didn't let her pick up any prostitutes."

"Jesus," I mutter to myself. Then I tap Abby's shoulder. "Come on, peanut. We have to go to Nana's for dinner."

"Can Dean come?" she replies excitedly.

I quickly shake my head before glancing over at him. "No, honey. I doubt he wants to." When he doesn't immediately turn it down, I add, "Do you...want to go to my mom's for dinner?"

"Do you really want me to?" he asks Abby.

"Yes!" she replies, hopping up and down on the couch cushion. "Come on. Please!"

"If it's okay with your dad," he says with a shrug.

I'm frozen for a second. Dean and I alone together? For some reason, it feels both terrifying and exciting. A few days ago, we were at each other's throats. He's still harboring resentment toward me for what happened over a decade ago, and now he's going to come with me to dinner at my mom's like everything is fine.

"Of course, it's okay," I stammer, looking down.

"Nana is such a good cook," Abby replies, tossing the controller on the couch.

"I know that," Dean says flatly.

She screws up her face. "How do you know?"

"I used to eat dinner at your Nana's house all the time when I was a kid."

She throws her head back in exaggerated shock. "You did?"

"Yep. I was good friends with your dad's brother," he replies, but I start to tense. The conversation is growing far too close to the one topic we don't talk about.

"Uncle Adam?" she says excitedly.

"No."

"That's enough," I say with a low growl.

"Your uncle Isaac," he finishes, and it feels like all of the air is sucked out of the room.

"Oh," Abby replies, sinking into the sofa. "I haven't met him."

Dean's eyes cast up to me, that familiar grief in his gaze. "Yeah, I know," he says lowly.

I let his hurt-filled expression burn for a moment before I swallow and turn away. "We should get going," I mutter.

In the car, Abby talks the entire time, but Dean and I stay quiet. When she distracts herself by singing to the song on the radio, I turn toward the man in my passenger seat.

"Don't bring up Isaac at dinner, please," I say softly.

"I won't," he replies while staring out the window.

"This dinner is going to be awkward enough," I finish. My hand grips the steering wheel a little tighter. Dean turns toward me, looking offended.

"Why? Because I'll be there?"

My brows pinch inward as I shake my head. "What? No."

"Then why will it be awkward?"

Tilting my head to the side, I look at him again, trying to read his expression and decipher whether or not he's joking.

"You don't watch the news, do you?"

"Fuck no."

My jaw clenches, and he must be able to see my contempt because he quickly corrects himself.

"Sorry. I mean, heck no. Why? What's going on?"

I let out a sigh. I'm not entirely sure how much I want to get into on this car ride, but what the hell? I already let the man get a blow job from my wife. Might as well let him in on the family drama while I'm at it.

"On Friday, my father made a statement that I would be taking over his defense in getting him a lesser charge." I spit out the truth. Just saying it makes me sick.

"You can't seriously..." he starts.

Appalled, I glare at him. "Of course not. I could never..."

"Have you told Adam that?"

"Not yet," I confess.

"Your family is great at communication."

"Very funny." I groan, side-eyeing him.

"So just tell him," Dean suggests.

"I plan on it, but you know Adam and Sage. When it comes to her, my brother can be a little hotheaded. I know my brother, and I know he's angry. Which means he will want to lash out."

"And you're just going to let him?"

Turning toward him, I give him an expression that is, for once, not full of spite or anger. "What choice do I have?"

When we reach my mother's house, I pull into the drive, and Abby is already bolting out of the car before I even have it in park. She rushes into my mother's waiting arms. My mom is sitting on one of the white rockers on the porch, and she gives Abby a long squeeze as Dean and I climb out of the SUV.

The moment my mother spots Isaac's old best friend, I see her expression change.

"Oh my," she says with a gasp. "Is that little Dean Sheridan? I haven't seen you in ages."

Standing from the chair, she hops down the front porch steps to pull him into a warm embrace.

"Hi, ma'am. Thanks for having me for dinner...again."

She laughs as she releases him, squeezing his arms and staring up into his eyes. I had wondered if seeing Dean would be hard on my mother, but then I forgot just how strong this woman is. Is there anything she hasn't endured? She takes it all in stride—with a smile and Southern charm to boot.

"Oh, of course!" she croons. "You are welcome anytime. My, how you've grown!"

I can see her squeezing his arms as if she's testing out the firmness of his muscles.

"Mother, stop it," I mumble with a laugh as I lean down and press a kiss to her cheek.

She finally releases Dean and welcomes us into the house.

"You're the first ones here," she says, leading us toward the kitchen. "Let me get you something to drink. Sweet tea or lemonade?"

"Sweet tea, please, ma'am," Dean says with a polite nod. Seeing him use his manners is pretty endearing, and I have to bite the inside of my cheek to keep from smiling.

"Oh, stop it with that ma'am stuff," she replies with a laugh as she pulls out the pitcher from the fridge. "Caleb likes sweet tea too."

With a wink, she pours two glasses for us. Abby climbs onto the tall stool by the kitchen island.

"And my little gabby Abby likes sweet tea and lemonade mixed together, don't you?" my mother says with a smile.

Abby nods with excitement.

After our drinks are poured, my mother looks at me over the rim of her glass. "And how are you doin', baby?" she asks.

My mom's concern for me always makes me feel like I'm seven years old again. It's as if she worries about me more than she worries about Adam, Luke, or even Isaac. Adam is older. He's always thrived under the wing of our father until recently. And Luke flew the nest as soon as he could, paving his own path in the world without ever looking back.

But me? I stayed. Close to home. Close to her. My life never strayed from the road I was meant to take.

Find a nice girl. Get married. Have kids. Live a good life.

And Briar made that life *so* easy. I was meant for her and the family we've created.

But it doesn't change the fact that my mother often looks at me like I'm the one who never grew wings to fly. And it's not until recently that I've started to wonder if she's right. I was too scared to take the leap. Time and time again.

A car door closes loudly in the driveway, and the three of us standing in the kitchen all freeze in anticipation, waiting to hear if it's Lucas or Adam.

Angry footsteps echo up the gravel pathway.

"Caleb!" my brother barks from the front door.

Adam.

He marches up the stairs to my father's office because he knows better than to start an argument with me in front of my daughter or our mother. So he's doing what my father often did. Reserve hard conversations for the confines of his office, pretending the things that happen behind those closed doors don't affect the rest of the world.

"I'll be right back," I say lowly as I set my glass of tea on the counter.

My mother gives me a sympathetic expression as I turn and leave. I pass Sage on my way up the stairs, but she forces a tight, uneasy smile, which I can't bring myself to return.

Before I disappear into my father's office, I feel a hand on my arm. Turning, I find Dean standing right behind me.

"I'm coming with you," he says.

"What? No. It's between my brother and me."

His demeanor doesn't falter. "I don't care. I'm coming with you."

Accepting that he won't change his mind, I walk into my father's office and close the door behind me. Dean is standing so close to me his arm brushes mine as we face Adam, who doesn't seem to care that I brought someone else into the room.

"Tell me this isn't happening," he barks at me. "Tell me you're not helping our monster of a father get out of this charge. Tell me he's a fucking liar, Caleb."

I shove my hands in my pockets and turn to face my brother. I want to tell him that when he acts like this, full of rage and animosity, he looks so much like Truett.

"He's a liar," I say calmly.

"What the fuck?!" he shouts.

"Keep your voice down," I reply.

"Why would he say that? Why the fuck would he think you're going to help him? He tried to kill the love of my life. He nearly did!"

I see the anger in my brother's eyes, and I understand it. If it were Briar who had been hurt and any of my brothers dared to even tiptoe to my father's side, I would lose my mind with rage. So I get it.

But that doesn't mean I know how to make him feel better.

"Because I met with him," I say flatly.

Immediately, Adam's eyes go wide. "You *what*?"

"I met with him last week. I didn't tell him I would help him, but I heard him out."

"The *fuck*, Caleb?" Adam shouts.

Luke warned me that Adam wouldn't want to hear that. But I won't lie.

"Calm down," Dean breaks in with the same authoritative tone he used the other night.

"Don't tell me to calm down," Adam snaps. "How could you do this, Caleb?"

"I didn't do anything, Adam!" I argue. "He's lying, probably to pit us against each other, which is what we're doing right now. You're playing right into his hands."

"Fuck you, Caleb," Adam shouts, and I notice Dean tensing at my side.

Then, for some reason, I decide to throw an accelerant on the fire. Maybe deep down, I want to see how angry I can get my brother. Maybe I want to see how much of this I can take.

"You do realize," I start, taking a step toward my brother. "That a lesser charge would be easier to convict and faster to get him into prison."

Adam's eyes go wild as he marches toward me. "I know you didn't just say that to me."

I'm waiting for our argument to turn into an all-out brawl like it did when we were kids. If he punches me right now, I deserve it. But that doesn't mean I won't fight back.

Before he can reach me, a tall figure steps between us. Standing tall and immovable, Dean takes a protective stance in front of me.

My lips part as I stare at him in astonishment.

"That's enough," he mutters to my brother.

"This doesn't involve you, Dean," Adam growls in return.

"If you plan on laying your hands on him, it does."

It feels like the floor gives out beneath me. Even my brother's face morphs into surprise. He stares at Dean with confusion as he takes a step back.

I replay the words that just came out of Dean's mouth to gauge if they're as protective and intimate as I think they are. Or maybe it's all in my head. Maybe I'm hearing things the way I want to hear them.

Adam doesn't ask questions or demand to know why my tenant is suddenly so defensive of me. He lets the anger drain from his face as his gaze dances back and forth from Dean to me and back again.

His rage doesn't dissipate entirely, but he gets control of it as he mutters at me ruefully, "Promise me you won't help that man, brother."

I stare at Adam with assurance. "I would *never* help him."

As Dean steps aside, giving my brother and me some breathing room, the three of us take a moment to compose ourselves. And when I expect questions or someone to address the elephant in the room, no one does.

Instead, Adam opens the door and vehemently storms downstairs. Left alone with Dean, I glance in his direction before he has the chance to leave. When his eyes meet mine, it feels like the underwear situation all over again.

A thousand words and possibilities exist in the long moments of silence when the things we should express get left unsaid.

And just like that, he walks away and heads downstairs.

Twenty-Seven

Dean

This family is so fucking weird. Granted, I don't have a lot to compare it to. It was just me and my dad growing up, and we never did *family* shit.

So I have no clue if this is how normal families behave. Yelling at each other in private rooms one minute, then saying grace and talking about the weather around the table the next.

This is how they were when we were kids, and I see nothing has changed.

Abby asked to sit next to me, which made Sage grumpy because, apparently, she always likes to sit next to *her*.

"She has a new favorite," I brag across the table, to which my pink-haired boss just sticks her tongue out at me.

Abby giggles and leans in closer to me.

After that outburst in the office, everything is mostly normal. There is still a thick tension in the air, but I think most of that is just from the situation of their patriarch being a slimy, villainous creep.

I like Adam, I do. But the way he yelled at Caleb got under my skin fast. Maybe it was what happened the other night with Briar, but I feel closer to Caleb now.

I'm still mad at him for what happened, but as I get to know him more and see just how complex his life has become, I think I understand him a bit more than I did when I was fourteen.

I *think* I'd consider him a friend, although friend doesn't seem the right word. He's something to me now. I just wish I knew what.

At the end of the table is Caleb's twin brother, Lucas—although they're not identical. Caleb is so much broader and taller, whereas Lucas is built more like me. He's slender and quiet. I notice the way he watches the room as if he's studying us but doesn't bother to weigh in much.

I wonder if he and Caleb are close. When Lucas arrived, he seemed to be able to tell immediately that Caleb was worked up. One look and he was approaching his brother with concern. For that, I stepped away, letting Caleb have a little privacy with his twin.

But now, as we sit at dinner, I feel Adam's eyes on me every few minutes, but he doesn't look as angry as before. He looks curious, which I can understand. I was acting like Caleb's boyfriend in there, practically pounding my chest like some overprotective gorilla.

That shit is just not like me.

"I hope none of you have forgotten about the charity gala next week," Caleb's mother, Melanie, says from the head of the table.

"We'll be there," Sage replies sweetly.

Melanie grins at her before touching her hand.

"I think it's good for the public to see us together, standing strong amid all of this," Adam adds from the opposite side of the table, sitting at the head where I assume his father once sat.

"I agree," his mother replies. When her eyes scan in my direction, I tense.

"Dean, I hope you know you are invited."

"Oh, that's all right," I stammer in response. "I appreciate the invite, though."

"Of course," she says with a gentle smile. "The invitation is always open."

I want to ask why, but I don't. I'm not part of this family, and the longer I sit here, the more I realize how much it feels like I'm filling Isaac's seat. He's not here, but I am.

Once that thought enters my mind, it becomes harder to relax. I end up pushing around the food on my plate and drowning out the rest of their conversation.

What would he think about this if he were here? What would he think about me, Caleb and Briar? Would Isaac and I have stayed together if it wasn't for Caleb driving us apart? Would we still be together today?

My gut says no, but it doesn't change the fact that, at the time, Isaac was everything to me.

That memory just hurts.

After our dinner is done, the family mingles for a while. We help clean up the table, do the dishes, and end up in the living room. I don't sit on the couches with them, though. I linger somewhere near the door.

Caleb notices me standing alone as he glances up from the recliner. With Abby sitting on his mother's lap, he says, "Mom, do you mind if I take a look through Dad's office before we go? I just need to check for something."

"Of course, baby," she says with her sweet Southern drawl.

As he passes by me, up the stairs toward the office, he nods in my direction, signaling me to follow. I feel Adam watching us as I jog up behind Caleb.

Once we reach the office, Caleb closes the door behind us, and my blood pressure spikes. For reasons I don't understand, I like the idea of being alone with him. I *wanted* this.

"You want a drink?" he asks, going to the shelf along the wall.

"Sure," I reply, watching as he opens the cabinet and pulls down a bottle of bourbon. He pours two glasses and hands one to me. When he moves to the large chair behind the desk, I take a moment to admire how handsome Caleb has become over the years.

He was always good-looking, but when I knew him before, he

was hot in a young, college-athlete way. Now he's sexy in a mature, aged way with a short beard and crow's-feet around his eyes.

I see the stress he carries, and if he were my client, I know exactly how I would help him relieve it.

Neither of us says anything for a while as he sips his bourbon.

"You seem stressed," I say after taking a drink of my own.

He chuffs. "You think?"

"Why do you care about your father's statement? Your dad lied. So what? Just tell everyone the truth."

"It's not that easy," he replies, rubbing his forehead.

"Why is it on you, though? It's like...you're carrying the emotions of everyone around you—your wife, your daughter, your mother, your brother, your family, the whole fucking world. But who's taking care of you?" I ask, taking a step forward and leaning against the desk with the glass in my hands.

"I didn't bring you in here so you could lecture me about how I'm doing everything wrong," he snaps.

"Then why did you bring me in here?" I ask, tilting my head.

He quickly averts his eyes, taking another drink. "I don't fucking know."

After a moment, he picks his head up and glares at me with a furrowed brow. "No, I do know. I brought you in here because I want to know what that was earlier. Why did you defend me to my brother?"

"Because I wanted to," I reply plainly.

"And why did you kiss me the other night?"

"Because I wanted to."

His eyes meet mine, blazing with something desperate and wild. "And what else do you want?"

Setting my glass down on the desk, I take another step toward him until my legs are brushing his.

"I think you know what I want."

His nostrils flare as he forces in a shaky breath. "Well, too bad. I'm married, so knock it off."

"That is too bad," I reply in a low murmur.

"Dean, stop it," he says with a plea in his tone. His resolve is fading, and it's not that I want him to do something he doesn't want to. I do care about his wife, so I'm not forcing him to do anything that would hurt her.

It's just that Caleb and I have been teetering on the edge of something for a while, and I'm tired of pretending it doesn't exist. We have chemistry, but he just likes to pretend that that chemistry is hate. At first, I guess I thought it was hate, too. I haven't forgiven him for what happened with Isaac, but as I get to know him more, there's a pull between us that has me forgetting about all of that.

"Stop what?" I reply.

He glares up at me as he says, "You know damn well what." But as the words leave his mouth, his leg brushes mine again. Then he's leaning into me as if his body is sending a different message than his words.

Leaning down, I rest my hands on the arms of his chair. This brings our faces mere inches apart.

"No, Caleb. I'm afraid I don't know what you want me to stop because you were the one who brought me in here with you. You were the one who stuffed my underwear in your pocket."

"I—" he starts, but his words quickly get lost the moment my hands move from the chair to his thighs. Sucking in a gasp, he freezes and waits for me to make the next move.

"I know you're married," I whisper. "And I know you don't want to cheat on your wife, but you're lying to yourself if you say you don't want this."

"My family is right downstairs," he replies, glancing toward the door.

"Then stay quiet." Slowly, I move to my knees between his legs, and I feel him tense.

"What—what are you going to do?"

"I'm going to take care of you for once," I reply.

He stares into my eyes with trepidation as I move my hands to the waistband of his pants. I carefully slip the button through the hole, and my cock throbs in my pants when I think about having his hard length in my hand.

I want to be his reckoning. I want to be the one to make him come undone.

His hands grip the chair as he watches me. "I can't do this," he whispers. "Fuck."

"But you want it, don't you?" I ask.

He lets his head hang back. "God, yes," he replies, his voice strained.

How long has he held up this lie about himself, probably *to* himself? How exhausting that sort of life must be. I wish I could dismantle every single lie he's told himself.

"I'm married, and I know I shouldn't, but fuck, Dean. I need your mouth. I need it so fucking bad."

Hearing him say that is like warm honey dripping down my spine.

"Tell me to suck your cock, then," I whisper.

He doesn't hesitate. "Suck my cock."

"Good boy," I reply with a smirk.

I can see him shiver with anticipation. After easing down his zipper, I tug on the elastic of his boxer briefs, and his aching cock springs out. As I wrap my hand around it, he winces.

"Fuck, fuck, fuck," he murmurs.

"Relax, let me take care of you."

"Okay," he breathes out.

Sitting higher on my knees, I stare up at him as I run the length of my tongue along his shaft. When he feels my lips wrap around the tip, he turns his gaze downward, locking eyes with me as I suck him into the back of my throat.

His mouth falls open, and his eyes roll as I hollow my cheeks and bob my mouth up and down on his cock.

I love every single second of watching him lose his mind. I'm fairly certain I'm the first man to ever have Caleb's dick in their mouth, and I love it. I want to be the last, the *only*. I want Caleb

Goode to treat me like his own personal fuck toy, his dirty secret, his guilty pleasure.

Tightening my hand around the base of his cock, I squeeze as my mouth and hand pump, bringing him closer and closer to the edge.

I realize our time is limited, and someone could walk through that door any minute and find me blowing him under the desk like his naughty secretary. That thought has my own dick leaking at the tip.

As if he can read my mind, he mutters, "Are you hard?"

I pull my mouth from his shaft, keeping up the movement of my hand as I reply, "Hard as a rock."

"Stroke yourself," he commands.

Putting my mouth back around his dick, I flick open the button on my pants and ease my own rigid length out. My hand is moving rapidly, stroking myself as I suck his cock, flicking my tongue under the head as I go.

"I'm going to hell for this," he whispers, running his hand over the short, buzzed hair on my head. "But God, it's worth it."

If I could smile, I would.

"Can I come in your mouth? Will you swallow it for me, baby?"

I nod eagerly.

Fuck yes, please. Give me all of it. Let me feel your pleasure sliding all the way down my throat.

A moment later, the head bulges, and he moans quietly into the crook of his arm as the warmth hits my throat. I let him fill my mouth before I pull my lips from his cock.

Grabbing his arm from around his face, I make him look at me as I show him my open mouth, my cum-covered tongue, and my seed-lined lips.

He lets out a whimper at the sight. Then I close my mouth and swallow, licking my lips and savoring the taste of him as he becomes a part of me. Rolling down my throat like he belongs there.

I've given up on my own cock at the moment. I'm not interested in jacking off under his piece-of-shit dad's chair.

No, tonight is about Caleb.

Releasing my cock, I stuff it back in my pants and rise from the floor.

Caleb is staring straight ahead, focused on nothing as the last ten minutes replay in his mind. I know he's already reeling with guilt. I knew that would happen, as did he. I just hope it was worth it. I hope *I* was worth it.

Twenty-Eight

Caleb

Oh God, what have I done?

Rising from the chair, I quickly zip up my pants and shoot back what's left of the bourbon. When Dean senses my panic, he grabs my arm and pulls me toward him.

"Relax," he whispers.

"Relax?" I bark back quietly. "I made a vow to my wife, and I just broke that vow."

"You don't think Briar will understand? She'll forgive you. Just *talk* to her."

With a scoff, I shake my head. "Sure, I'll tell her about how important it was to come in your mouth at my mother's house while our family was just downstairs. I'm sure she'll understand."

We're chest to chest, his hand still on my arm. And at the very mention of my cum in his mouth, I find myself slipping again. I want to feel that mouth again. I want to explore everything that this means, how good he feels. How much I want him.

Before I know what's happening, I wrap a hand around his neck and jerk him toward me, crashing my lips against his. He opens for me, clutching my jacket as I taste every corner of his mouth, finding traces of what we did on his tongue.

"What are you doing to me?" I mumble under my breath as our lips part.

"I could ask you the same," he replies.

I pull his mouth to mine for one more kiss, keeping it brief and tame. It's a little unsettling how easily I slipped down this adulterous path to sin. And how badly I want to do it again.

Stepping away from Dean, I let my eyes rake over his face and body. Arousal bolts through my bloodstream like lightning at the thought of what he and I could do together.

He seems to notice because he gives me a sly smirk, holding his head up higher. "Are you going to keep eye-fucking me, or are we going to go downstairs and face your family?"

"Fuck," I mutter with an eye roll.

As Dean and I leave the office, I pray we were quiet enough. Judging by the laughter coming from the living room that we couldn't hear on the other side of the house in the office, we're safe.

When we reach the living room, I do my best to look casual and normal, but suddenly, I don't know what normal is. I just let a man blow me in my father's office. How do I pretend everything is normal after that?

"Daddy, can I spend the night? Me and Nana are gonna stay up late and watch a movie." Abby bounces on the couch next to my mother.

"Of course, peanut," I reply with a forced smile.

Across the room, I feel Adam's narrowed eyes on me. I have nothing left to say to my brother, but I hate that he thinks I would ever take our father's side. A brother's bond should be stronger than that.

"Well, we're gonna take off then," I say, pointing to the door.

"I hope Briar is feeling better," my mother says. "Send her my love."

"I will."

"Thank you so much for dinner," Dean adds with a polite grin, waving at my mother and then at everyone else.

When Dean and I get to the car, I take another deep breath, trying to calm myself. The nagging reminder of *I cheated, I cheated, I cheated* plays on repeat in my head.

The closer we get to home, the sicker I feel. How am I going to face Briar now? What do I say?

Dean is silent the entire way there, and I can tell he's feeling some apprehension, too. After I pull the Volvo in the drive, we sit in silence for a few moments.

"I have to tell her," I whisper, my eyes focused on nothing as I stare straight ahead.

"Of course," he replies.

More silence. More tension-filled moments of reliving what we just did.

"Maybe it would be better if I moved out."

My head snaps in his direction. "What? No. You can't move out."

"Come on, Caleb. You have to admit what a mess this is."

"She'll understand," I say, forcing myself to believe it. "We're not going to kick you out on the streets."

He chuckles, scrubbing a hand over his head. "It's sort of funny when you think about it. You thought Briar was going to cheat on you, but you—"

"Don't say it."

Shutting his mouth, he slips out of the car, closing the door behind him. As I watch him walk away, disappearing around the back of the garage, I feel everything truly sink in.

This entire time, I thought he was the home-wrecker, the one who would ruin everything I have here. But it turns out that person is me. I've denied my feelings for him, pulled away from my wife, and avoided standing up to my father. I've even failed at giving Briar the child she wants.

I've ruined my own fucking life.

Dean has known he was bisexual since he was a teenager, or

maybe before that. And here I am, a thirty-three-year-old man still grappling with the truth of my own sexuality.

I'm not ready to say those words yet. I don't fully understand what any of this means for me. But I love my wife. That's all that has ever mattered. Why would I need to come out if I was happily married?

But maybe that's what got me in this mess in the first place. It's like I've suffocated a part of myself, and now it's clawing to get out. There's no excuse for what I've done tonight, but it feels like I understand myself a little more for the first time in my life.

Now, it's time to face the music.

I climb out of the car and walk steadily into the house. I hear the TV on upstairs, so after locking the door and dropping my keys in the bowl, I head up to the second floor to face my wife.

"Hey," she chirps from the bed. She's in a pair of light-pink pajamas with her hair pulled into a bun on her head. "How was dinner?"

Standing in the doorway, I stare at her for a moment. She is so beautiful and perfect and *mine.* How do I possibly deserve her? I don't. Ten years ago, I must have done something right or I've conned her into being my wife for this long. I just know that I love this woman more than anything, and no matter how much I don't deserve her, I refuse to lose her.

I clear my throat, tugging off my jacket as I reply, "It was fine. Abby is staying with my mom tonight."

"She already told me," Briar replies.

I kick off my shoes and unbutton my shirt as I approach the bed. I'm wound tight. At any moment, I could blow. And I just need to hold her before everything explodes.

"Well, hello," she says with a sweet hum as I climb onto the bed, positioning myself between her legs. Wrapping my hands under her knees, I jerk her toward me until she's lying on the bed.

"Caleb," she gasps in surprise.

Ripping off my shirt, I throw it on the floor as I lower myself over her. As my lips meet hers, she hums into the kiss, running her fingers through my hair.

"You should leave Abby at your mother's more often," she says with a giggle as I grind myself between her legs.

Then, because I don't know any other way to approach this, I ask, "Would you let Dean fuck you?"

She stiffens, trying to push my face from her neck. "What?"

"You said he tried to have sex with you that day at the museum. Why didn't you let him?"

"Caleb, what are you talking about?"

Lifting up, I stare down into her eyes. "I want to understand why you stopped him. How did you resist it if you wanted him so bad?"

Looking perplexed, she tilts her head. "Because I'm married to you. I don't want to sleep with anyone else."

"You don't want to sleep with him?" I ask.

She tries to push me away again, but I don't budge. "You're acting weird. What's going on?"

"What if you could? What if I said you could sleep with him?"

"What?" she stammers. "Why would you..."

When I don't respond, staring at her as if I've seen a ghost, her face falls. "What happened? What's the matter?" she asks, sounding desperate as she tries to shove me away again.

"Dean and I..."

"What did you do?" she asks, her voice flat and emotionless.

"He gave me a blow job in my dad's office."

Briar stares at me for so long. Her lips part and she searches my face as if she's waiting for me to explain or tell her it was just a joke or something.

"Say something, Briar," I plead.

"Get off of me," she snaps, shoving me again.

This time, I climb away, allowing her to get up. She throws her feet off the bed and stomps away.

"Briar, talk to me," I call.

"I can't," she barks back.

Jumping from the bed, I follow her out of our bedroom and down the stairs. "It just happened, Briar. I think what we did Friday night got to my head."

She spins on me, pointing a finger in my face. "What happened on Friday was different, Caleb, because we were *together.* Because I was with you. Don't you dare use that as an excuse now."

When she tries to spin away again, I grab her arm. "Please, listen to me."

"I'm too angry to listen," she argues.

"Then yell at me. Tell me why you're angry. Just don't give me the silent treatment."

"You don't get to decide how I react to this, Caleb," she snaps.

I release her arm, and she paces the downstairs floor of our house, fuming and breathing heavily as she lets everything sink in. Then, the moment I was dreading comes.

Briar stops, puts her hands to her face, and starts crying.

"Oh god," I mutter, going to her. "Please don't do that."

My arms engulf her as I pull her to my chest, rubbing her back and wishing I could take it all back. Wishing she never had to feel an ounce of pain.

After a moment, she lets out a frustrated grunt and shoves me away. "I can't, Caleb. I can't...let you touch me right now."

"I never wanted to hurt you, Briar."

Dropping her hands, she stares at me with tear-soaked eyes. "I don't know how I feel right now, Caleb. I don't know if I'm mad that you were intimate with someone else, hurt that you didn't share this part of yourself with me, or if I'm worried that all of this could lead to me losing you."

I take an eager step forward, holding her face in my hands. "*Nothing* could do that, Briar. Nothing."

"Then what does this even mean? Do you have feelings for him, or were you just curious?"

It's like she's just reached into my chest and pulled out something I was trying to hide. My mouth opens, and I try to say the words, but I can't.

“I don’t know, Briar,” I whisper. She blinks, and a tear falls over her cheek.

“I don’t know either.”

With that, she pulls away and leaves me standing alone in the living room. When I hear the bedroom door shut upstairs, I drop onto the sofa and place my face in my hands.

It feels like the pieces of my life have scattered in disarray, and I’m afraid I don’t know what it will look like when we put them back together.

Twenty-Nine

Briar

I don't sleep much. The bed feels so cold without Caleb in it with me. He clearly isn't sleeping much, either. I can hear him moving downstairs all night.

The more time that has gone on through the night, the more my anger turns into sadness.

Am I angry that Caleb cheated because I think I should be angry? Or am I angry he cheated because *I* had the opportunity to be with Dean, and I turned him down?

Or am I sad that my husband and I seem to want the same man, and I'm afraid it's tearing us apart? Or even worse...that my husband has kept his sexuality from me this whole time?

When morning finally arrives, I pretend to be asleep as Caleb gets ready for work. I feel him approach, brushing my hair from my face before leaning in and pressing his lips to my head.

It guts me, but I'm not ready to talk to him yet. I just need to figure out how I feel first.

After he leaves, I finally climb out of bed. It's futile to try and sleep now.

Instead, I shower and replay everything. I can't deny that when I take away everything else in this situation, the thought of Dean and Caleb together is more alluring than I expected it to be. I think the truth is, I'm not mad about it—just curious.

What were they like? Rough or romantic? Did Caleb tell him to do it, or did Dean gently force it on him in his own special, charming Dean way?

Did Caleb like it? Does he want more?

How long has he had these feelings and never told me?

By the time I get out of the shower, I realize that the only thing I'm truly angry about is the fact that I wasn't included in any of this. I'm mad at *both* of them. What if they have feelings for each other and Caleb leaves me for him? What if our marriage is a lie?

I'm full of questions, and there's only one person home right now who can give me answers.

After getting dressed and drying my hair, I march across the yard to the garage, climbing the stairs in silent frustration. I bang twice on the door.

"Dean, open up."

I hear movement inside, followed by footsteps before the door opens. He looks tired and weary as he holds the doorframe and waits for me to talk. As he stands before me, I curse internally at how goddamn handsome he is, and the anger bubbles to the top again.

Shoving him inside, I slam the door shut behind me. Pointing a finger in his direction, I sneer. "How dare you?"

"Oh, so he told you," he replies dryly with sarcasm.

"Don't be coy with me," I snap.

Then, without thinking, I let my hand fly as I slap him hard against the side of his face. His head turns, and he freezes as the sound echoes through his apartment. My hand stings, but it's a good pain. It's exhilarating, a welcome relief from everything I've built up for so long.

"First, you try to seduce me," I shout. "Then you seduce him!"

My hand flies, and I slap him again. With a wicked smirk, he licks his lips.

"Careful. You should know how much that turns me on."

Ignoring how sexy that sounds and the way my blood is starting to boil under the surface, I continue, "It's not funny! What are you doing, Dean? Why are you doing this to us? Caleb was vulnerable last night; this is the last thing he needs right now. Not to mention the way this hurts *me.*"

When I move to strike him once more, hoping to get a rise out of him or, I don't know, to turn him on some more, he snatches my wrist. Taking a step toward me with my arm in his hand, he backs me up to the kitchen counter.

"You think *I'm* doing this?" he exclaims. "That *I'm* the one to blame?"

"This is what you want, right? To get between us. To drive us apart because you have some resentment toward my husband. Isn't that right?"

When I try to yank my arm from his grip, he only tightens his hold and leans into me. "Sure, at the *beginning,*" he argues, bringing his face close to mine. "But it's *you two* who have been getting in my head ever since. You think this is just sex to me, Briar? You think I got a moment of sleep last night after what happened with Caleb? Fuck no!"

His voice is loud now, and I can see the rattled demeanor in his tired eyes. He's erratic and desperate as he moves my held wrist behind my back, gathering the other along with it so that I'm fully pinned.

Part of me starts to tremble, but I trust Dean. I know he won't hurt me. The adrenaline and fear are laced with arousal to the point where I feel like I'm crawling out of my skin.

Bringing his nose to my cheek, he continues, "I couldn't stop thinking about you last night. About how much you'd hate me for what happened. I worried I'd lost you for good. You seriously think I'm trying to drive you two apart? I know that at the end of all of this, you two will stay together. I see how much you love each other. Only one person will get left behind, and we all know that person is me."

"No," I whisper, gazing into his eyes.

"What am I to you?" he whispers. "Just someone to help you fix your marriage."

"You know that's not true," I argue, struggling against his hold. "I see the way he looks at you. And the way I feel about you, you're so much more than that."

With his free hand, he grabs me by the throat, holding me gently as he brings our faces together. "Then what did you expect me to do, Briar? Wait until you both need me again? Sit on the sidelines while I watch you get the man I want...or watch him get the woman I want?"

My eyes widen, and it becomes impossible to breathe. Is this really how he feels?

Staring back at him, everything becomes so clear. Dean has latched on to us this past month. He's filled the spaces in our lives that I didn't even realize were there, and as my heart has started to grow tender for him, I've brushed it off and avoided facing the truth —that I'm falling in love with him.

"I'm sorry that Caleb cheated on you, and I hate that something I did brought you pain," he murmurs against my lips. "But that's how I felt the day you turned me down."

"It was never because I didn't want you, Dean. I wanted you so bad," I reply softly.

"Do you still want me?" he mumbles against my lips.

"I'll always want you," I say on a gasp as his mouth crashes against mine.

Tightening his grasp on my wrists, he holds me in place while his mouth devours mine. Our tongues tangle in a desperate dance as I bite his bottom lip, and he lets out a yelp.

This kiss is the breaking of the dam. It's the fire on the fuse. It's the tidal wave that drags us from the shore.

We're lost to the current, both of us letting out so much frustration and helplessness. The want and desire that we've built up is finally overflowing, and we let it carry us away.

Dean's mouth is ravenous, soft friction against my own. As his kisses move their way across my jaw, I know there is no stopping us now. I'm too far under. I need him. I need his comfort, his touch, his body.

"Dean," I gasp as his mouth nibbles on my neck and warmth floods between my legs.

"What?" he mumbles against my clavicle.

"I need you," I cry out, trying to spread my legs. My hands are still pinned against my back, and he has me practically bent over backward against the counter, the edge bruising my spine as he grinds into me.

Dean pulls his mouth from my flesh and releases my wrists. Taking my face in his hands, he stares down at me with desperation.

"That was a hard line, remember? I can't fuck you, Briar."

"I don't care about lines or rules or anything anymore. Haven't we done enough to blur those by now? When it comes to you, there clearly are no limits for Caleb and me."

His mouth crashes against mine again, nipping at my bottom lip as he whimpers into my mouth. Then, without warning, he pulls his mouth away and hoists me over his shoulder, carrying me across the small apartment to the bed against the wall. Tossing me on the mattress, he doesn't waste a second before climbing over me and positioning himself between my legs.

"Do you have a condom?" I ask, feeling a tremble in my bones. I haven't needed to use a condom in over ten years. It feels reckless and strange to ask for one now.

"Yes, of course," he replies, kissing my neck again.

He presses his forehead to mine as he notices me reeling with thoughts and indecision. "Are you sure you want to do this? We can stop."

"More than anything."

The more he touches me, the more I'm swept away by this lust. Tearing his shirt from over his head, I run my hands over his chest. This feels wrong, but the more wrong it feels, the more I want it.

It's inappropriate to want another man. But knowing how Caleb felt last night makes me feel closer to him. He wanted this, too. He felt the same temptation to sin that I'm feeling now, and we're taking this leap together. All three of us.

In a frenzy of desire, Dean works off my top, and I unclasp my bra. As he works off his pants awkwardly, I slip mine off as well, pulling off my underwear, too. Then, I'm naked. And so is he. And suddenly, it feels so real. I can't stop shaking with anticipation.

On his knees between my legs, he stares down at me as if he's in awe. "You're so fucking beautiful," he says, running his fingers along my belly and down my thigh. Over the stretch marks and patches of cellulite. Every inch of my body that I criticize, he relishes in, touching me as if I'm something special.

I keep waiting for the voice in my head to tell me to stop, but it never does. There's no voice. No presence of God or an angel on my shoulder or fear of hell. There is just me and this man and a million complicated emotions that require so much more than the black and white of right and wrong to determine whether or not we should be doing this.

Reaching down, I stroke his cock, watching his mouth go slack as I bring him pleasure. I've already had Dean in my mouth. It feels like he and I have already done so much together, but sex feels monumental. Touching him like this while we're alone might as well be the craziest thing I've ever done.

He runs his fingers through my folds, and I moan with pleasure at the sensation. Those are not Caleb's fingers.

"Fuck, you're so wet," he mutters, leaning down to press his lips to mine. "You're ready for me."

"I'm ready," I cry, wrapping my legs around his hips to pull him into me.

"Wait, wait, wait," he stutters, pulling away. "I need a condom."

And as much as I hate to wait another moment for this, he's right. I can't let another man come inside me when we're trying so hard to conceive. This situation doesn't need to be messier than it already is.

He dives for the nightstand, and I watch with impatience as he slides a condom over his fat cock. In the space of a few moments, as he gets himself ready, I feel the passion dissipate, and the anxiety creeps in.

Is this wrong of me? Even if I know I'm not doing this as revenge against Caleb, it feels that way at the moment. Is that how I want my first time with Dean to be? Nothing more than a revenge fuck. It's so much more than that.

Once he has the condom secure, I feel the warm, thick tip of his cock at my entrance. The tip slides in, and I panic.

"Wait!" I shout, grabbing his hips and holding him there.

His eyes widen as he stares down at me with concern. When he tries to pull away, I stop him. With just the tip of his cock inside me, I freeze so neither of us can move.

"This isn't revenge, you know?" I say, staring into his eyes. "I want you to know that."

His brows furrow as he gazes down at me. "Then what is it?"

Tears spring to my eyes as I reach for him, interlocking our fingers as I bite my bottom lip. "Dean, I care about you. I want this with you, and it has nothing to do with what happened last night."

Slowly, a smile stretches across his face.

"I'm...falling for you," I add.

"I've already fallen for you, Briar. From that first night you came into my apartment, I've been crazy about you."

Without pressing his cock farther into me, he leans over and kisses me. I want to hold his face here and live in this moment forever.

"Record it," I say. "I want to see it."

He smiles wickedly against my lips. "You want to send this dirty video to your husband and show him what a bad wife you've been?"

The idea sends a thrill through me, and he's right. I do. I want Caleb to see this side of me.

"Yes," I whisper against Dean's lips.

After pulling away from our kiss, he reaches for his phone on the bed from where it fell out of his pocket. Still pressing just the tip of his cock inside me, he aims the phone down at the spot and hits record.

I love the look on his face as he stares at the screen. "You ready?" he mumbles sexily.

"Yes, please," I reply with a rasp in my voice. "Fuck me."

Grabbing my thigh with his free hand, he stares down at his cock as he yanks me toward him, impaling me on his length. I let out a cry as he fills me.

Canting his hips back and forth slowly, he moves in and out, and I can't take my eyes off his face. His expression is tight with ecstasy.

"Fuck. You're tight." He groans as he leans over and presses his lips to my mouth. The phone is still aimed at us, but he quickly props it against the nightstand as he gives me his attention.

He thrusts in deeper, and I love how he feels so different from Caleb. His body is different. Even his dick is different. The way he moves, the way he kisses, and the sounds he makes. It's all so unique to him, and I soak up every single bit of it.

Pressing my thigh up, he looks down as he fucks me, reaching a spot inside me that has my toes curling. He pounds harder, and I lose the ability to breathe.

"God, I don't want to ever stop fucking you."

"Then don't," I reply breathlessly.

His mouth latches on to my neck again, sucking hard. I know he's doing it to leave a mark, and I don't stop him. I want him to mark me, make me his, make this moment last forever.

"Harder," I groan, running my fingers over his buzzed head. "Fuck me harder, Dean. I need it."

My body is on fire. It's as if he's fucking out everything I've been keeping in—the regret, the disappointment, the trying, the losing, all of it. I want him to make it hurt. I want him to take me apart and put me back together again.

With a roar, he pulls out in a rush. Then, without warning,

Dean flips me over until I'm on all fours. Then he thrusts back inside me. I let out a scream as he hits a spot that burns so good.

I need to come. I need to feel this release. I need it more than I need to breathe.

When he spanks me hard against my ass, I let out a gasp of surprise. "That's for slapping me," he says between grunts. The second slap hurts just as much but makes my body crave the pain. It only intensifies the pleasure.

Looking back at him, I notice him staring down at my ass. Then I watch with parted lips as he spits, warm saliva landing in the crack.

When I feel his thumb caressing the tight ring of muscle, I let out a filthy-sounding cry of pleasure. Gently, he presses his finger inside me, and I begin to tremble.

"Has Caleb ever been in here?" he asks seductively.

I shake my head as I stare back at him. He smiles at my response.

"Good," he replies. "I'm taking this, then."

He pulses his finger in my ass as he fucks me, and I lose control. My body tightens and then explodes with pleasure. Burying my face in the mattress, I come so hard it brings tears to my eyes. I've never felt anything like this.

"Oh fuck. I can feel you coming. Milk my cock, angel."

I let out another howling groan as the sensation courses through me again and again.

When he begins to grunt and moan behind me, I know he's coming too. A few more violent thrusts and I feel him shudder against me.

As we pause in this position for a moment, each of us catching our breath, I wait for the regret to sink in, but it doesn't. In fact, I feel better than I've felt in a long time.

It's not about cheating or Caleb or our sins. It's about giving space to this part of me that has been begging for a voice for as long as I can remember. It's about connecting with a person who instills the confidence in me that I need.

After he pulls out and disposes of the condom, Dean and I

collapse on the mattress together. I lie on his chest as he reaches for the phone on the nightstand.

While I'm lying in his arms, he replays the video for me. I'll be honest. It's hard to watch. To see myself so sexual like that, it's like I'm looking at someone else. But that is me. And I like what I see.

Dean sends the video to my phone. "If you want to send it to him, I'll leave that up to you. But for what it's worth, I bet he would like to see it."

Nuzzling closer to him, I let out a deep breath and allow my eyes to close. Before long, we're both asleep.

Thirty

Caleb

"Okay, how about this?" Jules asks, reading from the notepad in her lap. "The statement made by my father, Truett Goode, this past Saturday was made in error. While I have spoken to my father recently, neither I nor my legal team have made any commitment to defend or represent the defendant in a court of law. The charges brought against him are charges I take very seriously as the victim of this offense is also a member of my family, and therefore, I cannot, in good conscience, act as the legal representation for anyone involved in the proceedings."

Jules looks up from the notepad and gives me an uneasy expression. Something about the statement doesn't sit right with me. Letting out a sigh, I rub my brow.

"I sound too complacent."

"You have to be passive," she replies.

"Do I?" I ask.

"Caleb," she says in her stern, motherly tone. "You have a legal firm and a reputation to protect. You are simply withdrawing your name from the conversation to protect yourself. That is reasonable. You don't need to be heroic."

I know she's right, but I don't feel any better about it. "I don't even know what the heroic thing would be in this situation."

"Nothing," she states flatly. "The heroic thing to do is to let the justice system do their thing and hope he goes to prison for a long time."

There's a tension headache forming in my frontal lobe as I rub my forehead again. "I know," I reply.

I can still see the furious expression on Adam's face last night. Last year, when he and our father had their big fallout, my brother made a huge spectacle of himself publicly rebelling and speaking out against our father. It was a mess. But my brother does not have a wife, a child, and a business to protect. He wanted to ruin his own life, and in some ways, that's exactly what he did.

But I am not my brother.

"Type it up," I say to Jules, waving her off. "I don't care anymore. Just run it. Call one of our contacts at the paper and give him our statement."

"You got it," she replies enthusiastically, jumping up from her seat.

When Jules leaves my office, shutting the door behind her, I recline in my office chair and stare at the ceiling. Ironically enough, this situation with my father is only the *second* most stress-inducing matter at this moment in time.

My homelife is also in shambles. Briar is so mad at me, and rightfully so. I lied to her, cheated on her, betrayed her, neglected her, and hurt her—all things I made a solemn vow never to do. My job is simple, protect her, love her, be truthful with her, and be loyal to her. And yet, I failed at every single one.

And for what? Because I found another person who seems to stare right into my soul as if he understands everything that I feel. Even when he hates me and even when I feel as if I hate him, we are still connected. I still want him in a way I've never wanted anyone except for Briar.

Half the workday has gone by, and I haven't heard a word from either of them. I don't know if they've spoken, or if she's approached him, or if he confessed. For all I know, they could be fucking or fighting or talking about me. I'm in the dark, and I hate it.

Last night, Dean suggested that he move out, and I have to come to terms with how much that idea gutted me. I couldn't stand the thought of it.

If Dean left today, could Briar and I return to what we had before? Would we be better off? How did we manage to fuck everything up in such a short amount of time?

My phone buzzes on my desk, and I flip it over to find a message from Briar. It's a long text.

I've had a lot of time to think today, and I know you've probably been ruminating on this as well. I know that the guilt is eating away at you, and I know you have regrets about what happened.

So before you come home, I just want to write out everything in this message.

First, you should know that I forgive you for what happened.

We can talk more when you get home, but what we talk about will greatly depend on how you react to this video. I want you to know that this is not a form of revenge. I didn't do this to spite you.

I think we both know that we are broken individually, and we've found someone who makes us feel whole again. I don't think that means that our marriage is broken. If anything, I think it means our marriage is strong enough to endure what we are putting it through at this phase of our lives. Not a lot of couples could handle this, but you and I have been through worse, and I believe we will get through this.

With that said, I am still angry at you. I'm angry that there was an entire side of yourself I never got to see. That I never got to love. I'm angry that you experienced something so profound without me, and in turn, I experienced something profound without you.

Dean said you would enjoy watching this video, and I hope you do. If watching this only makes you feel jealous and bitter, then we have more work to do than I first thought. Something tells me that's not how you're going to feel.

I love you.

I'm staring, perplexed, at my phone as I read her message. None of it seems to make any sense until the video comes through and there, on a thumbnail image in the text message of my phone, is a picture of my wife naked on someone else's bed.

I hit play, and the video pans down to show Briar with her legs spread and the tip of Dean's cock pressed inside her.

Immediately my face flushes red hot as I hit the pause button. My chest starts to move in a deep, erratic, heaving motion as reality settles in.

She fucked Dean.

She fucked him, and they recorded it, and they sent me the recording. That's what I'm about to watch. Quickly, I go back to her text message and read it again.

. . .

...what we talk about will greatly depend on how you react to this video.

If watching this only makes you feel jealous and bitter, then we have more work to do than I first thought.

Jealous and bitter. How am I not supposed to feel jealous and bitter about this?

Is this because of what I said last night? How I asked if she would fuck him if I let her? So, she actually did it?

I set my phone face down and take a moment to collect my thoughts. I have to force myself to take slow, deep breaths so I don't lose it.

Is this how she felt when I told her what I had done with Dean? Even so, it's not like I sent her a *fucking video* of it.

Still feeling worked up, I pick up my phone again. I turn down the volume so my secretary can't hear it outside my office and hit play, this time letting the picture fill the screen.

"I'm ready," Briar purrs through the video. Just the sight of his cock teasing her entrance has me feeling hot and strange. With one quick jerk, he fills her, and my cock twitches in my pants. A grunt escapes my chest at the sight. He starts moving slowly at first. His thrusts are powerful but erratic.

I can't stop watching the movement of his hips. The way she reacts and the expression on her face. The longer I watch, the more enthralled I become. Until it feels like I'm in the room with them. Like they're doing this for *me*.

Dean quickly switches positions, propping the camera up on something to show their whole bodies as he fucks her harder. I can't deny the heat building inside me. I have to press pause to catch my breath, setting my phone down to adjust myself in my pants.

That's my wife, *my* Briar. And he's touching her, taking her, claiming her, pleasing her.

And I'm fucking furious about it. But at the same time... My God, it's so hot. I rub my own cock through the fabric, groaning quietly from the sensation.

Then I can't stop myself. I quickly unzip, undo the buckle, pull down my boxer briefs, and wrap my hand around the rigid length of my dick.

Pressing play on the video again, I watch as Dean flips my wife into a doggy-style position and slams into her. I'm stroking fiercely now, holding back the grunts and groans that want to come out because of the spectacle of such a depraved act. The two of them are both so exquisitely beautiful and sexy and *mine*.

They are *mine*.

That's the thought in my head that moves my hand. That brings me pleasure. That makes me so close to coming I can taste it. Without even thinking, I tear open my office drawer, finding the black satin briefs I stashed there.

Dean presses his finger into my wife's tight asshole as I drape his underwear across my face, stroking my cock and inhaling the scent of him.

And when she comes, I come.

I am depraved. I am lost to the passion of a video that should have me fuming instead of jacking off in my office like a pervert. I don't know if I should feel ashamed or relieved, but this moment unlocks something carnal and filthy inside me. It turns off the part of my brain that overthinks and overanalyzes, that worries and stresses—and turns on the part that *wants, craves, desires.*

When did I start behaving like the kind of man who lets fear control his life? *I* got my wife. *I* fought for her. *I* won her. I get what I want.

And now, I know exactly what I want. Consequences or judgment be damned. I don't care anymore. I don't care who my father is or what kind of man I'm *supposed* to be.

They put the ball in my court when they sent me that video, and I know exactly what I'm going to do now.

Thirty-One

Caleb

21 years old

"Big game this weekend," my father says, glancing sideways at me as he brings his fork to his lips.

I'm too distracted by my brother and his quote, unquote best friend sitting across from me and what looks like their hands linked under the table.

What the fuck are they doing? Dad is right there. Don't they know what he'll do if he finds them doing shit like that? He'll ruin Dean, and it wouldn't be hard. A few calls to CPS, and I'm sure he could have Dean dragged out of his father's house and put in foster care for neglect or some shit.

And Isaac?

My throat begins to sting as I imagine how that would play out. He's just a kid. Barely fifteen. There are camps out there that our father would gladly ship him off to if he thought it would fix this "problem."

I can't let that happen.

Tearing my eyes away from them, I turn toward my father.

"Yeah, big game," I reply with forced enthusiasm. Maybe I can distract him from the boys. "But I think we've got this one in the bag. TCU is three for eight on the road, and their defense just lost its biggest player."

My father nods, chewing his food as he glances proudly at me. It's easy to please him by acting interested in the things he's interested in—a skill I've watched my brother, Adam, perfect over the past twenty-one years.

"You keep your head in the game now," he adds. "You've been distracted lately."

My brows furrow. What is he talking about? My game is better than it's ever been, and my grades are nearly perfect.

"Don't think we haven't noticed your little friend who likes to make late-night visits." There's a playful smirk on his face as he takes another bite as if I've been caught, but I'm not entirely in trouble.

But why? Sure, I'm a grown man now, but I'm still living in their house. If Luke or Isaac pulled some shit like this, they'd be hounded.

"'Bout time," he adds, knocking my shoulder. "Your mother and I were starting to worry."

"Huh?"

"Truett..." my mother scolds delicately from the other side of the table.

"You were worried because I wasn't sneaking women into my room?"

This catches Isaac's attention, and he looks away from Dean to stare awkwardly at me. I force myself to swallow as the conversation grows more tense. Even if my parents think this is funny, I don't.

"No, baby," my mother says sweetly, and for the first time in my life, my molars clench at that pet name. I'm tired of feeling like her baby. I'm not even the youngest, but she treats me like I am. "Truett, let's just drop it."

"What?" my dad replies with a laugh. "I'm not hurting his feelings. I'm just glad he's interested in girls after all."

What the hell is that supposed to mean?

Keeping my mouth shut, I swallow down all the things I want to say, like how they should be glad I'm focused on things like school and football and not on girls and dating.

And how I had plenty of sex in high school. Just because I didn't have serious girlfriends doesn't make me some sort of freak.

"Regardless," my mother says, giving my father a stern glare, "I trust you are being a perfect gentleman." She turns that glare on me. "That you haven't been sinning under our roof."

She's keeping her language concise and innocent because of my younger brother and his friend at the table. If only she knew what they *have been up to.*

"No, ma'am," I reply with my head down.

My father snickers to my left because he knows the truth. No twenty-one-year-old man brings a girl into his room after hours for anything less than sinning, but it seems that he's relieved that I'm even having sex, never mind that it's before marriage.

"I sure hope not," she replies with a tight-lipped expression as she lifts her glass of sweet tea to her lips. "Why don't you invite her to dinner like a proper gentleman would?"

A proper gentleman. At this point, I should inform my mother that I'm not a gentleman at all. That my friend *has a boyfriend and that premarital sex is the least of our worries.*

"Yes, ma'am," I reply.

Glancing across the table, my gaze meets Isaac's, and I notice he seems more tense than before. As if seeing me get in no trouble at all for having sex in my room with a woman knocked some sense into him.

He won't be so lucky, and he knows it.

I try to convey that through my eyes, and when Dean's arm touches his as if he's trying to hold his hand under the table again, Isaac quickly pushes him away.

Present Day

. . .

Naturally, I leave work early.

Jules ran the statement to the press, but honestly, I don't give a shit about that right now. I just watched my wife have sex with another man, and I jacked off to it. Needless to say, I have bigger fish to fry than whatever bullshit my father has to say.

Jumping out of the car, I march up to my house. Slamming the back door, I climb the stairs to our bedroom. I need to lay my eyes on my wife. I just need to see her. And as I turn the corner into our bedroom, I pause in the doorway.

She's standing in the middle of the room, arms crossed, as if she is waiting for me. She's not wearing makeup, looking freshly showered, and just as beautiful as ever.

She looks bold and ready for a fight—I love it.

I wasn't entirely sure how I was going to go about this, but seeing her awakens my senses. I don't think—I just act.

Rushing across the room, I grab her face and pull her toward me for a bruising kiss. For a moment, she tries to push me away, but I don't let her. I kiss her harshly on the mouth, down her jawline, and to her neck.

She gasps and whimpers from the roughness of my mouth. This need is like nothing I've ever felt before. I'm desperate and dying for her.

"Caleb," she calls as I begin tearing off her clothes. I hear her shirt tear as I rip it over her head. Then, as if she's fallen into the same coursing river of desire I'm in, she starts pulling at my belt and the button of my pants.

Backing her up to the wall, I shove her against it as I suck and nibble on her neck some more, craving that purring sound of her pleasure. Moving lower, I sink my teeth into the soft flesh of her breasts, and she squeals for me.

Then I grab the waist of her pants and shove them down. She quickly kicks them off just before I hoist her off the floor and pin her against the wall.

Fumbling for my cock, I find her wet cunt and thrust myself inside her.

She cries out from the rough entrance, but it only urges me on. "You are *my* fucking wife," I growl, my face pressed against hers.

When she tries to shove me away, I only thrust harder. She moans in pleasure, her back arching.

"And you're *my* husband," she replies, an expression of vitriol on her face.

Still, she struggles to gain control, but I keep up my thrusts, fucking her into the wall. With my hands under her legs to hold her up, her hands are free, and she uses it as an opportunity to slap me.

It only makes me smile.

We are grunting and moaning; our anger is mixed with arousal, and it's almost too much to bear.

"Did you like letting him fuck you?" I groan angrily.

"Yes," she replies with a sneer. "Did you like letting him suck you off?"

"Yes, I did," I say before kissing her again.

While our mouths are fused, I come with a rasping moan, filling her as she tenses against me. She trembles and cries into my mouth.

By the time we're both done, I feel her heart hammering against mine as I slump against her. We're both panting and still fired up. I don't know if I'm angry or jealous or upset, but I know I needed that. Maybe she did, too.

Suddenly, someone at the door clears their throat.

Briar and I turn in a rush to see Dean leaning in the doorway.

"That was hot," he says with a smirk, and my eyes narrow angrily at him.

I pull out of Briar and drop her legs. She shoves me away and grabs her clothes off the floor. With a huff, she marches into the bathroom to get herself cleaned up.

Then he and I are alone in my bedroom, and one of us definitely needs to speak first. Where do we even start?

What the fuck do we say?

That things have gone too far? Or that they haven't gone far enough?

My head thinks the former, while my heart sides with the latter.

Silent, tense moments pass as we stare at each other.

When Briar comes out a moment later and finds Dean and I standing in silence, she rolls her eyes.

"Say something!" Briar barks at me, slamming her hands on her hips.

"I don't know what to say," I argue.

"Say what you want, Caleb. Say exactly what's on your mind. You're furious, right? You got that video, and you're so disgusted and angry with me that you want a divorce. Is that it?"

I flinch as if she's just slapped me. "A divorce? What the fuck are you talking about?"

"I don't know," she says with a shrug. "I don't know what to expect."

I know this is on me. I have to be the one to say what I'm thinking, and how I react to this is going to determine everything. Just like always, I set the tone.

So, closing my eyes, I take a deep breath and let everything out.

"I'm not furious. I'm not even fucking mad. I probably *should* be, but I'm not. You fucked another man, Briar. And it was the hottest fucking thing I've ever seen. And *you,*" I bark, turning toward Dean.

He takes a step closer, his expression so empty it makes me pause. It reminds me so much of Isaac that it hurts. It's the brave look he gave our father that night, pretending that the daggers of his hatred didn't nearly kill him.

Words fail me. Fuck, everything fails me at the moment. I don't know what to think or say. I just know how I *feel,* and I don't know how to express it.

But I don't want these two to be afraid of me or my reaction. I want them to know how badly I want them—both of them.

Reaching out, I grab Dean by the back of the neck and bring his forehead to mine. Emotion bubbles to the surface, and for once, I don't fight against it. He folds easily into my arms, melting into my touch as if he's grateful for it.

I'm so staggered by how good it feels to touch him, even just in a passionless embrace. It's liberating and invigorating, and I never want it to end. He breathes heavily through his nostrils as if he feels it, too.

Reaching the other arm toward Briar, I tug her into the fold. Just like he did, she slips comfortably into it.

I don't understand it. Hell, none of us do, but standing here like this feels right. It's as if something new is formed, this essence of *us*. I felt it that night in his apartment when the three of us were together, but I brushed it off as being a sexual attraction. But it's so much more.

This thing is magnetic, and the pull is too strong to fight against anymore.

My wife presses her face between our chests as her arms wrap around us like the glue holding us all together.

"I don't understand any of this," I whisper.

"Neither do I," she replies softly.

"I do," Dean adds. Briar and I look up at him simultaneously, but just as he opens his mouth to reply, the doorbell rings. We quickly leap apart as if we've just been caught.

"That's your mother," Briar says, looking erratic. "She's dropping off Abby."

"Fuck," I groan because we definitely need to talk about this, but we can't exactly do that with our six-year-old around.

"We'll just pick this up later then," Dean stammers, rubbing the back of his neck. "I have to...go to work anyway."

I let out a low growl at that statement, and Dean gives me a disgruntled expression.

"This feels like a strange place to leave things, but it's fine," Briar says. "We'll just...talk tomorrow."

"Fine," I mutter under my breath.

She rushes down the stairs to answer the door, leaving Dean and I alone. The air is still thick with tension that he quickly erases the moment he opens his mouth.

"You jacked off to it, didn't you?" he asks with a crooked smirk.

Fighting a smile, I shove him out of the room with a roll of my eyes. "Go."

"I'll take that as a yes."

I can't hold in my laugh as I follow him down the stairs.

My mother is already in the foyer with Briar as Dean and I walk down, and I notice the way my mom's eyes watch us.

"Hello again," she says politely to Dean.

"Hi, ma'am," he replies.

"It's nice to see you settled in so comfortably here," she says.

Briar makes a noise, averting her eyes as Dean replies, "Absolutely. They are fantastic hosts."

"Yes, they are," she says, glancing my way.

Abby breaks in to show me the drawings she made at my mother's last night, and I give her as much enthusiasm as I can muster. Then she launches herself into Dean's arms without warning, and he lets out a groan as he picks her up.

When she wraps her arms around his neck, I glance at Briar, and our eyes meet.

I don't know if she's thinking the same thing as me, but I often wonder if anyone overthinks as much as I do. Like how much Abby adores him, but also...how careful we have to be.

We're not just playing with our relationship here. Our entire family is involved, and our feelings for Dean affect everyone. We can't just bring a new man into our marriage and pretend every single person is going to accept that.

It might be in our best interest to set these feelings aside—as much as I hate that idea.

Abby kisses Dean's cheek with a giggle before he sets her back down. "Gross," he says to her, only making her laugh more.

Then she takes off in a sprint toward her bedroom.

"Thanks for bringing her back," Briar says to my mom.

"You're welcome," she replies before looking at Dean as if she knows something we don't. "Abby likes having you here. I hope you stick around."

Then, without another word, she turns, quickly saying her

goodbyes before leaving. The three of us are left in awkward silence again, with my mother's words hanging around us.

"Tomorrow," Briar says. "We'll talk about this more tomorrow."

"Yeah," Dean mutters.

And with that, the three of us disperse. Briar goes to Abby. Dean goes to his apartment, and I go to my office, trying to make sense of the foreign feeling in my chest.

Sitting in my chair, I pull the satin briefs from my pocket, inspecting the fabric and remembering how they felt draped over my face.

With a smile, I tuck them back into my pocket.

I'm feeling content at the moment—which is odd. Everything in my life is up in the air. My marriage is a mess. My career is on the brink of disaster.

But for the first time in a very long time, I feel pretty fucking good.

Thirty-Two

Briar

We'll talk about it tomorrow.

That was the deal on Monday. But then, tomorrow comes and goes. Dean has been working so late most nights that he sleeps half the day away while I'm busy entertaining Abby during her summer break with trips to the library, the children's museum, and playdates with my sister.

Before I know it, five full days have gone by since the day Dean and I had sex, and every passing moment starts to feel like hands tightening around my throat.

Caleb and I haven't spoken about the incident at all. Our conversations mainly revolve around Abby and his father's case. It feels wrong to talk about this whole thing without Dean, and I think some part of us is afraid to discuss it.

Each night, he crawls into bed next to me, and the truth of it all —he was intimate with a man, *and I slept with someone else*—hangs over us like a cloud.

On top of that, we're smack-dab in the middle of the two-week wait, which means it's almost time to test again. For the first time in a long time, I don't feel the overwhelming weight of that on my shoulders. The situation with Dean has been a welcome distraction from the baby-making endeavors.

Grabbing my calendar to count the days, I notice an event scribbled under today's date—Caleb's mother's charity auction.

"Shit," I mutter under my breath.

Quickly, I text Caleb.

Your mother's charity function is tonight.

He answers back almost immediately.

Dammit. I forgot about that.

Can we skip it?

I think it would mean a lot to her to have us all there together. Can your sister watch Abby?

I'm sure she can.

Neither of us texts for a moment, and I know he's thinking the same thing I am. He's the one who says it first.

We should bring Dean.

I agree.

Will you talk to him?

Yeah.

Abby is playing out back with her dolls in the playhouse. Watching her through the window, I send a quick text to my sister, asking her to babysit tonight, and she immediately replies with a yes. After checking my hair in the reflection on the microwave, I head out back to knock on Dean's door.

"Abby, I'm going to talk to Dean. Stay here, okay?" I say as I pass her in the yard.

"Can I come?" she replies enthusiastically.

"Not this time," I say. "Stay here."

With a pout, she settles back on the grass. Dolls in hand, she quickly distracts herself with whatever she is playing. My knuckles rap against his door, and I take a deep breath, realizing this is the first time I've really faced him since the *incident*.

He opens the door, looking freshly showered in nothing but a pair of tight black jeans. His buzz-cut hair is still wet, droplets cascading down his temples as he uses a towel to wipe them away.

"Hey," he says with a hint of a smile.

"Hey," I reply in a sort of dreamy, flirtatious way.

His eyes dance across the yard as he notices Abby playing outside, a clear sign that we won't be doing anything inappropriate today.

"What's up?" he asks, obviously wondering why I'm here.

"Melanie's charity function is tonight. My sister is watching Abby, and Caleb and I thought..."

His eyes widen as he realizes what I'm asking. "You want *me* to go?"

"Yes. We do." Chewing on my bottom lip, I give him a suggestive smile. I hope it conveys everything we *could* do tonight if he comes, especially since we left things at a standstill a few days ago. I don't think any of us truly wants this fire to die.

His eyes start to twinkle with excitement. "I don't have a suit," he replies with a grimace.

"I'm sure Caleb has one you can wear."

Leaning against the doorframe, he gives me a contemplative expression. "You sure this is a good idea?"

"His mother invited you," I reply. "Why would it be a bad idea?"

"What if I can't keep my hands off you?" he says with a smirk, and my heart starts to pound in my chest. Butterflies assault my belly as I bite harder on my bottom lip. Then he takes a slow step toward me, seductively adding, "*Either* of you."

Putting my hand on his chest, I gently push him back. "You need to behave."

He snickers to himself, clearly in a good mood. Normally, Dean is so broody and clearly thrives on being alone, but since this whole thing started, I've seen a change in him. As if he likes the idea of being with us. It makes me want to draw him in even more. I want to make him part of our family and shower him with all the love and comfort I know he must have been missing in his own life.

"Fine," he murmurs under his breath. As he glances down at Abby again, she waves up at him, and I catch a small smile on his lips that he quickly hides when he notices me watching.

"Come over and try on a few of his suits. And if you're hungry, I'm about to make lunch."

Seemingly touched by the gesture, he nods. "Okay. If you two want me to come, then I will."

Leaving him at the door, I feel his eyes on me as I descend the stairs.

"Abby, it's time for lunch," I say, going into the house. It's cool for July, but I'm practically burning up as I walk into my kitchen.

I'm in the middle of making sandwiches when Dean walks into the house. Abby is getting cleaned up in the bathroom as he leans against the kitchen counter, with a shirt on now—unfortunately. Crossing his arms over his chest, he smiles at me, and I feel my temperature rising again.

"What?" I ask, glancing over my shoulder.

"Nothing," he mutters with a shrug. "Sorry, I've been working so much this week. We haven't had a chance to talk. I've missed it over here."

Chewing on my lip, I try to appear nonchalant. "It's fine," I reply.

I know that it bothers Caleb more than it bothers me that Dean works so much. I could see the disgruntled wince on his face every time I mentioned Dean working late. And I'm not sure if it's *what* Dean does or how much he does it that bothers Caleb, although I have a feeling it's the former.

"Unless...things have changed," he says with hesitancy. Immediately, I spin around and stare at him with wide eyes.

"Nothing has changed," I state brazenly.

His lips quirk in a small smile as Abby comes bounding into the kitchen. "I'm hungry," she says as she clumsily climbs onto the chair.

"You're always hungry," Dean replies.

As I put her plate down in front of her, she playfully sticks her tongue out at Dean, and I don't even have to turn toward him to know he's probably doing the same.

I laugh at both of them as I turn back to the counter to make two more sandwiches. "You haven't been around kids much, have you?" I ask as I spread mayo on the bread.

"Is it that obvious?" he replies.

"You're good with her in your own way." Peeking over my shoulder, our eyes lock again, and I feel something warm trickle down my spine.

I hate how hooked on him my heart is feeling. With every casual conversation and tender moment we share, it's alarming to me how well we fit together. I don't want to get my hopes up. I don't know what we're even doing or what the plan is.

Caleb and I are married to each other. Where on earth does Dean fit into all of this? How long can we keep him in that apartment, keeping him a secret from the world as Caleb and I raise our children together?

As I finish the sandwiches, Dean steps closer, blowing gently on the back of my neck. It's a brief touch of his nearness, and it makes me feel both excited and scared at the same time.

He and I sit down at the table with Abby, and the two of them make awkward conversation as we eat. And I can't stop smiling, feeling as if things are so close to being perfect.

After lunch, Abby sits on the couch to watch a movie while I take Dean upstairs to our closet so he can look through Caleb's suits.

The moment we're alone upstairs, I feel the warm, arousing tension grow. It's a delicious combination of excitement and danger.

As I slide the hangers on the rack, finding one of Caleb's older suits, Dean steps up behind me, bringing his lips to my neck.

I hum with how good his lips feel on my skin. His hard body presses up against my back, sending waves of heat to my core. His hands grab me by the hips, grinding himself against me so I can feel the length of his cock against my ass.

"We can't get carried away," I whisper. The last thing I want to do is stop him, but I have to. If Abby were to come up here, it would be a disaster for many reasons.

"I know," he mumbles against my neck. "But I told you I wouldn't be able to keep my hands off you."

When he finally drags himself away, he does so with a pained sound. "Fine. Let's find a suit."

I laugh as I pull one down from the rack. "Here, try this. It's a few years old."

Taking the black tux from my hand, he checks around the corner for Abby and decides to just try it on in our closet. I stay by the doorway to stand guard. I mean, I'm not going to miss watching him take off his clothes.

Crossing my arms as I lean against the doorway, I replay some of the things Dean said the other day when we were together.

What did you expect me to do, Briar? Sit on the sidelines while I watch you get the man I want...or watch him get the woman I want?

Does he really want us?

"Can I ask you a question?" he asks as he buttons up the black pants.

"Yeah," I reply, straightening my spine.

"Did you know about Caleb?"

Dread swarms in my belly. This feels like such a hard topic to discuss because it means that I have to face the shame I feel. I never knew something so intimate about my own husband. What kind of wife doesn't know that sort of thing?

Solemnly, I shake my head.

Noticing my melancholy expression, he takes a step toward me. "Briar, look at me."

Apprehensively, I turn my gaze up to his face.

"It's not your fault. I mean, maybe *he* didn't even know. It doesn't make you a bad wife, you know?"

Forcing a sad smile, I close the distance and wrap my hands around his middle, nuzzling my face against his chest.

"Thank you for saying that," I mumble.

"It's true."

"I still feel bad," I reply without pulling away. "I'm sure even if he knew, he wouldn't have felt safe coming out. His father wasn't the most supportive parent."

Dean scoffs. "Trust me, I know. I dated his little brother, remember?"

Pulling away quickly, I stare at him with astonishment. "Dated?"

He laughs as he puts some distance between us, reaching for the shirt. "We were fourteen," he says. "It's not like we had sex."

"You don't need to have sex for a relationship to be valid," I argue.

"I know that," he replies. "Isaac was my first taste of love, but we were just kids."

"How did I not know this?" I ask, crossing my arms. "I thought you and Isaac were just friends."

"That's what everyone thought," he replies, buttoning it up.

"Even Caleb?"

That makes Dean pause. "He knew." He won't meet my gaze, and something unsettling burrows its way into my stomach. I want to ask what he meant by that, or if there's more to this story I don't understand, but I decide not to.

Right now, I just want to focus on the beautiful man in front of me and the possibilities this evening could bring.

Thirty-Three

Dean
14 years old

"Hey, kid," my dad says as he stomps his feet on the mat by the door.

"Hey," I mutter in reply, not looking away from the video game on the screen.

"Thought you were staying at your friend's tonight."

I shrug. "Nah."

He pauses on his way to the kitchen as if he's waiting for me to expand on that topic, but I don't.

The truth is that I feel less welcome at Isaac's house now that his brother knows about us. He used to take us places, and for a moment, it felt like Isaac and I had some freedom. We'd go to the movies or the mall or out to eat, but now Caleb watches us like he's waiting to catch us holding hands or kissing.

It bugs the shit out of me, and I'm fucking tired of it.

I thought he was going to be cool about Isaac and me, but clearly, I was wrong. And now it's getting to Isaac's head, too. I'm afraid he's going to break up with me.

Well, fuck that. I'll break up with him first.

My dad cracks open a beer from the fridge and slips off his boots before dropping into the recliner and putting his feet up.

"You two didn't break up, did you?" he asks.

My hands freeze, and blood rushes to my face. Glancing sideways at my dad, I try to remain cool as I reply, "What? Who?"

"You and that boy."

I have to force myself to swallow. "What do you mean break up? He's just my friend."

"Oh," my dad replies casually. "My mistake."

I turn my head toward him with my brows pinched together. I want to tell him I'm not technically gay, but my dad is old, and I don't know if he understands the difference. It feels like too much of a conversation, and I don't know where the fuck to start.

Instead, I just mumble, "We didn't break up."

He nods knowingly. "Good."

What the fuck is happening? Did I just come out? Does my dad even know what bisexual means? Should I tell him?

I'm so confused.

My dad was born and raised in Texas. It's not that I was afraid he was going to kick me out or anything; I just never expected him to be this nonchalant about it.

"Finish your game. The Longhorns are playing tonight." He points toward the TV with the hand holding his beer.

I glance back at my game, unable to focus on it now. "Uh...yeah. Sure."

Quickly saving my progress, I turn off the PlayStation. Instead of going to my room to hide, which is what I normally do, I find myself sitting in the empty recliner next to my dad.

†

Present Day

. . .

I've never worn a tux before. Standing in the mirror of my apartment, I stare at the man in the reflection. This feels reckless. Like I should know better.

Getting so attached to these two is dangerous, but I *know* it's dangerous, and yet, I'm doing it anyway. This isn't like me.

Before leaving my apartment, I take a selfie in the mirror. Then I send it in a text message to my dad. He's not great with his phone, but he loves getting pictures, so I know he'll enjoy this.

The family I'm staying with invited me to a charity thing.

Fancy people shit. I'm going for the free food and booze. How do I look?

Guilt assaults me at the reminder that I haven't gone to see him in over a week. I've been so distracted with everything, and that's fucked up. I went from taking care of him every day to barely seeing him and never talking to him.

The man is dying. What is wrong with me?

I'm halfway out the door when my phone buzzes. Glancing down at the screen, I smile.

Looking sharp, kid. It's nice to see your face.

Fuck. His response has me freezing on the stairs.

God, I'm such an asshole.

I'll come see you tomorrow, okay?

Don't worry about me. Have fun tonight. Send more pictures.

Okay.

I want to tell him that I miss him or that I love him, but as cool and as laid back as my dad is, he's not the greatest with emotions and feelings. We keep things simple.

By the time I reach the house, Abby is already gone. Briar's sister picked her up a couple of hours ago. The house is quiet, so I quickly jog up the stairs and creep around the corner to see Briar sitting at her bathroom vanity, applying her makeup.

The sight of her takes my breath away. Her blondish, brownish hair is down and curled at the ends. Her dress is dark blue and sleek. It's short enough that when she crosses her legs on the small chair, it exposes her soft, pale thighs.

My mouth waters at the thought of burying my face between her legs and feeling those thighs wrapped around my head.

Caleb walks out of the large closet, buttoning his shirt as his eyes collide with mine. Slowly, his gaze rakes down my body as if he's soaking in the sight of me in his clothes.

"Hey," he says, clearing his throat, and I enter the room, showing off the way his tux fits me like a glove.

Briar's eyes lift as she takes in my appearance. "You look so good," she says with enthusiasm.

"It fits perfectly," I reply, turning slowly.

"Yeah," he stammers. "You should keep that. It looks better on you than it did on me."

"I find that hard to believe," I reply with a wink.

He turns his gaze to the mirror, clearly uncomfortable with my flirty nature.

"So, if I come with you guys tonight, then I want to use this time wisely," I say, leaning against the wall.

"What do you mean?" Briar asks while putting on her earrings.

"I mean that I want you two to do as I say."

Her eyebrows lift. Caleb glances my way with a furrowed brow.

"You know my mother will be there, right?"

I let out a laugh. "Then I'll be sure to keep it discreet."

He makes his way toward me, his eyes on my tie. Once we're toe to toe, he undoes the messy job I did (which I had to watch on a YouTube video) and begins to retie it. My eyes are on his face as he does, breathing in the scent of his cologne.

"We asked you to help us spice up our marriage," he says calmly as he tightens the knot around my neck.

"Yes, you did," I reply.

His eyes lift and meet mine. "Then I guess that means we'll do whatever you say."

My heart hammers in my chest as we stare at each other for another moment. Then he steps away and I suddenly feel too hot for this tuxedo.

It takes them about fifteen more minutes to get ready, and soon, we're climbing into Caleb's SUV and on our way to the event. I can't help the nerves that settle in my bones. I don't belong here. I don't belong with a happily married couple, regardless of how comfortable I feel with them.

I'm the infiltrator, the third wheel, the home-wrecker.

I feel like I'm stuck in some gray area. I'm here to help a couple with intimacy issues, but at the same time...I mean something to them. They mean something to me.

Fuck, it could be more than that. I find myself so drawn to Caleb. I want to smother that broody, pensive nature of his just to see his disarming but rare smile.

And Briar—what a surprise she turned out to be. I want to be around her all the time. I want to know everything in her mind and see her kneel for me as if I'm worthy of her.

When we reach the event, I stay close to them. They walk in, hand in hand, while I trail behind. The event is nothing like I expected. Everyone is dressed up, but the energy in the room is more relaxed and fun than I thought it would be.

Immediately, we're greeted by Melanie at the door. She's wearing a silver gown and a bright smile. How this woman maintains such a positive and warm personality through everything, I'll never know.

She gives me a tight hug and seems genuinely happy to see me there, which is nice. Most people are only excited to see me in work settings, and that's never personal. This feels personal.

I really shouldn't get used to this.

After entering the ballroom, we head straight for the bar. Sage and Adam are hovering nearby with Caleb's brother, Lucas.

"Hey!" Sage says with enthusiasm. She moves toward me first as if we're kindred spirits, a couple of outsiders who need to stick together. "I'm so glad you came!" She squeals as she pulls me into a hug.

She's wearing a tight black sequin dress that seems far too sexy and revealing for an event like this. But she owns it, as Sage so often does.

I notice the way Adam reaches for her, even as he's talking to Caleb, as if he can't stand her stepping away from him for only a second. When he turns to greet me, he's not nearly as tense or resentful as I expected after the incident at his mother's house.

"Glad you could make it," he says cheerfully as he puts out a hand for me to shake.

"Thanks for having me," I reply.

He claps me on the shoulder and gives me a tight smile. Adam reminds me of a congressman, but like an edgy one who definitely has a very kinky, sexy side. And it's not even that hidden if you come to the club on the right night.

Sage and Adam get called away, and I stand around awkwardly as Briar and Caleb chat with Lucas. I'm only one drink in and I'm starting to feel antsy. Nothing is really happening. Everyone is standing around chatting and we're there nearly an hour before we make it to our seats and they start serving food.

During dinner, Melanie takes the stage and makes a speech about the charity. She keeps it short and casual, using her quirky humor and pretty smile to keep the crowd light and happy.

Briar is sitting on my left, and halfway through our meal, I feel her hand brush my leg. Swallowing, I glance her way, doing my best not to draw attention. She doesn't do much more than that, although I wouldn't turn down the idea of getting a hand job under the table. Instead, she touches me affectionately as if to say she's glad I'm here. That I matter to her.

It means more than a hand job, if I'm honest.

By the time dinner is over, people are starting to appear and behave a little tipsy. Which is a sight for such a middle-aged, affluent crowd.

"Let's go dance," Briar says, bumping me with her elbow and tossing her napkin down on the table.

"Dance?" I stammer, staring at her as if she's grown a third eye.

"Relax. It's not the waltz." She laughs as she drags me out of my seat and onto the dance floor.

Immediately, I feel like it's middle school again, and I'm expected to shuffle around the middle of the room with my hands on her hips.

Needless to say, I let her lead.

She presses my left hand to her hip and takes my right as she pulls our bodies close together. Then she moves us with the music in a slow motion around the floor.

"This isn't inappropriate?" I ask in a low mumble.

She shrugs. "Not really. I dance with Luke and Adam sometimes. It's just a dance."

I nod, loving the way her short satin dress feels under my fingers. It reminds me how soft her hips are and how good they feel in my hands. My cock twitches in my pants at the memory of her laid out naked in my bed, her legs wrapped around me, ready to give herself to me.

Not to be dramatic, but that was the best sex of my life. And I've had a lot.

The way she stared into my eyes as if I was more than a hot guy with a big dick. I was special to her. She *needed* me.

Deep down, I want her to always need me.

"Besides," she adds with a shrug. "Why not give them something to talk about? Who really cares what they think anyway? So we are all sleeping together. Who cares?"

I can't help but chuckle as I lean in and breathe in the soft, flowery scent of her hair. "Doesn't your religion have something to say about that?"

She scoffs. Then, after a moment of contemplation, she says, "I don't think I really care what my religion has to say anymore."

"What would make you happy?" I whisper, not daring to look into her eyes.

She lets out a soft breath. "I think you know what would make me happy."

Her body is pressed against mine as we spin around the room, and I can barely breathe with how much I want her. I know what would make her happy. It's the same thing that would make me happy.

Feeling free to do what we want. All three of us. Together. No restraints. No judgment. No expectations or labels.

"I wish I could kiss you right now," I mumble into her hair.

"Me too," she replies.

Then my eyes lift and I see Caleb watching us from across the room. He's standing by the bar with his brothers, but instead of talking, he's busy staring at us.

And the look on his face is anything but angry. In fact, he's wearing a proud smirk that lets me know he feels the same way we do.

Thirty-Four

Caleb

There's absolutely no reason for me to enjoy the sight of my wife with another man.

I was raised to believe that a good husband would put an end to this. A good husband would keep his wife to himself. A good husband would not daydream about the lips of another man. And he certainly wouldn't imagine those lips against his wife's.

But I do.

And I'm tired of believing that it makes me a bad husband.

So I don't cut in on their dance. I just watch from the outskirts, marveling at how perfect they are. When the song comes to an end, Dean and Briar make their way over to me.

Just the sight of him in that tux—*my tux*—does something to me. Like sniffing his underwear to make myself come, I feel this intense need to claim him. To own his body. To mark him as mine.

I need to get these thoughts out of my head. What's going to happen when Dean moves out or moves on or finds someone else? We can't keep him forever. He agreed to help Briar and me.

It doesn't matter that it's so much more than that now. We all know that, but honestly, what can we do about it?

By challenging me that day, he made me a stronger man, a better husband, and a better lover. He's brought out this dominant side of me that has lain dormant for so long.

And I can't help but fear that once Briar and I no longer need him as much as we do now, we're going to lose him.

Dread fills my gut as they approach.

I step away from my brothers to talk alone with my wife and Dean. The night is still so young, and as ready as I am to get these two home where I know we'll be alone, I'm not ready for it to end yet.

"So you guys come to these a lot?" Dean asks, casually placing his hands in his pockets. Briar sidles up by my side, and I wrap an arm around her shoulders.

"Sometimes more than we'd like," I reply.

"Do you ever have a little fun?" Dean asks.

Briar huffs with a laugh. "Do I even want to know what kind of fun you're referring to?"

"Oh, you know," he replies with a smirk.

My skin begins to grow hot. The neck of this tux is starting to tighten. I tug at my tie to loosen my collar.

"I'll take that as a no." Dean laughs. "Well, you guys wanted me to teach you a few things, so..."

"So..." Briar says, letting her voice trail.

"One great way of revving up that sex drive is a little exhibitionism," he says so matter-of-factly.

Briar's eyes widen, as does mine. Clearing my throat, I look away.

"My mother is here," I mutter under my breath.

When Dean starts to laugh again, he bites his bottom lip to keep it in. And I can't take my eyes off his mouth. I want to pull it free, lick it, and bite it myself.

"What exactly do you have in mind?" Briar asks with curiosity.

"I'm not saying you two need to fuck right here, but just a little tease will do it." His voice is low and husky.

My cock is already stirring to life behind my pants. There are people around us, but not close enough to hear what Dean is saying. To everyone else, it looks like we're just having a regular conversation.

"You both agreed to do whatever I say tonight, remember?"

Briar squares her shoulders and looks up at him confidently. "Yes, we did," she replies.

"If you want to stop at any moment, you say the word, okay?" Dean asks.

"Okay."

"Okay," I echo.

I'm standing near the perimeter of the room with nothing but some large flowers and plants behind us. Most of the people at the gala are on the dance floor or mingling in small groups. No one is looking at us or paying us any attention, not even my family.

"I want you to brush the back of her thigh," Dean whispers. Licking my lips, I stare into his eyes as I let my arm drift from her shoulder down her lower back. Briar's gown is short with a flowing satin skirt that stops midway between her knees and ass, which makes it all too easy to lift the fabric and tickle her softly on the back of her thigh.

She tenses in response.

"Can you feel him?" Dean asks softly, looking at her. With her lips parted, she nods. "Do you want more?"

Again, she nods.

Then Dean looks at me with a wicked smirk. "I want you to slip your fingers into her panties and find that pretty, sweet pussy and just tease her a little bit," he says, with that cool, authoritative tone he used with us before.

Holy fucking shit. I can't do this. But God, I want to. I want to finger my innocent, angelic wife right here in this gala without anyone knowing. The idea of being inside her in a public space like this feels so dirty and wrong but incredible and sexy at the same time.

"All right, Briar," he says, turning toward her. "Eyes on me."

She lets out a heavy sigh, and I notice the coy smile on her face as my fingers creep up the inside of her leg, finding the moist center of her panties. Dean cocks his head, hiding his smile. Staring at her like a wolf with its prey.

Briar keeps up a casual stance as I move her panties to the side and run my finger along the moist center. She lets out a small yelp when she feels me. "Steady," Dean says, staring at her. I notice the way her eyes dance around the room, looking to see if anybody is watching me defile my wife. My cock hardens at the thought of this perfect, precious woman behaving so indecently. My body thrums with arousal as I run my finger through her folds.

"Tell me how it feels," Dean says.

"Good," she replies with a pleasure-laced sigh.

"Should we stop, or do you want more?" he asks.

"More," she replies without hesitation. Dean looks at me. Then he turns his head back and forth, checking to see if there is anybody near us. To anyone else at the party, it looks as if my hand is just at the small of my wife's back. There's not a single person here who can tell that I have my finger in her panties and that I'm only an inch away from being inside her.

"You heard her," Dean says. "She wants more."

I have to clench my jaw to keep from smiling as I slip my finger inside my wife. She sucks in a breath with a dainty whimper. Immediately, I scan the room to see if anybody heard, but no one reacts.

When I turn my gaze back to Dean, I let my eyes rake down his body quickly, noticing that he, too, is sporting a raging erection.

Fuck, we can't do this here. I have Briar mostly in front of me to hide the evidence of my arousal, but if Dean turns around, nearly everyone will be able to see the state he's in.

At the same time, I fucking love it. Adrenaline pumps through my veins, making my dick even harder. I don't wait for Dean to tell me when I start pumping my finger, feeling Briar's beautiful little cunt tighten around me. She's soaking my hand. I fucking love how wet she gets, unabashedly aroused, my horny little angel.

"Can we please get out of here?" she whimpers.

"Where would you like to go?" Dean asks in a cool, flat tone.

"Anywhere," she replies.

"And what is it you want?" he asks, drawing the words from her lips.

"I want to be fucked," she says under her breath.

I nearly come in my pants, my cock leaking at the tip. I don't know if I've ever been more turned on in my life, and I'm standing here with a group of people in a very crowded public space. I love seeing Briar like this, so passionate and driven by lust. I've missed this side of her.

"Where can we go?" Dean asks, looking expectantly at me.

I've been to this venue enough to know there's a private bathroom upstairs. It's intended as a dressing room. But tonight, it should be empty.

Briar lets out a small yip as I pull my hand from between her legs. Still wet with her arousal, my fingers intertwine with hers as I drag her from the room. It's damn near impossible to remain casual at this point. And it's very unlikely that nobody will notice the way the three of us dash out of the room as if there's a fire.

Once out of the ballroom, we race up the carpeted stairs to the second floor. It's quiet up here, and although the lights are on, I don't see anyone around. At the end of the hall is the small dressing room, and by some miracle, it's unlocked.

First, I peek my head in to be sure we're truly alone, and then the three of us rush into the room, slamming and locking the door behind us. There is not an ounce of composure left. We are frantic and needy and consumed by desire.

I turn from the door to find Dean is already passionately kissing Briar. She has her arms wound around his neck, and it doesn't even cross my mind to be jealous. I don't care that she's kissing another man. In fact, I fucking love it.

Without a hint of reservation, I come up behind her, squeezing her between us as I latch my mouth on her neck, lifting her dress and tearing down her panties. I don't want to wait another second before I'm inside her.

She whimpers against Dean's mouth as I tug her hips backward and run my fingers through her wet folds again. With one hand playing with her pussy, the other quickly unbuckle my pants, stretching down the hem of my boxer briefs and pulling out my aching cock. It all happens in a frantic moment.

"Fuck, I need to be inside you," I mutter as I run the head of my dick along her soaking core. When I find the warm entrance, I thrust in, and she moans loudly against Dean's mouth.

"Fuck yeah, angel, let me hear you," he mutters against her lips. She's so wet I slide in easily. Pulling back to the tip, I pound into her relentlessly, and she squeals again.

I'm lost in the passion of the moment when a set of fingers touches my cock. My eyes flash upward at Dean and a fire ignites inside me. His hand is touching the place where I am penetrating my wife. My eyes are locked with his as I pick up the pace, slamming harder and faster into her.

If there is anyone on the other side of that door, they for sure can hear us. Briar is not keeping it down.

And I can tell when Dean begins to massage her clit because I feel her pussy tighten around me and her body tenses as she comes.

With a bruising grip on her hips, I slam into her as my own climax takes over. I empty my balls inside my innocent, angelic wife in the private bathroom of my mother's auction gala.

It feels perverted and depraved and sinful, and I love every fucking minute of it.

But I'm not done, far from it. I'm tired of hiding from the truth and pretending that this thing between us isn't incredible. And I'm tired of pretending that I don't want this.

What I want is to take these two home and have my way with them for the rest of the night. I want to own them and touch them and claim them and fuck them—*both* of them.

Thirty-Five

Dean

By the time we finish in the private bathroom upstairs, it's clear none of us are fully sated. We're all craving more. I know I am.

I need to see Briar on her knees again. I want to corrupt this precious angel some more.

And I want to see Caleb truly let go. He's right on the brink of giving in to his desires, and it makes me want to feel his hands on me. Or more.

I don't know if he's ready for that, and it's okay if he's not. I will be patient. But God, I hope he is.

The whole idea is to improve their sex life. And I feel a sense of pride swell inside me as I realize that I've done just that.

At the prospect of being alone, I get an idea. While Caleb is putting his softening cock back in his pants, I say, "I want to take you both to the club."

They both freeze and stare at me.

"Sage and Adam won't be there," I continue. "They're still here at the gala. And if we go to Sinners and Saints, we'll have access to more things."

"Things?" Briar asks.

"Toys, paddles, whips, lube, condoms. Everything we want."

Her throat moves delicately as she swallows. Neither of them speaks for a moment, and I can see their concern. Going to a sex club is a big step. It's outside their comfort zone.

"I can take you directly to my room, and no one has to know what goes on behind those closed doors," I say, hoping to ease their worries.

After a moment, they glance at each other. It's Caleb who replies first.

"Let's do it."

My body hums with excitement as we open the door and sneak out of the small room.

As we descend the stairs together and head for the exit of the gala, I can feel the eyes of others on us. I don't know these people, and I don't know if them seeing us together should be alarming, but Caleb and Briar don't seem worried, so I'm going to follow their lead.

Like Briar said, who cares if they know the truth? That a loving, faithful, married couple consensually engages with the same man. If people have a problem with that, that's on them.

Once we reach the car, the idea of being stuck in the back seat alone sounds excruciating to me. So I drag Briar in with me. I just need to touch her.

The door closes, and Caleb climbs hastily into the front seat. We're all just ready to be there. Desperate to be together again.

Briar giggles as I tug her onto my lap, finding her mouth and devouring it in a passionate kiss. I hear Caleb growling from the driver's seat as he takes off from the parking lot. Briar is straddling my hips as I kiss her, moaning into her mouth.

We're not even on the street yet when I tug up her dress and run my hands along the warm, soft flesh of her ass. I squeeze a handful before smacking her on the right cheek. She hums with pleasure into my mouth. Caleb growls again.

God, I can't get enough of these two. I've never felt more alive in my entire life. She's writhing on my lap, grinding herself against me as I peel aside her underwear and run my fingers through her wet folds. Moaning against her neck, I find Caleb's eyes in the rearview mirror.

Plunging my finger inside her, she cries loudly with her head hanging back.

"I'll never get over how fucking wet your wife gets," I say to Caleb. "She's still leaking with your cum too."

Lifting my wet fingers to my lips, I stare into the rearview mirror, locking eyes with him as I lick them clean, humming at the taste. He shifts in his seat as if he is once again fully aroused and struggling to compose himself.

"Can I suck you off?" she mumbles against my lips.

"Angel, I am never going to say no to that," I reply with a smile. "What do you think, Caleb? Can your wife suck my cock?"

"If she wants to be punished," he replies, and my grin grows wider.

"What do you say, angel?" I ask, tugging on her hair and exposing her neck. "Do you want to be punished?"

"Yes," she says with a strained cry.

"Then take my cock out," I reply before licking the length of her throat.

Draping herself over the back seat, she begins unbuttoning and unzipping my pants. I lace my fingers behind my head as she pulls out my cock. When she wraps her lips around me, my eyes begin to roll into the back of my head. It feels as if I've been edged all night, and the sensation of her mouth is like heaven. I'm not going to last long.

"Yes, angel, that's it," I mumble. She's slurping frantically on my dick. Her delicate fingers wrap tightly around the base of my cock as she strokes me along with the motion of her mouth. When I look up at the front seat to gauge Caleb's reaction, I notice that he's not watching her. He's watching *me.*

So, I make sure that my reactions are exactly what he wants to see—groaning, expressive, exaggerated pleasure. Holding the back of her head, I thrust my hips upward, meeting the back of her throat as she gags on my cock, saliva dripping down my shaft.

"You're a lucky man, Caleb," I mutter through the sensation. "Your wife gives great head."

When I feel my orgasm creeping in, I don't hold it back. I let it wash over me, drowning me in ecstasy because I know that there will be more tonight. This is nowhere near over.

"I'm going to come, angel," I mutter. "You gonna swallow me down?"

She nods in my lap. With my hand fisted in her hair, my body explodes with pleasure. My groans are guttural and deafening as I unload into her mouth. She takes every drop.

After months of not being able to come, it's like these two are my antidote. Now, I only come with them.

"Fuck," I say, melting into the seat as my climax subsides.

With a smile, I softly pet her hair. For the rest of the drive, she rests her face on my thigh. And I can tell that Caleb is restless.

When we reach the club, we're not quite as frenzied as before, but there's still an energy between us that is charged with arousal. It's not just the sex we're excited about, I can tell. It's about the experience of being together, of being truly in the scene again, the way we were the night in my apartment.

I don't know if I've ever felt as truly whole as I did in that moment, and I think they feel it, too.

I tell Caleb to park in the back, and I lead them through the back door. The security guard there waves us in. Caleb and Briar tense behind me as I lead them to my room. We have to walk around the bar, which is the busiest section of the club, but when we pass the open playroom, where everyone is naked and most of them are fucking each other, Briar pauses to watch.

My girl likes voyeurism—*noted.*

Sadie catches my eye near the VIP entrance, but I briefly wave at her before ushering the couple down the hallway toward the last door on the right, which is my private room. Sadie's eyes narrow before we disappear around the corner, but I don't think she's ever met or seen Caleb and Briar in person, so she has no reason to suspect anything.

Before unlocking the door, I take Briar by the hand and press her back against the wall. Taking her face in my hands, I press my lips softly to her forehead. Then I stare down at her as I say, "You've been a very bad wife, Briar. Hasn't she, Caleb?"

He runs a hand through her hair, tugging her head backward as he stares down at her. "A very bad wife."

Her breath hitches as she gazes up at both of us. "Are you ready to be punished?" I ask.

Emphatically, she nods. "Then I want you to go into this room and get naked. You should be kneeling on the floor, waiting for us. I want to talk to your husband for a moment alone. Do you understand?"

"Yes," she replies breathily.

Reaching down, I smack her ass. "Then go."

Unlocking the door, I open it for her and she scurries inside, leaving Caleb and me alone in the dark hallway.

I'd like to have a word with him before we proceed tonight. After everything that's happened, I don't quite know where his head is at when it comes to him and me. I just want to know what to expect and where to draw the line.

Once Briar is gone, I lean back against the wall and stare at him. He seems to expect the statement before I say it. "I just need to know where you and I stand."

"You mean physically?" he asks.

"Yes," I reply. His response stings a little bit because I'd also like to know where we stand emotionally and romantically, but I'm too afraid to ask that at the moment because I'm almost sure the answer would be absolutely nowhere.

To my surprise, Caleb slowly closes the distance between us, pressing his large body against mine. He grabs me by the back of the neck and brings our foreheads together.

"I've been thinking," he mutters. "I'd like to fuck you."

If my dick had a mouth, it would be screaming, "Yes, absolutely, do it now."

But my brain is telling me to think about this because letting him fuck me is going to have consequences. And I'm the one at risk of getting hurt here. I don't want to be someone's experiment. I don't want to be the guy a married man uses, but I don't exactly know how to ask for reassurance.

What if he can't give it to me? What if this is just an experiment to him? Do I still want it?

The question doesn't even leave my lips as Caleb holds my face in his hands. There's a tremble in his touch, and I wonder if it's because this is the first time in his life he's allowed himself to be this close to another man—to *touch* another man. To explore and express a part of himself that he's kept hidden his entire life.

And I know that he's bad at expressing himself with words, and I'm too afraid to ask the important questions, so he answers them with his mouth on mine.

The kiss is consuming and visceral, as if he's licking his way into my soul. Speaking directly to my heart, finding the innermost vulnerable parts of myself and devouring them. I melt into his hands, surrendering myself to his touch. I let him lead the kiss because I want to empower him in this moment. I want him to know that he can take whatever he wants from me, and I will give it to him.

When we finally come apart, we're both breathless, resting our foreheads against each other's. His hands are still on my face, and mine are clutching tightly to his tuxedo jacket as if I'm afraid he might float away on a breeze.

"Yes," I reply breathlessly. "Yes, fuck me."

His response is the same familiar growl I've come to love as he grinds himself against me. And as excited as I am for him to be inside me, first, I want to punish Briar, and I know he does, too.

The punishment isn't meant to be cruel or even true discipline. It's an expression of trust, and there's nothing quite as hot as that.

"Follow my lead," I tell him as we move away from the wall and head into the room. Briar is kneeling naked on the floor, just as we told her to. It's still such an exquisite sight.

While Caleb stands in front of her, softly stroking her hair, I head toward the toys on the wall. This is obviously their first foray into this sort of thing, so it's best if I go easy on them. If we do any sort of impact play, I can keep it soft so I don't overwhelm her.

When I spot the nipple clamps hanging from the wall, I smile to myself as I retrieve them. Then I grab some leather cuffs and the riding crop.

Taking the supplies over to the bed, I drop them on the mattress as I turn toward the beauty on her knees. "Briar, look at me," I command.

Her eyes flash toward me as she waits.

"You'll need a safe word for this, but I don't want you to be alarmed. If you ever need us to slow down for any reason, I want you to say *yellow*. Do you understand?"

With a hint of a tremble, she nods.

"Use your words, angel."

"I understand," she states proudly.

"And if you want us to stop completely, you say *red*. Got it?"

"Got it."

"You're being punished, do you understand?"

"Yes," she replies with a needy look on her face.

"I want you to show us what a good girl you are," I add. Her cheeks blush with that phrase. "It's just like when you say your Hail Marys at church. Pay your penance, and you'll be forgiven."

Biting her lip, she smiles up at me.

"If you take your punishment, you'll be rewarded," I say. Kneeling in front of her, I add, "Do you want to know what your reward will be?"

She nods with a smile in her eyes.

"You get to watch your husband fuck me."

Astonishment crosses her features. Then, her eyes dance to Caleb, and I can see the excitement she's expressing. Turning my head, I see he's wearing a coy smirk.

"That's a good reward," she replies softly, gazing up at her husband.

"I think so, too," I reply.

Thirty-Six

Briar

It feels as if I'm living another woman's life, and yet it's a life I've always wanted to live.

Good Christian women don't come to sex clubs. They don't kneel naked on the floor between two men. Good Christian women don't love every single second of this.

But even when I know I should feel shame, I can't seem to find it. Maybe it's because the love and trust I feel for both of them has me wrapped up in a blanket of security and comfort so I'm free to truly express myself—as are they.

This is the life I always wanted with Caleb, where we feel comfortable sharing every side of ourselves with each other—every flaw, every desire, every vulnerability.

At times, our marriage felt like roles we were forced into, with lines we never fully memorized.

As I stare into his eyes now, a sense of pride swells inside me. My husband is fiercely loyal and loving. But I know deep down he has spent so much of his life in fear—fear of his father and of judgment, but mostly fear for the ones he loves.

He would protect us at all costs, and that's why I think Dean is so good for him. He supports him and carries that burden. Dean's confident and carefree nature is like a mirror placed in front of Caleb, reminding him that everything is going to be okay.

Kneeling between two tall, confident, powerful men the way I am now, I wouldn't expect to feel as comforted and secure as I do, but that's what we are for each other. Even as we embark on this quote, unquote *punishment*, I can surrender to the lust because they would never truly hurt me.

After they each remove their shirts, draping them on a hook by the door, Dean retrieves something from the bed. It's a delicate metal chain with two clips on either side. Shivers roll down my spine with anticipation.

He drapes them over his fingers, holding his hand out toward Caleb. "Care to do the honors?" he asks.

"Gladly," Caleb mutters, taking the clips.

Moisture begins to pool between my thighs. Every moment with these two is the hottest of my entire life. I will never tire of being the center of their attention.

Caleb squats in front of me with a hint of excitement beneath that broody exterior. When he stares into my eyes, it almost feels like breaking the fourth wall. For a moment, it's just us—out of the scene. We're both silently expressing how much we both love this.

"You've been a bad wife," he whispers to me. His brows flick upward playfully. I have to bite my bottom lip to keep from grinning.

When I hear the chain rattle, I glance downward to see him pressing open one clip and letting it close around my right nipple. I hiss as the pain shoots through me. For a moment, I wonder if I'll be able to endure it. But with an exhale, I lean into the throb, and it begins to subside, drawing more arousal from my belly.

The pain makes me feel alive, causing the blood to stir in my veins. I want more.

"Are you going to be a bad wife again?" he asks.

With a breathy whimper, I reply, "Yes."

"Tsk, tsk, tsk."

Just then, the other clip latches around my left nipple, and I squeal. My hands are clenched in fists on my lap. I have to fight the urge to pull the nipple clamps off, but I breathe through the ache again, letting it settle deep in my bones. I've never felt like this in my life—stunningly sexual and unashamed. It feels like a peek behind the curtain, and I want to see more. I want to try more.

Dean crouches behind me. "We're going to be very gentle with you tonight. Do you understand?" He whispers.

Without saying it, I understand what he's expressing. That, until I take a test, there is always a possibility that I could be pregnant. A thought now that leaves me feeling a mixture of dread and apprehension.

I don't like the reminder that I could be pregnant. I don't want to stare into the eyes of that possibility because I'm afraid of what I might find. We started all of this with Dean to improve our sex life so that baby-making would be easier, but what we've really found is so much more. We found a person who fits so well that our relationship has become something new entirely. Sexually, emotionally, intimately.

And maybe...with this new development, our old dreams aren't the same as our new dreams.

"I understand," I whisper to Dean.

"Tell me, Briar," he says, stroking my hair across my bare back. "Do the nipple clamps hurt?"

"Yes," I reply.

"How do you feel about that pain?"

"I like it," I reply.

"That's a good girl." His voice changes as he says, "Go sit on that bed," and I can tell he's talking to Caleb.

I glance up to see my husband stand and walk to the bed against the wall. He sits, wearing nothing but his black tuxedo pants. I love seeing this side of him, looking so confident and sexy.

The soft hand petting my hair turns painful as Dean buries his fingers at the base of my scalp, grabbing a handful of my hair, causing me to let out a hiss.

"Crawl to your husband," he mutters in a deep command.

I move on to all fours, the nipple clamps hanging nearly to the floor. As I move slowly across the room toward Caleb, he licks his lips at the sight.

When I reach him, Dean says, "Get on his lap. Face down."

Climbing onto the bed, I do as he said. My ass is in the air as I press my belly across Caleb's thighs. Dean takes my wrists in his hands, gathering them against the small of my back. I feel the leather cuffs tighten around my wrists, holding my hands in place. I am completely surrendered to them, but I feel no fear, only excitement.

"Your wife likes a little pain, Caleb," Dean says.

"I noticed," Caleb replies coyly.

"Let's see how much she likes it," Dean adds. "We're gonna start with six, Briar. Okay?"

"Okay," I reply.

"How are you feeling? Can you give me a color? Green, yellow, or red?"

"Green," I reply, staring at the floor.

The riding crop lands against my ass cheek with a resounding smack, and the pain is more intense than I anticipated. The sting travels all the way down my leg and up my spine. I suck in a gasp.

"Look at that red spot already," Caleb says, rubbing my ass and massaging the place where Dean just smacked me. I feel him fidget beneath me as if he's already getting aroused. "That was one," he says softly.

When he takes his hand away, the riding crop lands again, this time on the opposite cheek. It hurts just as much, but like the nipple clamps, I breathe into the pain. I let it consume me and flow through my veins. It feels like my body is waking up, making my arousal ten times stronger.

Caleb massages it again, this time squeezing a little tighter as if he's hungry for me. As if he can hardly wait to take me. My squeals turn into moans as his fingers begin to creep between the cheeks of my ass, delicately teasing the rim.

The next few smacks alternate between my cheeks, and the more sore my flesh, the worse the sting. With every hit, Caleb fondles and squeezes my ass, teasing me without penetrating.

And by the sixth, I'm so desperate for it, I could cry. His cock is rock hard against my belly, and he can hardly hold still now.

"Look how much our filthy little angel loves to be spanked," Dean says, his voice growing husky with arousal. "How are you feeling, Briar? Give me a color."

I have to think for a moment about my response. The pain is getting harder to manage, but I don't want to stop. Part of me wants to say *green* because I know how much they want to keep going.

But they trust me to be honest and tell them when I need a break. We wouldn't be able to do this without trust.

"Yellow," I mutter breathlessly.

Caleb takes his hand from my ass quickly and starts stroking my hair. "Okay, baby. We'll slow down."

"Do you want to take a break?" Dean replies.

I quickly shake my head. "I just need a minute."

"Of course, baby," Caleb says, stroking my hair. "I'm so proud of you."

"You're a very good girl for telling us that," Dean adds, his fingers stroking my spine. He's standing so close I can feel his legs pressed against Caleb's.

I love feeling nurtured by them. Their hungry attention is my aphrodisiac, and I can never get enough.

Dean steps away for a moment, and I begin to panic. I really don't want this to end. I hope I haven't ruined it by saying *yellow*, but he returns a moment later, helping me to sit up with my hands still bound behind me.

"Take a drink," he says, lifting a bottle of water to my lips. When my eyes meet his, he smiles. "You're doing so good."

The praise goes straight to my core.

"I want to keep going," I say, staring into his eyes.

He nods. "Okay, angel."

"Maybe just four more?" I ask.

"You still need a little more punishment?" he replies, the corner of his mouth lifting in a smirk.

Biting my lip, I nod. "Yes."

"Okay, then." Taking the water from me, he stands up and backs away. I get back into the position I was in over Caleb's legs.

"Four more strikes for our dirty little angel," Dean states with confidence. "Tell me how wet she is."

Caleb runs his fingers through my folds, and I let out a whimper. "She's so fucking wet," he mumbles with a growl.

"Good. Maybe after these four hits, we'll let her come."

"She's earned it," Caleb adds.

"All right, angel, you ready?" Dean asks.

I nod and then remember that he wants me to say it out loud. "Yes."

"Give me a color, baby," Caleb purrs, the vibration from his deep voice traveling through my body. I love hearing how comfortably he slips into this role as if it's made for him.

"Green," I say, my body tightening in anticipation.

The first smack of the crop on my ass feels better than I expected it to. Like my body has already translated the pain into pleasure. Caleb massages my ass again, this time letting his fingers slip all the way into my soaking cunt. I cry out a loud, animalistic groan, nearly screaming with the need for more.

"Oh my god, please fuck me," I scream.

"So eager, sweet angel," Caleb murmurs as his fingers continue to plunge inside me. I'm writhing on his lap, knowing that I'm not going to get what I want yet.

As soon as he pulls his hand from between my legs, the second smack lands against my flesh. I scream, dying to feel his touch as sweat drips down the nape of my neck.

Caleb does the same thing again, teasing me with what I want before quickly taking it away.

"I can't take it, please!" I cry. "Please fuck me." I can hardly recognize my own voice. I feel as if I exist only for pleasure now. My sense of self is wrapped up in this desire.

The third hit is practically unbearable—not for the ache but for the yearning. I scream against Caleb's leg as he plunges his fingers back inside me, thrusting them so hard, and it feels so good, but it's not what I want.

The fourth and final hit feels like a climax in itself. My body erupts with a sensation that I've never felt before, and when Caleb shoves his fingers back inside me, my orgasm drags me below the surface.

It's so intense that I can hardly breathe. My body seizes against the rapture, and it's everywhere, all-consuming, like nothing I've ever felt before. Pain and pleasure. Dull and sharp. Quiet and loud.

I'm practically convulsing on Caleb's lap as he continues thrusting two fingers inside me, riding out my orgasm.

In the distance, I hear Dean quietly muttering to himself, "Holy fucking shit."

By the time it comes to an end, my ears are ringing, my skin is buzzing, and it feels as if I'm waking up from a dream. I'm left gasping on Caleb's lap.

He softly mutters, "My hand is fucking soaked." I don't even remember him pulling his fingers out. I don't want to move.

I don't want to ever move.

"What a good fucking girl you are," Dean whispers, coming up to our side again. Resting his hand on my head, stroking my hair.

He rubs his rigid length against my arm. "Do you feel that? Do you feel what you fucking do to me?" he says in a deep, raspy tone. Pride bubbles to the surface.

"I'm so fucking proud of you," Caleb adds, and I smile against his lap.

My body feels like melted wax, my muscles like rubber. Lifting anything is impossible at the moment. One of them unbinds my wrists while the other gently removes the nipple clamps. Then I'm hoisted into Caleb's arms as he brings me to the bed. I'm pressed between them when someone hands me water and another wipes my face.

No matter what, the pain was worth this—an earth-shattering orgasm and being cared for by two people I love so much.

Realizing I love Dean already is not a revelation. It came to me as naturally as my love for Caleb, expected and easy.

And while this is amazing, I still haven't forgotten about the reward that awaits me.

Thirty-Seven

Caleb

Briar has never looked so beautiful to me. It took everything in me not to come in my pants, watching her lose herself in the moment as her cunt tightened around my fingers. It was exquisite.

Lying between us, she seems so at peace now, as if she's exhausted and alert at the same time. Neither Dean nor I can stop praising her, how perfect she is, how proud we are, how much we care about her.

Whenever the three of us are together, it seems there is this energy that is undeniable. He brings out this side of me—this *dominance*—and Briar eats up every crumb. Each of us gives as much as we take, and we seem to exist in perfect harmony, something I have longed to find in my marriage for years. Briar was never once at fault, but I can see now that something was always missing.

"You are so perfect," I whisper to her before dusting my lips over hers. I feel her smile against me.

"That was amazing," she whispers.

"*You* were amazing," Dean adds. With a soft grip on her chin, he turns her face toward him, taking her mouth with a delicate kiss, and I savor the sight.

"Does that mean I get my reward now?" she asks shyly.

Immediately, my cock twitches and my heart starts to pound. When my eyes meet Dean's, I begin to wonder if he might change his mind. And he's probably thinking the same thing about me, but there's not a chance in hell I've changed my mind.

Ever since that blow job in my father's office, I haven't been able to stop thinking about being with him, taking his body, making him mine, and fucking him until neither of us can take another second.

Dean has inspired me to be honest with myself about my sexuality and what I want. And now that I see things so differently, I don't understand why I kept this part of myself hidden for so many years and not just hidden from the world but hidden from *myself*.

I don't understand why the fuck I thought that once I married Briar, my sexuality didn't matter anymore, but it matters. As much as my attraction to her, this attraction to him means just as much. Being attracted to men and women never went away because I married a woman. It didn't change who I was.

"Of course, you get your reward," I whisper, watching his eyes light up with excitement. I reach for Dean, and leaning over Briar's body, I find his mouth with mine, kissing him with the same energy that he kissed me with in the hallway.

I feel Briar's delicate fingers run across my cheek, and when my kiss with Dean ends, we both look down at her at the same time. As he takes her mouth, I kiss a line across her jaw, down to her neck, and she hums with pleasure between us.

After a few moments, Dean rises from the bed. "Take your clothes off," he says to me while unbuckling his own pants. "I'm going to grab a couple of things."

My blood pressure spikes again as I consider what those *things* are—assumedly, lube and condoms. As I watch him retrieve those two exact things from a drawer against the wall, reality sets in. *This is happening*. But there's not a hint of fear or hesitation in my body. I want this to happen more than I've wanted anything.

I need him to know how serious I am and how much he means to me. This is not just about sex. He is not an experiment to me.

Once he retrieves the items and sets them on the nightstand, he looms over the bed next to me, completely naked. His cock is hard and jutting straight out from his body.

"It's been a while since I've bottomed," he says, lazily stroking his cock. "I'll need you to prep me. Can you do that?"

Swallowing down my nervousness, I nod. "Just get over here," I growl.

With a lopsided grin, he climbs onto my lap, straddling my hips and leaning in for another bruising kiss.

The moment I feel his cock against mine, a shiver rolls through me. As much as I wish this could last forever, I'm already so aroused that I know it won't take me long.

Dean wraps a hand around both of our cocks and begins stroking.

"Fuck," I mutter. Grabbing his hand, I freeze his movement. "I'm not going to last long if you keep doing that."

With a chuckle, he releases his grip. Sitting up, Dean grabs the lube from the nightstand and squirts a dollop onto my fingers before placing them on his ass. My mouth goes dry as I begin to circle around the ring of muscle. When my middle finger spears the tight hole, he lets out a hearty groan.

"Fuck yeah," he mumbles. "You don't have to take it slow."

His ass is so tight around my finger that I can hardly wait to be inside him. Briar moves into a kneeling position next to us. With her bottom lip pinched between her teeth, she watches with a lust-filled gaze.

It doesn't take long before I'm able to add a second finger and then a third. His body opens beautifully for me. Carnal shivers run through him as I thrust in and out, searching for the spot that drives him wild.

I may have done this to myself a few times to know where to find it.

When my fingers graze his prostate, his cock drips with precum, and a helpless moan escapes his lips. His eyes light up with surprise, like he didn't expect me to do that. Making him feel such pleasure goes straight to my head. I love this power over him. He is *mine*, which means it's up to me to make him feel good. I can hardly wait another second to be inside him.

Thankfully, he immediately replies, "I'm ready. Fuck me."

Taking my fingers from his ass, I reach for the condoms on the nightstand. I rip one open, but he takes it from my hand.

I watch with rapt attention as he places the condom in his mouth, forming it into a perfect circle. Then he slides his mouth over my dick, rolling the condom into place and engulfing my shaft in warmth.

"Jesus Christ," I growl, squeezing his hips. "You are so fucking sexy."

He smirks down at me and the need to fuck him becomes unbearable.

"Do you want me in another position?" he asks, his voice strained and raspy with arousal.

"No, I want you like this," I say. "I want you to ride my cock, and I want to see your face while I fuck you."

Briar whimpers next to us, her hands softly sliding over our chests and stomachs. When Dean lifts up, Briar takes my cock in her hand and helps to guide me into place. He begins to lower his weight, easing down on me. And when my cock breaches the opening, he and I gasp in unison.

The first thought in my head is that I'm *in him*. I'm fucking him. There is no turning back now.

I let him control how deep and how fast I penetrate him, which is good because I can hardly think straight with how amazing this feels. His ass is strangling my dick, so tight and warm, and the look of his body on top of me is almost more than I can handle.

Slowly, Dean rises before lowering again, each time taking me deeper until he's seated completely down on my cock. Grabbing his hips, I hold him there for a moment, savoring the sight. He is so beautiful, with thick muscles and perfect skin. Everything about this is a new sensation—from the weight of his body to the texture of the hair on his legs. My thoughts ring with one word over and over—*perfect.*

"Holy fuck," I mutter through clenched teeth. "You are amazing. You are so fucking amazing."

Lifting up again, he goes just as deep as he drops his weight on me, pounding himself harder on my rigid length. His hard cock bobs between us, aching and leaking from the tip.

"Ride my fucking cock," I say. His hips grind back and forth as his thighs lift him up and down. His movements are rough and aggressive, so within minutes, my orgasm is on the brink.

"Briar, stroke him," I command.

Her hand wraps around his length, stroking to the rhythm that he bounces.

"Fuck yes," he cries out. "Oh god, I'm going to come."

When he lifts again, I grab his hips and hold him there until each of us can compose ourselves and catch our breaths. This is all happening too fast. I'm not ready to be done yet. But I also don't know how much more I can take.

My hands move from his hips to his ass, massaging the muscled globes. "You're so perfect," I say in a deep mumble. "I can't believe I'm fucking you."

He leans down to kiss my lips, and I reach for Briar, pulling her in so she is a part of this. Our kiss turns messy as his lips find hers and mine find his.

It's clear we're not going to evade this orgasm. It's too fucking hot.

When he sits back on my cock, rocking to a steady rhythm, I do my best not to let myself get too worked up this time.

"That's it," I say. "Let me come inside you. And I want you all over my chest." His movements pick up speed as Briar strokes faster. Our groans become deafening, a jumbled mess of words and curses and pleas, the sounds of our bodies coming together, creating a perfect, sexy symphony.

Dean and Briar are devouring each other's mouths as she pumps him. And finally, with a roar, his release shoots across my body. The warm splashes of his arousal make me wild.

Using my grip on his hips, I slam him down on me harder and faster until my release quickly follows. With a long, drawn-out grunt, I fill the condom, coming so hard that I nearly lose my vision altogether.

After my cock is spent, Dean collapses on my chest, the sticky mess pressed between us.

"Goddamn," he murmurs into the crook of my neck. Wrapping my arms around him, I hold him there, loving the feel of him against me.

Nothing about this feels forbidden or sinful or wrong. Not that I ever really thought it was. But I realize now how the opinions of others have guided my own actions and my own thinking, even when I disagree.

There was never anyone else for me. I loved Briar from the minute I saw her, and I knew I would spend the rest of my life with her.

But having Dean now in my arms, I've never been more grateful for him, for us, for this opportunity, and for everything that this means. I don't know what our future holds, and I don't know how we could ever keep him, but we'll always have this moment and this memory and the way it's changed me.

And that can never be taken away.

Thirty-Eight

Dean

We lie together in bed at the club until nearly three in the morning. We don't say much, but at this point, there's not much to be said. I think we all know where we stand with each other. But there's not much we can do about it.

If I tell them how much they mean to me and how fast I'm falling for them, it'll just expose me to the inevitable hurt. This is why I don't do relationships.

Sex is easy. Feelings are not.

I can tell them how much they turn me on and how much I love fucking them, but I can't possibly tell them that I think about *being* in their marriage. In their family. I think far too late into the night about sleeping in their bed, holding their hands in public, telling the world how much they mean to me.

But what is the point?

So I'll just keep those things to myself.

My only real concern is—how long we can do this before it gets too serious. If I stick around in that apartment for five years, what happens when they get pregnant and have another baby? I will always be the odd one out.

There is no real future for me here.

And that reminder is like a stain on an otherwise perfect night. I just wish I could enjoy it more.

"Let's go home," Briar whispers with her head on my chest.

Caleb stands first, finding his underwear and pants. He smiles down at us as he pulls them up and buttons them.

Isn't he wondering the same thing I am? Isn't he as worried as I am about where this is going?

Of course not. He ends up with a beautiful wife either way.

The entire ride home, I stay quiet. When we get out of the car, I go toward my apartment, but it's Caleb who takes my hand and drags me toward the house.

"We have the place to ourselves tonight. Stay with us," he says quietly in the moonlight.

"Are we sure that's really a good idea?" I reply, unable to meet his eyes.

"If you don't want to..."

"I do," I say, cutting him off.

I hate my stupid heart for how much I want this. Even knowing there's no more sex in the cards tonight, I want to sleep between them, nestled in the warm comfort of their bodies.

So I follow them both inside and up the stairs. We get undressed together, not saying much. And when we crawl into the bed, I end up in the middle.

Briar makes a pillow out of my arm, facing me with her bent leg resting on my thighs. Caleb lies close behind me, a strong hand wrapped around my chest.

No matter what a mess my head is at the moment, I can't fight how comfortable this is and how tired I am. Within minutes, I drift off to sleep.

†

I wake to the smell of bacon and a warm arm under my head. Peeking my eyes open, I see 10:37 displayed on the clock on the nightstand.

Caleb's hand is on my hip, and his body is pressed against mine. When I begin to stir, pressing my hips back against him, he hums lowly in my ear.

"Good morning," he mutters, tugging me closer to grind himself against me some more.

Then his hand reaches down and grips my morning wood, giving it a stroke over my briefs.

"First time waking up with a man in your arms?" I say with a smile as I push my hips back.

He chuckles, the deep sound vibrating through my chest. "Yes, why?"

"Just curious," I reply. That's one conversation Caleb and I have not had yet. How long has he known he's attracted to men? The only reason I don't bring it up is because then we'd have to face the hypocrisy of what he did to Isaac. And I'm not ready to do that.

There are voices downstairs, which means we definitely cannot let this get out of hand now. So we stop stroking each other. Instead, I roll toward him, but his hand stays on my hip.

When our eyes meet, it feels like electricity. I quite like his morning look, mussed-up hair and unkempt beard. It's both masculine and tender at the same time.

"That was the best I've slept in a long time," he says quietly.

"Me too, actually," I reply, feeling a little surprised by that. I can't remember the last time I've slept with anyone, let alone squeezed between two bodies.

As we stare at each other, I wonder if he's thinking the same thing I am—that waking up like this again would be nice, but how long could it really go on? Are we playing with fire or just having fun?

His eyes drift closed, and he exhales, looking relaxed and at peace. "That bacon smells good, but I think lying here is nicer."

I hook my leg around his and scoot in closer. "I vote we stay here."

"Okay, you convinced me."

He rubs his thumb intimately over my lower back, and I find myself burrowing closer to him. Who knew Caleb was a cuddler? Everything he does takes me by surprise. I could get used to this.

"Caleb!" Briar calls from downstairs. "Breakfast!"

He groans, pulling me closer. "I guess we should get up."

"Okay," I reply, but neither of us moves for a few more minutes.

In here, we're safe from consequences and the real world. In here, it's just us.

Eventually, we roll away from each other, but I miss his nearness immediately.

"I'll go down first and you follow after a few minutes. It sounds like Briar's sister has already dropped Abigail off," he says.

"It's okay that I'm here?" I ask.

He shrugs. "It's fine."

When he climbs out of bed, I prop my head on my hand and watch him cross the room in his underwear. The sight of his broad shoulders and patch of hair on his chest has me wanting to drag him back under the covers and remind my tongue of what his cock tastes like.

He catches me watching and shoots me a playful smile before pulling on a pair of sweats and a T-shirt. Then he pulls out some clothes for me, tossing them on the bed.

"Here," he says. "I like seeing you in my clothes."

That sends a jolt of warmth to my chest. "I like wearing them," I reply.

It's more than just clothes, though. It's the sense of belonging that comes with them. He owns me.

After he disappears from the bedroom, I get dressed and wash up a bit in the bathroom. Then, I descend the stairs before turning toward the kitchen. Abby spots me immediately.

"Dean!" she squeals as she jumps from her chair and sprints

toward me. When she launches herself into my arms, I can't help the way my lips pull into a smirk.

So what if I love how she's always so excited to see me? Anyone would love that.

It's just one more thing that's going to hurt when I eventually leave.

"Did you spend the night?" she asks with a head tilt.

"Uhh…" I look toward Briar at the table and Caleb at the counter, getting bacon. Neither of them seems too worried about it so I just give a shrug as I set her back down. "Yeah, so?"

"Can we have a sleepover?" she asks, hanging on my arm like a monkey.

"No."

"Why not?" she whines.

"Because I said so. Go eat your breakfast."

With the attention span of a squirrel, she jumps from my arm and dashes back to her seat.

"There's coffee," Briar says, standing up to get a mug down for me.

"Thank you." As I fill the cup, my phone rings in my pocket.

Retrieving it, I see my dad's name on the screen and quickly answer while placing the coffeepot back in the machine. "Dad, hey."

"Hey, kid," he replies. His voice sounds bad—*really* bad.

"How are you feeling?" I ask, keeping my back to the family.

"Like shit." He tries to laugh, but it only makes him cough. I wince at how wet and deep into his chest the sound is.

"I'm coming to see you today," I state. "I'll leave as soon as I finish my coffee."

"I'd like that a lot, son," he replies. "Bring that new family of yours. I want to meet them."

My eyes widen as I stare straight ahead. Glancing behind me, I notice Briar watching with concern.

"I don't know about that, Dad. I'm sure they're busy today."

My dad responds with a disgruntled hum, but he doesn't push the issue anymore.

"I'll be there in a couple of hours. Want me to bring you anything? You must be dying for some Whataburger."

"You know I'll never turn down a burger," he replies, breaking out in another coughing fit. "But just a little one. I can't eat much these days. Don't have the stomach for it."

"Okay. You got it. See you soon."

"See you soon."

When I hang up the phone, the kitchen is silent. Taking my cup of coffee to the table, I sit down, and Abby bounces excitedly on her chair. "Do you ever sit still?" I ask, smiling over the rim of my mug.

"No, she doesn't," Briar replies warmly.

Turning toward her, I admire how beautiful she looks today. Something about her lazy smile and relaxed demeanor makes her even more stunning than she was the day I met her. It's as if she's more at ease now.

Do I give that to her? Do I make her happy?

The same goes for Caleb. He smiles more than he used to. Even with the shit show that is his father's case, he's not so tense about his family or his marriage.

They did ask me to help them. I've done that, haven't I?

"How is your dad?" Briar asks gently.

Looking down at my coffee, I reply, "He sounds bad. I don't know how much time he has left."

"I'm sorry," she says, placing her hand on mine.

"I wish I knew how to help or what to give him. He's done everything for me. Raised me by himself. He's been my only family."

"If it were me," Caleb adds as he sits in the seat across from me, placing the bacon and eggs in the middle of the table. "I'd want to know my family is going to be okay. That would bring me peace."

I shrug. "My dad knows I'll be okay. I've always been independent. I can take care of myself."

"I'm sure he knows that," Briar responds as she passes out breakfast plates, giving me a soft smile.

We dish up our food, and I can't stop thinking about my dad

and what Caleb said. How do I convince him that I'll be okay? I'll put on a brave face today. I'll be strong for him so he knows he doesn't have to worry about me.

Would I worry about my child if I knew they were going to be alone after I left? Even if they knew how to take care of themself, would that be enough?

As I glance around the table, my eyes land on Abby. She's grinning up at Briar as she tells her a story. Briar reaches over and brushes her hair out of her face.

And I realize what I have to do.

"Would you guys like to come with me today? I think if he meets you, he'll know that I'm not alone. I think it will make him feel better."

Briar has tears in her eyes as she smiles. "Of course we will."

"I'd love to meet him," Caleb replies.

It dawns on me how odd it is that he never met him before, not even when we were young and I spent the majority of my time at his house. We really did come from two different worlds.

"I'd love that, too," I say while staring into his eyes. "Thank you, guys."

After we eat our breakfast, the four of us get ourselves cleaned up and ready to go. It's about a forty-five-minute drive to my dad's nursing home.

Once we get a bit closer, we go through the Whataburger drive-through to pick up some food, a cheeseburger for each of us, so he doesn't have to eat alone.

There's a subtle tremble in my bones as we get closer, and I don't know if it's because of my nervousness to see him for the first time in a couple of weeks or if it's because I'm bringing them to meet him.

I hope he likes them. I hope *they* like *him*. I've never brought anyone home to meet my dad, and while bringing this family of three is hardly the same as bringing home a new girlfriend or boyfriend, it's how it feels to me.

Of course, he'll have no idea that there's anything like that among us. As far as he knows, we're just friends, and I'm living at their rental property.

But it means so much more to me.

When we get to the home, we check in at the front desk, and the same nurse I met when I brought him here meets me in the lobby. Her name is Rhonda, and she's a sweet older woman with a comforting smile and kind eyes.

"Mr. Sheridan, can I have a word with you for a moment?" she asks with a thick Southern drawl.

My body tenses as my heart drops to the floor. "Yes, ma'am," I reply, following her.

A soft hand wraps around my arm, and I turn to find Briar walking next to me. "I'm coming with you."

"Thank you," I whisper. I glance back to see Caleb and Abby waiting in the lobby with the bag of food. Naturally, Abby is already climbing on the couches like an animal. I smile to myself as Rhonda opens the door to a private room and ushers Briar and me inside.

"I don't want to alarm you, Mr. Sheridan, but I want to make you aware of the situation," she says with a softness that makes me want to cry.

Emotion forms a lump in my throat as I nod.

"We look for certain signs in our patients to know when the end is near. Your father, while still able to walk around and speak, is showing a couple of those signs. His appetite has gotten very low, and he has moments of delusion. These are normal in patients with very little time left."

Briar squeezes my arm and leans in closer. My eyes sting with tears, and I have to force myself to breathe. When I blink, a tear slips over my cheek.

I don't know why this is taking me by surprise. We knew this was coming. We knew he was dying, but it's still so jarring to hear that it's *real.*

He's really dying.

"How much time?" I ask.

"I can't answer that," she replies as she reaches out and touches my arm. "Could be days. Could be weeks."

I choke back a sob as another tear slips over my cheek. I can't seem to think as the news rushes over me like a tidal wave.

"I just wanted you to be aware of the situation. I was going to call you today, so I'm glad you came in."

"I should have come sooner."

Rhonda smiles softly at me. "For what it's worth, everyone here has loved having him around and will miss him greatly."

"That's so sweet," Briar says, and when I hear the emotion in her voice, I turn to find her crying. It takes me by surprise. Why is she crying? She doesn't even know him.

"Take a few moments if you need them, and then come to his room. He'll be so happy to see you."

With that, Rhonda walks out, leaving Briar and me alone. The moment she's gone, Briar wraps her arms around me. The comfort of her embrace drags more tears from my chest.

"I've been off having a blast, living my life, and he's been in here dying," I say.

She pulls away, taking my face in her hands. "Don't say that. He would be happy to know that you're living your life, Dean. I speak as a parent when I say that's all we want. To know our kids are living their lives. You understand me?"

I quickly wipe my eyes as I nod. "Yeah."

"You're here now. And we're going to give him the best day we can."

A smile stretches across my face, and I'm suddenly so glad I brought them.

"Okay, let's go."

When we open the door, she slips her hand into mine, intertwining our fingers to show me comfort and solidarity. And it doesn't feel strange or wrong.

It feels like love.

Thirty-Nine

Briar

Dean leads us to his dad's room, and I'm impressed with how quickly he's composed himself. Feeling him cry in my arms shattered my heart to pieces, but I'm so proud to see that he's not afraid to show emotion.

Bringing us with him today is such a good sign. It means he's willing to give us a chance—whatever that means. And maybe there's no name for what this is, but we love him, and we want to be there for him.

I know Caleb feels the same.

Abby clings to Dean's other hand as we enter the room. His father is sitting in a hospital bed, but he's lying on top of the blankets in a pair of blue plaid pajama pants and a sweatshirt. He's so gaunt and nearly ash-colored that it takes me by surprise.

"Hey, Dad," Dean says as he enters the room.

Immediately, the man lights up. He begins to try and stand, which has Dean rushing over to help him. And when he wraps his arms around Dean, tears prick my eyes again.

The love between them is evident.

"Dad, I want you to meet my friends," Dean says, turning toward us. "This is Caleb and his wife, Briar."

"Nice to meet you," I say, going in for a hug.

"Oh, it's so great to finally meet you," he replies. His voice sounds so weak. Like it's been shattered into a million little fragments. There's an oxygen tank at his side and tubes strapped in place around his head.

Caleb puts out his hand with a smile. "Likewise." He squeezes Dean's dad's hand tightly as he places an arm around Dean's shoulders.

"I'm Abby!"

Dean's dad looks down and smiles at her brightly as he puts out a hand for her. "Well, hello, Abby! I'm Sal," he says.

"We brought you burgers, Sal." She holds up the bag to show him.

"Oh, thank you so much," he replies excitedly.

There's a small table in the room, so I take the food there, unbagging it while Abby helps me pass out everyone's burgers.

The entire time we eat, I can't take my eyes off Dean. This concern for him is visceral. How could his entire family be one person? He's only twenty-six, and he's about to lose everyone. It's not fair, and my heart breaks for him.

No matter what happens with him and us, I can't stand the thought of him being alone. No one should be alone.

Abby sits on Dean's lap while eating her food. After unwrapping her burger, she holds it out to Sal and says, "Cheers!"

He laughs heartily before touching his sandwich to hers. The laughter turns into coughing, and Dean grows concerned, patting his father on the back.

"I'm okay, I'm okay," Sal says, waving him away. "Just happens sometimes."

"I'm sorry," Abby murmurs.

"It's not your fault," Dean says, squeezing her shoulder.

Across the room, my gaze connects with Caleb's, and we just

stare at each other for a moment. I wonder if he's thinking what I'm thinking.

After we're done eating, Sal says he'd like to take us for a tour of the center. He wants to walk, but Dean insists they take a wheelchair. As soon as Sal sits in it, Abby asks if she can sit in his lap.

"Of course you can!" he replies, helping her up.

As we walk past the exercise room, the library, and the game room, Dean pushes and tells his father about everything he's been up to. He tells him about the museum I took him to and the swim races with Abby—of course, she brags about how she beat him that one time. Then he tells him about the charity gala.

"My son knew them," Sal says. "The Goode family."

"What?" Dean asks.

"They seemed like a nice family, and I wanted him to have that, you know? A mom and a dad and brothers."

Dean freezes. "Dad, what are you talking about? That was me."

Sal turns and looks up at Dean as if he's shocked to see him standing there. Then, he starts to fidget, seemingly upset by his mistake. "Yeah, that's what I meant. I was talking about you."

I glance over at Caleb, but his expression stays tight and guarded. His eyes don't leave Dean.

Then Caleb approaches him, placing an arm around Dean and squeezing him comfortingly.

Dean resumes pushing with Caleb by his side, but I can see the way he swallows and blinks away his tears. "You don't have to say that, Dad. I had a nice family. You and I were a family, remember?"

Sal clears his throat. "Yeah."

I have to look away to hide my tears.

As we walk a bit farther, Sal's mood begins to brighten back up as Abby tells him all about how Dean let her play his video games, watch *Friends*, and made her spicy ramen. He laughs at her stories and holds a hand affectionately on her back.

It's a beautiful day so we venture for a walk out back in the garden. When Sal sees someone he knows, he waves, and the elderly woman comes walking over.

"Oh my, Sal!" she says with excitement. "Is this your granddaughter?"

"Yes, it is," he replies. "This is my granddaughter, Abby."

When I notice Dean lean in to correct him, I grab his arm. He turns toward me with bloodshot eyes and an expression of confusion. I quickly shake my head.

"Let him," I whisper.

I watch as his jaw tightens, and he swallows down the urge to cry.

Sal is beaming as he introduces Abby to the woman and the few others who gather around to meet her. She smiles excitedly on his lap as she tells them that she's six and a half and about to go into first grade.

They fawn over her, and Sal sits proudly in his wheelchair. He introduces them to his son, and Dean shakes their hands using such good manners they practically faint over how perfect they are.

Sal's perfect son and his perfect granddaughter.

As Caleb and I step away to allow them to have their moment, I feel his lips against my head.

"We can't let him be alone, Caleb," I whisper. Sadness bubbles to the surface as the words leave my lips.

"We won't," he replies, squeezing me tighter.

I turn my head to stare up at him. "I'm serious."

"Me too," he replies.

We spend the rest of the day with Sal. He watches me and Caleb play against Abby and Dean in a game of pickleball. We watch a few innings of the Rangers game on the TV in Sal's room, and when dinnertime comes, we join him in the dining room so he can show off his perfect family some more.

As I pick at my food, I remember the looming situation of my two-week wait about to end. Which means I'll have to test in the next couple of days. I don't know if what I'm feeling is excitement or nervousness.

I rest my hand over my lower belly as I sit silently and ponder the situation. Somewhere deep in my heart, I know there isn't a baby there. It's a strange intuition, or maybe it's just some form of self-preservation, but somehow I just know.

How do I feel about this?

The thought of a baby growing inside me, *Caleb's baby*, is a comforting thought. But then what comes after that? A miserable pregnancy. Sleepless nights. Another two years of my life when my body belongs to someone else, growing and feeding another person. It's exhausting but rewarding.

If only having a baby were as simple as my mother seems to think it is.

How much longer can we keep doing this? One disappointment after another, what is going to be left of me by the time I do get pregnant? My life is ticking by, day by day, and I'm terrified of filling these years of Abby's childhood with the grief and pain of one negative test after another.

At what point do I just let it go and live?

My feelings are all over the place, made even more complicated by the prospect of Dean and everything he means to us.

There is a small part of me that wants to take a break from trying if this test is negative. Not to say I wouldn't be ecstatic for the baby if it's there. How would Caleb feel about that?

I can't help but feel like these years of trying have been more about a positive test than an actual baby. But could I say that to him? Would his heart be broken? His hopes are up, and I can't let him down.

After dinner, it's time to say our goodbyes to Sal. I can see he's exhausted from a long day. He slips in and out of lucidity, agitated with himself and getting more and more quiet as the time passes.

Abby hugs him tightly once he's in his bed. The picture she drew for him at dinner is taped to the wall next to the TV so he can see it.

Dean struggles to leave his dad's side, hugging him and holding his hand as if it's the last time. Knowing it very well could be. They say their tearful goodbyes, and Dean promises to return tomorrow and the next day, while Sal insists that he doesn't need to.

"Go have fun," he mutters to his son as he squeezes his hand.

When Dean finally leaves the bed, I see how his lip trembles and his eyes moisten. Once we reach the lobby of the nursing home, I stop in my tracks.

"I think I forgot my phone," I lie. "I'll be right back."

I run back into the room. Sal is lying in his bed, staring listlessly at the TV (or Abby's photo) with tears in his eyes. I rush to his side and lean down to meet his gaze.

He smiles softly when he sees me, giving me a gentle nod. I don't know if he's with me consciously or if his mind has taken him somewhere else.

"We're going to take care of him," I frantically whisper. "I promise. He'll never be alone."

His eyes fill with tears as he smiles, and I know he knows. "Thank you, thank you, thank you."

I squeeze my arms around him, letting a sob rack through me. When I stand up, I quickly wipe my eyes.

I feel a kindred adoration for this man I just met today. My mother would say that feeling is God's presence, but I think it's love's presence. He and I love the same person, and that binds us.

As I step away from his bed and to the door, I know I've given him something no one else could. I gave him peace.

I think about Abby and how I would feel in Sal's position. Peace is all I'd want for my child.

As I walk back down the hallway toward the exit, I let my hand rest on my lower belly again.

If I want peace for my daughter, and for Dean and Caleb and even Sal, then why can't I want peace for myself?

"Did you get it?" Caleb asks, putting an arm out for me.

"Huh?" I stammer. "Oh, yeah." I reach into my pocket and pull out my phone. Of course, I never left it in there. I just knew I couldn't leave this place without telling Sal that we have Dean.

As we reach the parking lot, Abby takes my hand and lets out a yawn. Reaching down, I pick her up as she rests her head on my shoulder. She's getting far too big to carry, but I'll still do it while I can.

Stroking her hair, I kiss her head.

"Mommy," she whispers. "Why did that man call me his granddaughter?"

I smile to myself as we walk a few feet behind the guys. Turning my head toward her, I whisper, "He was just confused, peanut."

"He can be my grandpa," she replies with a yawn. "He was nice."

"Yeah, he was."

As her eyes close, she adds, "I love Dean. I hope he never moves away."

My heart aches as I squeeze her closer. With my lips against her head, I say, "Me too."

Forty

Caleb

21 years old

After the last game of every season, Sean throws a big party at his house. It's not normally something I would go to, but Briar will be there. And I sure as hell can't leave her alone with so many drunk guys.

It's been weeks since she and I first started sleeping together, and while I don't blame her for not wanting to tell Sean, there's a part of me that worries that maybe I don't mean as much to her as I thought. Maybe she won't tell him because she doesn't want to lose him.

But when Briar and I are together, it feels real. I love her. More than I've ever loved anyone in my life. And it's devastating to think about a future where she and I don't end up together.

When I enter the party, half the guys here are already drunk. The music is loud and most people are in the backyard, so I make my way out there, scanning the crowd for Briar.

I spot her in the yard, standing by Sean's side with his arm slung over her shoulders. Her gaze meets mine, and I notice the sympathetic melancholy on her face. Even she knows this has to come to an end. Either she breaks up with him, or she ends things with me.

But I need to be the one to make that ultimatum.

I have to believe that the only reason Briar hasn't left Sean is because she's afraid, and I can't blame her. This is a tough situation. He's manipulated her and gotten into her head, so she thinks she can't do anything without him, but she has me. I will do everything I can to keep her safe and make her happy. She just has to see that.

"Goode!" Sean shouts, and the guys around him cheer. My face remains emotionless as I make my way over because I know their enthusiasm is fake. They don't like me. Sean and his friends fucking hate me, and it's obvious. They respect me on the field because I can throw, but that's all. Outside of the games, they treat me like shit.

And I don't care.

"Grab a beer," Sean says with a slur to his voice.

I take a red Solo cup for the sole purpose of not causing a scene. My eyes land on Briar's face as I lift it to my lips.

"I'm going to the bathroom," she murmurs softly before leaving his side and heading into the house.

I give it a few minutes before I ease out of the group conversation. Glancing behind me, I make sure no one watches as I slip into the house, following Briar.

Sneaking through the long hallways, I find the bathroom, but a girl I don't know emerges.

"Psst," a soft voice calls, and I spin to find Briar, turning down another hallway to the back of the house. When we reach a dark room, she pulls me in and closes the door behind us.

The moment we're alone, I gather her into my arms and hold her, breathing in the scent of her hair. There is another man's cologne there, too, and it grates on my nerves.

"This is dangerous here," she whispers against my chest. "But I couldn't take another minute."

The room we're in is dark, with only the light of the moon through the window. So when I pull away and take her hands with mine, I can barely make out her perfect blue eyes.

"Then leave with me," I plead. "Let's go right now, Briar."

"I can't," she cries.

I press my lips to hers. "Yes, you can. You don't belong to him."

"Who do I belong to, Caleb? You?" she cries.

"No, Briar. You belong to you. This is your choice. Your call. Even if you don't come with me, don't stay with him. He doesn't appreciate how beautiful and how smart you are. You deserve so much more than him."

She hiccups on a sob and buries her face in my chest again. "Why would you wait for me?"

Suddenly, that stupid ultimatum I thought I could give her floats away on a breeze. I could never force her to choose. I love her too much.

"I'll wait forever, Briar," I mumble against her hair.

"I don't deserve you," she whispers.

Pulling her face back in my hands, I stare into her eyes through the darkness. "You deserve more than me. You deserve everything, and if you came with me, I'd spend the rest of our lives making you as happy as I possibly can."

Sliding her hand through the hair at the back of my head, she pulls me in for a kiss, mumbling against my mouth, "I love you."

I try to mutter my reply, but our kiss grows too heated, too fast. I wrap my arms around her waist, holding her against me. Hope courses through my veins. She loves me. Everything is going to work out.

Lifting her off the floor, her legs wrap around me as I carry her to the bed. When I lay her on the mattress, she hums into my mouth.

In the back of my mind, I realize I should have locked the door. I was too focused on her to care. I thought I was invincible.

But when the door flies open, and the room is bathed in light from the hallway, I know the dream I had in my hand was too fleeting to hold on to.

"I fucking knew it!" Sean bellows as he marches angrily into the room. His hand latches around the back of my shirt and hauls me off the bed. I stare in shock at Briar, concerned only for her, when a fist pummels against my chin.

I stumble backward, hitting a wall as pain radiates through my skull.

"Sean!" she screams, and I open my eyes to see her reaching for his arm to hold it back from swinging again. Then everything happens in slow motion when he turns and slaps her so hard across the face that she flies to the floor.

Burning hot rage courses through my veins. My ears begin to buzz as my vision goes blurry.

Lunging from the wall, I fly toward him. I lose focus as I close my hands around his throat and slam him against the wall. My fist flies, connecting with his face. I don't feel the pain in my hand. At the moment, I don't feel anything.

There's a commotion down the hallway, and a foreboding feeling of dread settles in my stomach. I'm fucked.

A crowd of guys burst into the room, finding me holding Sean against the wall. His face is bleeding. My hand is bleeding, and Briar is crying.

They won't give me an ounce of mercy, and I don't expect them to.

Hands close around my arms as someone places me in a choke hold, forcing me to the floor.

"Take him outside. I don't want to get blood on the carpet," Sean mutters from above me.

"Stop!" Briar screams.

When I hear her voice, I try to fight them off, but it's useless. There are too many of them, and with alcohol coursing through their veins, they have no restraint. To them, I'm the enemy—the home-wrecker. It's not just that I've broken some code or done something wrong, but these guys have seen me as different since I got here.

And now I'll be punished for it.

I'm manhandled by at least six guys as they drag me out of the house and into the yard.

My face hits the concrete as they drop me onto the ground. There are so many hands on me that I can barely budge. It dawns on me in this moment that they could kill me. Briar would be left alone with them if that happened.

Roaring like an animal, I fight to get up, thrashing and shouting when someone kicks me hard in the ribs. The air is knocked out of me, and I nearly vomit on the cold ground.

"You piece of shit!" Sean shouts, just before another kick explodes against my side. I feel my ribs crack from the toe of his shoe, and pain pulses through me. "You don't think we see the way you stare in the locker room? Now you want to touch my girl? You fucking pervert. You freak!"

In the distance, Briar screams again.

Fighting against their arms and my broken ribs, I struggle to get away. I need to get to her, but it's useless. They're too strong, and there are too many of them.

"Break his fucking hand. He doesn't deserve to be on our team anymore," Sean mutters.

I try to fight some more, but everything happens so fast.

With my cheek pressed against the cold cement, I'm staring down my outstretched arm as someone's heel lands so hard on my knuckles that I feel the bones shattering.

My vision cuts to black for a brief moment before another shoe stomps on my fingers. The pain is no longer something I feel, but it becomes something I am. *I am made of pain. Excruciating, sharp, white agony seeps into my bones like it's changing the very structure of my conscience.*

I'm screaming, but I can't hear anything anymore. Again, everything goes black, but I wake up too quickly.

This time, the shoe lands against my forearm and the crack of the bone forces my stomach to heave and tears to sting my eyes. I can't scream or breathe. They stomp and howl like animals in a slaughterhouse.

There are sirens in the distance, and the hands holding me down release my body so I can finally suck in air again, but it's too late. I am broken and shattered into a million pieces.

With my face still pressed to the ground, I watch the feet of the scattering partygoers as they run. Shrieks and screams fill the night air as I lie in pain, waiting for my mind to allow me to pass out again.

Then, the face of an angel fills my vision, and I stare through the tears in my eyes as Briar lies on the ground in front of me.

"Oh my god, what did they do to you?" she cries.

"Did they hurt you?" I mutter, although my voice is broken; nothing but a wheezing whisper scrapes its way out of my throat.

"Me? Caleb, look at you. Oh my god, your arm!"

I try to pull my arm to me so she doesn't have to see the grotesqueness of it, but the slightest movement has me wanting to vomit again, so I hold still and wish for mercy.

"This is all my fault. Caleb, I'm so sorry. I'm so, so, so sorry," she sobs.

I feel her face pressed softly to my side, and I don't bother telling her how badly my ribs ache. Just to feel her close to me is enough. I wish I could reach for her or touch her, but I can't. She just keeps repeating, "I'm sorry, I'm sorry, I'm sorry."

Moments before the police arrive with the ambulance, she stares into my eyes as I softly murmur, "I'm not."

Present Day

Sitting at my desk at work, I flex my right hand, staring at the old scars and feeling that phantom ache that comes and goes now, and I can't help but think about how far Briar and I have come.

This gets me thinking about Dean and how amazing the other night was. I had sex with a man, and I don't feel one bit different. But I looked into his eyes and realized how much I care about him, and now I hardly recognize myself.

Dean is so much braver than me. He's unapologetic, and he doesn't dull his own shine for the sake of others. I love that about him, and for the first time in my life, I feel inspired to do the same.

But he's not invincible, and I worry about him the same way I worried about Isaac. Dean needs me, and it feels so good to be needed. He won't ask for help because I know how vulnerable he feels when he does that, but I can be there for him even when he doesn't ask.

I had to fight for Briar, and I did. I nearly died showing my love for her. But when did I stop?

If I allow another man into our relationship, does that mean I've stopped fighting for her? Or does it mean I still am?

I've never met a poly family in my life. No one in our community would approve. My father would have disowned me if he hadn't already burned the bridge between us. My mother would struggle, for sure.

Our community. Briar's family. My career. There is so much at stake, and for what? Because Briar and I found another person we love? Someone who's good for us. Someone who is already a member of our family.

What could be so wrong about that?

My mind is so full of questioning, overthinking, worrying, and calculating that I can hardly work. My father has yet to make a statement in response to mine. Honestly, I hope he never does. He should face trial and serve the time he's sentenced.

He won't find any mercy from me.

My phone flashes with a notification, and I glance down to see the message: Theo Virgil is going live on Instagram.

I've never moved so fast in my life. After quickly hitting the notification, the app opens on my phone, and just like that, I'm staring at my brother's face.

But it's not a picture. It's a video, and it's him at this very moment.

He looks nervous, quietly staring at the screen with a hint of a smile on his face.

"Oh man," he stammers. "You're all here."

The sound of his voice brings tears to my eyes. I cover my mouth with my hand and watch as he addresses his fans. Propping my phone up against my coffee cup, I stare at him.

"How are you enjoying your tour?" he says, reading one of the questions. Leaning back in his chair, he bites his bottom lip as he stares up at the ceiling as if contemplating his answer. When he brings his attention back to the screen, he says, "I'll be honest. It's a dream come true. Even just playing at bars and small venues, I'm living the dream. I couldn't be happier."

Blinking again, another tear rolls down my cheek.

Just then, I remember the tour stop he has nearby, and I scurry to open my calendar on my computer to check the date. With relief, I notice that I haven't missed it. He'll be here next week.

I can see him next week.

But then I glance back at the video on the screen, and I see how happy he is. He's living his dream. Would it be wrong of me to invade that peace? He doesn't owe me anything, but can I really see him play without invading his space?

It doesn't seem fair.

Not to mention, I'm currently engaging in sexual acts with his ex-boyfriend. His *first* boyfriend. I know Dean hasn't had contact with Isaac since the day I drove Dean away, but I know how much they meant to each other.

What if Dean was to Isaac then what Dean is to me now?

What if they see each other while Isaac is in town and reconnect?

Once again, I'm the infiltrator. The one that is breaking up friendships, relationships, and families. I'm the home-wrecker.

All the more reason to ignore all the voices and judgment of others. If I bring Dean into our marriage for real, I'm not wrecking our home. I'm healing it.

For once, I know how to fix things. And I know exactly what I need to do next.

Forty-One

Dean

"Dean!" Abby shouts from the living room as I walk into the house.

It's nearly eleven when I decide to come see Briar. Caleb is at work, but at this point, I feel comfortable just walking into the house.

The night before last, when we got back from the nursing home, I just needed to be alone. Seeing my dad like that was a lot. I didn't expect it to hit me so hard. Especially the moments when he looked at me as if he didn't know me.

I knew this day was coming, but feeling its presence now is more than I can handle. A part of me wants to feel this pain alone. I want to grieve and be in anguish by myself so they don't see the dark parts.

But at the same time, the way they covered me in love and support meant everything.

Abby bolts from the couch, wrapping her arms around my legs. "Hey," I say, patting her head. "Where's your mom?"

"Upstairs, I think," she replies.

I wait with Abby in the living room for Briar to come down, but when there's no sign of her after a few minutes, I get concerned.

"Stay down here," I say to Abby, who jumps back onto the couch to watch TV.

Then I rush up the stairs, taking them two at a time.

"Briar?" I call with concern. Scenarios flash through my mind—like, what if she fell and hurt herself? Or she's sick?

When I hear sniffles coming from her room, I pick up my pace, bolting around the corner.

As I reach the doorway to the en suite bathroom, I freeze.

"Go away," she cries.

I can't move as I stare at Briar, trying to make sense of it all. She's sitting on the toilet, her face wet with tears.

"What's wrong?" I stammer, coming toward her.

"Dean, go!" she shouts, clearly erratic and emotional.

"Why?"

"Because you don't want to see this," she replies. I've never seen her so angry, and it has me scared. Is it something I did?

"See what?" When I take a step toward her, I spot a streak of blood along her inner thigh. Then I notice the underwear around her ankles bears a giant, wet, red spot.

I release a sigh, my shoulders melting away from my ears as she covers her face with her hands and cries. Then everything clicks into place.

"Fuck," I mumble, dropping to my knees in front of her.

"Please go," she cries.

"No," I reply. Resting my hands on her thighs, I rub her softly, hoping I can give her at least a little bit of fucking comfort. "Briar, I'm so sorry."

I know how long she and Caleb have been trying, and I know how hopeful they were that *this* time would do the trick. Her disappointment guts me.

She cries some more. "I knew it. I fucking knew it."

I pull some tissue paper from the roll and blot at her face. When she opens her eyes, she tries to shove me away again. "Dean, stop. This is disgusting."

"No, it's not," I argue, leaning closer. "You think I'm afraid of a little blood?"

I take the wadded-up tissue from her and throw it in the trash. Then I get another piece and clean her face some more. Her eyes are bloodshot with swollen bags under them, and it breaks my heart to think about how long she's been in here crying alone.

She's staring at me as her eyes and nose continue to leak. Once the crying has stopped, I pull the underwear from around her ankles, shoving them into the trash, too. I'll buy her new ones, but she shouldn't have to see them anymore.

Then, I pull more toilet paper from the roll, folding it up delicately and easing her thighs apart. She lets out a small hiccup of surprise as I begin to wipe her clean. There is more blood than I expected, but I don't react. I just keep wiping as gently as I can.

"Dean..." she whispers. "You don't have to do this."

"I know I don't," I reply, throwing the paper in the toilet and getting some more. "But it seems cruel to make you do it." Then I glance up and stare into her eyes. "You've been through enough."

Her lip trembles as tears fill her eyes again.

With delicate care, I wipe her until she's clean. Then I place a soft kiss against each of her knees, rubbing her thighs softly.

"Where do you keep your tampons?" I ask.

She sniffles. "Bottom drawer."

"Don't move." Rising from the floor, I go to the bathroom cabinet, pull out the tampon, and take it back to the toilet. She's still wiping her tears when I kneel back between her legs.

I unwrap the applicator and gently insert it for her. She stares at me in shock as I care for her, but I just want to give her *something*. Some comfort or relief. I wish I could fucking help her so she never had to feel this pain anymore.

A little period blood doesn't faze me, but I know how much it breaks her heart. Helping her is the least I can do.

I won't ask her to talk about it now. I'm sure she needs time, but there's a part of me that is protective of her. And I hate that she's putting herself through this. When will enough be enough?

After she's clean, I wash my hands and find her some fresh underwear and sweatpants from the dresser in the bedroom. When she stands from the toilet, I ease the underwear and pants into place. Then, I kiss her head.

She buries her face against my chest. "Thank you."

"You don't have to thank me, Briar. I'd do anything for you. Why don't you lie down for a little while," I say. "Can I bring you anything?"

She shakes her head before walking to her bed and lying on top of the covers.

"Just try to relax, okay?" I say.

She nods. "I will."

"Mo-om!" Abby's small voice calls from downstairs. I stand from the bed.

"I've got her," I say, leaving Briar's side. I turn off the main light and close the curtains so the room is dim for her.

"Where's Mommy?" Abby asks when I reach the bottom of the stairs.

"She's not feeling well. Leave your mom alone for a while." I ruffle the hair on top of her head.

"I'm hungry," she says, clutching her stomach like she's about to die of starvation.

"You're always hungry."

"Will you make me something?" she asks.

"Sure. What do you want?" I reply, leading her to the kitchen.

She hops up on the dining room chair. "Um...macaroni and cheese."

"Good choice."

Rummaging through the pantry, I find the box of mac and cheese. While I cook, Abby colors at the table. Watching her while the water boils, I feel this strange warmth in my chest.

She's annoying as hell and messy and gross and can't hold still for one fucking second, but dammit...she's pretty cute at the same time. And if anyone hurt a single hair on her head, I'd kill them.

While Abby and I eat our lunch, I send a quick text to my dad.

Hey, something came up. I don't know if I'll be able to stop by before work. But I'll be there tomorrow.

He doesn't respond, but I don't think about it too much. After lunch, Abby wants to play outside. Before we go, I jog up the stairs to check on Briar. She's sleeping peacefully on her bed, nuzzled up in a thick, white robe. I drape a blanket over her legs and kiss her head.

Forty-Two

Briar

When I come downstairs from my nap, I stop at the bottom step, admiring the scene in the living room. Dean is lying on the couch asleep with Abby curled up at his side.

As the bottom step creaks, his eyes pop open. He holds up a finger to signal me to be quiet as Abby naps.

"Thank you," I whisper, leaning on the arm of the couch. "I needed that."

"I already told you you don't have to thank me," he replies quietly. "What time is it?" he asks, looking for his phone.

"It's three thirty," I reply.

Letting out a sigh, he looks despondent. "I have to work tonight. I can cancel my appointments, though, if you need—"

"No," I say, shaking my head. "Don't do that. Caleb will be home soon. And I'm fine."

The moment those two words—*I'm fine*—leave my lips, I feel how untrue they are. Dean seems to notice as well, his brow furrowing as he gently works his way out from behind Abby.

When he stands, I fall easily into his arms.

"Do you want to talk about it?" he asks, his lips pressed to my hair.

"I don't know what to say," I whisper. "I don't know how I feel."

Gently, I pull Dean from the living room to the kitchen so we don't wake Abby. I quietly start to make a cup of tea, pouring water into the kettle to boil. He stands behind me, stoically keeping close and patiently waiting. He asked if I wanted to talk about it, so I do.

"When I saw that streak of blood on the toilet paper today, my first reaction was relief. And then guilt for that relief," I say, facing away from him. The moment I say those thoughts out loud, I feel a weight lifted off my shoulders. Something about Dean is safe. So I continue.

"My emotions ricocheted so fast in my mind that I started to feel crazy. How could I possibly feel relief when we have been trying for a baby for so long? How *dare* I?"

"Let me stop you right there," he says coldly from behind me. "You are allowed to feel however you feel, Briar. You don't owe anyone an explanation for your emotions."

I scoff. "My mother says God has a plan. It will happen when God intends it to." My face twists in anguish. "What kind of God would do this to us? To *me*? God does not decide. *I* decide. Caleb and I decide."

"And what would you decide?" he whispers. "If it were up to you, what would you choose?"

I'm getting so angry my hand is gripping the counter, my knuckles white from the intensity. "I felt relief, Dean. I felt relief because deep down, I don't want a baby anymore."

Saying that out loud leaves me feeling cold and empty. As if the lie I've been telling myself for years has been the only thing keeping me alive. But I'm not sad. A single tear doesn't fall from my eyes. Not even when his arms wrap around me from behind and he holds me tightly. I lean into his embrace, feeling free for the first time in a very long time.

It's like I've just handed myself my own life back.

"You may change your mind, and you may not," he mumbles against the side of my face. "But you don't have to feel bad either way. There's no right answer here, Briar."

Spinning around, I wrap myself up in his embrace. We stand there for a while when the teapot starts to whistle and we both jump from the sound. He releases me, and I retrieve a cup from the cabinet, and he watches as I stir honey in with the tea.

"I meant what I said," he adds. "I can reschedule my appointment."

I shake my head. "Dean, you love your job."

"Yeah, well..." His voice trails off, and my hand stills as I stare at him. Lifting his fierce blue eyes to my face, he adds, "I love you more."

I nearly drop the mug in my hand as I set it clumsily on the counter and rush back into his arms. It feels wrong to hear another man say he loves me, but God, I needed to hear it. I already knew I loved Dean, but I would have never said it to spare him from the complexities of everything between us.

I look up at him as he takes my mouth in a warm, tender kiss. The feel of his tongue sliding against mine nearly makes me forget everything.

"You don't have to say it back," he whispers. "I know how hard and complicated this is."

"But I do, you know," I reply.

His lips stretch in a smirk before kissing my cheeks, one at a time. "I know you do."

†

The door closes, and I glance up from the book in my lap to see Caleb walking in from work. He yanks at his tie as he walks over to the couch and kisses me on the head.

"Sorry I'm late," he mutters with a yawn. "Work piled up."

"It's okay," I say, resting my head on the back of the couch. "There's leftovers in the fridge if you're hungry."

"Is Abby in bed?"

"Yeah," I answer softly, and he looks disappointed. I know how much he hates working late and missing evenings at home.

"Where's Dean?" he asks as if he's already expected to be living in our house and not out in his apartment where he technically lives.

Caleb wants things to seamlessly fall into place without any tough conversations or acknowledgments.

I close my book and turn toward him. "He's at work."

Immediately, Caleb's expression changes, frustration washing over his face as he marches toward the stairs and up to our room. Standing from the couch, I follow him.

He's tearing off his shirt, looking aggravated when I enter. I lean against the doorframe. Clearly, he's upset about the idea that Dean is still a sex worker and Dean still *works*. But right now, we have bigger things to discuss.

"Caleb..." I say carefully.

He spins toward me. "He can't seriously keep working, can he? That's not right."

"Caleb..." I repeat.

"I can't stand the thought of him at the club, letting people use him for his body like that."

"I have something to tell you."

He flings his tie across the chair and lets out a disgruntled sigh.

"I started my period," I mutter softly. Everything about his demeanor softens.

"Oh, Briar..." He crosses the room quickly, pulling me in for a tight embrace. "I'm sorry."

"It's okay," I whisper into his chest. "Dean was here."

His hands rub comfortingly on my back as he kisses my head. "I'm glad."

"But I need to talk to you," I murmur.

Holding me by the shoulders, he stares into my eyes. A sense of contentment and security washes over me. Just having him close and feeling this connection between us makes me feel as if I can say anything.

We've been through so much together, and we'll go through so much more, but it will always be us. No matter what, we'll have each other. In sickness and in health. In good times and bad. Those vows rang with truth, and they always will.

"I can't do this anymore," I whisper. His brows furrow and I feel his fingers tighten around my arms.

"Do what?"

"I don't want to have another baby."

With a sigh, he rests his forehead against mine.

"I'm sorry," I whisper, fighting off tears. "I know you really had your heart set on—"

"You don't have to apologize, Briar," he says gently.

I peel him away from me and force him to look at me. "You're not upset?"

"How could I be upset?" he asks. "I have everything I've ever wanted. Another baby would have been great, but I want you to be happy even more. Not to mention..." he adds, placing a kiss on my shoulder. "When you said you couldn't do this anymore, part of me worried you were talking about us."

I jerk backward, staring at him in shock. "Caleb, how could you think that?"

"Come on, Briar. We haven't exactly had the best couple of years. I feel you slipping away, and I don't know how to fix it."

Grabbing his face, I force his eyes to mine. "Caleb Goode, all marriages have hard times. We have been through a *lot*. But I love you so much. I would never, *ever* leave you."

A smile pulls on his lips as he gathers me back into his arms. This time, I squeeze him back until we're holding each other so tight it feels like we're one. We stand there for so long, embracing tightly, neither of us speaking the entire time.

There is so much we need to speak about and so many feelings to be expressed, but right now, just *feeling* is enough. Feeling his love and letting him feel mine.

Through everything in the past few weeks, we've changed. We are a different couple than we were before. There is a new energy in our relationship, and we are stronger than ever.

When he lifts me from the floor and carries me to the bed, it takes me by surprise. After laying me on the mattress, he takes off his pants and crawls in next to me. Pulling me into his arms, he lets me lie against his chest as he softly strokes my hair.

And I don't expect him to speak because it's not like Caleb to start the conversation, and I certainly don't expect him to be nostalgic or emotionally vulnerable. But when he starts talking, I'm pleasantly surprised.

"The day we got married was the best day of my life," he says with his lips against my hair. I lift up and stare at him.

"It was?"

His brow furrows. "Of course it was. Until that day, I kept thinking I would lose you. That you'd change your mind or that our relationship was just a phase for you. I seriously thought there was a chance you would go back to *him*."

"Caleb," I say in a scolding tone.

"I'm serious," he replies. "You were the best thing that ever happened to me, and I kept waiting for my luck to run out. But then you said your vows at the altar, and I knew it was real, and it was forever. It felt like the first day of my life."

Tears prick behind my eyes as I lean toward him and press my lips to his. "I love you so much."

"And if you want to stop trying, we'll stop trying," he says, stroking my hair and pulling my face to his chest. "I wanted a baby, but I *need* my wife. And I need you to be okay and happy."

This freedom to speak our minds, no matter how wrong or unconventional our thoughts are, is why I fell in love with Caleb in the first place. I am safe with him.

"I just wanted to give you so much more," I whisper.

"Why are you taking the blame, Briar? You can't help this any more than I can. And I refuse to put you through any more pain for something we don't even have. This life is perfect. We have Abby. We have each other. And now..."

His words trail as if he's too afraid to speak this into existence. This affair with Dean already feels like so much more, even if we don't acknowledge it.

The question that haunts me even more than whether or not Dean truly wants to be with us is the question of what happens to our marriage if we add him in. Are we strong enough to withstand this? Will we still be *us*?

I stare into Caleb's eyes as our minds both reel with thoughts and worries. But rather than keep them hidden away in my mind any longer, I finally feel free enough around Caleb to let them out.

"I'm scared of how bringing him into our marriage will change us," I say.

"Yeah, me too," he replies, letting his eyes cast downward. "But I'm even more afraid of what losing him will cost us."

My breath hitches as I gaze into his eyes, tears soaking my vision. Caleb holds me closer as he continues.

"Briar, he fills a piece of our relationship I never knew we needed. And I don't care what anyone has to say about it. The three of us fit. We were made for each other."

"It's so amazing to hear you say that, Caleb." When I blink again, another tear falls as I bury my face against him again.

As we lie there, with a bright future beaming on the horizon, I don't think about what we lost but what that loss has granted us. With every moment of darkness and grief, there is a moment of rebirth and hope.

And while there is still so much for us to discuss and work on for our future, I know that we will build this new life together, slowly, brick by brick.

Part Four
The Lover

Forty-Three

Caleb

Briar sleeps peacefully at my side, and I love to see her so at ease. My heart aches for the years she spent in frustration and pain, blaming herself and her body for things that were completely out of her control.

How did I not know this sooner? Why did I keep this up for so long?

I thought it was what she wanted, but I should have known sooner that she needed a break for herself. That *we* needed to weather that storm together rather than battling each other through the hardest periods of our lives.

I'm just grateful now that we are coming out on the other side, stronger and more connected.

Still, after everything, I can't sleep, and I find myself tossing and turning, thinking about Dean. I still don't know where his head is at with all of this. And I fucking *hate* that he's with someone right now at that club.

Someone is touching him.

Kissing him.

Making him feel good.

Maybe they think that he's theirs. That they can lay some sort of claim on him. What if he does care about them? What if that's all we are to him? Just another client.

Clearly, I'm spiraling. And I don't want to wake Briar to express any of this. But if I lie here another second, I'll explode.

Climbing out of bed, I get dressed quietly. I sneak out of my own house, knowing Briar could track my location if she woke up and was worried about me. As I pull out of the driveway, I know that this is crazy and reckless, but I don't know what else to do.

When I park in the lot across from the club, I start to worry that I've completely lost my mind. What if I go in there and see him with someone? I have no right to be at his place of work. And I know that I could very well ruin things between us if I fuck this up, so I need to get my head on straight.

I'm going in there to see him. To *understand*. And if he really wants me to, I'll find a way to accept that this is his job.

Getting out of my car, I head to the front entrance. Even though I've been here before, and my brother basically owns the place, I still feel like an outsider. Like I don't belong here.

But when I walk in the front door and meet the young man at the host stand, he gives me a shocked expression as if he recognizes me.

"Good evening," he says softly, pasting a fake smile on his face.

Under my breath, I mutter, "I'm just here to see Dean."

He glances down at the iPad on the stand. "Do you have an appointment?"

My molars grind together as I force myself to breathe. "No, I don't need an appointment."

The man's lips part in surprise as he straightens his spine. "Well, he is between clients right now. If he's not on the floor, he'll be in his room. Number four."

"Thank you." I brush past the host and into the club, ignoring when he calls after me for something.

The main floor of the club is dark and loud. There are soft-pink lights ahead that keep the space bathed in a warm hue. There's a bar in the middle and tall tables stationed around it.

My eyes scan the crowd for someone familiar. I don't spot Adam or Sage, which is a good thing. But I also don't see Dean, which *isn't* a good thing. What if he's with someone?

I make my way to one of the high-top tables and stand there alone, surveying the room. I'm in the corner, so I'm out of the light, watching like some sort of voyeur. No one is doing anything particularly dirty out here. In fact, it's surprisingly tasteful. There is a room I can barely see from here that is labeled *Open Play*. We passed it on our first night here, and Briar seemed especially interested in it.

What if Dean is in there? Does he have sex here that's *not* part of his job?

No, he wouldn't do that. He knows we have something special between us. We might not have set up boundaries or expectations in our relationship, but he knows we're not just casually hooking up.

Yes, I technically cheated on Briar to be with him, but he wouldn't do that to us. That's different. *We're* different.

"Can I get you something to drink?" a woman with long red hair braided over her shoulder asks.

"Whiskey neat," I reply, pulling out my credit card and handing it to her. My eyes continue to scan the crowd as she disappears and returns a moment later with my drink and my card.

Slowly sipping it, I start to feel more and more worked up. Where is he? If I don't see him before I finish this drink, I might break down the door of room four, and I don't care if they have to take me out in cuffs.

Finally, he appears, coming from a dark hallway in the back. I bolt upright, standing taller, as I watch him walk across the floor by himself. He's wearing a tight black T-shirt, his nipple piercings showing through the fabric, a pair of holey blue jeans, and black boots. The way his shirt strains against the muscles of his shoulders and chest has my mouth watering.

I hate that someone else gets to touch him. Someone else gets to peel that shirt off. Someone else gets to kiss the soft skin underneath it.

My fingers tighten around the glass. I'm being irrational, and I know it. But I have to draw the line somewhere, and I can't just sit by and allow this when he belongs to us.

He doesn't see me as he reaches the bar, leaning on the surface and speaking to the bartender. There's something different about him. He's missing that charismatic Dean smile. In fact, he looks almost disgruntled and worried.

I want to go to him, but I also want to keep watching. It's like seeing a whole new side of him. And I can't take my eyes off him.

Then, a man sidles up to the bar next to Dean and gives him a look that curdles my blood. I set my drink down and watch as the man says something and Dean only replies with a polite nod and clipped response. I can't hear them from here, but I can read body language enough to know the man is making advances and Dean is shutting him down.

The man doesn't seem to get the message as he continues to talk to Dean. But when he places a hand on Dean's lower back, I snap. Marching across the room, I grab the man's arm at the wrist, squeezing tightly as I sneer in his face.

"Keep your fucking hands *off*," I say with a growl.

"You're hurting me," the man howls before I shove him away. Security guards rush over and crowd us.

"Caleb?" Dean's voice drags my gaze from the man currently being escorted away. "What the fuck are you doing here? Where's Briar?" he asks.

"You just let random people touch you like that?" I shout, ignoring his questions.

His eyes widen as he glances around, clearly not wanting to cause a scene here.

"Jesus," he mutters under his breath before grabbing my arm and hauling me away from the bar. When I spot Sage coming out of the dark hallway, she gives me and Dean a shocked look. "What is going on?"

"Nothing. I'm handling it," Dean mutters, sounding angry.

I don't say anything to her but I know, in her head, she has to be spinning so many questions.

As we reach Dean's room, he uses his key to unlock it like last time, and once the door opens, he grabs my shoulder and shoves me in.

The door slams behind him, and neither of us wastes a second.

"What the fuck are you doing here?" he shouts, putting far too much space between us.

"How can you let people treat you like that?" I bellow, taking a step closer.

His nostrils flare as he lets out a heavy breath. When he puts a hand up to stop my advance, I halt in my spot. "You can't just come into my place of work and start manhandling our patrons because someone *touches* me, Caleb!"

"Yes, I can," I mutter.

"Why? Because we've fucked, you think you have ownership of me?"

That stings, but I try not to let it show. "Is that all it was, Dean? A fuck? Tell me right now that that's all it was to you, and I'll walk out this door right now."

He rubs his hands over his head, letting out a grunt of frustration. "Jesus, Caleb! Of course, it was more than that, but it still doesn't mean you own my body."

"I own *something*," I yell, taking a step closer and pressing my hand to his chest.

He averts his eyes, and I see the pulse in his throat pumping hard as he fights the urge to argue with me. "Now what?" he asks coldly. "Where do I truly fit in all of this, Caleb? You and Briar are *married*. I'm not going to spend the rest of my life being the dirty secret you keep in the apartment above the garage."

"I would never—"

His gaze is fierce as he stares into my eyes. "So, what, you're going to tell everyone I'm your boyfriend? Are you going to move me into your house? Into your bed? What about your daughter?

Your mother? Your career? What happens when all of Austin finds out you and your wife share a sexy little fuckboy?"

I slam him against the wall. "You are not a fuckboy."

"This isn't going to work, Caleb. Besides, you can't stand my job, and I don't plan on quitting just because I'm in a relationship. Would you stop being a lawyer?"

"That's different, and you know it," I reply with a growl.

"I won't give up my life for you," he spits back. "And if you truly loved me, you wouldn't ask me to."

"It's because I love you that I'm asking you to," I argue, slamming his back against the wall again.

The room grows quiet and thick with tension as we stare at each other. The anger between us is laced with passion, and it's come to a head.

I can't stand the space between us, so I keep him pressed to the wall as I take his mouth in a brutal, hungry kiss. He opens for me, sliding his tongue against mine. I press my entire body against him, moving my hands around the plane of his chest, feeling every muscle, every ridge and ripple.

"Mine," I growl into his mouth, and he answers with a groan.

We are a frenzy of hands and lips, taking and claiming. I yank up his T-shirt to feel his skin against my fingers. My hands run over his pecs, toying with the silver barbells on either side. He reaches for the buckle of my pants, tearing it open like he can't live without my dick. Goose bumps erupt all over my body as he undoes the button and reaches his hand inside to wrap his fingers around my already hard length.

I whimper in response, resting my head against his shoulder as he strokes me and nearly brings me to my knees. Kissing my way along his neck, I suck hard against his flesh, drawing blood to the surface to leave a mark.

"Mine," I growl, licking the already red patch.

My hands rush down to his jeans, working open the button. Grabbing another man's dick is still foreign and new to me, but I'll never tire of the way it feels to stroke his velvet-smooth length. Hearing his gravelly groans of pleasure is my reckoning.

"Fuck," he mutters before kissing me again. We're stroking each other, and it's like heaven, but it's not enough. I need more. I need him to reassure me that we mean more than all the rest.

I'm too scared to ask for that reassurance. The idea of his rejection terrifies me.

"God, Caleb," he mutters before biting my jaw. Then he releases my cock and pulls me against him so our dicks are aligned, squeezed tightly between our bodies. Moving by instinct, I begin to rut against him, and the warm sensation of his shaft against mine is like heaven.

"Say it again," he whispers in my ear as we move against each other. "Tell me what you just said."

My brain is mush, so it takes me a moment to realize what he's referring to. And when I finally remember the last words I said, my heart soars. Grabbing his neck, I put my lips against his ear as I growl, "What? You want to hear it again? I love you."

He whimpers, holding me tighter. Then he nibbles on my earlobe, driving me wild.

My rutting grows more frantic, and I know I'll come soon if I don't slow down. He must feel the same because he shoves my hips away, catching his breath as his head hangs, staring down at our leaking cocks.

"Come here," he whispers, reaching for my dick again. I'm breathless as I stare down with my mouth hanging open.

When he rubs the tip of his cock against mine, I feel the cum leaking from his tip.

"Hold still," he whispers, and I watch in lustful awe and a little confusion as he slowly slides the foreskin of his uncut length over the spot where our cocks meet. An uninhibited gasp flies from my mouth as the crown of my dick is engulfed in warmth.

With a wicked grin, he glances up at me as he strokes us together, one tight sleeve of pleasure bringing us to the brink. He's watching my reaction as I melt into the rapture of feeling him slide against me. It's all too fucking filthy and perfect. I can hardly breathe.

"Say it again," he commands.

Speak? I can hardly breathe. But with what he's doing to me right now, I'll sing it for him if he wants. I force the words through my strained lungs. "I love you. Fuck. I love you, I love you, I love you."

He looks up at me with a wink. "Look at you. You're a mess for me, aren't you?"

"God, yes," I reply weakly.

"I love you, too," he whispers. It feels amazing to hear it, but I sort of wish my dick wasn't in this tight, warm heaven right now because there's not enough blood left for my brain to process him saying those words. "Does this feel good?"

"Fuck yeah, it feels good." My hands grip tightly on his neck and arm, squeezing as he strokes us in tandem. My hips keep up their rutting as I hold on to this sensation for as long as I can.

"God, I'm about to come." He groans. He's gripping my arm tightly as he jacks us faster.

"Me too," I say, my voice tight and gravelly. "Don't stop."

"Let me see you come first," he says. "You come so pretty."

I actually fucking whimper at that.

Staring down, I can't get over the vision of what he's doing to me. It's like we've become one. We're fused, feeling the same thing, our dicks aligned and covered as one.

How the fuck is Dean so good at this? And I don't just mean the magic trick he's pulling with his dick right now, but all of it. It's the dirty talk, the attention, the knowing exactly what the other person wants and needs. If making people feel good is his job, then fuck...he was made for it.

Who am I to take that away?

My toes begin to curl, and my eyes squeeze shut as the pleasure ignites in my bones, sizzling like a fire from my head to my toes.

Reaching down, I grab my cock at the base, my fingers grazing his as I feel the warm pulse of his cum filling the same pocket of foreskin I'm filling. He quickly releases, and we continue to stroke ourselves as the mess covers our hands. We're moaning and breathing the same air with our foreheads together.

It feels like a long time passes as we stand there, dripping onto the floor and onto our pants. I don't give a shit. I'm in euphoria that I'm here with him, and for the moment, he's mine.

Forty-Four

Dean

I break all my rules for Caleb. Or rather, he breaks all my rules for me.

As we stand here, our hands coated with a mixture of our releases, I realize how royally fucked I am if I think I'm going to be able to walk away from him or Briar.

"I can't get enough of you," I whisper, placing my forehead on his shoulder.

"The feeling's mutual," he replies.

After a moment, he pulls away. I show him to the sink, where we both get cleaned up. It's so weird to see Caleb in this environment. It was different when he and Briar were here together. That was under much different circumstances.

But now, he's here for just me. And I'm not used to it.

Relationships don't end well for me. So I don't bother trying. The first one was a disaster *because of Caleb*, so it's ironic to me that now he's the one vying for my heart.

After we're cleaned up, I take his hand in mine and pull him deeper into the room. "Lie with me," I say, but his feet freeze when I reach the bed. He stares at it ominously.

"You've been in this bed before," I say, glancing back at it.

"Have you been with someone else tonight?" he asks and lets out a huff of frustration.

"Not that it should make any difference, but my only client tonight was a Dom/sub appointment. We didn't have sex."

"But you have sex with other people here," he mumbles sadly.

"I had sex with *you* here!"

He stares at me with a melancholy expression on his face, and it kills me. Letting out a heavy breath, I tug him toward me again. "Just lie with me so we can talk, okay?"

Feeling my hands against his chest, he seems to relax a bit. We each slip off our shoes first. Then I help him out of his shirt and pants as he does the same for me. We're not hurried, and it's not a sexual thing. It's more comfortable and emotional than that.

For me, I just want to feel that intimacy with Caleb that I miss with everyone else. We're in our underwear as he climbs in first, and I climb on top of him, resting my head on his chest and draping one leg over him. He holds me close, even though I understand that this is still so new for him.

Caleb told me he loved me today, and that was huge for both of us. I need to find a way to convey my feelings back to him while making him understand why things can't be as perfect as he wishes they could.

"I never come with my clients," I mumble, running my hand over the patch of hair on his chest.

He tenses and looks down at me with confusion. "Never?"

"Not in a long time," I reply. "I used to, but then something inside me just broke. That night in my apartment was the first time in months that I was able to finish."

"Is that supposed to make me feel better?"

He's so fucking stubborn, and something about it makes me smile. "This is my job, Caleb. It's not like I have feelings for these people."

"They have feelings for you," he replies.

"How do you know?"

"Because it's impossible not to," he says, and my smile grows wider.

"Well, that's on them. It doesn't change anything for me. I just do my job, and I come home."

"So, even if you do move into the house, you'll still work here?" he asks, and I feel myself wincing at those words.

"Caleb..."

"I can learn to live with it. It'll take me some time, but I'll try." The pleading sound in his voice hurts.

"I can't move into the house. You know it's not going to be that easy," I say, pressing my face into his neck.

"Then we'll take it slow."

Letting out a huff, I reply, "How slow? And for how long?"

"Whatever it takes, Dean. I'm serious." He presses his fingers under my chin and lifts my face until I'm staring at him. Gently, he kisses me, savoring the tender moment.

When we finally pull apart, I get the nerve to ask what I've wanted to know. "When did you realize you were into guys?"

He stiffens at my side. At first, I think he's going to avoid the question, but after a sigh and looking a little uncomfortable, he answers. "Probably...college. Before Briar, I wasn't really interested in anyone. I looked at guys the same way I looked at girls, but somewhere in my head, I think I knew I'd never act on any of those feelings. Then I fell in love with her, and I was actually...relieved. I know that's wrong, but it meant I never had to face those feelings. I could just forget about them."

"Did you...forget about them?"

He turns and faces me. With a smirk, he replies, "Of course not. Instead, I started to feel really bitter and frustrated."

"I understand."

"And Briar was always enough for me. I never needed anyone else, but I underestimated just how hard it is to be myself in this world."

Pride fills my chest as I stare at him, seeing how far he's come. Leaning in, I press my lips to his again. When I open my eyes, he says something I didn't expect to hear.

"I'm sorry about what happened with Isaac, but that was a long time ago, and I've changed."

Hearing him bring up Isaac sets my blood on fire. I rise from his chest, moving into a sitting position. My back is to him as I let those memories come flooding back.

"Why would you bring that up?" I ask.

"Because I don't want you to hate me anymore," he replies, sitting up against the headboard.

With a wince, I reply, "I don't hate you."

"You did."

"I was mad," I argue. "You pushed me out of his life," I mutter. "Out of all of your lives."

He leans closer, touching my shoulder. "I did it to protect my brother."

Spinning on him, I stare into his eyes. I hate that we're digging this up now. It feels like the one conversation we've avoided and maybe because it was so long ago and we've changed, but I'm still harboring more scars from what happened than even I know.

"Protect him?" I reply, appalled. "It was because of *you* that your dad kicked him out."

He looks as if I've punched him. "Because of me? I would *never* hurt my brother."

When he stands from the bed and paces the room, I watch him with confusion. "Caleb, you told me that day that...I had to leave Isaac alone. That I wasn't good for him. I thought you...told your father."

"I did that to *protect* him from my father," he argues, staring at me with shock. "I regret what I did to you that day, but I would have *never* outed Isaac. *Ever*. I was terrified our dad would send him to a conversion camp or something. I just had to keep him safe until he was old enough to move out."

Standing from the couch, I ask, "So how did your dad find out?"

Caleb freezes. "Isaac told him."

"He did?"

"Yeah, when he was seventeen, he just...came out. My dad was furious. He waved the Bible in his face and told him he was going to hell. Isaac just...took it. The next day, Isaac was gone."

"Where did he go?"

Caleb shrugs. "For a while, he kept in touch but never let me know where he was. Then he just disappeared. A few years ago, I started digging around, and I found out he lives in Nashville now. He's actually doing pretty well. A country music singer."

A chuckle slips through my lips. He actually did it. He ran away.

Meanwhile, I'm still here.

I let out a heavy sigh as I drop back down to the mattress. "All this time, I assumed you just...hated that your brother was gay. I assumed you were the one who told your dad. You broke us up, and he found out anyway."

"I did what I had to, Dean. I was young and stupid and scared. But Isaac...was never scared."

"Yes, he was," I mutter to myself. "When I knew him, he was."

When he kneels on the floor between my knees, it takes me by surprise. "Is that what you've thought of me this whole time? That I was a homophobe who sent my kid brother away? That I was like my father?"

Did I? Before I moved into that apartment, that's exactly what I thought. It was a theory I'd built in my mind for years. I was so bent on hatred and revenge that I never bothered to ask questions or have doubts. I wanted to hate Caleb Goode because it was easier than facing the truth—*Isaac let me go.*

Even when he ran away at seventeen, he never looked back, and while part of me was waiting for him and hoping that chapter of our lives wasn't over, he'd already closed the book.

Raising my eyes, I stare at Caleb. "It doesn't matter what I thought," I reply.

"It matters to me."

"I was wrong," I say, holding him by the back of the neck.

"So was I," he says as he presses his lips to mine. Our bodies meld together as we hold each other there, him kneeling between my legs and our arms wrapped around each other. "I'll tell everyone you're our boyfriend, and I don't give a shit what they say. I'll tell my father and my brothers and everyone. Just like Isaac did. And if they don't like it, they can fuck off."

He's mumbling into my neck, and I can't help the smile that stretches across my face. When he moves to stand, he pushes me back onto the bed, draping his body over mine. Then, he kisses me with all of the tenderness and passion I want from him.

For a long time, we just lie here and kiss, taking our time with each other. I think for Caleb, this is his chance to prove to himself that he's not afraid anymore. He's not hiding. He's accepting who he is and celebrating that acceptance with me.

When his kisses trail down my throat, I feel my heartbeat start to pick up speed. Then he reaches my abs, and I nearly stop him.

"You don't have to do that," I whisper.

"I want to," he says as he continues to make his way down my body. As he reaches my groin, he stares down at the rigid length hiding behind my tight black underwear. After easing the waistband down to reveal my cock, he smiles up at me. "I can't promise I'll be any good at it."

Biting my bottom lip, I run my fingers through his soft brown hair. "Are you kidding? Just the sight of those lips anywhere near my cock, and I'm happy."

His mouth opens, and his tongue peeks out, grazing softly along the underside of my cock. The hesitation on his face turns me on, especially as he kisses the tip of my dick. His warm, wet lips suck gently on the crown, and I hum with pleasure.

Wrapping his fingers around my cock, he strokes me softly, gently uncloaking the head of my cock as he takes me into his mouth. I glide along the length of his tongue until I reach the back of his throat. When he gags, I have to remind myself to breathe.

"Yes, just keep doing that," I say with a grunt.

He does it again, closing his lips around my shaft as he bobs his head up and down, getting lost in the desire to suck me off. He is relentless, exploring my dick as if it's the first one he's seen. Sucking, licking, and even gently biting until I rise off the bed and grip his hair until it hurts.

For a long time, I let him practice. And I watch as he works to perfect his technique, studying what makes me groan and tense. Before long, he has my climax at the tips of his fingers.

"Here's your warning," I say with a gasp. "I'm about to come, baby."

He continues to suck on my cock as my body seizes with ecstasy, but just before I shoot my load into his mouth, he pulls away and continues stroking, so I spill the mess all over my own chest.

I'm still recovering when he starts to curse himself. "Fuck, sorry. I panicked."

A laugh bubbles out of my chest. "I don't care. Expecting you to swallow on your first blow job would be too much."

"How was that?" he asks, desperate for me to grade his performance like I'm not lying here staring at the ceiling and waiting for my ears to stop buzzing.

Lifting my head, I smile down at him. "Are you fucking kidding? That was incredible."

His head cocks to the side. "Don't patronize me."

My laughter gets louder. "I'm not! You can't take a compliment. Once you got the hang of it, it was great."

There is a deep wrinkle forever indented on Caleb's forehead from his permanent scowl, so when he frowns at me now, it only makes me smile. He clearly thinks I'm just blowing smoke up his ass, but the blow job was phenomenal for a first-timer.

When his gaze lands on the cum pooling in the divots of my abs, he leans down and sticks his tongue out. I watch with my mouth hanging open as he licks up one spot to taste me.

Bringing his tongue back into his mouth, he swallows down the small amount and takes a moment to consider how he likes it.

Then, to my surprise, he leans back down and licks his tongue across my entire stomach and chest in one long stride. I gasp as he cleans my body with his mouth. My fingers are in his hair, and by the time he brings his face to mine, there's not a trace of cum left on my skin.

"Holy shit, that was hot," I whisper before hauling his mouth to mine. The salty taste on his tongue has my cock twitching, even though I know it's spent for the night. Or at least for the next twenty to thirty minutes.

And as I wrestle him onto his back, I think I know exactly how I'll pass the time.

Forty-Five

Briar

21 years old

"I'm not."

Those were the last two words Caleb uttered before passing out and being hauled away by the paramedics. I stayed by his side for as long as I could. But eventually, they slammed those ambulance doors in my face.

I sobbed the entire way to the hospital in my car. All I kept thinking as I drove was that this was all my fault. If I had just told Sean sooner, or if I'd broken up with him when I had the chance, none of this would have happened.

Why was I so afraid? It's because of me that Caleb is in the hospital right now. It's because of me that his arm is broken and his hand is shattered.

And yet, after all of that, he still uttered those two words to me after I said how sorry I was.

I'm not.

It baffles my mind how someone can love someone else at all costs, regardless of the sacrifice. Knowing what it cost him to be with me, he still did it. Caleb and I both feared Sean's reaction when he found out, but Caleb took that risk anyway.

I'm not.

The nurses in the emergency room wouldn't let me back to see him, no matter how much I cried and begged. So I slept the night away on the weathered, dirty vinyl seats of the emergency room waiting area.

By the time someone finally shakes me awake, it's early morning.

"Hey," the man says gently. He looks oddly familiar, but I'm sure I've never met him before. "You must be Briar," he adds as he takes a seat in the chair opposite mine.

I wipe the drool from my mouth as I move into a sitting position. "Yeah," I reply.

"I'm Luke, Caleb's brother."

"Oh." I glance around the waiting room, looking for his mother or someone else. Panic sets in as I stare at the triage desk, waiting for an answer. "How is he? Have you talked to him?"

"They've put him in a room, and he's being prepped for surgery."

"Surgery?" I ask in a panic.

"It's nothing major," he replies, trying to calm me. "They just have to put a few screws in his arm to set the bone."

I slap my hand over my mouth. The grotesque sight of Sean's foot stomping on Caleb's arm reenters my mind. "Oh my god."

"They're only letting his family back right now, but the nurses said you slept out here all night."

Suddenly, I want to cry. Exhaustion, fear, and adrenaline have my head pounding.

"I had to," I wail. "The ambulance came and got him, and then they said to wait here, but it's been all night." My voice is shaking with emotion.

"Okay, okay. It's all right."

"I just want to see him," I cry.

"I know you do," he mumbles. "Let me see what I can do."

Wiping the tears and streaks of makeup from under my eyes, I watch Caleb's brother walk to the triage desk of the emergency room. He leans down and gives the nurse behind the counter a flirtatious grin. She glances my way, giving me a stern look before turning back toward him.

After a moment, she nods and gestures at me. I scurry from my chair, and when I reach them, Lucas wraps an arm around my shoulders.

"If anyone asks, you're his wife, okay?"

"Okay," I stammer nervously.

The nurse stands up and walks us through the large door leading to the emergency room. We go down a long hallway and up the elevator until we reach the third floor. When she opens one of the doors on the right, and I see Caleb lying there, I begin to cry again.

"Caleb," I sob, rushing to his side.

His mother is there, holding his good hand in hers, and it looks as if she's praying quietly to herself.

When she lifts her eyes to look at me, I can tell she's been crying too. Wiping away my own tears, I brush his hair from his forehead. The bruises and swelling around his face make my heart ache with remorse.

"They've pumped him so full of pain meds he's not waking up right now," his mother says softly.

"As long as he's not in any pain," I reply.

When I feel his mother's skeptical eyes on my face, I want to say something, but I don't know what. I want to apologize because this happened because of me, but I don't quite know how much they know. I'm sure they have questions as to why their son was so badly beaten at a party after a football game. But if they knew the truth, that it was because of me, would they hate me?

If it was my son, I would.

Luke scoots a chair up behind me and allows me to sit at Caleb's side. His mother holds his left hand while his right is bandaged and resting against his chest. Since I have no hand to hold, I just continue brushing the soft hair away from his face.

And in my mind, the apology echoes over and over like an incantation. I'm sorry, I'm sorry, I'm sorry.

Present Day

I'm standing at the edge of the pool deck, staring down at the man currently sitting at the bottom, waiting for him to come up for air.

Glancing down at my watch, I time him.

"Almost four minutes. That's actually pretty impressive," I say as his head pops up, and he shakes the water from his face.

He spins toward me, looking surprised. "Oh, hey."

I prop my hands up on my hips as I stare down at him. "Care to tell me why my husband is still sleeping at eleven a.m. in the morning?"

A coy laugh slips through his lips. "He's still sleeping?"

"Well, yeah, Dean. He didn't get home until nearly four o'clock this morning."

Dean shoots me an apologetic smile. Lowering myself, I sit on the edge of the pool and let my legs dangle in the water as he approaches. I shake my head at him in mock disappointment as he plants his hands on either side of my body.

"It's not my fault he decided to surprise me at work," he says.

"Uh-huh," I reply. "And what exactly did you do at your work in the middle of the night?"

With a wince, he turns his sexy smirk away from me. "I mean, do you really want to know?"

Biting my bottom lip, I fight a smile. "No," I reply, "as long as I get payback."

His brows shoot upward flirtatiously. Then he glances behind me at the house. "Where's that little monster who is bound to interrupt us?" he asks.

"My sister picked her up this morning to take the girls shopping."

"Oh, so we're alone then?" he replies as he tugs me closer to the edge of the pool.

I place a hand on his chest. "Let me stop you right there."

"I already told you a little blood doesn't scare me," he says with a wink.

"We are not having sex in my swimming pool in broad daylight," I reply obstinately. But as he begins unbuttoning my shorts, I can't help the giggle that escapes.

"Are you sure about that?" he replies in a sultry tone before dragging me into the pool. I let out a shriek as water soaks my clothes, but he quickly quiets my screams with his lips against mine.

When I'm with Dean, it's like nothing else exists. He treats me differently than everyone else, like an entire person, separate from a mother and a wife. I'm lost to the world when I'm in his arms, which is probably why I don't hear the car door slam in the distance.

"Knock, knock, we're back early—"

Dean tears himself away from me as I turn to see my sister standing in the yard, staring down at us with her mouth agape. It feels like she stands there forever, just staring. Then she quickly turns away nervously.

Shit.

"Felicity had a little accident, so we had to cut our shopping trip short." Juliet starts pacing wildly as if she doesn't know how to behave.

"It's okay," I stammer as I climb out of the pool. I glance back at Dean awkwardly, who exits from the other side, grabbing a towel to dry off.

"I'll be...uh, over there," he stutters as he disappears toward his apartment.

I wrap one of the spare towels around myself as I stare at my sister, waiting for her to acknowledge me.

"Abby's already in the house," she stammers without looking at me.

"Juliet," I say, trying to get her attention.

"Um, I'll just... I'll just go," she says.

"Juliet, wait," I say, calling after her. "It's not what you think."

She spins toward me, meeting my gaze with hers for the first time. "Not what I think? Because I *think* what I saw was your new tenant with his hands all over you in the pool and the two of you making out like teenagers."

I let out a sigh. I don't want to lie to my sister, and I promised Dean that we would make this work, that we would make people understand. So, hiding the truth and lying as if we have something to be ashamed of is not how I want to handle this. And who better to launch the whole idea with than my sister?

"Yes, I know that's what you saw, but I'm telling you, it's not what you think," I reply calmly.

"Okay, so it's *not* you cheating on Caleb?" she asks, astounded.

"It's not," I say.

She scoffs as she lets her hands slap against her legs. "Okay, then, what exactly is it?"

"Caleb knows," I say softly.

Juliet's eyes widen as she stares at me. "Oh god."

She sounds appalled, as if she's just discovered that we are some alien life forms. And finding out that we have somewhat of an open marriage is the worst possible thing she could have just discovered.

"Calm down," I say.

"Are you guys, like..." her voice trails as she glances around to make sure that we're alone, "swingers?" She says it like it's the punch line of a joke.

"No," I reply. "We are not swingers."

"So, you just have an open marriage?" she asks.

"Not really."

"I'm so confused," she says, looking at me, waiting for some sort of clarification.

"Okay, we've never told anyone this." I start as I take a step forward and cross my arms. "But technically, Caleb and I are *both* with Dean, or rather, he's with us. We are all together."

Once I'm done speaking, she continues to stare at me, her mouth parted and her eyes wide. After a moment, she finally turns away, taking a moment to breathe and think.

"Oh my god, Briar," she hisses, "aren't we a little old for this?"

"A little old for what?" I ask, feeling offended.

"I don't know—threesomes and partying like you're in college. You're supposed to be trying to have a baby, not screwing around with some twenty-six-year-old."

She sounds so pretentious and judgmental; it hurts to hear her talk to me like this. Sure, my sister does live on a high horse from time to time, but I hate hearing her talk this way.

"Okay, first of all, we're not partying. This isn't a phase. And we're not just screwing around with him, Juliet. We love him."

"What do you mean *we*?" she scoffs. "Caleb is..."

It's not really my place to tell, but there's no way to hide it now. "Yes, Caleb is with him too. But I'm asking you to keep this to yourself for now."

Her mouth hangs open, and the way she looks almost *offended* grates on my nerves. How dare she judge Caleb or me. How dare she act like this somehow hurts her.

"You made a vow, Briar," she snaps. "To *each other*. In front of God, you made that vow. Does that mean nothing to you?"

"Caleb and I have kept our vows," I reply. "Bringing more love into our relationship doesn't change that. Besides, I'm done trying to live my life to please God."

"How progressive of you," she replies with scorn.

"I thought you were going to take this a lot better," I reply, letting my brows pinch inward as I glare at her.

"Take what?" she shrieks. "This is ridiculous, Briar. Do you even hear yourself?"

"I do hear myself, Juliet," I reply in a clipped tone. "What I'm struggling to hear and understand is why on earth you're so upset about this. You're acting like what I've just told you somehow affects you at all when it doesn't."

She scoffs. "You're kidding yourself if you think this doesn't affect everyone around you. What about your daughter? What sort of example are you setting for her?"

"That she can love anyone she wants and be in any kind of relationship that makes her happy," I argue.

"A relationship? That's what you call this?"

"Yes, because that's what it is."

She lets out an exhale through her nose and shakes her head at me. "I don't think Felicity and Abigail should play together for a while. I can't expose my daughter to...whatever this is."

Bile rises in my throat as I fight the urge to scream or vomit. This isn't fair. But it's clear I can't make her understand that.

I don't respond to that. Instead, I just avert my gaze and mutter under my breath, "I think you should go."

"Yeah, I do, too," she replies, sounding angry.

She stomps out of my yard, but before she can leave, I call after her. "And for what it's worth, Juliet, we're not trying for a baby anymore."

She presses her lips together and gives me a nod. I'm already feeling sick from the response, as she adds, "At this point, I think that's probably for the best."

Her words sting and there's a burning behind my eyes, but I won't let her see me cry. My sister and I have definitely butted heads before. We don't always see eye to eye. But I never expected this.

For some reason, I felt as if she would have had my back before anyone. I expected my mother to be the one so appalled. Not my sister. But it always was them against me. Now, I truly feel it. I have no doubt that my mother will react the same way as Juliet, tenfold.

But to know that I don't have a shred of support from my sister hurts more than I ever expected it to. Even after I hear her car door slam and her tires against the gravel as she pulls out of the driveway, I stand on the back patio soaked to the bone, holding the towel over my body as I let that entire interaction wash over me.

It dawns on me now that Caleb and I have been in serious denial. No one is going to just accept our relationship without doubts and judgment. Those who do accept it likely won't take it seriously. They'll see us, as my sister said, like it's some partying threesome phase we're in.

The road ahead of us feels daunting and insurmountable if that's the choice we choose to make.

I'm sitting in one of the patio chairs and staring straight ahead, letting my mind ponder and reflect when I hear the apartment door closing. Dean appears in front of me after a few moments. I lift my gaze to his face as he gives me a sympathetic smile.

"Did you hear that?" I ask.

"Every word," he replies.

Then he crouches down in front of me, placing his hands on my thighs as he stares into my eyes.

"That's how it's going to be with everyone, Briar. We don't live in a perfect world. I'm terrified about what this relationship might cost you both."

I reach for his hands as I lean forward.

"I'm not," I reply with confidence.

Forty-Six

Caleb

"She said that?" I ask.

"Yes," Briar replies, chewing the inside of her cheek.

She's upset, I can tell, and for good reason. I always knew Juliet was a pretentious bitch at times, but I had no idea it was this bad.

I've seen families turn on each other before over love, of all things. Briar is a little less familiar with what this feels like. And maybe that's why this doesn't faze me at all.

I was there the night my father threatened my little brother with eternal damnation. I knew going into this that people were not going to accept us. I knew they would form their own opinions, talk behind our backs, judge us for our personal choices, and even judge us for things that were out of our control—like who we are attracted to and who we love.

Dean is standing across the room, leaning against the kitchen island and staring at the floor. I can practically feel his sense of discomfort swelling from over here. I know he's scared. And I know he doesn't want to be the cause of any harm.

In his mind, he thinks that if he just leaves, then everything will go back to normal. We'll have nothing to expose, nothing to be judged for, and nothing to worry about, but he'd be wrong.

I know it. Briar knows it. And deep down, he knows it.

We don't sacrifice who we love just to make our lives a little easier.

"Well," I say, lifting my arms in a shrug. "Telling your sister is out of the way."

Briar lifts her eyes and glares at me. "This is not a joke, Caleb."

"I know it's not a joke," I reply. "I'm taking this very seriously. But I also know that we cannot control their reactions, and their reactions are going to be fucking absurd. We control what we can control."

Dean turns his eyes up toward me as I continue.

"What happens here at our home is our business. And people may not like it once they find out. But I'm not willing to give up either of you because of *their* reactions."

Briar continues to chew on her bottom lip as she watches me, arms crossed in front of her. "We have to all be on board if this is what we're doing," she says softly.

I keep my eyes on Dean. "I know," I reply, waiting for him to answer.

He knows what I want. I made it very clear last night at the club with how many times I told him I loved him.

When Dean finally does speak, he does so with a lighthearted tone in his voice. "I was just supposed to help you guys, remember?" he says. "I was supposed to fix your marriage, not ruin it."

"You didn't ruin it," I reply.

"Well, either way, this isn't really how I expected things to turn out."

"None of us did," Briar replies.

My phone starts buzzing in my pocket, and I look down to see it's my secretary, Jules. It's bad enough I had to reschedule my morning meetings because of my late-night rendezvous with Dean, but I can't put off work forever.

"Listen, we don't need to figure this out right now. We have time. But I have to get to work, or I'll lose my cases."

"Of course," Briar replies with a soft nod and a smile. She steps toward me, kissing me on the lips.

I cross the kitchen toward Dean and stand in front of him, waiting for him to relax. As my lips curl into a smile, so does his. "Relax," I say. "Everything will be fine."

Then I lean forward and press my lips to his. Feeling him soften and kiss me back gives me hope.

By the time I'm in my car, I feel lighter. Fuck, this might be the first time in my life I've actually felt optimistic about everything. My mind isn't swirling with worry and indecision. Which is crazy because none of this will be easy, but honestly, how can I complain?

I have a beautiful wife, a hot fucking boyfriend, a perfect daughter. My family couldn't be better.

We'll weather these storms together, and I know we'll make it. If we have to, we'll move. I'll take them far from here, maybe somewhere where our family will be more accepted. There has to be a better place to be a poly family than Texas.

My phone rings again, and I glance down to see Jules's name again. If she's calling twice in ten minutes, it must mean something important has come up.

"Hey, Jules," I say as I answer the call through my SUV's Bluetooth.

"Caleb," she replies. Immediately, I hear the tension in her voice.

"What's going on?" I ask, gripping the steering wheel tighter.

"Your father is here." Her voice is low, a mere whisper into the phone line.

The blood drains from my face. "What? Why?"

"He said you're his counsel and that he got explicit permission from his probation officer to visit his lawyer. And he won't leave until he sees you."

What the fuck?

"Okay, Jules. I just left the house, but I'll hurry. I'm sorry."

"It's okay," she mumbles.

"Jules, do not let him in my office alone."

"I won't, sir."

When she hangs up the call, I press my foot on the pedal, speeding down the freeway to get to the office faster. The good feeling I had when I got into my car is suddenly gone.

By the time I park, I have myself convinced that my father is officially delusional. There's no way he didn't hear my statement. He's here to argue with me, which means I need to prepare for a fight.

Truett Goode doesn't take losing well. His ego is too large to let him admit defeat, so he won't go down easily.

As the elevator dings and I walk to the doors of my office, I can hear his voice booming from out here. Opening the door, I shove my shoulders back and hold my head up high.

If he thinks he's come here today to bully me, he's wrong.

"I'll go wherever I damn well please," he shouts.

"Sir, please wait in the lobby," Jules says in her sweet voice as she follows him into my office.

"Dad," I bellow, catching them both off guard. "Stop yelling at my secretary."

"I'm your father," he argues. "I won't wait out here like some regular client."

Ignoring his outburst, I coolly reply, "I wasn't aware we had a meeting today."

"Where the hell have you been?" he says, staring at me as if I'm still sixteen and he still has control over me.

The first thing I notice about my father is that his suit is wrinkled, his cheeks are gaunt, and his hands have a shake to them I pick up on immediately. For a man who was once a revered pastor, broadcast around the world every Sunday, and builder of one of the biggest megachurches in Texas, he fell from very great heights. Now, it's just sad to look at him. Especially since I know he's hiding an ankle monitor under those dirt-stained slacks.

"Why don't you keep your voice down in my office?" I mutter, passing him by. When he enters the office space, I start to close the door behind him and mouth a silent *thank you* to Jules. She waves me off as I shut myself in with my father.

"Sit down," I say to my father as I move to the chair behind my desk.

"You got bourbon or something?" he asks.

"This is where I work," I reply flatly. "I don't drink at my office."

He huffs, staring in disgust as he drops into his chair. Seeing him sitting there, I fight the urge to smile. I bet he doesn't often get to sit in *that* chair. He was always the man behind the desk. The one who called the shots, holding the control and making others feel inferior.

My, how the tables have turned.

"What do you want?" I ask, placing my arms on my desk and staring at him without a hint of compassion on my face.

I watch as his molars grind, and he fights some sort of emotion bubbling to the surface. Then his expression changes, and it's as if the cloak is whisked away. Beneath it is a sad, lonely man staring at his son and wondering what went wrong.

I could ask myself the same thing.

"I need your help," he says, and when his voice cracks, it takes me by surprise.

Never in my life have I heard my father cry. Not for real, at least. In his sermons, he would perform. Pulling at the heartstrings of his congregation, I have heard him pretend he was so overcome with emotion and vulnerability that he was brought to tears.

I saw right through that charade.

But now...this feels real.

He's here begging me for mercy because I am the only one who can help him. This is not what I prepared myself to face.

Before I can let him change my mind, I look away and remind myself internally to stay strong.

"I can't help you," I say plainly.

"I know I messed up," he continues. "Lord, I pray every day for forgiveness, but what I've done is between me and God. I will face my justice on the day I meet him, I know that. But I can't go to prison, son."

He places his hand on my desk as if he's reaching for me, and I make the mistake of turning toward him. There are real tears streaming down his face.

"I can't help you. You know I can't," I say, but the moment the words leave my lips, I hear how weak they are. I'm letting him win. I've lost the confidence in my tone, giving him the upper hand.

"Your brothers are not without sin, Caleb. Before you pledge your loyalty to them, consider the mistakes *they've* made and have some compassion. You have the power to save this family, Caleb."

I lean back in my chair, losing the fight in me. For a moment, I actually consider the consequences of defending my father's case as if it's a choice I would actually make.

Protecting people is what I do. That has been my first priority for so long. Protect my family above everything else.

"Perhaps I could have a word with the judge," I say, my knee bouncing under the desk as anxiety swells inside me.

My dad quickly wipes his tears. "If you think that would help, son, I'd be so grateful."

"But I can't do much more than that," I say, but it feels like a lost cause. I gave him an inch. And I know my father will try and take a mile.

In my head, I keep thinking that if I just get him out of my office with empty promises, then I can brush this entire thing off. I'll go back to my family and the bright future ahead of us and pretend this never happened.

"Let me see if I have his information," I say.

As I pull open the top drawer of my desk, looking for my contact book, I freeze. Sitting at the back of my open drawer is a pair of black silk underwear—*Dean's black silk underwear.*

I'm frozen in place, just staring at them, and it's as if they are fingers snapping in front of my face.

What am I doing?

I'm actually considering helping the man who would ruin my

family if he knew Briar and I are in love with a man. How could I possibly defend him? He's a threat to our entire way of life.

He *is* the enemy.

It's like Isaac all over again—trying to protect him and only doing more harm than good. I hurt so many people with my actions because of *this man*. But I don't have to take that road again.

I can do better this time.

I slam the drawer shut.

"I don't have the contact," I mumble under my breath.

"What?" he snaps. "You didn't even look."

"I don't have to."

He glares at me skeptically from the chair. "Why not?"

"Because I'm not going to help you," I say, standing from my chair. It's like seeing the underwear finally gave me the confidence to let everything out. I'm tired of hiding. "And do you want to know why?" I continue. "Because you're a hypocritical, selfish, greedy, ignorant bigot who wouldn't even help his own *son*."

My blood is coursing through my veins so fast I feel it thrumming in my ears. I've never said anything like that to my father before. I'm getting worked up, and it feels a lot fucking better than I expected.

"What the hell has gotten into you?" he bellows, standing from his chair.

"You drove my seventeen-year-old brother away after he confided in you," I shout.

"Isaac ran away. I didn't do anything to him."

I want to scream at him.

"You never take responsibility for your actions! You never learn, and you always act like you're so much better than the rest of us, like you have some holy relationship with God, but if God could see the way you treat your own family, he'd send you straight to hell."

"Caleb Goode, you watch your mouth," he says in a deep, grumbling tone. "I am your father."

My skin is tingling, and this feels too good to stop. I'm just getting started.

"And one more thing, Dad," I reply, planting my hands on my desk and glaring at him with a mad, wild sort of look in my eye. Adrenaline pumps through my veins as I prepare myself for everything I'm about to say. It feels as if I'm coasting down a hill without brakes. Even if I could stop, I don't think I'd want to. "You wouldn't want my help if you knew that I'm queer too."

He flinches as if I've punched him. "What on God's earth are you talking about?"

"I'm bisexual, Dad. That's right. You were blessed with *two* queer sons. Not only that, but I'm in love with a man. And so is Briar. He's moving in with us, and we're going to be one big happy, polyamorous family."

His face is frozen as he stares at me, stunned. "You're joking," he replies, trying to force a laugh. "You're fucking around to get back at me for Isaac."

"You wish that, don't you? Because you can't stand the thought of accepting your children the way we are." I tear open the drawer and yank out Dean's underwear. "Well, too fucking bad!" I shout as I wave them in his face.

I look crazy, and I *feel* crazy. But, for the look on his face right now, it's worth it. It feels good to finally go mad.

"These are my hot boyfriend's underwear. I keep them in here to remind me of all the filthy, wonderful things we've done."

"You've lost your mind," he mutters, but I only laugh.

"Oh, and for what it's worth, he sucked my dick in your office." I shoot him a wink as I toss the underwear at him. He bats them away in disgust, but I only find myself laughing harder.

My father's look of astonishment quickly transforms into a sneer. "What kind of man acts like this?"

"Your son, Dad," I reply. "Aren't you proud of me?"

"First Adam and now you. You've both gone crazy."

"The only crazy thing I could do at this point is to help you. Now get the fuck out of my office and never call me again."

He moves for the door before turning back toward me with a finger pointed at my face. "If I find out this bullshit is true, I'll have my granddaughter taken away from you for raising her in a home of perverts. You should be ashamed of yourself."

"Come near my family, and I'll kill you," I mutter without a hint of a smile on my face before grabbing him by the back of the neck and tossing him out of my office.

Jules lets out a scream when he puts up a fight, but I manage to haul him out and toss him onto the floor before slamming the door in his face.

Forty-Seven

Dean

Standing in the kitchen, I stir the pasta sauce on the stove while Briar cuts up vegetables for the salad behind me. I didn't have any clients at the club tonight, but even if I did, I don't know if I would have wanted to leave this house.

I meant what I said to Caleb last night. I'm not changing my life or quitting my job if I decide to stay here with them and try to make this work. Plenty of sex workers keep up their jobs after they enter relationships. It's nothing to be ashamed of, and as long as we communicate and come to an agreement, it can work.

It feels like a lie I keep telling myself. We can make this work. Everything will be fine.

But Caleb and Briar's optimism is infectious.

"How is it?" she asks, coming up behind me and leaning into my side. I lift the spoon from the pan and blow on it before carefully bringing it to her mouth.

She takes a small bite and hums. I find myself fighting the urge to kiss her, but Abby is running around the house and could stumble in here at any moment.

"You're a good cook," she says as she turns back to her salad.

"Thanks," I reply. "I'm self-taught. My dad was a terrible cook, and if I didn't want to eat microwave dinners every night, I had to learn how to make something better."

"How resourceful of you," she replies with a smile.

"And how are you feeling?" I ask. "After that conversation with your sister."

Leaning against the counter, I watch her as she shrugs. Then she glances up my way with a forced smile. "I'm sad, but I hope she'll come around. But Caleb's right. It's going to be like that for a while."

"And it's worth it to you?" I ask.

Her smile isn't forced anymore. "Is it worth it to *you*? You're the one trading a life living alone in your apartment for family dinners and a suburban life."

Just then, as if on cue, Abby shouts for Briar from the downstairs bathroom. "Mo-om! I need you."

We both laugh at the same time. "It's messy," she says as she wipes her hands on the kitchen towel. "But it's fun."

While Briar is in the bathroom with Abby, the timer goes off on the stove. So I drain the noodles in the sink. Once I'm done with that, I set the table with plates and bowls.

As I'm retrieving the glasses from the cabinet, the door opens, and Caleb walks in. Immediately, I can tell something is different about him. Normally, Caleb is guarded and subdued, but within seconds, I can tell there is a frenetic energy about him. He's different from when he left just a few hours ago.

"What happened?" I say, holding a plate in my hands as he nearly ambushes me next to the dining room table. Grabbing me by the sides of my face, he pulls me in for a kiss, and I quickly push him away, worried that Abby might see.

"What are you doing?"

"I'm kissing you," he replies casually.

My brow furrows in confusion. "What happened at work?"

"It's not important," he says, "but seeing you standing here in my kitchen right now is the greatest thing in the world."

I continue gawking at him. He's practically beaming.

"Daddy!" Abby shrieks as she comes out of the bathroom, flying toward Caleb.

"Hey, peanut," he replies, hoisting her off the floor. She wraps her arms around his neck with a cheesy grin on her face.

Briar comes out a moment later and notices what I've done. "You set the table," she says.

"Let's eat," Caleb replies enthusiastically before kissing Briar on the side of the head. Everyone begins to dish up their food, and a moment later, we're all sitting around the table about to dig into our spaghetti dinner. We don't say grace or thank God for this meal, which takes me by surprise.

Instead, we all sort of stare at each other for a moment.

"This is nice," I mumble quietly.

"It is," Briar replies, resting her hand on mine.

Naturally, Abby is bouncing in her seat, spaghetti stains already covering her cheeks.

And while we eat, I can't help but think to myself just how perfect this is. Whatever happened at work with Caleb or with Briar's sister exists only in the outside world, but when we're here in this house together, none of that matters.

For the first time, I realize that this could work. We can shut out the world and live in harmony here. The judgment of others doesn't have to affect us.

Being with them doesn't make me feel so afraid of commitment anymore. They make being in a relationship feel so natural.

"Can I ride my bike after dinner?" Abby asks, slurping up a spaghetti noodle.

"Of course, peanut," Briar replies.

"Will you watch me?" she asks, looking up at me.

"Uh...sure."

As she grins with excitement, I feel my mouth pulling into a smirk.

For the rest of the meal, we don't bother with stressful, tense topics of conversation. Instead, Abby talks about how excited she is for school to start back up—to which Briar replies how excited she is as well.

It's all so comfortable and pleasant and *normal*. It reminds me of being a kid and sitting on the couch with my dad while eating dinner together. Sometimes, we'd go on the patio if the weather was nice and talk about nothing and everything all at once.

It's family, and nothing in the world can compare to that.

By the time we're cleaning up the table, I don't feel like an interloper or an outsider. I feel like I belong here.

I do belong here.

"You know what?" Briar says while drying a plate. "I don't know why, but I feel like we need a cake."

"A cake?" I ask.

She shrugs. "Yeah. We've had a rough few days and I just think we need to celebrate all being here together. It's a beautiful day. Why not have dessert?"

Caleb wraps his arm around Briar's shoulders. "I think that's a perfect idea. I'll run to the store."

"I'll come with you," she adds. "If Dean doesn't mind staying here with Abby."

Making a puzzled expression, I stare down at Abby as she hangs on my arm with glee. "I guess."

"Yay!" she squeals.

After the kitchen is clean, Briar and Caleb leave and I turn toward the bouncy six-year-old dancing around the kitchen.

"All right. Show me this bike of yours."

Abby hops excitedly as she takes my hand and drags me to the garage. When I hit the button to open it and see the pink-and-white bicycle in the corner with a little white basket and pink tassels on the handlebars, I glance down at her with concern.

"What is that?"

"That's my bike," she replies with a giggle as she drags it out of the garage.

"It has training wheels!" I say, pointing to the two extra wheels attached to the back.

Looking down, she hides her embarrassment. "I'm not good at riding without them yet."

I let out a breath as a feeling of shame washes over me. I can't be such a jerk to her all the time.

Kneeling down beside her, I lift her chin so she looks into my eyes. "I can help you ride without them if you want. I bet you're better than you think."

Her tiny lips purse together as she frowns at me. "But I don't like falling down."

"I'll catch you. You won't fall down."

"Promise?"

"I promise," I reply. "Go get your helmet on, and I'll take these off."

A minute later, I have Abby on her bike out front. She's scared at first. I can tell by the way she shakes and timidly hits the brakes every time the bike starts wobbling.

"Don't stop," I say, looking her in the eye. "You've got this, Abby. Just keep going."

"Okay," she replies with a quiver in her voice.

"You're a tough, strong, brave little badass, okay?"

She giggles. "Okay."

As she takes off again, I jog beside her, but when I notice her wanting to stop, I push her faster. "Pedal, Abby. Don't stop. You got this!"

When her little feet pick up speed, and she starts drifting away from me, I start to feel more excited than I've been in a long time. Stopping on the side of the road, I raise my hands in the air, shouting in excitement for her as she pedals all the way to the end of the street.

"That's it, Abby! Go! Go!" I yell.

When she reaches the stop sign, she manages a shaky turn and rides back toward me. I'm still cheering her on as she comes to a stop at my side, planting her feet on the ground as she shrieks.

"I did it! Did you see me? I did it!"

"Fuck yeah, you did it!" I shout.

When she hops off her bike, letting it fall to the ground, I hoist her into the air, swinging her triumphantly. She squeals with excitement, and when a couple passes by walking their dog, I place Abby on my shoulders and point to her.

"Look at this badass. She just learned to ride her bike without training wheels."

They smile at us and congratulate her as Abby laughs uncontrollably.

"Natural born talent," I continue as the couple passes by. "Watch out, Tour de France. Abigail Goode is the next bike-riding champion!"

She waves her arms in the air as we both laugh, jogging around the front yard like it's a victory lap. When I finally put her back down, she runs to her bike and climbs back on. Without any struggle, she starts riding around again, flying down the street like she's been doing it for years.

I watch with pride, a smile stretched across my face.

When a black car turns down the street, coming toward us, I shout for Abby to stay on the sidewalk. I expect the car to drive past our house, but as it comes to a stop at the end of our driveway, I stare in concern.

Abby rides back toward me, stopping near the parked car.

"Abby, get over here," I bark.

"Who is that?" she asks as she ditches her bike and rushes up to my side.

"I don't know," I reply, waiting for someone to get out. I push Abby behind me, just in case.

The driver's side door opens, and my jaw drops when I see a face from my past emerge. Truett Goode does not look anything like the booming force of a man I knew twelve years ago. He's withered away since then.

"Grandpa?" Abby murmurs tentatively. I keep a hand on her shoulder, holding her there.

"You," he mutters, his fierce gaze colliding with mine. When he makes his way to the front of the car, I notice the clumsiness in his movement. He's drunk. "What are you doing here?" he slurs.

"I live here," I argue.

He scoffs. "Where is my son?"

"He's not here, so why don't you go?"

"Dean, what's going on?" Abby whines behind me.

"Go in the house, Abby," I mutter.

Of course, she doesn't budge, clinging tighter to my side. I can feel her hand squeezing my arm in a death grip. The fact that he's scaring her makes my blood boil.

"You're the one my son was talking about, aren't you? You turned him into a—"

"Watch your mouth," I bark, shouting over his slur and hoping Abby didn't hear it. "Leave now, or I'll call the police."

He laughs. "This is *my* family. You may have already turned my son into a pervert, but I won't let him raise my granddaughter like this. Abby, come to Grandpa."

She trembles behind me, and my teeth clench together in rage as I stare at him. I'd like to break his nose right now for even talking to her, but I don't want to scare her. Instead of walking toward Truett, I back Abby up toward the house.

In my periphery, I notice neighbors watching, and I wonder if they're calling the police already.

"Stay by me, Abby," I say softly.

"I'm scared," she whimpers.

"You think you can keep my granddaughter from me?" he shouts. "I'll have the police take you away."

"You're drunk, Truett. Why don't you go home now?" I say, struggling to keep my cool.

He's advancing on us, and I keep waiting for him to attack. I'm not worried for Abby's safety because I know I'll have his face in the cement before he lays a hand on her. But I don't want it to get that far.

"Shut the fuck up," he mutters, throwing another slur at me that I try not to react to. "Abby, come with Grandpa, *now*." His voice booms with his anger, and I lose it.

Shoving Abby farther behind me until she's in the garage, I step toward Truett. Pushing my chest against his, I get in his face.

"I don't want to bloody your drunk ass right here for her sake, but if you yell at her again, I swear I will."

"Are you threatening me?" he replies with a sneer. His breath reeks of bourbon.

When I notice red and blue lights down the street, I turn my attention away from him for a split second, and he takes it as his opportunity to act. He lunges toward Abby, and she screams in fear.

It's bloodcurdling, a sound I'll never forget as long as I live.

I tackle Truett to the ground with the force of hatred built up over a decade. He lands hard against the concrete of the driveway. As I stare down at his ugly face, thinking about everything he's done to Isaac, I want to pummel my fist against his face. I'd like to feel the way his nose cracks or hear the way he cries in pain.

But Abby is crying, and I refuse to be the reason she cries any more.

The cops ambush us, making her scream again as they haul me off the old man's chest. When one of them tries to bind my wrists behind my back, I just see Abby crying in the garage. Tears are streaming down her face, and I shout at the officer behind me.

"Wait! I live here!"

"Dean!" Abby shrieks.

"Sir, calm down!" the police officer shouts, but all I see is Abby. She's so scared and alone, and I can't stand it.

"Please, that's my little girl!" I scream.

It takes the cops a moment to register that I'm not the one trespassing here, and they release my wrists. I bolt across the driveway and yank Abby into my arms. She wraps her whole body around me while she sobs into my shoulder.

"It's okay," I mumble as I stroke her back. "It's okay. We're all right. I've got you."

Over and over, I repeat those words, mostly to comfort her but also to comfort myself. We're all right. Everything is going to be okay.

Everything *has* to be okay.

FORTY-EIGHT

Briar

When we turn into our neighborhood and see the police car parked in front of our house, I let out a scream. "Caleb!"

He gasses it to our front yard, and it's nearly impossible to make sense of what I'm seeing. My eyes only look for one person—Abby.

I bolt out of the car before it's even in park, and when I spot Dean on the front porch with Abby wrapped around his neck, I take off in a frantic sprint.

"Oh my god. What happened? Is she okay?" I shriek as I brush my daughter's hair from her face, looking for any signs of harm or pain.

There's a police officer standing nearby with a clipboard in her hands. Dean looks at me, and I notice the fear in his eyes.

"He just showed up. Scared the shit out of us, but we're okay."

"Ma'am, is this your house?" the officer asks.

"Yes," I stammer. "I live here."

"Me too," Caleb replies, placing a hand on my back and

checking Abby. She won't leave Dean's arms. "Someone, please explain what happened."

The officer steps up. "We received a call from one of your neighbors that there was an altercation on your property. When we showed up, Mr. Sheridan assured us that he was a resident here and that Mr. Truett Goode was trespassing and making violent threats against him and your daughter."

"Oh my god," I gasp, putting my hand over my mouth.

Dean holds Abby tight against his chest while he looks like he's seen a ghost. In the short time since we left, he's been through so much. It breaks my heart to see it.

Beside me, Caleb tenses, turning toward the police car parked on the street in front of our house.

"He's in there?" he asks.

"Yes, sir," the officer replies.

"I'm going to fucking kill him," he mutters under his breath.

"Caleb, don't," I say, reaching for him, but he's already gone.

Marching toward the car, the police officers step in his way to keep him from opening the door. A despondent Truett sits behind the glass, staring straight ahead instead of turning toward his son.

"Leave him," I say, grabbing Caleb's arm and holding him back. "Stay with us."

It takes Caleb a moment to relax, turning back toward Dean, Abby and me.

"I think I have everything for the report. We'll have his car towed off your property, but for now, we'll be taking your father into custody. If you have any more questions or need anything, I'll leave my card here with you," the police officer says, handing her card to me.

"Thank you," I reply.

Once she's gone, Dean stands from the porch and takes Abby inside. Seeing how tightly she's clinging to Dean is both touching and terrifying. She must have been so scared. I've never seen her like this.

"What about my bike?" she says, lifting her face from his shoulder.

"We'll get your bike, peanut," I reply. When her eyes meet mine, she finally releases Dean and reaches for me. I pull her into my arms, holding her tight as I kiss her head.

Leaving Dean and Caleb to talk downstairs, I carry Abby up to the second-floor bathroom. Running her a bath, I carefully help her undress and step into the bubbles. She seems a lot calmer now as I pour warm water over her head.

"Would you like to talk about what happened?" I ask.

She shakes her head. But then, after a moment, she says, "Grandpa was scary."

"I know he was, and I'm very sorry he scared you."

"He doesn't like Dean. He was so mean to him."

I swallow the lump building in my throat as I settle onto the floor next to the bathtub. "Grandpa was wrong to be so mean to Dean."

"Why doesn't he like him?"

"He doesn't know Dean like we do," I reply. Stroking her head, I think about how innocent she is. I love that, and I wish I could preserve that forever. I want my daughter to make her own judgments on what is right and wrong in life without me or anyone else forming those opinions for her. I want her to hold on to this childhood innocence forever, but I know eventually she'll have to cut her own teeth on dealing with ignorance in the world.

"You know how we love Dean, and he's like a part of our family now?" I say.

She nods. "Yeah."

"Well, some people won't like that. Some people think families shouldn't have Deans. But it's only because they don't understand. Our family will look a little different than everyone else's, and that's okay. We just have to be patient, but no matter what, Daddy, Dean, and I will always protect you."

She nods again.

After her bath, I carry Abby to her room and lie with her for a while. We take turns reading books to each other. There is a sense of peace inside me now, knowing that Abby might be the only child I have. It makes me want to slow down time and savor every moment with her.

And maybe, down the line, I'll have a change of heart or be open to other avenues of parenthood, but for this moment right now, I want to be present with her.

Before she falls asleep, Caleb comes in and kisses her on the head while Dean watches from the doorway.

"Daddy, will you lie with me?" she asks, and he smiles down at her.

"Of course."

I climb out of her bed, and he lies in my place. Abby makes herself comfortable on his arm, and I know that Daddy sleep magic will only take a few minutes to kick in.

Dean and I slip out of the room, and he pauses in the hallway outside our bedroom. "Come on," I whisper, taking his hand and tugging him into our room.

"Are you okay?" I ask, feeling the tension in his body. He won't meet my gaze as he stares at the floor, deep in thought. Worry builds in my gut.

"This was all my fault," he mutters, and I quickly grip his arms, forcing him to look at me.

"Dean, stop it. It's not your fault at all."

"Yes, it is," he argues. "Briar, I don't want Abby's life to be like this, constantly having to hear people's bullshit and be the victim of their ignorance."

"Her life won't be like that—"

"Yes," he snaps, glaring at me. "It will, and you know it. We don't live in a perfect world, and loving each other isn't going to make everything better. At the end of the day, we have to protect *her*."

I'm staring at him, my eyes wide and beginning to moisten. "I can't believe you're saying this right now," I mumble as he walks away. "Dean, you *protected* her."

"I shouldn't have had to," he replies.

"You're just upset," I say, coming up behind him. Placing my hands on his arms, I rest my forehead against his back.

Just when I feel like everything is coming together, he's slipping away. If I could hold him tighter, hug this fear out of him, and force him to stay, I would. But deep down, I know that's not right. This has to be his choice. I refuse to let him resent us for what happens once we're together.

Every harsh glare from someone. Every judgmental comment. Every laugh behind our backs. Dean is right that nothing we do will shield us from those people, but if that's truly something he doesn't want to endure, then Caleb and I cannot force him to.

My dreams are shattering right in front of my eyes.

"Let's sleep on it," I say. "We don't need to make drastic choices."

"Okay," he murmurs.

A moment later, Caleb joins us, but judging by his sour mood, he and Dean already had this same conversation while I was bathing Abby.

"Stay with us tonight," I plead. "Just sleep here."

Dean turns toward me, running his thumb over my cheek. "Just tonight."

The mood is somber as we each take off our clothes, climbing into bed together. Dean lies between us, and there is no need for sex tonight. We just absorb this feeling of togetherness that exists only when the three of us are here.

I kiss Dean without urgency or desire. But I feel the sadness in his touch. The way he holds my face as if he's memorizing the feel of my lips against his.

As I run my hands up Dean's rib cage, I find my husband's fingers there too. Intertwining them, we embrace him together. Dean's mouth casually moves from mine to Caleb's and back again.

Before it can grow too heated, the three of us stop and just hold each other. My eyes find Caleb's, and we stare at each other for a moment. There's a sense of failure in our gazes. As if we both know we started celebrating too soon. We had everything for a brief moment, but now it's gone.

Tomorrow, we will be in this bed again, but Dean won't be between us. Things will go back to the way they were. And we'll have to figure out how to survive without him—the way we did for years before.

Forty-Nine

Caleb

21 years old

My head is foggy, and the lights are too bright. As I peel my eyes open, I quickly clench them back together, blocking the buzzing fluorescent bulbs from stabbing my skull. Everything hurts, which means the drugs are wearing off.

But I've been in such a haze that I don't want any more drugs.

My lips hurt as I peel my mouth open to grumble out a weak, "Briar?"

"I'm here."

Her sweet voice fills my ears, and I let out a sigh. A straw is pressed against my lips, and I suck in ice-cold water, which might be the best drink I've ever had in my life. I feel it going all the way down, saturating my tired, aching body.

Squinting my eyes open, I stare at the most beautiful girl I've ever seen. Blonde wisps of hair surround her head, making her glow like an angel. Shutting my mouth, I stay quiet as I just stare at her.

"Are you in pain?" she asks, touching my forehead.

I lie and shake my head. No more drugs.

If I so much as twitch my arm, searing hot pokers radiate up my entire arm and down my spine. I had no idea breaking your arm could hurt so much.

"You're here," I whisper.

"Of course I'm here," she replies. "Caleb, I couldn't leave you."

"What about Sean?" I ask, my voice splintering like a tree in a storm.

Briar's eyebrows pinch inward as she leans toward me. "Forget Sean," she mutters coldly. "I was so wrong for staying with him as long as I did, but I was afraid. I was a coward. But he and I are done for good now. I will never speak to him again. I mean, look what he did to you." She starts to cry, her nostrils flaring and her eyes tearing up.

"I don't care," I mutter. "I'm fine."

"Caleb, you're not fine," she replies. "Your hand..." Her voice trails as she looks away, wiping tears from her cheek. "You're going to lose your scholarship, and they don't think you'll be able to play college football anymore."

Staring into her eyes, I wish I had the strength to move so I could wrap my arms around her. All I can manage is to lift my left arm to her face. Gently holding her chin, I force her to look at me. "I don't give a fuck about football."

"And your scholarship?"

"I'll get a student loan. I don't care, Briar. I really don't."

She presses her lips together as she grins at me. "I was afraid you'd never want to see me again."

"Are you crazy?" I ask. "They could break every bone in my body, and it would be worth it just to wake up and see you sitting there."

She starts to cry again. "Oh, Caleb."

As she buries her face in my chest, I use my good arm to softly stroke her hair. My right arm still screams in pain, but it doesn't matter.

A moment later, the door opens, and a nurse walks in. "That husband of yours is finally awake," she says sweetly before dimming the lights.

"Husband?" I mumble.

Briar lifts her face and laughs. Then she glances at the nurse as if they have some inside joke I'm not privy to. "The only people allowed to stay in the room outside of visiting hours are parents and spouses."

"So it's a good thing y'all are married," the nurse replies with a chuckle as she draws the curtains open, letting in the early morning light.

Briar bites her bottom lip, trying to hide her smile. "This angel lied for me so I could stay all night. I didn't want you to wake up alone."

"Thank you," I say to the nurse as she comes over to check my vitals.

"I know love when I see it, and this girl was not leaving your side."

My heart picks up speed in my chest, and I wonder if the nurse can see it on the monitor what hearing that does to me. Briar told me she loved me, and then she showed me. Honestly, there's not an ounce of pain on this planet that could make me regret that.

"You're a lifesaver..." I say, glancing at her name badge before adding, "Abigail."

Present Day

It's been a week since my father's visit. I haven't spoken to him since, and I don't care to. Last I heard, he found a new lawyer who posted his bail, and his hearing has been moved up. Any chances of getting his charges dropped now are gone. The man can't even help himself at this point.

Dean has hardly left his apartment. He's putting distance between us because he thinks it's what we need.

Abby started school again yesterday, and he at least came out in the morning to see her first day of school dress.

But as for us, things between us, I think it's over. It feels like I've failed. And I don't know if I'll ever get over the heartbreak this has caused my family—all of us.

Briar is despondent. She drinks every night, crying alone in the bathtub, and there's nothing I can do to fix this. If I tell her that I'll get him back, she just argues that we can't force him into this.

But that's just not good enough for me. I know when to accept defeat, but this is so much more than that. This is my family. And I can't lose my family.

Abby has asked about Dean every day since, but we just cover it up with him being busy, having to work, or needing rest. If this truly is the end, and he moves out, then will she forget him? Do I want her to?

Lying in bed, Briar is sleeping beside me, and I'm scrolling through Instagram again, looking for a distraction from the mess that is my own life.

And there he is—Theo Virgil.

He's on tour, playing on a stage in some historic-looking venue with huge rustic chandeliers in what looks like some old speakeasy. The place appears packed, filled to the brim with people.

Let's do this, Austin, it says in the caption.

My eyes nearly bug out of my head. I quickly glance at the date, realizing a moment too late that my brother's show was *tonight*.

I don't know why, but I immediately fly out of my bed. Briar doesn't move as I run into our closet and grab the first pair of jeans I see. I'm not even sure what I'm doing. This is crazy. I've already missed the show, but that doesn't matter because he's *here*.

Isaac is in Austin, just a few miles away. I can't just go to sleep knowing that.

In a frenzy, I slip on my shoes and tiptoe down the stairs. I'm in my SUV and driving down the road, still without a plan. I don't need a plan. I just need to *try*.

It takes me about thirty minutes to get to the venue. Checking the time stamp on his last story, he started his set about an hour ago. It's not likely he's still playing, but if I'm lucky, I can try to catch him coming out.

Quickly, I park across the street and run toward the brick building squeezed into one of Austin's more quaint and artistic districts. The vibes here are young and hip, with coffee shops and vintage clothing stores around the corner.

By the time I reach the building, it's clear the show has ended, and very few stragglers are still coming out of the venue. I look around for a back entrance or a place where the artists might come and go. On the side of the building, there's a tall fence to keep people from getting to the doorway in the back, but I know this has to be it.

A small black van is parked near the exit, and there are people coming and going, packing boxes and equipment into the trunk.

I check every face, looking for the familiar one, the one who shares my DNA. The eyes of my baby-face little brother. The sweet kid who once cried to our mother for hours after I kicked over an anthill.

My skin is buzzing, and my heart is pounding. He's here. *Isaac is here.*

As I watch the band members and roadies come and go, a few girls congregate around me. They're giggling and taking pics, clearly fans of Theo and just hoping for a glimpse.

Suddenly, as I stand there waiting for my brother, I get a feeling of regret washing through me.

What am I doing?

This is his life. His escape. His safe space. And I'm here infiltrating it like I have some claim to every aspect of his life just because he's my brother.

Isaac doesn't owe me a damn thing, and Theo Virgil might as well be a stranger to me.

Just because my life is a mess doesn't mean I need to bring any of that into his. He's safer with distance. I'm always so concerned about keeping everyone safe, but this is one instance when walking away is how I protect him.

Before I'm spotted, I quickly back away from the fence. Pulling the cap farther down on my head, I shove my hands in my pockets and turn to make my way back to my car.

This was stupid. I'm an asshole for even coming here.

"Theo! Theo! Over here!" The girls cheer excitedly, flashes illuminating the night sky as they take photo after photo.

And I can't help myself. I have to at least look. I need to lay my eyes on him, even if that's all I do.

So I turn.

His head is tilted down, with a cowboy hat hiding most of his face. The brightness of his smile stops me in my tracks. He approaches the fence line, beaming at the women. With shoulder-length brown hair and a rugged blue jean jacket, he looks like a star. He looks like he was made for this.

"Hey there," he says in a Southern drawl with a mixture of confidence and shyness. I smile to myself as I watch him interact with his fans.

They gush over how much they love his songs, and he blushes in return, thanking them for coming.

As I watch from across the street, I try to find traces of my little brother inside this country music star. He's there. In the dimples in his cheeks. The way he fidgets with his hair. The way he looks right into their eyes when they're talking to him.

For a moment, I'm at peace. I don't need anything from him to feel better. He doesn't need to acknowledge me or let me in. He's happy. And I refuse to ruin that.

So, with that, I turn away from him and head toward my car.

I only make it three steps before I hear his voice call...

"Caleb?"

Fifty

Caleb
21 years old

My arm is in a sling, and I'm lying on my couch next to my brother Isaac. There's a football game on, but I'm not paying much attention. Instead, I'm scrolling on my phone, trying to get used to doing anything with my left hand.

I hate the way meds make me feel, but the pain is worse. The screws in my arm are at least keeping it steady, but the bones in my hand will have to heal on their own.

I wouldn't wish this on my worst enemy.

"Wanna play Gran Turismo*?" Isaac asks. "You could probably steer with one hand."*

He gives me a sympathetic smile, and I force one in return. Ruffling his hair, I reply, "Nah. Thanks, though."

When his gaze drifts down to my blue and swollen fingers peeking out of the cast, he winces. "I hope I never get in a fight. Does it hurt?"

Staring at my little brother, the image of him going through what I went through makes me sick. His face pressed against the concrete. Cruel feet stomping on him. Relentless kicks against his rib cage.

Bile rises in my throat.

I want to tell Isaac that it wasn't a fight. It was a slaughter.

My little brother might not survive that. I want to make him understand that people can be cruel and hateful, and like-minded ignorance is stronger in numbers.

Around here, they would do worse to him for less.

I have to swallow down the lump building in my throat.

No. I'll protect him. I can keep him safe—at least for as long as I'm around.

"Listen to me," I reply soberly. "I don't want you ever getting in a fight like me. You just keep your head down and don't go thinking you're tough enough to take them because you're not. Don't do anything to provoke them or give them a reason to hate you."

"Jesus," he mutters, clearly scared by my sudden humorless demeanor. He tries to laugh it off, so I grab his arm with my good hand.

"I'm serious, Isaac. High school can be brutal, and I won't be around forever to protect you. Just...blend in, okay?"

His expression settles as he stares into my eyes, and that's when I can tell he gets what I'm implying. I hate that I have to ask my brother to conform because of the close-minded world we live in. It feels wrong, but I refuse to let him go through what I did.

"Relax, Caleb," he says softly, patting my arm.

Forcing myself to breathe, I rest against the back of the sofa and stare numbly at the TV. We watch the game for a while. I order a pizza while he puts some headphones on and hums a tune I've never heard before.

When there's a knock at the door, I stand from the couch and go to answer it.

I expect it to be our pizza, but when I open it to find young Dean standing on the welcome mat, my eyes narrow, and I close the door a little to block Isaac from view.

His eyes rake over my broken arm and bruised-up face.

"Hey..." he stammers. "Is Isaac here?"

"No," I answer coldly. "He's, uh, off with some friends."

Pain crosses Dean's face and I hate myself. His molars clench, and I know he can tell I'm lying.

"I don't believe you," he mumbles.

"You don't have to believe me," I reply.

He stares at me with hatred, but I don't care.

"You just don't like your brother dating a guy," he says like it's supposed to hurt my feelings.

"No, I don't like my brother dating someone that's going to get him hurt."

"I'm going to get him hurt?" he replies.

I step outside, closing the door behind me. "Yes, Dean. You're too reckless. You think we live in a world where it's safe to be yourself, and we don't. Hate me if you want to, but you need to stay away from my brother."

I can see his fists tighten at his sides and his nostrils flare as if he's fighting off tears.

"Fine," he mutters before backing away. Before leaving, he lets out a dry and emotionless, "Fuck you, Caleb. You're an asshole."

That's fine, *I think as I watch him walk away angrily. I'll be the asshole. Anything to keep my brother safe.*

†

Present Day

"Is that you?"

When I turn back around, the fans are mostly scattered, and Theo Virgil is standing alone on the opposite side of a tall chain-link fence. He's staring at me quizzically.

"It's me," I mutter as I take one single step toward him.

Our eyes meet. One city street and nine years between us. Time slows as I take another step.

"Did you come to my show?" he asks.

Shamefully, I shake my head. "I missed it. But I thought if I hurried, I could at least see you."

His eyes dart around, looking behind me as he asks, "Are you alone?"

I nod.

Then silence settles between us. His smile fades and in its place is a tense, flat-lipped expression. He should yell at me, tell me to never come back, leave him alone. He should swear me to secrecy and be furious at me for even showing up.

Instead, he shrugs. "Wanna grab a beer?"

I could cry as a laugh slips through my lips. Without letting the emotion brewing inside me bubble over the top, I clear my throat and stare at the pavement. "Yeah. I'd like that a lot."

"I'll meet you around the front. There's a bar next door."

"Okay," I say, my voice cracking.

As he disappears, I blow out a heavy breath.

Get it together, Caleb.

With my hands in my pockets, feigning calmness, I walk to the front of the venue. And then Isaac is standing right in front of me. I nearly forgot how tall he was, probably a few inches taller than me.

He traded his cowboy hat for a trucker hat and his jean jacket for a hoodie.

And now we're just staring like two old friends who ran into each other. I want to break down, grab him, and haul him into a hug as I sob into his shoulder. But I don't. I keep my cool.

His eyes are glued to my face. "You look good," he mumbles. "You're so grown up."

"So are you," I reply, struggling to keep it together.

We're strangers. My little brother and I are strangers, and it hurts so much I don't know if I can get down a beer without sobbing.

"Come on," he replies, leading the way to the hole-in-the-wall bar next door. As we enter, Isaac walks directly to the bar, grabbing a stool as I take the one next to him. We order a couple of beers like this is just a casual drink.

I'm practically shaking inside.

The bartender hands us two longneck bottles and I hold it up to my brother. "Cheers," I say.

He taps his against mine. "Cheers."

When we drink, we keep our eyes on each other, and I decide that I want this entire encounter to be about him. I want to hear everything. And I don't want him to know about Dad or Adam or any of that bullshit.

"So, Theo Virgil," I say with a smile as I turn toward him. "How did this happen?"

He laughs to himself bashfully. "I moved out to Nashville with a friend. I started bartending at a place with live music, and after a while, I started writing my own songs, and a few years back, I got on stage for the first time and started playing them."

I can't stop smiling. "That's amazing. I'm so proud of you."

He tips his bottle toward me before taking a swig. "And how did you find me?"

It's my turn to look bashful. "I'm a lawyer now. I find out everything."

He nods with a laugh. "You and Briar are still together?"

"Yep," I reply, wanting to turn the conversation back toward him, but then I realize something.

Abby.

I quickly pull out my phone, the picture of her on the lock screen. When I point it toward Isaac, his lips part as his eyes gaze at the smiling little girl on the screen. It's an old picture. Abby was only about three, with a big cheesy grin. I think we took it on Easter when Briar put her in a flowery pink dress and placed her in a big flowerpot in our front yard.

"Oh my god," Isaac whispers.

"Her name is Abby. She's almost seven now. Hang on. Let me find some more pics."

My phone is full of photos and I must scroll through a hundred of them, showing Isaac. He devours each one, smiling from ear to ear as I tell him all about her.

"Caleb, she's incredible," he mumbles. "I can't believe you have a kid."

As I put my phone back in my pocket, I don't point out that I'm thirty-three now and I've been married for ten years. Having a kid isn't all that surprising for guys like me, but for Isaac, I'm still twenty-three, just out of college, and newly married. That's where I was in my life before he left.

Couple years later, Briar was pregnant.

Things grow silent between us for a moment. I wonder if he's curious about the rest of the family. Does he want to know how things are with Mom or Dad? Does he know about what Adam has been through this year? Is he curious about Luke?

Or is all of that too heavy? This is just a casual beer. It's not the time to get into all the family drama and face the hard truth that nearly a decade has gone by since I've spoken with my brother.

He picks at the label of his beer when I finally decide to face the elephant head-on.

"I nearly messaged you so many times."

He looks up and stares into my eyes. "Why didn't you?"

"Because I felt bad for even knowing your secret," I reply. "And I don't want to mess up everything you have going for yourself, Isaac."

He flinches at the use of that name. Does no one in his business even know the real him?

"I understand," he replies sadly. "And I appreciate that."

"But fuck," I say in a low grumble. "I've missed you so much."

His head snaps up as he stares in shock. "You have?"

"Of course, Isaac," I reply in an urgent whisper. "I hate myself for not protecting you that night. I should have defended you—"

"I don't want to talk about that," he snaps, closing his lips tightly.

I freeze, letting the words hang there. I don't know if he's referring to that night or our father or coming out.

But it doesn't matter. I said this night was going to be about him, not me or our past. So I quickly drop it.

"I'm sorry," I say. "Of course. We don't have to talk about any of that. I just want to hear about you. Tell me everything."

He takes a drink, looking uncomfortable as he shrugs. "There's not much to tell. But I'd appreciate it if you wouldn't tell everyone..."

"Of course," I reply confidently. "Your secret's safe with me."

"Thanks."

Then, with a pause, I add, "I can tell Briar, right?"

"For sure," Isaac replies with a shrug.

My jaw clenches before quickly throwing in, "And Dean?"

Isaac freezes, his eyes narrowing before glancing at me. "Dean? *My* Dean?"

Biting my bottom lip to keep me from grinning, I reply, "Well, he's sort of *my* Dean now."

Isaac couldn't look more shocked. "Really?"

And that's how I end up telling my little brother everything about how I pushed Dean away twelve years ago and how he reentered my life recently. I leave out the dirty details, of course.

"So, you're..." he starts.

With the beer bottle at my lips, I finish the sentence for him. "Bisexual, I guess."

This makes him laugh. "You guess?"

"Listen, this wasn't supposed to be about me," I argue, setting my drink down. "This was supposed to be about you."

"No," he argues. "I like hearing about you. I've...missed a lot."

"Yeah," I mumble to myself. "You have."

Before I know it, our beers are gone, and it feels like time is slipping through my fingers. I'm not ready to let him go again.

I pay the bartender, and we slide the empty bottles to the inside edge of the bar. Then we stand and face each other for a moment. He walks to the door first and I follow.

This whole thing feels like a fever dream. Did any of this really happen?

As we stand on the sidewalk in front of the bar, we shuffle our feet a bit, putting off this goodbye. I need to say something, but I don't know how to express this.

"Thanks, Caleb," he mutters under his breath. "I appreciate you coming."

"I'd come to all of them if I could. But I want to give you your space, Isaac. I'm just happy that you're free now."

His head pops up. With a scoff, he says, "I'm not free."

"What do you mean?" I ask.

"You think because I ran away from our dad that I'm free? You think there's anywhere I can go to be free from him and people like him?"

"I—" The words are caught on my lips.

"Caleb, I didn't run away to feel free. I ran away because I knew that if I stayed there, I'd hate myself just like he wanted me to."

My chest is heaving as I receive this information. This entire time, I thought Isaac was free. And meanwhile, I've been trying to promise my family that same sense of freedom. To hear him say he'll never have it is devastating.

"So we just have to live with his voice in our heads forever?" I ask. "Constantly telling us we're not good enough."

Isaac shrugs. "Music helps me drown the voices out."

Glancing away, I stare unfocused at the glow of streetlights on the dark buildings. What is my distraction? What helps me drown out his voice?

There's no hesitation—Briar, Abby, Dean.

We were never going to outrun other people's judgment or my father's hatred. There's nowhere we could move that would give us that freedom. But we can give each other peace.

If we let Dean go, we'd be letting them win. Truett Goode would get exactly what he wants.

I can't let that happen.

"Everything okay?" Isaac asks.

"Yeah," I say, clearing my throat. "I just...realized something."

He nods, a lopsided smirk on his face. "Well, you should go...be with your family."

"I am," I reply, placing a hand on his shoulder.

Before I have a chance to go in for a hug, he closes the distance, wrapping his arms around me. Feeling how tightly he holds me shatters my resolve.

In the blink of an eye, my tears are staining his hoodie as I let the emotion roll through me. A sob escapes when I feel him do the same.

"I love you, Isaac. And I'm so fucking proud of you."

"I love you, too," he replies, his voice cracking as he cries.

When we pull away from each other, our faces are a mess. Turning away, we quickly wipe our tears and compose ourselves.

"You know you can message me anytime," he says, shoving his hands in his pockets.

"I will," I reply.

"Send me pictures of my niece. I'd really like that."

Stepping backward, I smile at him. "I promise I will."

"And uh...tell Dean I said hey." He scratches the back of his neck as he smirks.

Laughing, I clear my throat. "You got it."

"Bye, Caleb," he says, waving at me as he walks toward the van at the back of the venue.

"Bye, Theo," I call, making him laugh. "Good luck on the rest of your tour."

"Thanks," he replies before turning away.

One of his bandmates claps a hand on his back before Isaac jumps into the van.

And then that's it. I'm in my car, driving home, tears streaming down my face as I replay that entire thing. It still feels like a dream, but a great dream.

For a brief moment, he gave me a piece of his life, and if that's all I can get for now, I can live with that.

I keep thinking about what he said about feeling free. How we never truly escape our father's judgment. And it makes me realize that if I'll never escape the thoughts he's planted in my head, then what is the point of running?

Just like the day I woke up in that hospital, swearing to Briar that I'd endure far worse for her, I want to be able to promise Dean the same thing. Whatever the world wants to throw at us, we can take it.

Toss us into the fires of hell if it wants to. For this love we share, it would still be worth it.

Fifty-One

Briar

The front door closing wakes me up. I pop up in bed and look at the clock to see it's past midnight. Caleb isn't beside me, so I wait until I hear his familiar footsteps on the stairs before I relax.

When he steps into the room and sees me awake, he pauses. "Sorry," he whispers. "Did I wake you?"

"It's okay. Where were you?" I ask.

He's in jeans and a baseball cap, definitely not what I'm used to seeing him in. With a sigh, he drops onto his side of the bed and stares at me.

"I saw Isaac," he whispers.

I let out a gasp. "What? Where?"

As he explains everything, how he's been following this country singer, who is actually his estranged brother, on Instagram and found out he had a show in Austin tonight, I feel grateful and regretful at the same time. On the one hand, I'm glad Caleb is at a place where he feels comfortable sharing these secrets with me, but at the same time, I hate that he had secrets in the first place.

"I realized something tonight," he says softly. "We can't just let Dean go."

"Caleb," I start with the tone of a warning. "We can't—"

"I know," he says, cutting me off. "We can't force him, but we have to fight for him, Briar. Because if we don't, then we're basically letting people like my father win."

"But...what if he resents us?" I ask. If I had any tears left to cry, I would, but I'm exhausted. Every ounce of energy to feel anything has been spent.

"Then we'll cross that bridge when we get there, but we have to try. What a waste to throw love away to try and be free. We may never be free, Briar. But this way, we can at least be together. I fought for you, and I'll fight for him just the same."

He grips my hand in his, squeezing tight. His eyes are rimmed red, which I know means he's been crying. Deep down, I know he's right. It's a mistake to let this go.

"Come to bed," I whisper. "We can talk to him tomorrow while Abby's at school."

With a sigh, he finally relents. I watch as he undresses and climbs into bed beside me. I place my head on his chest and stare up at him. Pressing his lips to mine, he kisses me softly.

Before long, I drift off to sleep, but I can feel Caleb beside me, restless all night.

†

"Don't forget your lunch box!" I shout toward Abby as she bolts for the front door. The long yellow bus can be heard from all the way down the street as it heads toward our house.

Jogging behind Abby, I hand her her lunch and kiss her on the head as she runs to meet the other kids getting on the bus on our street.

She giggles excitedly with her friends as the bus rolls up and stops in front of them. It's still so hard to watch her go to school every morning. Not being there to protect her at every moment takes strength and faith as a parent I never prepared for.

Putting on a brave face, I watch from the porch as Abby climbs onto the school bus. Once she finds her seat, she waves at me through the window, and I wave back.

I'm so deep in thought as her bus rolls away that I hardly notice the car missing from our driveway. As I head back toward the house, I glance toward the apartment above the garage, where I know Dean is currently sleeping.

But I stop in my tracks and glance back toward the driveway for a sign of his car. Dread rolls through me when I realize it's not there.

"Caleb," I call, moving quickly toward the house. As I enter the back door that leads to the kitchen, I find Caleb pouring himself a cup of coffee. "Do you know where Dean is?"

He pauses. "He's not in his apartment?"

"His car's gone," I reply.

When our gazes meet, I recognize the instant fear in his eyes. I rush out the door first, jogging across the yard and up the stairs. I bang on his door, hoping he'll answer and put this fear to rest. I'm aware there are a hundred possibilities of where he could be that is nothing to worry about, but my gut tells me something is wrong.

There's no answer. Caleb comes up the stairs a moment later with keys in hand. As he unlocks the apartment, I dash inside and find it empty.

"Where could he be?" I ask.

"Let's not panic," he replies. "His stuff is still here, so he's coming back."

"What if he's hurt, Caleb? What if there was a car accident or someone hurt him while he was alone? No one would know to call us."

"I'll call him," he replies in a rush, pulling out his phone. I can hear it ringing through the speaker, but after a few unanswered rings, it goes to voice mail.

I pull out my phone and shoot him a text.

Just let us know you're okay.

In the back of my mind, I know there's a possibility that Dean is perfectly safe and that he's just found someone else to keep company overnight and into the early morning hours. That realization hurts, but could we blame him?

Caleb and I have each other. If Dean is alone, he has no one.

"Adam," Caleb says, holding his phone to his ear after calling his brother. "Did Dean come into work last night? He's not home, and we're a little worried."

I stare, waiting for a response.

Caleb looks at me, his expression shrouded in disappointment. "He didn't? Okay. Yeah, if you hear anything, let us know."

He hangs up his phone, and I bring my hand to my forehead.

"Where could he be? He never goes anywhere this early in the morning."

"It's too early to start panicking," Caleb replies, and I turn away from him, annoyed with that response. All of a sudden, he's the calm and collected one. Normally, it's the other way around.

As the minutes roll by and Caleb and I spend the next hour pacing around and waiting, the worry starts to congeal and turn into guilt. I promised his father I wouldn't let Dean be alone. I promised that we would always have him. We would always be there to protect him.

Suddenly, I stop pacing and quickly pull out my phone. It's a long shot, but I do a quick search of the nursing home where we met Dean's father. Biting my lip nervously, I hit the call button. After a couple of rings, someone picks up.

"Hi, I'm looking for information for one of your residents, Sal Sheridan," I say, trying to remain calm.

"Can I ask who's speaking?" she replies.

"I'm...his daughter-in-law."

The line goes quiet for a moment before the woman says,

"Unfortunately, I can't give you any information about a patient over the phone."

I let out a huff of frustration, ready to call it a dead end.

Then the nurse continues, "But I remember you. You came in with Mr. Sheridan's son, right?"

"Yes, Rhonda," I say, holding a hand to my chest as I remember the kind woman who spoke with us. Somehow, I know where this is going.

"I was the nurse who spoke to you and your...husband. It was a good thing you signed that release for your father-in-law while you were here. Otherwise, I wouldn't be able to tell you anything."

My brows furrow as I try to think back to that day that we visited. I definitely didn't sign anything, but judging by the nurse's tone, I think she's trying to tell me she can help me.

"Yes!" I reply. "I did...sign that release. And I'm just looking for my...husband. Have you, by chance, seen him?"

"Your husband is here, Mrs. Sheridan," the nurse replies somberly.

"Oh, thank God," I mumble.

"And I don't think he should be alone right now."

"He's alone?" I cry.

There's movement on the line, and Rhonda replies in a hushed whisper. "I'm so sorry to have to tell you this over the phone, but Mr. Sheridan passed late last night."

A yelp escapes my lips as I press my fingers over my eyes. I have to breathe for a moment, gathering the strength to speak again without sobbing.

"Thank you for telling me."

"I wish I had your information to call you sooner. Your husband is not doing well. We've let him stay because we feel terrible, but he won't leave Mr. Sheridan's room."

"Oh god," I cry.

Caleb is suddenly by my side. I give him a quick nod to signal that I know where Dean is. He runs to grab his keys as I finish with the nurse on the phone.

"Thank you," I say through my tears. "We're on our way."

Hanging up the phone, I run out the door to the car, climbing in the passenger seat as Caleb starts it. After I tell him what Rhonda told me, we don't say much else on the drive. We just keep our hands held together over the center console.

I know he's feeling as anxious to see Dean as I am. We won't feel whole until we're all together.

As we reach the nursing home, we park in a rush and jog toward the entrance. Rhonda spots us immediately. Giving us a nod, she leads us down the same hallway we walked before and stops at the same room Sal was in the last time we were here.

She slowly opens the door, and the sight is like a knife to my chest. Sal is gone. His bed has been removed and in its place, our sweet Dean sits on the floor in the corner alone, sobbing with his hands in his hair.

Nothing in the world could stop me from running to him. When he hears us coming, he looks up just before I drop to my knees in front of him. I wrap my arms around his neck and feel his face rest against my shoulder. His warm breath is on my neck as I softly stroke his buzzed hair.

"What are you guys doing here?" he asks. His voice sounds cracked and tired.

"You shouldn't be alone," Caleb replies, dropping onto the floor next to Dean.

"But I am alone," he cries.

"No, you're not," I say, holding him tighter.

"I didn't expect it to hit me this hard," he says. "The nurse called last night and told me it was time. I watched him take his last breath. And then that was it. I realized I have no one. No family. Nothing."

Pulling his face away from my shoulder, I force him to look at me. "Stop saying that. You have us, and we love you."

"But—" he starts.

"No buts," Caleb argues. "We are your family, and families stay together. Running from us isn't going to make anyone's life easier. You belong with us, Dean."

He takes Dean's hand in his, intertwining their fingers and bringing the back of his hand to his lips.

"I'm so sorry about your dad, Dean," I say, wiping away his tears. "He was a wonderful man."

Sadly, he smiles. "He was."

"And he wouldn't want you to be alone."

Finally, his eyes meet mine. They are tear-soaked and raw and seeing the pain in them makes me want to hold him in my arms.

Still grasping his face, I bring his lips to mine. "We love you."

The kiss is soft and tender, and after we pull away, he gently replies, "I love you, too." His eyes dance back and forth between me and Caleb.

I've never felt anything more pure in my life. These *I love you*s are real because they are hard fought and triumphantly won. It's a love worth celebrating.

"So come home with us," I reply.

"Where you belong," Caleb adds.

"Are you guys sure about this? This is a serious commitment. People won't like it," he mutters with anguish on his face.

"They'll get over it," I reply.

He manages a hint of a smirk. Then he stares at the floor before finally nodding. "Yeah. Let's go home."

Fifty-Two

Dean

Briar's hand in mine is like an anchor. It's holding me to the earth so I don't float away into space, light enough to drift off on a breeze. I'm not made of enough at the moment for gravity to keep me down.

I'm weightless. Empty. Void of life or feelings or sense.

Right now, I'm made of nothing.

My eyes burn as we drive home. Briar sits with me in the back seat. Letting me lay my head in her lap as she holds my hand.

Her touch is my existence, and I need more. I want to bury my face in her hair, wrap my arms around her waist, and tether myself to her so she can never let me go.

I know shock and grief are behind the wheel. My mind has shut itself off to protect me from the pain. I watched my father take his last breath. I stood with him one moment, and the next, I was just... alone. It was just me and his lifeless body in a room.

Now, I am officially nothing to no one. No one's son. No one's husband. No one's father.

I should have felt this coming. We had warning. I knew he was dying, but there is nothing that prepares you for the moment they're just gone.

Maybe that's why I'm holding so tightly to Briar. I want to be something to her. And to Caleb. In the life-filled array of things that matter to them, I desperately want to be listed as one.

The caressing touch of her hand tells me I am.

I matter to them.

They want me.

But I need to feel it.

I don't even realize we've reached the house until the door opens and Caleb reaches for me. The moment my feet are on the ground and he's standing in front of me, his arms around me, he's squeezing me so tight I can hardly breathe.

Please don't let go.

I'm crying again, more tears streaking down my face, and when he lets me go, I feel myself drifting away again, so I link my hand with his, and I let him guide me into the house. Briar is in front of us as she leads us up the stairs to the second floor. We go directly into their bedroom and then into the bathroom.

"It's not big enough for all three of us," she murmurs.

"I'll get in with him," Caleb replies.

Their voices sound far away, but I distantly register that they're speaking about me. I'm too busy staring numbly at the floor, trying not to absorb anything they're saying. I want to feel as little as possible. I don't want to see anything, hear anything, feel anything—but them.

The water in the shower starts, and Briar holds my face as I stare into her eyes. *Angel.*

"Let's get you in the shower, okay?"

"Okay," I mumble. She pulls my shirt over my head and wipes her thumbs across my cheekbones. Then, with sympathy in her eyes, she leans in and kisses me softly on the mouth. Then on each of my cheeks.

She pulls down my pants, and I don't even have the mental capacity to be self-conscious. My dick hangs lifelessly between my legs, and nothing about this is as sexy as it usually feels when I'm naked with them. I'm just this sad, vulnerable thing they want to take care of.

And I let them.

"We've got you," Caleb's deep voice whispers in my ear as he tugs me into the shower. The water is hot, but I wish it were hotter so it would burn.

Caleb presses his bare chest against mine and holds me tight against him, stroking my back as I rest my head against his shoulder.

As I stand there and focus only on the sweep of his hand and the feel of his heartbeat, I let him slowly bring me back to life. The contact between us is everything to me in this moment. My entire world.

I press my lips to his neck. At first, it's a soft peck. Then I open my mouth and lick the moisture from his Adam's apple up to his jaw. The prickle of his cropped beard against my tongue stings with just enough friction to awaken my senses.

When I reach his mouth, I lick the seam of his lips, and when he parts for me, I plunge my tongue into it, searching for the familiar give-and-take exchange of our kisses. He kisses me back with hesitancy, so I grab the back of his neck and force him to give me more.

There's a twitch of life in my dick, enough to remind me that I have one. That I'm alive.

"Bite me," I mumble against his mouth.

I can't look him in the eyes, but he pulls back enough to stare at my face for assurance. *This is really me talking. Please, just give me what I need.*

Then, he brings his mouth back to mine, forcibly kissing me before sucking my bottom lip between his teeth and biting until I whimper in pain.

Yes. More.

As I'm gasping for air, I mutter with need, "Again."

This time, his teeth clench around my jaw. And then my neck and my shoulder.

Every time he brings me to the brink of pain, I feel my blood grow hotter and my heart beat faster. And suddenly, I'm not trying to blink out the world, but I'm rushing headfirst toward him.

I almost don't register that my cock is now hard until my hips rut of their own volition against Caleb's.

"Let's slow down," he whispers in my ear.

I don't want to slow down. I desperately want to keep going. But I don't feel like myself at the moment. My head is a mess. So when he pulls away, I let him.

Shutting my eyes, I force my brain to focus on nothing as he lathers up my hair and rubs soapy bubbles all over my body, running the washcloth under the pits of my arms and between the crack of my ass. My cock begins to deflate, and I slip back into a mentality of nonexistence again.

I'm not here. I'm nowhere.

When he finishes rinsing my body, he goes to turn off the water, but I stop him. "Please," I croak, sounding pathetic and helpless.

"What do you need?" he asks.

"I need you," I reply, hearing my voice crack.

He closes the distance between us, holding my face in his hands. Caleb's eyes are so genuine. They don't hide secrets or lies. They are as real and as pure as his soul. It's why he keeps them so guarded. And why it feels like such a gift when he lets me in.

"I'm here," he replies. "You've got me. As much as you want."

My heart aches as I run my hands over his hip bones, tugging him closer. "Just distract me."

His expression turns sad as he plants a kiss on my forehead. "Come on."

After turning the water off, he opens the shower door and reaches for the towel hanging on the hook. First, he wraps one around me, delicately drying my head and face, working down to my feet. Then he grabs another for himself and does the same, tying it around his hips when he's done.

As I step out of the shower, Briar comes into the bathroom. I spot a folded pile of my clothes on the bathroom counter. She must have retrieved them for me from my apartment.

"You need some rest," she says.

No. My mind refuses the idea of rest. Rest is not distracting enough. It's too much free space in my head to think and feel.

When she opens her palm to reveal two blue gel pills, I glance up at her face. "They'll help you sleep."

I shake my head. "I don't want to sleep."

Looking concerned, she closes her hand. "What do you need, Dean? Tell us what to do."

I feel like a fool for what I'm about to say. Why is it so hard to be vulnerable? To ask people to take care of me. To expose my deepest, most personal wishes.

"I just want you two to be with me," I say, my voice sounding so sad and lifeless. "Just fucking hold me."

In a rush, Briar tosses the sleeping pills in the sink and wraps her arms around me. "You don't ever have to ask for that."

Stepping on her tiptoes, she presses her lips to mine, and I focus on nothing but her kiss. The softness of her lips. The hesitant way she licks into my mouth. The delicate friction of her tongue against mine.

It was only a week without them, but it was enough to leave a chasm of doubt in my heart. How could I think I could live without them? Was I really so stubborn I thought I could walk away from this?

Her kiss comes to an end, and she lightly peppers my jaw and then my chest with more. My grip on her arms turns desperate.

Caleb comes up behind me, pressing his chest to my back.

"I don't want to feel anything but you two," I say. Staring down at Briar, I kiss her face again. First on the forehead, then on the lips. "If I asked for your body, would you give it to me?"

Her pupils dilate as she stares up at me, and there is no hesitation in her voice. "Yes."

In a needy rush of desire, I run my hands down her back to her thighs and I hoist her off the floor. Her legs wrap around me, and I press my face to her chest.

This. This is what I want.

Her body in front of me and his behind, so they are the only things that exist.

I carry Briar to the bed, dropping her on the mattress. I don't waste a second. I'm not savoring or being cautious. I'm throwing myself into the only place I love.

Tearing off her shirt and tugging down her pants, I need her naked in my hands.

When I feel Caleb's absence behind me, I reach for him. He answers the call, his fingers sliding down my spine and ripping off my towel.

We're all naked, and they're giving me everything I need. Just them. Just us. Nothing more. Nothing less.

Leaning down, I rub my face down the length of her perfect body, covering her in my scent as if she's territory I can claim. My tongue finds her breasts, and I bury myself between them. As I lick a circle around her left nipple, I feel Caleb spread my cheeks with a growl. Then my mind practically shatters when the warmth of his tongue prods my asshole.

"Fuck," I groan out before biting Briar's tit. She squeals, and it's like we're all animals, ignoring the complexities of being human with heavy thoughts and feelings. We just want to be wild with each other, indulging in the sensations only our bodies can give us.

Caleb licks circles around the tight ring of muscle as I move my way down Briar's body. Lifting her thighs, I wrap them around my head as I dive into the heady scent of her cunt. Spreading her lips, I lick the sweet length of her pussy, driving her to pleasure the same way her husband is doing to me. When Caleb reaches around and finds my cock, I groan against Briar's body.

We are in a frenzy of hands, mouths, cries, and screams. He takes his fill of me as I take mine of her. There's no end. No racing toward a climax. We settle comfortably into the place between arousal and orgasms when sex is not just a means to an end but literally heaven on earth.

Fifty-Three

Briar

I could tell Caleb was hesitant about this at first. He thinks it's not right to let Dean have this distraction, but we all know that the grief and pain will be waiting for him when all of this is over. For now, Dean wants to put off those feelings and indulge in something only we can give him.

I'd give him anything.

But, to be honest, after a week apart, I need this as much as he does. I spent the last seven days thinking that we were losing Dean to please others. What a waste that would have been.

So now that he's here, I'm not letting him go.

As he flips me onto my stomach and yanks my ass into the air, I know what Dean wants. My core flutters in anticipation at the thought.

His touch grazes my back entrance, and I practically melt.

"Remember telling me I could have this?" he asks.

I nod with a whimper.

"It's still all mine, right?"

It's so dirty and sexy. I swear I could come from his words alone. "Yes," I purr in return.

"Can we fuck you at the same time, angel?"

My heart hammers in my chest. I've wanted this for so long. Both of them inside me at once. Being the glue that holds us all together. Being one.

"Yes, please," I cry out.

"Do you have lube?" Dean asks, turning back toward Caleb.

"Yeah," he replies, climbing off the bed. It takes me by surprise. Caleb didn't tell me he bought lube, but he must have been thinking about being together again. Another shot of excitement shoots through me. We're all getting what we want.

Caleb opens the drawer of his nightstand and retrieves a bottle of lube, tossing it to Dean.

"Lie down," Dean says to him.

Caleb drops onto the bed next to me before yanking me on top of him. My legs straddle his hips as I lean down and kiss him. I've never been more in love with my husband. We struggled for so long, and now I feel closer to him than ever.

All it took was falling in love with the same person.

Dean's fingers slide through my core as he lets out a hum. "So wet, angel."

I love letting Dean use my body to get what he needs. I want to fulfill his every need.

Caleb nibbles and kisses my face when I feel something cool drip down my crack. I moan into Caleb's mouth when Dean's finger rubs and massages the tight ring. I can't help but tense up.

"Relax for me, angel," he murmurs, rubbing his hard length against my leg. "Feel that? That's how hard you make me, looking so sexy like this with your perfect ass in the air for me."

"You *are* so sexy," Caleb adds with his lips against my ear. "And you're all ours."

More moisture pools between my legs from their praise.

"Lift up, angel. Let me see you take your husband's cock."

Biting my lip, I raise my ass in the air as Caleb lines himself up with my soaking core. Dean's hands are there, touching me and touching him, so we feel like one. And when I lower my hips, letting Caleb sink deep inside me, I let out a strained moan of pleasure.

"That's my girl." He moans, kissing my neck. "God, I love being inside you."

"I love it too," I reply with a breathy whimper.

"You two are so fucking hot," Dean adds from behind me. He's still gently massaging and playing with my asshole, gently trying to relax the muscle to let him in.

Having Caleb inside me, moving slowly on top of him, helps to relax my entire body. So, without even trying, I feel myself open for him, and Dean slips inside.

"There you go," he says, his voice deep with a sultry growl. "Good girl."

It's just his finger at first, but I'm eager to take more. So I thrust backward, chasing the sensation. I feel him stretching me and then adding a second finger.

"How are you doing, angel?" he asks. I can't stop moaning with each tiny thrust.

"I need more," I reply quickly. "I need you both."

My voice doesn't even sound like me. It's too raspy and sexy. As if I've been corrupted into being this sexy vixen, and I never want to go back.

Right now, I'm not playing the part of the sweet angel, mother, or wife. It's like I've added a new role and uncovered a deeper part of my personality—this erotic side of myself that does not shy away from sex or know shame. She is not a lesser version because she's dirty and loves being fucked or dominated. She is more.

She is me.

"Fuck me," I cry out, pushing back toward Dean and taking Caleb deeper.

There's a click from the bottle of lube, and more cool liquid drips between my cheeks. Then I hear the wet sound of Dean stroking himself.

"I need to be inside you, angel. I need it so fucking bad."

His voice is strained and desperate as I feel the blunt tip of his cock against my back entrance. It's foreign, and for a moment, I think there is no way this will fit. I'm already so full.

But with just a little pressure, he breaches the tight ring and fills me even more.

My body is buzzing with excitement and arousal as he slowly inches his way inside.

"Oh fuck." Caleb groans beneath me. "I can feel you."

"You should fucking see how beautiful this is." Dean groans, gazing down at the place where he's buried inside me. "She's taking us both so well."

I can hardly breathe. I am overcome with *them*. And when Dean's hips are against my backside, and I know his cock is as far in as it can go, I let out the air from my chest and ease into this sensation.

We are one.

I almost don't want to move. I'd rather stay this way forever.

Dean places his hands on my hips and inches me forward and then back in a slow rhythm. For a while, it's just me moving very slowly. I'm savoring the newness of this, committing it to memory. It's like nothing I've ever experienced.

But then I feel us all growing restless for more. We're all strung so tight, needy for the explosion of pleasure awaiting us at the end of this. There is tension and angst to get out, and I am ready to be fucked hard.

Relaxing my face on Caleb's chest, I melt into his arms. "Use me," I say, kissing the soft patch of hair between his pecs. "And make it rough."

Caleb grabs my face and kisses me fiercely.

Then Dean tightens his grip on my hips and slams into me harder. I let out a filthy-sounding cry as pleasure erupts inside me, cascading up my spine.

"More," I moan.

Suddenly, they are unleashed. Dean pounds relentlessly behind me as Caleb thrusts upward, and all I can do is claw at the sheets and hold on.

The three of us are caught in a storm of moans, cries, bodies, and flesh—clinging to each other as if our lives depended on it. The current of this lust is powerful and godly. And we are exquisitely doomed to ride this wave forever. It's a storm I never want to escape.

My orgasm begins to build with every violent thrust and every hint of pain. Burying my hand between my legs, I massage my clit, intensifying everything until I nearly explode from the pressure.

I let out a scream as the climax rolls through me, wave after wave. My body trembles and shakes as I try to hold on to this sensation, wanting this pleasure to never leave my body.

Caleb roars out his own release, a punishing grip on my ass as he roughly thrusts upward.

Dean is the last to come, and when he finally lets the sensation win, his cries are strangled and exhausted. They sound like relief and euphoria combined.

I know the moment he's done because he sinks down on top of me, and I feel his chest quake. I don't know if they are tears or if he's just trying to catch his breath, but I know this is what he needed.

We lie like this for a long time, recovering and holding each other. When they each pull out of me, I become empty without them. Their cum leaks from each hole until I'm a mess—a filthy, beautiful mess.

Dean collapses onto the mattress, pulling me down so I'm in the middle. Exhausted and sore, I let them dote on me, each kissing me and whispering sweet nothings into my ear. Back and forth, they mumble their praises until I don't know one voice from the other.

"You are incredible."

"How do you feel?"

"What can we get you?"

"We love you so much."

"Our angel."

I must nod off for a moment because I wake to Dean carrying me in his arms. When he sets me down, I sink into a hot bubble bath. I open my eyes to find Caleb lifting cold water to my lips and stroking my face.

There's something so lovely and perfect about being roughly fucked and then tenderly nurtured. It's that dichotomy of getting to be both, and it needs trust and love, something we all share. I trust them to use me, hurt me, and control me because I *know* that they love me and will be here to take care of me when it's done.

It's the same way we feel for Dean. We trust him to go to work and let others touch him because we know that his heart is ours, and at the end of the day, it's *this* relationship he's devoted to. And when the grief of his loss hits him, we will be here to support him however he needs.

And the same with Caleb. Dean and I both know that while he struggles to express himself, he loves us and will always protect us, no matter what. Because a time will come when he needs us to love and protect him, and we will be there.

This relationship was forged by trust. It was thrown into the fire of sin and infidelity until it was melted and softened before being hammered into something new. Something stronger.

Something I know in my heart will last forever.

Fifty-Four

Caleb
21 years old

"I'm nervous," Briar mumbles to herself from the driver's seat.

I reach over with my good arm and touch her leg. "Why are you nervous? They're going to love you."

She shrugs while chewing on her bottom lip. "I still blame myself for what happened. And I think they should blame me, too."

I squeeze her leg. "Stop it. It's not your fault. Besides, you were at the hospital longer than anyone. I'm sure my mother already loves you."

With a sigh, she forces a smile. Then she leans over the center console and presses her lips to mine.

It's been two weeks since the incident and Briar has hardly left my side. I never pressed charges against Sean or his friends. They don't matter to me. Seeing them punished for what happened won't erase anything we did or justify our sins.

"You know," I mumble against her lips. Pulling away, I stare into her eyes. "We haven't really made things official between us."

Her brows pinch inward. "What are you talking about?"

"I haven't even asked you to be my girlfriend yet."

Her pearly white teeth shine as she grins with a blush to her cheeks. "I'm not your girlfriend," she replies. "Remember?"

It's my turn to look confused. She runs her fingers along my jaw and holds my face as she brings my lips back to hers.

"I thought we already settled this in the hospital. I'm your wife."

My lips stretch into a smile. I know she's just playing, and I love that that story is part of our history now. And at this moment, we both know without a doubt in our hearts that Briar will be my wife someday. There is this certainty between us. This is it. We are forever.

"That's right," I reply, kissing her back. "You're already my wife."

†

Present Day

Briar stares up at me lovingly from the bath as I sit on the edge of the tub.

"You're so amazing," I whisper, stroking her hair.

She smiles to herself. "Why? Because I can take two men?"

"No," I reply with a shake of my head. "Because you let us love you and because you've stuck by me through so much, even when I wasn't a very good husband."

"You were a good—"

"No, I wasn't," I say. I won't let her spare me from what I need to own up to. "I didn't know how to let you in. I was so afraid of losing you that I thought I had to bear everything on my own. I wanted to protect you, and all I really did was shut you out. I'm sorry."

Her expression softens as she stares up at me. "I love that you always try to protect me. It makes me feel like I'm never alone, and with everything we're going to have to face in the future, I love that I feel safe with you."

Leaning down, I press my lips to hers. "I love you."

"I love you too," she replies with a smile.

Letting Briar enjoy the rest of her bath, I go in search of Dean. After getting himself cleaned up and dressed, he disappeared and I don't like the idea of him feeling left out or being alone.

When I finally find him, he's sitting on the edge of the pool in his underwear, staring at the water. I walk up quietly and sit beside him without a word.

"Hey," he mutters.

Glancing his way, I ask, "You okay?"

It takes a moment before he shrugs. "Yeah."

"Wanna talk about it?"

He turns toward me with a quizzical brow. "*You* want to talk about it?"

I can't help but laugh. "That's just the effect you've had on me. I want to talk about things now."

"I've ruined you," he replies. "I liked you better when you just scowled and grunted at everyone."

I laugh some more. "I'll still growl and grunt at you if you'd like."

"Okay, good."

When our clipped laughter comes to an end, he lets out a loud sigh. Then, without warning, he rests his head on my shoulder. It's intimate and wonderful. The way he's so unafraid to be vulnerable and the trust that must take guts me.

I will always protect him so he can continue being so vulnerable.

Turning my head toward him, I press my lips to the top of his head. Then I wrap my arm behind his back.

"You know..." I say softly. "I don't know if this is any consolation, but you were lucky to have such a good dad. I hate that you lost yours while mine is still living, but I also wish I had a dad like yours."

His body shivers as he cries. "That does make me feel better."

I squeeze him tighter. "Sometimes I worry that I'll never be a good dad because I didn't have one as a role model. So I'm glad Abby has you."

He cries some more. "You're crazy," he replies. "You are a great dad."

"Thank you," I whisper with my lips against his head.

After a moment, he seems to have dried his tears, but his head is still resting on my shoulder. It's then that I realize that with everything that's happened this week since my father's arrest and Dean's father's death, I never got to tell him about the conversation I had with Isaac.

And while I told Isaac I wouldn't tell everyone about his whereabouts, Dean is as close to me as Briar now. It would be wrong to lie to him.

"I didn't tell you..." I start. Dean lifts his head and stares at me as he waits. "I saw Isaac."

His face tenses in confusion. "What? When?"

"Last night. He...was in town for the night, and we had a beer."

Dean smiles. "Holy shit. What did he say?"

"It was so weird. He was like a stranger to me. But he gave me some really good advice. And I realized that I should have never tried to hide him or push you away to protect him. I should have stood with him. I always wanted Isaac to pretend he was straight so my father wouldn't be angry with him. And maybe that's why I always pretended to be straight."

"And how do you feel now?"

Looking out over the water, I let out a sigh. "I feel ready to finally come out. I think I knew my entire life that I was attracted to men and women, but I tried to brush that part of myself off. I figured that if I was married, I didn't need to worry about it."

He nods, resting his hand on my leg. "I think a lot of people make that mistake. You're not alone."

"And maybe if I come out first, Isaac will be ready to come home. I'm ready to do what I should have done nine years ago."

Dean reaches over and grabs my face, kissing me hard on the

cheek. "For what it's worth, I'm proud that you've finally made it here. I love you so much."

Turning toward him, I smile as my lips press against his. "I love you too."

Fifty-Five

Dean

"How are you feeling?" Briar touches my hand as I stare down at the program in my hand. My dad's smiling face stares back up at me. The picture was taken on his boat when we went fishing one day, not too long ago.

"I'm feeling okay," I reply. I squeeze her hand and fight the urge to kiss her. There are too many people here, and that's not a conversation we want to have right now. At least not until later.

"Your eulogy was beautiful, baby," she replies quietly.

"Thank you." Briar stands and moves toward the food table in the back to help Sage and Melanie.

Next to me, Abby is coloring on one of the programs. It's a picture of her on my dad's lap under a rainbow. There are some unicorns and cats in the picture too.

Leaning over, I softly stroke her head, careful not to mess up her perfectly-styled braids. "That's a nice picture," I say, admiring her artwork.

She smiles up at me before climbing onto my lap and finishing her drawing. "I'm sorry your dad died," she says, and I have to fight a smile.

"Thanks."

I press my lips to the top of her head. "Done," she says, showing me the masterpiece.

"I love it."

"Will you hang it in your apartment?" she asks.

Flatly, I reply, "Obviously."

As she hops off my lap to run to Caleb, I silently wonder how long I'll live in that apartment. I'm not ready to move into the house yet. We all know this transition will take time, and if we rush anything, it will only put unnecessary pressure on our relationship.

But at least I've accepted the fact that this *is* a relationship, and I'm not leaving. This is my family. There is no question about that.

Glancing up from my chair, I nod at Caleb, who's standing with his brothers by the front of the room. It pains me to see them all together and know that Isaac is missing.

Adam immediately offered to hold my father's funeral at his church. It's really more of a celebration of life since that's what my dad would have wanted. Food, music, family.

This was his dream for me. He didn't want me to be alone, and thanks to these people, I'm not, and I never will be.

Currently, I'm sitting alone at this table, so I decide to stand and make my way toward the front, where the Goode brothers are talking. Immediately, and maybe by habit, Caleb wraps an arm around my shoulder, pulling me to his side.

Adam's eyes track the movement first. Meanwhile, Luke has this all-knowing look on his face as if nothing surprises him.

The four of us make small talk together for a moment. Adam brings up the renovations they're doing at the church, and Luke talks about his new course load at the university and his prospects of reaching tenure.

Meanwhile, I feel Caleb tense beside me. He's growing restless, and I get a sinking suspicion that he's thinking about his plan to come out today.

Glancing around the room, I notice that most of the guests have started to trickle out. Some were friends from my dad's work or nurses from the senior living center.

"I'm ready," Caleb whispers to me.

Turning toward him, I shrug my shoulders. "I'm ready when you are, but no pressure."

"Fuck it," he mutters, squeezing my arm. Then, he looks across the room at Briar. She smiles at him as she sets down a tray of food. "Briar, Dean, and I have an announcement to make," he says loudly.

The small, quiet conversations in the room quickly come to an end. Suddenly, all eyes are on us.

I watch him in awe of how courageous he is in this moment. There's not a hint of doubt on his face as his hand squeezes mine.

Abby looks up from where she's playing with some toys in the corner. She beams at us before going back to what she was doing.

"We understand that this might come as a shock to you all, and it might take some getting used to, but we want you all to know that Dean..." Caleb looks at me, and my heart soars in my chest. To be so loved and wanted is like nothing I ever thought love could be. "Dean is a part of our family now."

In the corner of my eye, I see everyone glancing around confusedly. But I don't care about them. I'm still staring at this man that I've fallen in love with.

I used to think relationships weren't for me and that I would never be able to give my all to anyone. Because love was nothing more than a risk. But that was before I found a love worth risking it all for.

Briar joins us, taking my hand in hers and squeezing it tightly as she smiles at Caleb.

"What we mean," she says, "Is that Caleb and I are in a relationship with Dean. We...love him. And he loves us."

"And we don't want to hide it anymore," Caleb adds.

Silence envelops the room as the three of us share intimate glances.

"I knew it!" a voice out of nowhere shrieks from the back of the room. We turn to find Sage hopping excitedly behind the food tables.

Meanwhile, Caleb's mother, Melanie, looks as if she's just been struck by lightning. I sort of figured she'd be the one to take the news with a little more apprehension, but it seems the rest of the Goodes are trying to be as supportive as possible.

Adam claps me on the back. "We're happy for you all. This is excellent news."

"Yeah," Luke adds. "I haven't seen Caleb this happy in a while, so you must be doing something right."

"Don't make it weird," Caleb says to him, which makes everyone laugh.

"How am I making it weird?" he argues.

And for the most part...that's it. It's only slightly awkward. People are still obviously curious, and I'm sure they have a ton of questions. We have a very long road ahead of us, but at least we don't have to face it alone.

†

Briar is stacking dishes in the dishwasher as I come behind her and wrap my arms around her waist. Leaning against her, I press my lips to her neck, and she hums, letting her head fall to the side.

"I love being able to do this whenever we want now," I murmur against her skin.

"Me too," she replies.

"Let's go to bed." I moan, skating my lips up to her ear.

She gasps when my hand slides around and slips between her legs. "The sooner we get these dishes done, the sooner we can go to bed," she replies sweetly.

I let out a groan.

But she ignores my complaints and hands me a towel. "Here. You dry."

Disgruntled, I snatch the towel away and start drying the pots and pans on the counter. She's wearing a smug grin.

"You're a tease," I mutter, which makes her laugh.

"This is domestic life, my love. You'll learn to love it." Standing on her tiptoes, she reaches up and plants a kiss on my lips.

Smiling to myself, I reply, "I already do."

Once the dishes are done, Briar jogs up to our bedroom, and I go in search of Caleb. Slipping down the hallway to Abby's room, I hear a gentle lullaby playing and a soft blue light coming from her room. Peering around the corner, I lean against the doorframe and take in the sight of him, engulfing her tiny bed with her snoring lightly on his chest.

Moments like this, I wonder if I'm dreaming. How did I end up here, with a sexy man *and* a sexy woman *and* the greatest kid on earth? And how on earth did I come to love this so much?

If someone had told me a year ago that I'd be here and this life would make me so fucking happy, I'd tell them they were out of their mind.

"Hey," he whispers from across the room.

"Hey," I reply softly.

Very slowly and carefully, Caleb maneuvers Abby off his chest and tucks her into her bed before slipping out of the room. When he reaches the doorway, he stands in front of me.

"Do you ever just stand here and watch her for hours?" I ask, unable to take my eyes off the little girl across the room.

"It's tempting," he replies lightly.

I'm not surprised how quickly I fell in love with Caleb and Briar, but I am absolutely shocked at how quickly I fell head over heels for that little girl. It feels like a piece of my heart is constantly outside my body, and she's not even technically my kid.

But in every way that matters, I guess she is my kid now. I'll love her like mine until the day I die, no matter what happens. That's for sure.

I still don't like kids. They're gross and rude and *so* much fucking work.

But I would die for this one.

"Come on," Caleb whispers, pulling me from the doorway. "There's something even better waiting for us in our bedroom."

My interest is piqued as I turn away from Abby's room, gently closing the door before following Caleb across the house.

When I enter the room, I stop in the doorway and gawk at the woman in front of me. Briar is on her knees, staring at the floor with a light-pink collar clasped around her neck.

"Call it a welcome gift," Caleb whispers in my ear from my side.

"For me?" I ask with a sly grin as I take a menacing step toward the prize on the floor.

I tug at the buttons of my shirt as my mouth waters. Stopping in front of Briar, I touch her chin and force her to look up at me. Her gaze is soft and loving.

Leaning down, I press my lips to her forehead.

"You want to please me, angel?" I mutter darkly.

"Yes, I do," she replies.

"How bad do you want it?" I ask.

Caleb stands just on the other side of her, watching her with lust in his eyes.

"I want it so bad," she replies sweetly.

"But your husband is watching," I say, adding a little more role-playing to this already sexy-as-fuck situation.

Briar tugs her bottom lip between her teeth as if she's ashamed.

"That's okay," Caleb growls as he buries his hand in her hair and forces her head back. "If you want to please him so bad, then do it. But I'm going to watch."

She whimpers in response as I begin to unbuckle my pants, eager to free my aching cock.

Caleb moves to the chair in the corner, dropping into it and watching us with carnal interest.

Looking down at the woman in front of me, I can't help but smile.

Seriously, how the fuck did I get so lucky?

"This is a very dirty little wife you have, Caleb," I say as I ease my cock toward her mouth.

She gives me one last smile as Caleb replies, "Yes, I do. And she's all ours."

Epilogue

Caleb
One year later

Abby slams the side of her hand down on the thin board with a loud "Hiyah!" It breaks with a resounding crack.

"Fuck yeah," Dean cheers quietly in the stands next to me.

"Good job, peanut!" Briar squeals.

I'm holding my phone to record the entire thing as she bows to her sensei with a beaming smile on her face. When she spots the three of us in the crowd, she waves while practically bouncing in place.

I wave back, making sure to look her in the eye instead of at the screen of my phone. I want her to *know* I was watching. When she looks back at her childhood and all of her accomplishments, she'll remember us being here and cheering her on.

As they take her white belt and replace it with a yellow one, Abby looks so excited I feel myself starting to get emotional.

Everyone applauds, all of the students on the mat bowing together.

Afterward, Abby comes running toward us. "You are such a badass," Dean says as she wraps her arms around his legs.

"Can we get pizza?" she asks excitedly.

"Sure," Briar replies, taking her hand.

As the four of us leave the gym, Abby and Briar in front, I place a hand on Dean's back affectionately. I don't miss the way other people, specifically dads, glare contemptuously, but I've learned to brush it off by now.

Since Abby joined karate almost a year ago, the other parents have shown their curiosity every time we've shown up with our daughter. Sometimes, it's just me and Dean. Sometimes, Dean and Briar. And sometimes, all three of us.

Briar says I show off too much, never shying away from holding their hands or showing affection, but deep down, I do it for the version of myself I kept quiet for so long.

I won't change myself to make room for other people's close-minded biases.

With that, I squeeze Dean a little bit closer.

As we reach the parking lot, I kiss Dean on the side of the head. The sleeve of my shirt rides up, exposing the large black-and-white angel tattoo on my forearm.

There's a matching one on Dean's arm. We take our angel with us wherever we go.

†

After pizza, the four of us head home. As we pull into the driveway, there's a new Theo Virgil song playing on the radio, and I smile to myself as Dean and Abby sing along.

I've messaged my little brother nearly every day since that night, mostly with pics of Abby.

His new album has been a huge success, and I know this is going to mean a lot for his hidden identity, but for now, I try not to be the overprotective (to a fault) pain in the ass I was before. I simply cheer him on and offer support where I can.

The only person in my family who knows about my brother, as it turns out, is my mother, who revealed to me that she's known his whereabouts this entire time. I can't say I was surprised, though.

There's nothing Melanie Goode can't do.

My father's case continues to drag on, but it's a footnote in my story at this point. If I remember to check the news, I might hear about a new development. But as far as I'm concerned, that day he threatened Dean and Abby, he stopped being my father.

And the peace I feel now is astounding.

Like Isaac said, I'm not entirely free. The cancer that is Truett Goode burrowed its way into my psyche, but at least this cancer has a cure—the three people in this car with me.

"What do you say we do some renovations in the apartment tonight?" I ask as we climb out of the SUV.

Doing renovations is our code for sneaking out after Abby's asleep and doing ungodly, filthy, and exquisite things to each other in Dean's old apartment. Since he's officially moved into the house, the space has essentially turned into our sex den of sin.

"Can't," Briar replies as she leads the way into the house.

"Why?" I ask.

"I have book club tonight."

She's been reading the same dusty old bodice-ripper romance novel that Sage has, and once a month, she attends their little Laundromat book club and margarita night.

It was her Bible study replacement.

And since her relationship with Juliet and her mother is still not repaired, we encourage her to get out and be with better people who actually lift her up instead of tearing her down.

"Oh yeah, I forgot about that," I say as we reach the kitchen. When we get inside the house, Abby bolts up to her room to play.

"What about you?" I ask, smacking Dean's ass. "You're off tonight, right?"

He gives me a sly smile over his shoulder. "I am, and I could be down for some renovations."

"Not fair," Briar whines, leaning against the kitchen counter.

Taking her in my arms, I offer her a kiss on her pouting lips.

Working out the boundaries and rules of this relationship has been interesting, and we've definitely hit some bumps in the road along the way. It's hard to be in a relationship like this and not feel left out sometimes, but according to our new poly friends, that's normal.

But, to be honest, seeing them love each other fills me with so much peace and happiness. I love to see Dean and Briar together, and instead of feeling jealous when they're alone, I take such pride in knowing that if I'm not around, they have each other.

Of course, first and foremost, we carve out time to be sure we're feeding *this* relationship the most. It's the one that means more.

I still like time with Briar or time with Dean alone, but it's nothing compared to the times when all three of us fill the same space. That's when this love shines the brightest, and I feel most at home.

But if Briar is going to be gone for tonight, you best believe I'm going to indulge in some time with my sexy fucking man.

†

After pouring myself a glass of red wine, I cross the yard toward the apartment, where I know he's waiting for me.

Opening the door, I find the room already dim, with the string of lights around the ceiling illuminated in a magenta haze. Dean is standing near the record player, flipping through the selection of vinyls.

He's in nothing but a pair of black pants, and I lick my bottom lip as I take in the sight of him.

"What's the mood tonight?" I ask as I set down my glass and begin unbuttoning my shirt.

There's a scratch of the record through the speaker before the sultry, sexy sound of jazz echoes through the room.

"Vintage," I say with a crooked smirk. "I like it."

He turns around and smiles at me. Crossing the room, I slide my hand along his jaw, holding his face as I pull him in for a slow, sensual kiss. He's been growing his hair out lately, and I love that I can run my fingers through it. Hold it. Pull it.

"Lie down," he mumbles, his soft lips against my neck.

"Why? You got something for me?" I ask.

"As a matter of fact... I do."

My brows lift as a myriad of possibilities run through my mind. "You have my attention," I reply.

He shoves me toward the bed, and it does something to me when he takes control. "I said, lie down."

With a growl, I do as he said. When I start to pull my clothes off, he stops me.

"No. Let me."

"Yes, dear," I reply as I drop onto the bed. Resting my back against the headboard, I watch him with lust-filled anticipation as he begins to unbutton his pants.

Biting his lip, he says with a wince, "God, I really hope you like this."

I find myself chuckling. "If it's on you, I will."

He flicks open the button, and I narrow my eyes curiously. Then, he slowly eases his pants down his legs, and at first, I don't notice anything.

Then, as he stands, I get a look at his underwear, and a whimper slips through my lips.

He normally wears briefs, and with his strong thighs and tight ass, they always look amazing.

But tonight, his briefs are special. They are black lace and delicate. They hug his cock and balls, and when he turns, revealing the soft, see-through lingerie around his ass, it's so hot I could cry.

"Oh...baby," I mumble as I sit up and reach for him.

"You like 'em?" he asks as he climbs on top of me, straddling my hips.

"Are you fucking kidding me?" I ask, running my hand over the back, his tight little cheeks peeking out the bottom. "I think I've found something new to keep in my office drawer."

He laughs as he leans down and kisses my neck, slowly sliding my shirt from my shoulders.

"You're so beautiful," I murmur, gliding my fingers over the crack of his ass.

I can't stop touching him, running my hands over the lace to cup his hardening cock. The music continues playing as Dean works his way down my body, tugging down my pants until I'm naked.

Then, he lays his outstretched body between my legs and puts his mouth on my cock. Licking, sucking, and nibbling on my dick, he fondles my sack and even teases my ass as he brings me to the brink of heaven.

Staring at his perfect ass in that black lingerie, I come down his throat with a grunt, pulling his short hair as I thrust up into his mouth.

It's just the appetizer for the night, I know. As he rests his face on my thigh, my cum still wet on his lips, I say a little prayer of thanks that he came back into my life. If it weren't for that fire, I'd still be living in denial, bitter and lost. My marriage would still be suffering. My wife would still be unhappy.

Instead, his father lit a match that burned down more than just his house. My life, built on lies, was left in ashes.

But with fire comes renewal, and what we've gained is better than anything heaven could ever offer.

Epilogue

Briar

The bell chimes over the door of the Laundromat as I open it, carrying a tray of brownies in my arms. The delicious scent of Mary's enchiladas greets me as I creep toward the back of the building where the rest of the ladies are waiting.

"Hey there!" Gladys says as she sets the margarita glasses on the table.

"Hey," I reply, placing the brownies with the rest of the food.

Sage bounces out from the back and throws her arms around me. "So glad you could make it!"

"Thanks again for inviting me," I reply.

After coming out last year, my mother and Juliet nearly cut off communication with me immediately. They both chose to play the victim as if their choice not to accept my family somehow hurt them. My mother cried on the phone with me for an hour about how I was denying her time with Abigail because she couldn't possibly come over and see me with two men.

Two men who love me and have committed themselves to me.

Two men who will raise my daughter with more compassion and support than I've ever seen in my entire life.

My family can't seem to accept that and would rather place their faith in God's word than their own sister and daughter.

So, needless to say, I stopped going to Bible study. And I started coming to book club instead.

The reading is better, anyway.

As I set down my thrifted copy of *Torrid Affair*, I greet the other two women—Mary and Sylvia.

The door chimes again, and I look up to see Sadie stroll in. She has a backpack hanging from her shoulder and two grocery bags in her hands. I see her in the club setting so often that it's always interesting to me to see her in regular, everyday clothes.

With a cropped crewneck riding up to expose her belly and a pair of loose joggers hanging on her hips, I'm envious of how she manages to look like an adorable mess and a sex goddess at the same time.

She wears her curves with a confidence that I admire.

"Sorry I'm late!" she stammers as she ambles in, knocking her bags against the dryers as I rush over to help her.

"You're not late," I say, taking the groceries.

"I am always late," she replies. "I had a huge test today in my lit class and a paper due tomorrow, and I'm going to be a bad book club member because I totally didn't finish the book."

Laughing, I give her a smile. "You're fine. We'll fill you in."

"How do you do it?" she asks as she drops her backpack. "You're getting your master's and raising a kid and fucking two guys at once. You're a superwoman."

Everyone laughs. "Well," I say, clearing my throat. "Those *two* men help a lot. I couldn't do it without them. Besides, you're managing a sex club and getting your degree. Give yourself some credit."

"I need to find a man." She groans as she picks up a brownie.

Just then, the door chimes again, and to my surprise, it's not a woman who walks in but Caleb's twin brother, Lucas. He's carrying a large box and struggles to get through the door.

"Oh my god, you're a lifesaver," Sage exclaims as she jogs across the Laundromat to take the box from Luke.

"Don't mention it," he replies sheepishly, glancing up at the rest of us. When his eyes meet Sadie, he freezes for a moment. Something intense passes through their gazes before he shakes it off and looks away.

"The library at the university donated a bunch of old books for our next meeting," Sage says as she drops the box onto the floor. Reaching in, she pulls out a yellowing copy of *Forbidden Desires*.

"This was at the university library?" I ask, picking up another and smiling at the dramatic artwork on the cover. It's a couple in a historic setting. Her hair is swept away by the wind, and the man holds her in his arms, his hand resting on her stomach.

Luke clears his throat. "The librarians kept them in the back, but they said no one's touched them in years. When I heard about your book club...I thought you might be interested."

"You're the best," Sage says, squeezing his arm.

"Are you hungry?" Sadie asks, gesturing toward the food.

Luke tenses, looking anywhere but at her as he shakes his head. "Kind of you, but, erm, no. Thank you."

With that, Lucas waves at us before making his way back to the door.

Then, we dig into the food and find our seats around the card table. Gladys pours the margaritas, and we all start gushing about the book.

"What did you think, Briar?" Sylvia asks at one point, and I don't miss a beat, answering with how romantic I thought the entire story was.

"I loved the part where they just gave in to their desires. I know it was wrong, but it all worked out in the end. That's what I love about these books; they always end happily. It proves that love really just...conquers all," I say before taking a drink.

"Cheers to that," Sage says excitedly.

Grinning, I lift my glass to theirs, and we clink them together in unison.

+

I cut myself off after one drink so I could sober up to drive home. When I reach the house, I smile to myself when I spot the pinkish-purple light through the window of the apartment.

After I quietly climb the stairs, I press my ear to the door. The muffled groans coming from inside set my body on fire, sending a swarm of butterflies to my belly.

Opening the door, I bite my bottom lip as I walk in quietly before pressing my back to the door after I've closed it.

Dean's gripping the headboard as Caleb pounds into him from behind. He didn't even bother taking off Dean's underwear—they're just slipped to the side to accommodate Caleb's cock.

I helped Dean pick them out last week, and by the looks of it, Caleb approves.

"Hello, angel," he mutters, pausing his thrusts to turn and smile at me.

I drop my purse on the floor and tug off my jacket as I cross the room toward them.

"I see you two are having a good evening," I murmur when I reach the bed. Kicking off my shoes, I climb onto the mattress and pull Dean's mouth to mine for a kiss.

There's a sheen of sweat and goose bumps on his skin. When I reach down and slip my fingers into his lace underwear and wrap my hand around his length, he throws his head back with a hiss.

"Mind if I join you?" I ask, slowly stroking him.

Caleb grabs Dean by the throat, kissing his ear as he mutters darkly, "Don't you dare let him come yet."

My hand slides up Dean's chest, and he grins at me.

"I'll be good," I reply.

As Caleb thrusts in again, Dean's smile fades into an expression of carnal pleasure.

Before long, I'm naked right along with them—except for Dean's underwear—and we're indulging in the pleasure only we can give each other.

I can't stop thinking about that book we read for tonight's meeting and how hot it was to see that couple break the rules for each other. There's nothing hotter to me. Love doesn't live in perfect little boxes and abide by arbitrary rules. It grows and spreads, and we are all just pawns in its game.

Living with these two, I'm so glad we didn't fight against that love. It might not have been an easy road, and we will face scrutiny for years to come, but there's not a day that goes by when I'm not eternally grateful that we let love win.

†

Ready for The Heartbreaker? Luke's story is coming August 30th.

Preorder now!

ACKNOWLEDGMENTS

Holy shit.

That was intense. I had no idea this would be my longest, spiciest, and most emotional book when I set out to write it. Thanks for sticking with me through this story. I know it was a lot. I hope it was fun.

Somewhere in the process of writing, I said to my friend, "I don't want four spicy scenes in a row."

For that, I should really thank her for saying, "We do."

So, I went ahead and did it anyway—twice.

Thanks, Jill. I'm pretty sure everyone is grateful to you for that.

This seems like a good place to thank everyone for their help in making this book happen.

My beta readers—Jill, Becca, Janine, Phil, and Adrian. Thanks for the encouragement, insight, and perspective. Love you all.

My assistant—Lori Alexander for keeping me in line and on time.

My agent—Savannah Greenwell.

My editor—Rebecca for being so flexible and amazing.

My proofreaders—Rumi and Rosa.

My cover designers—Lori Jackson and Emily Wittig.

My PR company—The Author Agency

My friend and assistant—Misty Frey for stuffing a thousand PR envelopes.

My forever hype girl and friend—Amanda Anderson.

The lovely Kristie of read_between_the_wines for a beautiful plotting sesh.

The moderators and members of Sara's Salacious Readers.

All of my readers for staying with me through this new series and letting me try something different.

Thank you all!

Also by Sara Cate

Salacious Players' Club

Praise

Eyes on Me

Give Me More

Mercy

Highest Bidder

Madame

The Goode Brothers series

The Anti-hero

The Home Wrecker

The Heart Breaker - coming in 2024

The Prodigal Son - coming in 2025

Age-gap romance

Beautiful Monster

Beautiful Sinner

Wilde Boys duet

Gravity

Freefall

Black Heart Duet

Four

Five

Cocky Hero Club

Handsome Devil

Bully romance

Burn for Me

Wicked Hearts Series

Delicate

Dangerous

Defiant

About Sara Cate

Sara Cate is a USA Today bestselling romance author who weaves complex characters, heart-wrenching stories, and forbidden romance into every page of her spicy novels. Sara's writing is as hot as a desert summer, with twists and turns that will leave you breathless. Best known for the Salacious Players' Club series, Sara strives to take risks and provide her readers with an experience that is as arousing as it is empowering. When she's not penning steamy tales, she can be found soaking up the Arizona sun, jamming to Taylor Swift, and watching Marvel movies with her family.

You can find more information about her at
www.saracatebooks.com

Made in the USA
Las Vegas, NV
03 November 2024

11002345R00267